BLACK HILLS MOON
ANTHOLOGY VOLUME I

Cover Design by T.S. Huntzicker

Printed in the United States of America

First Printing, 2019

ISBN: 978-1-7334435-0-0

Published by: Brilliant Sanity Media 2019
            Storm Lake, IA 50588

This book is obviously a work of fiction. Any names, characters, places, or incidents are just figment products of the author's imagination and used fictitiously. If any resemblance to actual events, or locals, persons living or dead, is strictly coincidental. It is important to note that B.A.M.F. Pixies do exist and the do make for excellent stew meat!

Embrace the suffering...proudly wear your scars!

CONTENTS

DEDICATION

To Maria whose impassioned voice along with the music of "In this Moment," inspired the creation of the Black Hills Mocn Universe. To my son Eric; although you are not at my side each day, you are on my mind and in my heart every moment!

-TSH

To Rowan, to the Woods, to the Wilderness, and to the Moon!

-BH

PROLOGUE:
CRYPTIDS AND CRYPTOZOOLOGY

AN EXCERPT:

(An Excerpt from 'Cryptids and Cryptozoology: A Call for Relevance and Instrumentalism' by Dr. Gimlin Patterson, PhD, Anthropological Studies)

The controversy over the limits of science and rationalism are a hotly debated subject, especially in the current era of post-truth politics in America. Nevertheless, I feel it is my duty as an academic and a seeker of truth to illuminate a generally-scoffed-at avenue of Anthropology. We are talking, of course, about Cryptozoology. Classified under Anthropological Studies, the practice began in academia as an offshoot of gathering folk tales—hoping that oral relics of human culture, such as spirituality and spoken word, were codified and written down for further study. Illuminating even the false avenues of human path and their cultures would give future historians and studiers of mankind an idea of the delusions that mankind suffered from.

And yet, a curious thing began to happen. The more data was gathered, the more pieces of a larger mythos began to accrue. Folk books and accounts began to become indistinguishable from one another. Variables common over numerous geographically disparate locations began to show themselves. Clerical error? Naïve undergrads digging in too deep and going, to use a rather dated colonial term, 'native?' This and many other "rationalistic" excuses pushed by an Old Guard of Academics desperate to prove their so-called enlightened predecessors and their own personal theses as correct have squashed efforts that could be used to further the study of a vast swathe of esoterica.

In short, this paper hopes to prove the validity of the working theory known as "Cryptid Concept," and will attempt to focus on the two sets of four main 'global footprints' of genuine Cryptid sightings: There are 4 Physical Footprints, and 4 Folkloric Footprints that quantify a specific biological specimen as a Cryptid.

The Four Physical Footprints:
A.   Cryptids are usually animals, or animal-like beasts, commonly associated with negative feelings or violent actions tied to a region's local geography, though in some rare instances more active vegetation has been discovered.

B.   Cryptids are usually not defined in current biological sciences. In other words, if there is a lack of biological information on a specimen, it's likely a Cryptid of one sort or another. If there are no biological or genetic genus or subgenus matches connected during or after a dissection or genetic analysis, it is likely to be Cryptid in origin, in other words, not native to this world. Again, this is subject to formative theories.

C.   Cryptids are typically ecosystem-independent; that is, they exist, and can alter the natural 'ecosystem' of an area, but are not integral to its continued function. A wolf, for instance, is important in keeping down populations of deer; yet it is, in and of itself, perhaps a rogue, but not a Cryptid, because it has a normalized place in an ecosystem on Earth. Cryptids are typically invaders in an ecosystem, with no natural place in the food chain.

D.   Cryptids are often linked with certain cosmic cycles or geothermal patterns—specifically, Erickson et. al. report a causal link between Moon phase and appearance, in particular a high recurrence/visibility rate during occlusion events. In other words, Eclipses and Blood Moon phenomenon seem strongly connected to the appearance of a Cryptid. Strange weather patterns or other astronomical events seem to preclude Cryptid sightings. The scientific nature of such measurements and a statistical analysis representing a detailed overview of sightings from the 1960's onwards is included on the final Errata portion of this document.

The Four Folkloric Footprints:

A.   Cryptids are usually 'said' to be witnessed with an intrinsic odor to them that sits at odds with the human nervous system—it is surmised by Brown et. al. that this is a biological defense mechanism on the Cryptid's behalf, and that, if they are 'biological creatures,' whose genesis is one of evolution in-line with Earth's, perhaps it was developed directly counter to Earth's typical biological patterns. This, however, is still a tricky subject even within Cryptid studies: the argument of counter-evolving is one usually sidled with Intelligent Design; and Intelligent Design is a debate not many scientists are willing to dive into, even in a subject as fraught with controversy as Cryptozoology. The main takeaway is they are reported to have an 'irredeemably foul' stench that causes numerous neurological and biological hazards.

B.   Cryptids are said to be violent—on occasion communicating ill intention, and their appearance is usually a prelude to a mythic influx of bad luck. Their negative nature casts the Cryptid into the typical role of 'villain' or 'harbinger of doom' in folkore. Hence, Cryptids are typically associated with a pattern of bad luck, ill-omens, and general unpleasantness, including but not limited to violence against naturally occurring bio-organisms—in specific, humans. (Please see Addendum B.XVI regarding counter arguments.)

C.   Cryptids are said to have their appearances coincide with dates and patterns—appearing only during certain times. While this is strongly tied with Folklore and sociological examination of stories, Erickson et. al. have provided a number of studies that indicate astronomical event patterns suggest appearance during Blood Moons and Lunar Eclipses. (Recent debate has gone back and forth on whether or not this is a Physical or Folkloric footprint, though there are aspects of both. A rare creature that one can hardly see can be found, whereas a Cryptid will make itself hidden from view.)

D.   Cryptids are said to be from 'somewhere else.' The nature of their other-ness is again, hotly contested. Some cultures speak of a Fairy World; some speak of a ghostly plane. Still others talk of interplanetary travel, from cracks between dimensions. This is all mostly conjecture, though the prevailing nature of such creatures and a discussion on the suggested origin are found in Appendix C.XXV

PART 1: LEGENDS

CHAPTER 1:

THE LEGEND

The three of them were sitting at the café, some nineties alt music playing softly on the radio in the background. It was their normal Wednesday hump-day early morning extended coffee break from work. All three of the girls had grabbed iced coffees; makeup was still flawless, per usual group code, but damn if it didn't smear from sweat on the way into the building. The cement sidewalk outside was starting to hum with the heat. Andi was pretty positive that if she dropped some of her drink outside it would evaporate before it touched the ground.

"It's Memorial Day weekend coming up," Andi said. Andi was ginger and proud of it, even if she thought she looked a bit like the square-patty hamburger lady from certain angles. "And I don't know about you, but I need to beat the heat and float this weekend."

"Andi, the city girl through and through?" Cheyenne asked, sardonic tilt to her eyebrows. Cheyenne was originally from mid-Oklahoma, and her voice had a very casual twang to it. Her brown hair was high and tight on her head; if it weren't for her usual work makeup, she would pass easily for a man at the twenty feet mark. Andi was pretty positive Cheyenne could take down a bear, well, bare-handed, so to speak. "Ain't that something. When's the last time you floated the river?"

Andi rolled her eyes at her friend.

"It's been a while," she said. "Do *you* have any better plans?"

"Me and Levi had plans," Rheighna said softly. She was a perpetual optimist, soft-spoken and ground down by childhood and the patriarchy. The fact that Levi worshipped the ground she walked on was the only reason Cheyenne and Andi allowed the relationship to begin with. "But water sounds better. Especially this weekend, this weather is nuts."

"I swear I saw a lamp-post melting the other day," Cheyenne said. "We have got to get out of this city. Maybe hit some trees. Let Mother Nature shield us from the sun's deadly rays. We could make a trip of it—carpool out together in the 4x4."

"Is it out of the shop yet?"

"Yeah, it's doing great," Cheyenne said. "Just takes a minute or two to get started on account of the ignition, but it's pretty much all tuned up and ready for the road. Big enough to pack enough shit for the three of us."

"Four of us," Rheighna reminded them.

Cheyenne rolled her eyes.

"I don't know about you all, but if I don't leave this city this weekend I feel like it's gonna be the death of me," Andi said.

"Agreed," the other girls said, in stereo.

And so they left that Friday; Levi, Rheighna's current beau and single devotee of the Church of Rheighna, tagged along after skeeving off from work for the weekend. The four of them drove over hot asphalt blacktop highways that sizzled in the summer sun, windows down and sunroof open. At least the breeze was keeping them cool.

"So where are we going?" Levi asked, against the wind, arm waving with the breeze out the window. His other hand and Rheighna's hand were interlocked.

Andi wanted to throw up at the sheer saccharine level of their sweetness, but only a little. The two of them gave her hope for a future herself.

"Black River," she said, instead. Her hair was up in a tight ponytail and her bangs were held in place with a visor. She looked a bit like a soccer mom, or perhaps a blackjack dealer at a shady casino. She frowned at her reflection and paid attention to the mile markers again. Only eighty miles left to go now…

"What's there to do at Black River?" Levi asked.

"Andi was talking about floating the river," Cheyenne said. "There's a little outlet at one end they call Black Hills Lagoon. The water is about as blue as you can get. We can set up a little campfire… I brought a tent and some fishing poles. We can swim, fish, roast marshmallows. I even brought my rifle if you want to go hunting deep deep in the woods. Whatever you want."

"That sounds pretty cool," Levi said.

"I know, doesn't it?" Rheighna asked.

"You're telling me you decided to come out here and didn't even know what we were going to do?" Cheyenne asked.

"It doesn't matter what we do, as long as we do it together," Levi said.

He leaned over and kissed Rheighna, and they disappeared into each other's faces for a while.

"Disgusting," Cheyenne said, but it didn't sound like she was serious.

They arrived shortly before dusk had set in, and a full bright moon was hanging out on the edge of the sky, waiting to fill in.

"Dear God," Cheyenne said suddenly when they rounded the bend.

The place was packed. Wall to wall people, tents, grills, the crisp bitter smell of beer and charcoaled meats, and laughing and crying children splashing in the lagoon greeted them. The four of them stared out at the water with something akin to dismay. It was like some festival right on the edge of the lake.

"I left the city to get away from people," Andi muttered.

"Yeah," Cheyenne said. "Man I hate it when people find these cool little spots."

"We could still try swimming at least," Levi said. "Drive a little further into the campgrounds and set up a tent somewhere farther out when we're done."

"Yeah, it's probably not so bad if we cut through the beach," Rheighna said. "We don't need a whole tent setup to get wet."

Andi shook her head.

"You two have fun," she said. "This is a lot of freaking people. I'm not sure I'm feeling this."

"Might want to get started on the tent before we get wet or it gets dark and we can't find somewhere to set up," Cheyenne said.

"We can split up, then," Rheighna said. "Me and Levi at the beach."

"You girls sure you don't need some help setting up?" Levi asked.

"I don't need a man to help me set up a tent," Cheyenne said, and her normal twang was sharp on the edge. It softened at the end. "You two lovebirds go get wet. You have your phones on ya?"

"Yeah," Rheighna said.

"You know what we're driving," Andi said. "Worst case scenario stumble on out to us. We'll try to go for that one campsite we saw on the way up here, the Badger route."

"Aye aye, captain," Levi said, saluting.

"Ladies," Cheyenne said to the couple.

Rheighna and Levi held hands and ran off into the crowd of people, towels hanging over their backs and swimming packs full.

"They are so cute together," Andi said. "Is it bad that I wish they'd drown?"

"No," Cheyenne said. "Normal human response to that level of unadulterated fluff. Let's go set up this stupid tent already."

Andi nodded, and they climbed back in and headed off to Badger route.

There was a relatively empty space way out in the middle of the woods, off a seemingly awkward path that spiraled into nowhere. Nobody was there, and there weren't even signs that indicated it was a campsite. Their only clue was a freestanding metal grill.

"No people," Andi said. "Quietude and seclusion."

"Perfect place for a human sacrifice," Cheyenne said.

"Don't joke like that!" Andi said. "I'd like to be able to sleep sometime this evening."

They lugged the sleeper tent out towards a relatively smooth patch of land next to a huge oak. Cheyenne dropped the kit and walked up to the tree.

"Check it out," Cheyenne said. "Lookit these gouge marks. Antler marks."

"What are they from?" Andi asked.

"Well," Cheyenne said. She paused. The woods were growing darker around the two of them, the moon getting higher and higher in the sky. "There could be two explanations. One mundane. One weird."

"Mundane," Andi said.

"Could be a stag in mid-rut," Cheyenne said. "Look, you can see a little bit of blood in the gouge marks here. Makes sense. Antlers are covered in a fine skein of fur and tissue, so when the males lock horns they start to bleeding out. If he's marking his territory here, like I assume, it would make sense for there to be a little blood."

"So bloody damage on a tree is normal, is what you're saying," Andi asked.

7

"Yeah, and it's not even that big of a problem if a big buck comes up and gives us grief. I brought my rifle," Cheyenne said. She paused again, hands in her pocket, boyish face staring out at the trees surrounding them. She blew out air in a big sign. "But."

"I don't like that word."

"Have you heard the stories about this place?" Cheyenne asked. "The Black Hills area."

"If this is some ploy to scare me out of my panties and somehow get some lesbian action out of me I swear to God," Andi said. Her tone changed. "It's actually a pretty good plan. It might work."

Cheyenne grinned at her.

"Come on, tent first, urban legends second," she said. "Gotta tell this story over marshmallows."

True to form, Cheyenne did most of the work herself. Andi knew there was a joke somewhere in there about tent-pegging but she didn't have the mental clarity to work out the logistics of it. She knew she had a crush on Cheyenne, in an abstract way, but she also knew it would likely never work. For one—Cheyenne was a girl, even if only technically. For two—well, there was no two about it. Her list of reasons why she wouldn't date Cheyenne was very limited in scope, when she really thought about it...

Distracting herself from her weirdly budding sapphism, Andi went and gathered firewood as dusk settled in. By the time she'd wandered back the newly erected sleeper was up and secured; a circle of stones nearby had some twigs and some fuel burning gently, and Cheyenne had even went and grabbed some of her own firewood to boot.

Soon the ladies had marshmallows up and roasting, and Cheyenne stared at her with all the gaunt grotesquerie of the Crypt Keeper from across the fire.

"So there's word that this whole land is cursed," Cheyenne said. "They say that the woods are haunted—supposedly there was a huge mansion owned by a very rich man long, long ago. He was a famous illusionist, they said, and supposedly it was an illusionist's guild, but the locals all said it was a front. In reality he was a devil worshipper, and his comrades were all fellow supplicants in league with Satan. They came out under the light of a full blood moon and did weird rituals, like summoning the dead, or raising devils to walk the earth. They say that one day one of their rituals went wrong, that some of the demons escaped and stalk the forest."

"Well," Andi said, and she blew out her marshmallow. It was blackened, and not at all appealing. "That sounds like a big bunch of nope."

"Oh but there have been a lot of sightings," Cheyenne said. "Weird, man-sized bird creatures with no hands. Huge stinking man-apes. Giant flesh-eating deer creatures that walk on two legs and have huge antlers they gouge trees with..."

Andi felt the hair on the back of her neck stand straight up. There was movement and noise out in the woods suddenly; she and Cheyenne turned and stared at the moving shadows.

Cheyenne slowly reached down to her feet to grab her rifle...

A piercing shriek tore through the night sky, and Cheyenne raised the rifle to her sights.

"You have five seconds to turn around, mother fucker!" she called out.

"It's just me!" Rheighna's voice shrieked.

"Oh dear God." Andi's shoulders slumped.

Rheighna, Levi, and an older man with long graying hair walked up together, and when they got into eyesight, Cheyenne lowered the rifle and sat it at her feet. Andi noticed it was still well within reach, however...

"We got so lost," Rheighna said. "The water was really cold, and the forest was even colder when we got out. This guy helped us get our bearings and find you."

He was an older man, weather-beaten with age, and his long steel-gray hair hung to his shoulders. He smiled at them all. It was almost imperceptible behind his feathered hair, but when the wind caught it he seemed to have an eyepatch over his right eye.

"Why don't you guys introduce us?" Andi asked.

"Oh, yeah," Rheighna said. "Mr. Eyepatch, this is Andi and Cheyenne. We work together. Andi, Cheyenne, this is our lifesaver."

"I wouldn't say that," Mr. Eyepatch said, barking out a laugh. "I'm just an old fart that's familiar with these woods. Saving the lost is kind of what I do. I guess you young people call it being an empath nowadays. I'm just drawn to suffering, and seek only to find its source. I'm… ah, this might sound a bit esoteric, but I'm drawn to it like a moth to a fire. And speaking of fires… it is a very chilly night this evening. May I sit and banter for a spell with you? Hard being old. Your joints like to stiffen up in the slightest breeze."

Andi and Cheyenne locked eyes. Cheyenne's hand edged almost imperceptibly to her side. Andi knew without words being spoken that Cheyenne would have this guy's head exploded if any fuckery happened.

"Yeah, sure," Andi said.

"Wonderful," he said, sitting on a nearby log and warming his hands.

Rheighna and Levi chattered on non-stop, toweling off and getting clean, the old man sitting and listening and nodding his head occasionally, turning his hands carefully. The moon overhead was bold and bright; as big as a city in the night sky, with crimson chasing its edges.

"Andi, can you come with me to get some marshmallows?" Cheyenne asked.

"Sure," Andi said.

They disappeared into the tent together, and Cheyenne zipped the zip all the way to the top behind them.

The fire's glimmer cast a shadow through the tent walls, and Cheyenne looked like a dark spirit standing in the gloom.

"Okay," Cheyenne said. "On three, we say what we're feeling."

Andi nodded.

"One… Two… Three."

"I'm getting serial killer vibes—" Cheyenne hissed.

"I think we might make a good cou—" Andi began, then coughed. She spoke in a whisper as she continued. "Yeah, serial killer vibes. Totally."

Cheyenne stared at her for a few seconds more.

"If things go south, I need you to grab the other two, run for the car, and just drive," Cheyenne said. "Keep your cellphone on you at all times. Don't stop until you hit civilization."

Andi nodded.

"But you don't think he'd actually do anything, do you?" Andi whispered.

"I fucking hope not," Cheyenne whispered back. "I've got my rifle, so I'll do what I can on my end. Remember. If you need it—the code word is rhubarb. That means run your ass to the car."

"Why rhubarb?"

Cheyenne threw up her hands.

"What fucking code word do you want to use, Andi dear?" she hissed.

"Rhubarb is okay, I just think it'd be kind of obvious."

"Isn't that part of the point, though?"

Andi thought about this.

"Yeah, you're right," she said. "Where are the keys?"

Cheyenne pulled them out and dangled them soundlessly. Andi grabbed them and put them in her pocket.

"Okay, now let's just try to get him to go away," Cheyenne said.

They nodded at each other and unzipped the tent, taking opposite spots at the opposite corners of the campfire.

"You seem a bit distressed," the old man said.

"Nope," Andi squeaked.

"Not distressed at all," Cheyenne said, fake smiling through her teeth.

"So you'd say you have your suffering in check?" the old man asked.

"'Scuse me?" Cheyenne asked.

"What do you mean 'in check?'" Andi asked.

Mr. Eyepatch paused and blinked, his visible eye carefully taking them all in.

"I suppose that's a bizarre sounding thing to say. Ah. What fortuitous timing! We appear to be experiencing a blood moon."

He gazed at the sky, and the other four stared up with him.

It was a lunar eclipse, Andi thought. The crimson that had been threatening to overtake the wide moon at its edges was now a full-blown red orb staring down at the earth.

"The Native tribes on this land used to call this a blood moon because of its coloring, but it's a total eclipse. Fascinating, isn't it? You know what they say about a blood moon, don't you? That it amplifies whatever suffering you're experiencing tenfold. A terrible burden, that. You must keep your suffering in check on nights like these! It just may well save your lives."

"You keep talking about suffering," Levi said. "I'm not suffering."

"Me neither," Rheighna said.

"You're thinking too literally," the old man said. "Suffering is more than a brief moment of pain. Suffering is anguish—suffering is negativity. Pessimism. Lack of hope. The shadows that live at the edge of the human heart and provoke our sadness, our despair… that is true suffering! The depression that lays in wait, the evil thoughts that crawl in one's head and gives one nightmares. The endless beckoning of a life no longer filled with hope, *that* is suffering! The incalculable dread of a flat gray future one can feel suffocating one to death. *That* is suffering. The darkness in ourselves that we don't acknowledge—the shadows—that harden our hearts and our spirits. They cling to you, dragging you down, preventing your potential. Suffering is bad enough on its own. But they say a blood moon makes it worse. Makes you a target."

"A target?" Levi asked. "That sounds like a crock of shit."

"Ah, I am full of shit in a general sense, but in this case I must insist that I know what I'm talking about. There is evil that walks the face of this earth. Monsters, you know. They're drawn to your suffering. Your pain can be so exquisite that it calls out to them like a perfume."

Cheyenne and Andi looked at one another, thinking of their earlier conversation.

"Keeping your suffering in check could save your life, especially on a night like tonight," Mr. Eyepatch said quietly. He pulled back his hair, and showed off his hidden eye. It was covered with a patch. "That's how I got this."

"Earlier you were saying something about falling off a horse—" Levi said.

"You're not listening like you ought to," Mr. Eyepatch said. "Of course I got it from falling off a horse. I was riding like my life depended on it—the horse tumbled, and off I went, flying. But there was something that happened to cause it all. Something that caused me to ride through a forest much like this at lightning speed, in the dark, like a fool."

"And that was?" Andi asked.

"It was… a long time ago. Times were different then. The economy had tanked. We had a ranch, but the ranch was drying up, the water source had become foul, and the crops were turning up rotten for the third year running. Any extra money I made was from stabling horses for passersby. Just to make ends meet, my wife hemmed and sewed for a bit of extra cash on the side.

"I didn't keep my suffering in check then. Didn't know how, truth be told. I didn't address it like I ought. To acknowledge it. Instead it built up inside me and grew like some odious cancer, and all I could do was drown it in a bottle." He made a drinking motion with his hands. "All the while, our babies were starving and I was becoming more and more of a useless drunk. Do you know what it's like to see the light of love in your partner's eyes die out? To see them look at you and hate you? I was a failure as a husband and as a provider. After enough of this went on, and this darkness grew and grew, I decided to take matters into my own hands.

"I had taken out an insurance policy on myself, you see, and I was determined to come out here and end it all. They weren't so stringent on rules and regulations at that time. I got liquored up and after enough happy juice I had it all worked out. I was to blow my brains out, and fall into the river. They'd find my horse and my boots, and eventually my body. My hopes were that the falls would bash me up enough to cover any head injuries I may or may not inflicted on myself. Then they could collect the check, and all would be right in the world—one less miserable bastard, and my wife and children taken care of. You get the picture. Anyway, I had it all planned out in my whiskey wisdom. And right as my finger touched that trigger, and I summoned up all the nerve I could to just do it, I had this dawning realization. Even if things worked out the way I needed them to, or thought they ought, my family was going to remain miserable. I was still leaving 'em behind. It was such a revelation that I dropped the Colt right there in the grass and hopped on my horse, boots and everything off my feet as I rode hard homewards bound. My family needed me! The *me* I could be, the *me* I needed to be."

"And that's when you fell off the horse?"

Mr. Eyepatch shook his head.

"Now now, don't go putting the horse before the carriage, m'boy. I made it home safe and sound, and I felt the weight that had been building up for years in my chest fall away. It was like seeing the sun for the first time in years. I felt reborn, like I had been baptized! But life can be as cruel as it can be kind. There was another man's boots at my door. A very familiar pair, too. It was my best friend's boots, as I found out—when I found him getting intimate with my wife in our bed."

"Oh shit," Levi said.

"That's awful!" Rheighna said.

"It is what it is," Mr. Eyepatch said. "That's life. The important thing is you experience pain and you keep it in check. Because I didn't. My wife screamed at me to get out, so I did. I ran out of my house, ran back down the steps, and hopped on my horse again. I turned straight around back into the woods and kept on riding. I was after my Colt. If my wife didn't even want me then I knew, with a sudden certainty, that my best friend would keep her company even while my corpse was still warm.

"My suffering drew up around me, like a cloud. The forest started to get confusing. I was getting scared and angry. I couldn't quite find where I'd dropped my pistol. And just when I had remembered where it was again, all of a sudden I heard this noise. Like nothing I've ever heard before. It was so sudden, so terrifying, that I damn near wet myself."

"I bet he pissed himself," Levi whispered, to Rheigna. Rheighna elbowed him.

11

"I wasn't filled with that hate, those shadows, that suffering anymore at that point. It had all curled up in my chest like so much fear. My immediate gut instinct was that whatever was in the forest was ready to end my suffering for me, that it was going to do what I couldn't. But if it was gonna happen, I wanted it to happen on my terms. My way. Not pissing in terror."

"I fucking knew it," Levi hissed.

"I rode hard. My instincts knew where the Colt was, now that adrenaline was going through me. I hopped off the horse, listening to things crunching in the woods around us, slipped back into my boots, grabbed my pistol, and then carefully crawled back up the horse. Whichever way that thing was coming from, I was gonna take off in the opposite direction. The only problem was, I could smell it. It smelled like death, like a dumpster, like horseshit basted in an old spitoon left in the sun in an outhouse for a week. It was so thick I damn near upchucked. My horse was skittish, spooked as all hell. We danced in a circle, looking for where the sonofabitch was. My intentions were to discharge my sixth, fifth, fourth, third, and second to last bullet into whatever this thing was' skull and skedaddle, but that was before the trees parted and it roared. Of course, wet leather ain't comfortable, no matter how scared you are."

"Urine trouble now," Levi said.

Cheyenne rolled her eyes.

"The first thing I saw was antlers," the old man said. "Antlers made of bone, I reckon, for they shone in the moonlight a crimson bloom, as if they were stained with gore. Twelve-points like a crown extending backwards. Its face looked like a deer's, with a strange, atavistic expression in its eyes, as if it were *angry*. I still can't get the image out of my head, all these years later. The bastard was walking on two legs—it was as if someone had taken a deer and pulled it, broke its bones, reshaped it into a man, and filled it with a rage so powerful it burned from its eyes. Its long arms—talons spindly, grotesquely deformed—were reaching out to swipe at us already, but my horse, being an intelligent sort, whinnied and bucked, turning, damn near throwing me off in the process. I held on for my life and the two of us sped off into the night. Tree branches hung low, slapping at my face, and here and there I ducked.

"Now that it had revealed itself, it seemed not to want to let us leave alive. Roars and shrieks, the sound and noise of ancient trees bending and cracking all around us echoed as it tore ass after us.

"I turned around and discharged my pistol, but it didn't even flinch. Its eyes were like the devil itself in his fiery pit, and it roared, and before I knew it a jumping swipe launched it towards us, and swept my poor horse off its feet. I flew through the air, ass-over-teakettle, landing on the ground with a bone-shaking thump. And the world was suddenly looking very different, sort of distorted-like. I sat up, hesitating, and found something wet hanging by my cheek from a little cord, connected to my eye-socket."

Andi looked down at the naked, spherical marshmallow she had just peeled the black off of, then tossed it behind her into the bushes.

"So what happened next?" Rheighna asked.

Mr. Eyepatch shrugged.

"I passed out. But it was a curious thing. I saw something appear in view over me, some kind of bird-looking creature big as a man. *Its* eyes were glowing green. And the damn-dest thing was. Maybe it was just my vision. But it didn't look like it had hands. Just arms with empty stubs."

"What do you think it was?" Andi asked.

12

"Hell if I know," Mr. Eyepatch said. His tone here was completely different, as if hurrying through to finish. "I woke up and it was daylight and there was a man in charge of the property poking me with a stick and looking a bit sick to his stomach. On account of the eye, y'see. I don't know how I didn't see nothing when it was just there on my cheek. Guessing the optical nerve got snapped in the tussle."

"The thing didn't eat you?"

Mr. Eyepatch shrugged.

"It ain't a perfect story, but I am sitting here telling it," he said. "Call it luck. Call it what you want. I got patched up and never went back to my family, and I've been wandering ever since. Trying to ignore it all. To keep my pain in check, so I never come face to face with that thing again…"

"And how has that worked out for you?" Cheyenne asked.

"It's been a struggle," Mr. Eyepatch said. "But no monster thus far. The only problem we face now is tonight. The Blood Moon. More apt to manifest things like this. So let me ask you. Who here is suffering? And who here has their suffering in check?"

There was a very hungry look on his face.

Something snapped in the trees. Rheighna flashed her cellphone into the distance. Some kind of birdish creature in a hood stood outlined against the light for half a second, eyes glowing green, before it vanished from view.

"Did you see that?" Levi asked.

"Ugh, who cut the cheese?" Rheighna asked, holding her nose.

A hideous smell surrounded them on all sides, so thick and cloying it was like cologne.

"Okay, I'm done playing nice," Cheyenne said. She stood up, hefting her rifle up in one motion and pointed it at the man, sighting it across the fire. Rheighna gasped. "I don't know what kind of sick, twisted horror show you're running here old man, but I don't truck with cults or serial killers or whatever the *fuck* this bullshit is." She paused, and turned her head to Andi. "Hello! Rhubarb, bitch!"

Andi nodded in recognition, got up, moved quickly to Levi and Rheigna, then bent down between them, tugging at them and whispering to them.

"I'm just here for the show," the old man said, and he looked up, from the page, at You. "We all enjoy a little bit of terror now and again, don't we? Of course I mean you. Yes, you, the one reading this. We're here for the same thing, aren't we? Oh, don't be so shocked. You knew this was coming, surely. Or are you that naïve?"

The old man grinned, pulling back his eyepatch. A horrible, crimson light pulsed from it, geometric symbols swirling endlessly...

"And now the real story begins!" he cackled.

"Who are you even talking to?" Cheyenne screamed.

Levi and Rheighna stood, and Andi too, but something huge swiped at them from the forest, and suddenly a meaty thump slapped into the ground. The girls gasped.

Levi's mouth gaped, eyes rolling over as the top half his torso, gruesomely severed diagonally from his right shoulder down to his waist, slid onto the ground with a wet plop. Bizarrely, he was still alive—his hand scrabbled at the ragged edge of his pants, where his cellphone was presumably tucked into his pocket. What he was trying to accomplish, nobody could say—maybe call the police. His legs and the other half of his torso buckled and his lower half fell right on its ass. Van Morrison's "Moondance" blared as loud as possible from where part of him had fallen on his phone.

A scarlet fountain spattered blood over both Andi and Rheighna, who shrieked.

"What the fuck is that?" Cheyenne asked, looking at the creature. It stalked forward, murderous rage on its face and eyes gleaming vermillion, towards Cheyenne. Rifle on her shoulder, she aimed and released shot after shot at it, the impact ringing through the woods.

"Beautiful," Mr. Eyepatch said, clapping, face in awe. "It's so goddamn beautiful!"

Across the fire Rheighna was trying to pull Levi's upper half. Andi tried to pull her away and towards the 4x4.

"Come on, we have to go, you have to leave him—" Andi babbled.

"But we can save him!" Rheighna shrieked.

The creature stepped forward towards Cheyenne, talons grasping, unblinking even as shot after shot entered its rank hide.

Its large hands picked her up by her waist, raising her nearly six feet in the air, then squeezed and dug its nails in. Her ribs cracked; her lungs were pierced. She coughed, blood spilling from her mouth, and leveled the rifle at its right eye. She pulled the trigger—it dropped her, and she splatted on the ground like raw meat, and it howled as it recoiled. Half of its long, almost lupine face had exploded away. Now there was only a wriggling mass of flesh and a hanging tube of meat where its tongue hung nearly to its waist.

Andi was tugging at Rheighna's shoulders.

"Come on, Rheighna, we have to leave NOW!"

Rheighna turned and pushed her backwards. Andi fell backwards on her butt.

"Don't touch me, bitch!" Rheighna screamed, sobbing. "I can't just leave hi-"

The creature had loped over the fire as fast as a shadow, pouncing on her, even as the chorus of the song played. Rheighna shrieked, struggling as it started to rip into her with its teeth, and Andi turned over and scrabbled on her hands and knees to get purchase and get away.

The old man with one eye laughed and laughed.

The beast turned, attacking the cellphone in Levi's lower half's pants. Andi got to her feet, wobbling, and sprinted to the 4x4. She turned and saw Levi's hand waving, in horror, before she scrabbled and dropped the keys in the dirt. She picked them up with trembling hands, unlocked the door, and dove in, locking the door behind her.

"Okay, Andi," she whispered to herself. "Turn the car on. Turn the car on."

It whined, shuddered, refused to catch. She saw the creature hear the noise—saw its huge outline turn as slow as a juggernaut.

"Start bitch!" she shrieked, turning the key again. Whirr, fizz, dud. The engine remained inert. "Start already you stupid piece of crap!"

It tore towards her, and the car sprung to life just as it hit her like a mack truck.

"No," she muttered, the car shaking as it was lifted off the ground. "No no no!"

As the metal creaked and shrieked, she tore off her seatbelt, kicked open the door, and jumped to freedom. Or at least, she tried. Her ankle got caught in the seatbelt and she dangled upside down, squirming loose and falling at just the right angle to hear something in her neck snap, for good.

She lay frozen on the ground, paralyzed. She couldn't move anything below her chin. Not the worst way to go, she considered, in the half a moment before the creature tossed the SUV over her. At least she wouldn't feel it pierce—

A weird sense of euphoria overtook her as its talons entered her. And then her thoughts, mercifully, left her... except for the ongoing laugh of the one-eyed man, and the sight of the Blood Moon hanging overhead.

All she heard, as she was lifted into the air and lost consciousness, were the last few chords of Van Morrison playing...

B.A.M.F. PIXIES: AN A-HOLE STORY

Illustration by Anton Tolstobrov

CHAPTER 2:

B.A.M.F. PIXIES: AN A-HOLE STORY

The radar pinged and wailed in his hands as he entered the clearing. Well, it was evidence enough to know he was in the right place—even if he hadn't seen the small pile of toad and squirrel bones against the far tree, or the decomposing cat stretched out on its side.

He closed his eyes, breathed in deeply. Tried not to smell wastewater and muck and dead things.

"This is it," he said to himself, and there was an almost manic glee to his voice. He clapped his hands together, then poured a decent splosh of liquor down his throat. It splashed on his shirt. "Showtime."

His name was Grimm. He was a man on a mission, though if one didn't know him, they would say he looked a little like a nutjob. There was a frantic, frenetic air to him as he moved—staggering about like a scarecrow that had just been given some inhuman life, both legs dragging as he walked in a zombie lurch. How much of it was an act, and how much of it was him, was hotly contested, even with those who knew him.

The truth of the matter was that Grimm had always been a little off. At least, that's what his Aunt had always said. She'd found him in the basement one morning, attempting to perform a brain swap surgery on his cousin and the family labrador. He was all of ten years old. He did not get much further than shaving their heads and marking the prospective cut marks with a ballpoint pen. The ass-chewing he'd got then did not do much to deter him as the years went on.

He sat himself on a tree stump in the clearing. He was deep in the woods of the Black Hills, and after a moment or two of consideration, he put his face in his hands, shoulders slumped, and to anyone looking at him from the outside, he was clearly awash in despair.

A sticky bottle of liquor, half-empty, sat in a puddle of its own juices by his booted feet, near a pistol, which was primed and loaded. He looked, clearly, like someone who had seen better days—perhaps better months, years, lifetimes—and was someone whom life had seen fit to trod on, repeatedly.

"Stephanie," he said. "I wonder why I left you here. I wonder why life is the way it is sometimes. I know you're here. I know I can't see you. I know that… things could have been worse. But they could have been better. How long has it been, Stephanie?"

Small blue things buzzed from the trees, hovering, almost silently, lamp-like eyes staring at him.

He picked up the revolver, sat it in his lap, and considered it. He swigged another few mouthfuls of liquor, wiping a sticky hand across his mouth.

"It would be so simple just to end it all. I know you're here. I know there are more things in this world than either of us know. But I wonder. When the pain is going to end. When the pain is going to let up. When it's going to release."

He sat back, a penitent rogue staring at the blue sky.

"Fuck me," he said. "I have nothing left. You were the only light in this dark world, and now that you're gone. Well. It feels selfish to keep living. To keep striving. The most I can ever hope for is a half-life. Haunting these grounds like some phantom that's not quite all the way here. Not quite all the way there."

Buzzing closer now, with wicked eyes and tiny sharp teeth, with antennae and a lust for the desperation pouring from him, they swarmed in even closer.

"Help me, Stephanie. Can't you. Can't you just give me something? Some kind of sign? A whisper from beyond the veil. Hold my hand. Speak to me. Send me peace and joy. I'm struggling. I know it's selfish of me. I have my life still. But why did I survive? I'm this malformed freak of a thing. You. You were goodness and light. You were everything in this fucked up world left saving. And somehow... I'm the monster that got left behind. Some revenant, floating through his life..."

He stared down at the gun. Imagined cold metal in his mouth, the awkwardness of his thumb pulling the trigger while his hand held tight onto the muzzle. Imagined gunpowder and shrapnel slicing straight through his brain. He imagined silence... a vast void of nothingness, a womb of calm. Some way to end all thought, all pain, all suffering...

Voices came to him. The small blue creatures had crawled around the stump, their vile faces leering happily.

"There's nothing left for you here," one of them said.

"The only way to beat your suffering is to end it," another of the creature's voices said.

"End it. End your pain," another voice said.

He closed his eyes. Of course oblivion sounded nice. And wasn't that the best a scientist of any persuasion could hope for? An eternity of a quiet mind. An eternity of nothingness. And yet... the voices spoke to him all around. Cajoling him. Whispering to him. Coercing him.

"The only way you'll see her again is if you kill yourself, you miserable prick!" one of the voices hissed.

And, of course... that was what stopped him. Rationally, the only good part of a suicide was the part where you were wiped out. What good was being a ghost when he was already half-dead with longing and sadness? If there was someone to greet him on the other side... what would he say? What could he say? I wasted this gift I had. Hope you're happy to see me.

He stuck the gun under his chin. Felt the cold metal of the muzzle against his whispy stubble. Felt the cold, miniature pinpricks of pixie talons as they pierced his shoulder, his back, their little wings buzzing their lies.

"Just do it," one said.

"DO IT!" another one said.

"FUCKING KILL YOURSELF!" the last one said.

He swallowed, put his thumb on the hammer. Turned it, ever-so-slightly to the right... and released.

The gunshot echoed out into the clearing, and for a second, nobody moved. And then, from a far tree, a little blue body, smashed and beyond recognizable, fell off and hit the ground.

"Oh shit!" said another pixie.

Grimm stood, rising like a giant in the field of blue buzzing bloodsuckers before him. His fingers hit a mechanism on the pistol—what had before been a relatively cleverly concealed handgun was now turning itself into something that looked a bit like a crossbow made of chrome.

He loaded it with a bolt from his sleeve, then cocked another switch. The bolt split into three.

He grinned, and the pixies screamed…

"You should know the name of the man that's going to end your life. Grimm Grimtowsky. But you can call me Death, if you prefer" he said, laughing maniacally. "I'm as inevitable as taxes and suffering."

"Die motherfucker!" one of the pixies said, hoisting a small pitchfork. It rushed at Grimm on a kamikaze mission, wings buzzing angrily. Grimm knocked it out of the air with the butt end of the crossbow. It fell to the ground, wings fluttering weakly. He stomped on its body with one shoe, then leered down at it.

"I'm here to pop wings and kick some bitch-ass motherfucking pixie ass, and I'm all out of wings!"

There was a horrible bite-sized scream as he ripped, viscous fluid painting the ground in front of him… and a pair of sparkling wings shone tightly in his fist as he cackled triumphantly…

A cavalcade of three pixies in Vee formation flew at him, each holding one end of a sharp piece of clothes-line. The back two separated, flying in either direction around him, and before Grimm could aim he felt the line wrap around his throat. His feet started to lift off the ground, and he felt himself dragged backwards by his neck. He dropped his bowgun and clutched at the line, taking in deep, ragged breaths, and slammed into a tree.

One of the pixies stabbed a little pitchfork through his right hand, nailing him to the tree.

"You glittery little piece of crap!" he gasped, fighting for air against the clothesline.

He pulled his pitchforked hand off the tree, screaming, then used the spines sticking through his hand to cut at the cord holding him by his neck. His vision was starting to blur, but he dropped to his feet and rolled, coming up with a crossbow from earlier. Triple crossbow bolts nailed each of the little fuckers against a far tree.

Grimm tore off the corner of his shirt, hissing as he yanked the pitchfork out of his hand. Another pixie had started to fly in at him from behind, attacking like an angry bluejay, and he aimed the crossbow over his back without looking. Two more fell, one on top of the other, impaled with a bolt and landing on a third he'd stomped on earlier.

"I'm getting sick of these games," he screamed, and finished wrapping his hands. "I counted twelve of you little Fraggle Rock fuckers earlier, and I've already taken down seven. Come at me!"

He moved back towards the grove, a murderous look in his eyes…

A stump made great firewood, especially for a cauldron, especially when he stacked rocks around it and dumped gasoline on the damn thing. The smell of mushroom soup with sycamore leaves and pine needles was an awesome odor in the night air. Twelve little pixie bodies, sans wings, were lined up on a neat series of shishkebabs. They had been Vlad the Impalered—in the mouth, out the butt. A little like guinea pigs, Grimm considered.

The little shits got what was coming to them. They were attracted to suffering like hummingbirds to nectar. A suicidal drunk man in a forest was like a honey-glazed ham left out for a very hungry wolf.

Well, he considered, you can either eat or be eaten. And these were very delicious mushrooms that grew out here, he considered, placing one of the kebabs over the flame under the cauldron. Now, with these pixie wings, he could perfect that experiment he was working on…

SLEIGHT OF HAND

ILLUSTRATION BY ANTON TOLSTOBROV

CHAPTER 3:

SLEIGHT OF HAND

Henry Hudson first stepped foot on the land that would be called Gravesend, arriving on his ship the Half Moon in the late 1600's. Randall would come to appreciate the irony of the land that shaped him as a child much, much later in life. Gravesend proper was established by one Lady Deborah Moody around 1643. It was at times a harbor of sin—heretical sects of Protestantism came and flocked, and in time, the area would grow up to be the bustling center of seduction known as 'Sodom by the Sea.'

When he was but a boy of nine, his mother had taken him down to Coney Island and he witnessed his first disappearing trick. On the spot Randall Erickson fell in love with magic. What a way to go, he thought. Just a poof! And before you know it, the magician was gone. It was downright impressive. With another flash of smoke and roar from the crowd the man reappeared on the other side of the room. It was fantastic.

Equally impressive how his mother disappeared from Gravesend the same night. Poof! A clutter of noise from the kitchen, the smell of cigarettes and the sound of a scuffle. Maw went missing, with a tip of the hat from the mysterious magician that had rolled into town. Even more impressive—his father's new magic trick. How quickly the whiskey bottle showed up in the pantry! And the thing seemed to be bottomless—It was almost like no matter how much Paw drank, it perpetually refilled.

Poof! Watch how quickly people's eyes avoided them in public. Poof! With the arrival of Paw and Son Erickson at the church it seemed almost divine how quickly Bibles went to faces and handkerchiefs went to mouths, how quickly the women chatted with each other as they looked at the two with pity.

Magic had given, but it had also taken away. Magic gave Randall an escape; it gave his mother an escape. It took what it wanted, though—his time, his money, his efforts. His father's sanity.

Randall searched desperately for the secrets behind prestidigitation. He would sneak down to Coney Island at night when any new travelling stage-shows rolled through town, and would often scour the newspapers endlessly for the latest stories on his favorite illusionists: Robert-Houdin, Hermann the Great, The Great Wizard of the North. Mostly European, of course, but that was neither here nor there. His meager allowance was used on packs of playing cards, new hats, and specialty made gloves from one of any more Victorian-styled tailors in their little New York borough.

He'd have to hide the whole getup from his father, or else he'd get a beating.

"You're wasting your time," his old man often said, five whiskeys in on a Saturday evening. His breath reeked of liquor, and his eyes swam in his skull as he spoke, all iris and rage like a bull. "Magic's all smoke and mirrors, boy. Illusion. Deception. All it's good for is tricking people. Do you really want to be a liar for a living?"

Randall knew better than to say anything, and on good days he'd take the hand to the side of his face. On bad days, his father would grab him by the wrists, hard enough to cut off his circulation and make his fingers tingle, and shake him.

"Do you want to be a liar for a living? I asked you a question!"

Nothing Randall said ever helped. It was like a magic trick, getting hit—one second you're standing in place, the next you're on the floor and the whole world is spinning.

Here one second, gone the next.

Somewhere in Randall's heart of hearts he knew that there were two layers. There was a deeper meaning, an older mythos that spanned the course of human history. In the old days the Gods had fire stolen from them, depending on who you were reading. Fire itself was used for all things good and kind in human society. The ancient alchemists called fire one of the fundamental energies that composed the world. It was Old Magic, fire was. This fire—this Promethean flame—it was illusion and deception itself used for the highest of good.

Randall figured that if he kept studying, he might find something else like it, some other kind of Promethean flame that would solve all his problems.

His father had run afoul of the law in one of Gravesend's numerous saloons—drinking and fighting, leaving a man practically catatonic. Onwards they drifted, down country roads and through the woods of New England, out to the mid-west of the Dakotas, where evergreen forest took over. They stopped in Deadwood, where the land teemed with power, a land of casinos and money and opportunity.

His father sure had his particulars about towns.

The old man had taken to card-sharking. (And wasn't that ironic? Randall thought.) Tourists would come with greenbacks, then turn around and leave, divested entirely of their fortune. The old man had it down to a science.

Randall spent his evenings by candlelight at home, days spent at the public library and the bookshop. He was searching, ever-onward, for something more… though he wasn't sure when he would find it.

One thing he did find, though, was young love. A young woman, Margaret, whose father owned the bookshop had caught his eye. She was slim, petite, polite. Had the same interests as him, or at least feigned it well. Prestidigitation, folktales, the arcane, and the occult. She knew just what he was after when he needed something.

Life had seemed to be getting better in its own way…

His father's mood seemed to improve as well. At least, at first, with their new surroundings… but soon, just as it always had, the whiskey got to him. Some nights the old man would stumble home, smelling as bad as an outhouse, eyes crimson and bloodshot. He'd pick up Randall's latest research project, sneering at it.

"Magic," he said, laughing. "You're a feebleminded fool to believe in that idiocy. Work as a farmhand, tend to a stable! There's plenty of coin you could bring in, were you driven.

Do something with the two hands God himself gave you! Don't you know what they say? Idle hands are the Devil's providence! And if you aren't the spawn of Satan himself."

Mocking threats were easy nights. Not so easy were the other nights, when the shaggy form of his father would drunkenly bring yet another woman home. It all started the same—giggles, laughing, enjoyment... his father grunting like a horrible beast, and then the terrible screaming...

More than one young woman had come back to the house and left in tears. A few had not left at all. Doors had opened and closed... a foul stench on the wind, and the sound of his father dragging something out into the woods...

There was a fear that stole over Randall during these times. A terrible fear of things unknown and unsaid, of violence unaccounted for. It was a situation he knew nothing of—there seemed no logical recourse to it, no way to investigate. When he left in the mornings, there was nary a drop of evidence in his room—nothing untoward or out of place. No way for him to know what had happened. But the local papers had all found something to say—that there was a slew of missing women.

It was not, to Randall's greatest shame, until his father had found him in the bookshop that he considered there might be something he'd have to do.

His father was drunk midday again. He howled and caroused on the streets, spotting Randall through the front window, and carrying on like a jackass as he walked through the front doors.

"My son, ever the bookworm! What brings you here?"

"More research," Randall said, voice terse.

"More hokum, then," his father crowed. He paused, beady eyes staring, tracking something intently that had fallen in his sights.

It was Margaret. The look on his face, then, chilled Randall to the bone.

"She's a looker, ain't she?" his father said, knocking him in the ribs. "Why don't you introduce us?"

There was nothing Randall could say. He didn't seem to have the words for it.

"Margaret," he called, across the room, and felt his insides quaking. "This is my father."

"Delighted," she said, coming over and extending a hand.

His father began to speak. Margaret began to laugh.

Randall, beside himself, took to the alleyway, and began to cry.

He found one solution in a book on Voudoun practice in the Caribbean. Three drops of blowfish toxin in a victim's drink would make them catatonic, and appear dead. The victims would be buried, and the Doctor would dig them up after three days entombed in the dirt, with a shallow pipe to let them breathe. The brain-dead creature would find itself the unwilling servant of the Doctor. A truer magic Randall had never known before, and a far-away trip to the gambling halls for a bit of a trade gave him what he needed. And he'd found success, after a few days' worth of careful work and testing on the local rats.

"I think I've finally completed my best trick ever," Randall said, to his father, one weekend before Margaret had decided to come by.

"You know how I feel about that sort of lying, conniving business," the old man bellowed.

"Yeah, but this one's different," Randall said. "This one's real magic."

He waggled his pack of cards in his left hand, and slid his father a whiskey and tonic with his right.

Here one second, gone the next. What a shame, the ladies in town whispered at the funeral.

"Must have been the whiskey," Randall heard someone say.

He'd never performed a better illusion.

And of course, he never bothered about the whole digging his father back up part. Better to let the old bastard think about what he'd done, with what little was left of his brain, as the earth swallowed him alive.

Margaret, for her part, was stricken. She'd been quite fond of the old man. Randall hadn't known what to say to her. In time, she packed up and left for boarding school work further south. The last he'd heard, she married a nice young Lawyer from Alabama.

And as for Randall. He was a dab hand at words and tricks. There was nothing keeping him attached to Deadwood anymore. While working as a mobile telegram repairman and letter writer, he honed his act, making a decent living and studying just as hard as ever.

Here one second, gone the next. That's how he lived his life. He read and studied constantly. Blowing in from town to town, performing his act, and studying older spellbooks in his spare time. The secrets he managed to glean from the old texts were cyphers-puzzles locked away by his own lack of education, written in ancient metaphor, seemingly hidden beyond his hands.

Still, he improved. One particularly nasty tome told him the secrets of summoning the Ladies. The Ladies were ephemeral, phantasmal spectres that could be asked almost anything. One fasted for three days; they said the Lord's Prayer and sanctified the ritual chamber. (He had rented an old cabin in the woods, and hired a local boy to help him set up the space.)

After three days of penitence he prepared a dumb supper, dimmed the fire low, and chanted the incantation. The Ladies arrived at the table when he turned and faced the wall. He could smell them by the sulfurous noxiousness of their fumes; feel them by the way the air chugged and turned thick; hear them by their sonorous voices.

"What a brilliant little mageling," one of the Ladies said.

"A superior conjurer none have known," another Lady said.

"Shall we eat him for supper?" the third Lady asked.

"I have prepared a meal fit for a King," Randall stammered. "Eat and be merry, and know you are welcome within this house."

"He knows his manners," the third Lady said.

"Aye, he does," another Lady said.

"Shall we sup, then?" the first Lady asked.

They made a terrible noise as they attacked the spread, and Randall continued to stare at the walls, sweat dripping down his forehead. After some time had passed, Randall heard the Ladies start to stir again.

"A finer meal I've never had," one Lady said.

"A meal fit for a King," another Lady said.

"Aye, the lad has done his job," the third Lady said.

Silence, then, and then the one Lady spoke.

"And I suppose you shall be seeking an answer for a question?" she asked.

"Yes," Randall said.

"Probably another one of the League," another Lady tittered.

"Aye, yes, probably one of those foul Magicians," the third Lady said.

Randall, always very keen, decided to interject… carefully. The Ladies could be summoned and asked one question, exactly. That was the only safe way to ensure one lived throughout the summoning.

"Can't stand those lot," he said, trying to fish for information.

"What?" one Lady asked.

"You mean the League of Magicians?" another Lady asked.

"Of course I meant them," he said. "Which ones did you think I was talking about?"

"The vile hunters that live in the Black Hills," the third Lady said.

"Yeah, them. Never trusted a single one of 'em," Randall said.

"On that subject, we are agreed," the first Lady said. "Of course, that's beside the point. We must complete the contract."

There was a cracking noise; like that of a mouth whose teeth had perhaps grown too great for its skull. The sound of wet meat splitting open behind him was not a pleasant sensation. Randall felt very much that whatever presence was in the cabin's dining room had perhaps doubled, or even tripled in size; that whatever frightful forms the things he had fed had were replaced by some other, even more terrifying forms.

"What is it that thou wisheth from us, oh mageling?" the first Lady asked.

"And what would you give us in exchange?" the second Lady asked.

"Mind thee that thy words are careful," the third Lady said. "We take your token of offering in pounds of blood and flesh, and an agreement with us is not entered into casually."

"We will always collect," the first Lady said.

Her breath rushed over the back of Randall's neck—clotted, cold air thick with the smell of decay rushed out to greet him. He shuddered.

"I ask only for one answer," he said. "Give me the true secrets of magic, so that I may wield the power to work my will in this world."

There was a silence, then, for some time. Randall felt the sensation of serpents staring and waiting to strike at his back, as if he were being analyzed by some hungry creature waiting to leap and devour in the dark…

After some time, he heard one of the Ladies laugh.

"You clever little Mageling," she said.

"Knows the true secrets of the ritual and wants even more," the second Lady said.

"Yet asks it as a question," the third Lady said.

"Well?" the first one's voice was sharp. "What have you to offer?"

"I am an illusionist," Randall said. "I have only sleight of hand to offer. I ask for knowledge and I offer it in return. I shall teach you the tricks of my trade, if you but teach me the tricks of yours."

"What use have we for parlor tricks?" the second Lady asked.

"Our powers are beyond your ken, little illusionist," the third Lady said.

"And yet I have performed the ritual in accordance with the rules," Randall said.

A flurry of whispers burst out between them, and then, Randall saw a blast of light in every color imaginable against the cabin wall, and their three shadows in it. He could feel the edges and boundaries of where he was and who he was melting into the ripples of light, and the Ladies' raised cackles were all he heard.

"He makes his decision, then," the first Lady said.

"We have agreed to your terms," the second Lady said.

"You offer us sleight of hand, and wish to wield powers unimaginable to most of your kind," the third Lady said. "We give and we take. We shall grant thy wish, but take our flesh price."

"But you should know our terms," the first Lady said.

"You will wield great powers by your hand, but by your own hand will your downfall be complete," the second Lady said.

"You will rise like a shining star, and plummet like a meteor," the third Lady said.

"You will gain what you want, but in return you will lose that which is most precious to you."

"I've already lost all that is precious to me," he said, gesturing over his shoulders. "There's naught else you can take that would overly beleaguer me."

"We shall see," the first Lady said.

The Ladies cackled; the light rippled against the wall, and Randall found himself melting into the flow of something older than time itself.

Whatever they'd done worked, and worked well. Randall found sparks of insight in every tome he read. Whatever weird code the elders had written inside their spellbooks began to be legible. Soon he was mastering actual magic—the kind that tore reality in two and let him do what he wanted. The larger the spell, the more concentration it took—sadly, it wasn't as easy as snapping his fingers. But he was a simple man, with simple needs. The real work went into crafting illusions that looked like real magic.

He was able to materialize a pack of cards from nowhere. Manifest a rabbit from a hat. Literally disappear and reappear on the opposite sides of the stage. The realism of his act took him on the road, and propelled his career up and onwards.

He was hitting the headlines in every paper, packing the house down.

His last act before they found him? The old trick hands technique.

He had found his way back to Deadwood. Ah, the sights and smells and sounds of Deadwood. It called to him, nostalgic—a simpler era—and the place he'd buried his father. He always wondered if someone had dug the old bastard up.

A rolling hill dotted with trees on one end of town, overlooking a spattering of white houses. On the other end, there was the boardwalk, which he'd taken to walking in the evenings. Taking in the strip proper—gas lights, incandescent globes chasing away shadows in the evening. Hanging wooden signs calling out to thirsty patrons. And then, of course, the crown jewel of the boardwalk, the Gem Theater itself, rising from the brick storefronts, a two-storied amphitheater, resplendent in its beauty.

His old act had been becoming a bit... oh, what was the word? Stale? His own reserves of knowledge had been tapped out some time before. He could see the listlessness in his audience, and the small spark of his insight gave him some terrible intuition about what he would perform.

Everyone had their one gruesome trick. He and his assistant worked out the details, leaked it to the papers, and within weeks of working out the physical equations they had nearly the whole theater filled to capacity.

"Good evening Ladies and Gentleman," he beamed out at the audience. He started his patter up and let it fly through the air. "It has certainly been a pleasure to tease your senses with the wonders of the unseen world. It is well known that every great illusionist begins his career with the simple things..."

Randall waved his hands, and a deck of cards appeared, fanning wide.

"But tricks like these are simple sleight of hand."

Another wave, and the cards disappeared.

"Eventually the illusionist graduates on to slightly larger acts of grandeur." Randall pulled his cape off, twirling it around his shoulders and snapping. A white dove took to flight from beneath its wings. The audience oohed and ahhed. "And then with deeper study and an in-depth understanding of the universe, the true source of arcane knowledge is revealed to the patient seeker."

Randall snapped his arms out to his sides, palms open to the ground. Thunder crashed, and the floor rumbled. Flashes of light like lightning exploded from around the auditorium. There was a clunk from the eaves, and the lights shifted to deep blues and crimsons.

"And finally, after years of intense devotion to the taming of the ego, a man can begin to command the very nature of life itself. Suffering is inevitable, despite the life one leads—it matters not how good or bad, ugly or evil we are. Suffering is an inherent part of all walks of existence. However, the true master Magician can manipulate this flow of life and death, controlling it and ensuring that mere quibbles that impact lesser mortals never bother them."

His assistant, all smiles and curves and legs, walked out a pair of guillotines at arm's length from one another. Each sharp blade was clearly held up only by a rope-pulley mechanism knotted for safety. She moved them into place—one sharp blade dangling over his right hand, one over his left. Right on cue she snapped both of his wrists in through a locking mechanism and padlocked it; he jerked and tugged at both shackles, but was clearly stuck.

His assistant placed a candle under each of the rope knots. The kicker? A blindfold she wrapped around his eyes.

"And now, I'd say I have approximately one minute before the candles burn through the ropes and the blades come smashing down. They called these the Widowmakers in France, during the revolution. They're sharp blades, sharp enough to slice straight through bone, heavy enough to tear right through vertebra and decapitate their royal victims. They're definitely sharp enough to remove my hands right at the wrists. But as one who wields the true arcane force of Magic, I should be able to free myself from these bonds just in the nick of time. I ask you all for complete silence so that I can tap into the 'twisted realms' that are veiled to all but the few who know its secrets."

Silence in the auditorium then. The blind man struggled against his bonds, seemingly a fruitless endeavor. Flames licked at the knots; the burning smoke of the hemp ropes suspending the blades seemed to grow taller and taller, higher and higher.

There seemed to be panic on-stage. Randall's assistant looked at his struggle, face uncertain. She looked to the audience, then back to the candles. Randall pulled and yanked at each wrist cuff; his hands seemed to twist and turn, and suddenly a muffled noise came from his mouth.

"Get these goddamn cuffs off me you stupid slattern!" he screamed. "Can't you see I'm stuck?"

Snickt! The audience gasped. The left blade had fallen. An initial trickle of blood, and the sound of wet meat hitting the ground were all that could be heard. Someone, somewhere, shrieked.

The assistant ran forward and grabbed the other rope. Randall pulled against the righthand wrist cuff, then used the free shoulder from his missing hand's arm to nudge the blindfold off his face.

"Staunch the wound you idiot!" he shrieked, moving his bleeding stump over to her. Another gush of blood from the stump, spilling down her outfit and her hands. Blood caused her grip to slip; the rope fell and with it, his other hand was removed as well.

There were two thumps—one his remaining hand, the other the assistant passing out.

Men and women both were rising to their feet, mumbling and talking in low, astonished voices, but the doors had been locked. Children were shrieking. Someone behind the stage was calling for a doctor—anyone, his voice floated, anyone at all—

But the lights dimmed red. The ground shook again. Thunder and lightning roared. The pooled blood at his feet began to boil and bubble; a timed alchemical concoction made it evaporate into a misty cloud, so dense none could see him. As if connected by strings, his hands flew back to his wrists, accompanied by a wash of red mist, and a flash of white light as they sealed themselves where once they had been cleft in twain.

He rolled up his sleeves and waved. An aura of relief rolled over the audience. The illusion was complete. His assistant sat up and smiled, clearly uninjured. Randall Erickson bowed, but not a single person in the audience clapped. A roar of whispers and mutters exploded over the auditorium, and people began to trickle out of the room.

It was his most perfect illusion, he knew, and he thought of card decks in his left hand while his right hand slid poisoned whiskey into the hands of his enemy.

He was backstage smoking a cigar when the men arrived, as he figured they would. The room grew dark, and the door locked of its own accord; there was a movement in the air itself, and suddenly where there had been a plume of smoke from Randall's cigar there were two men staring at him with imperious looks upon their face.

"Neat trick," Randall said.

"Grinton Dulcini," the older man said, introducing himself.

"Harold Pavlov," the more fearsome of the two said, in introduction.

"Randall Erickson," Randall replied, bowing deeply. "I am the illustrious Erickson, Master of Mysteries—"

"We are well acquainted with your illusions," Dulcini said.

"Are you fans?" he asked, cheeky smile on his face.

Yet another magic trick. The heavier one of the two moved, the air fuzzed, and next thing Randall knew was darkness.

Here one second, gone the next.

He awoke in a conference room. A mounted head of a beast stared down at him, teeth bared and glorious antlers spread wide over its head. It was terrifying to behold, and unlike anything that Randall had ever seen before. It resembled a foul, evil stag, if the stag had six-inch long teeth. Randall carefully glanced around the rest of the room. He was in some sort of study, clearly… and opposite him was the grey-bearded imperious face of the old man that had appeared inside his dressing room.

"A Wendigo," Dulcini said, gesturing at the stuffed monster head. "Frightful things. Man eaters, you see. But of course you've never quite seen anything like it, have you? Welcome back to the land of the living, Mr. Erickson."

Randall's head was pounding.

"What happened to me?" he groaned.

"We knocked you unconscious," Dulcini said. "Well, Pavlov did, I should say. He has rather the temper. I like the man, mind you, but that temper! May well get him into trouble one day."

"Where am I?"

"The League of Magicians Headquarters," Dulcini said. "Located in the heart of Black Hills, the League operates itself here, in an old manse on a hill. We look like quite the abandoned estate, I assure you... so it's not likely any of your friends will come looking for you."

"And why am I here? Not that I assume it's anything good."

"Your flagrant disregard for the rules," Dulcini said, and his voice was acid. "You can't just go waving around your powers, man! I have to say, it's not often we find rogue magicians. Working their own magicks, learned from sheer luck I suppose!"

"Nobody told me any rules when I started," Randall said.

"Ignorance of the law is not an excuse for its trespass," Dulcini said. "You have no doubt trafficked with some rather unclean entities for these powers. And I can hardly blame you, either. Most people work with spirits right off the bat. It's not a bad thing, necessarily.... though the ease of access certainly can shortcut some of the more established boundaries most lawful magicians have when they learn how to work wonders. You need to understand that your gifts are a responsibility, Mr. Erickson. Not some shortcut to fame and success."

Randall shrugged.

"So, lesson learned?" he asked. "I take what you say to heart, and we part under mutually beneficial circumstances?"

"Certainly," Dulcini said. "On one condition."

He raised a pair of wristlets from his desk.

"You simply wear these," Dulcini said.

"Fashion has never been my forte," Randall said.

Dulcini shook his head.

"This is not optional, Mr. Erickson, and if you want to be able to control a modicum of your power still you will listen very carefully to what I say next. *You have no choice in this matter.* As an unlicensed, unmentored Magician you must wear these wristlets. They will dampen your powers."

Randall narrowed his eyes.

"I fail to see how that's fair or mutually beneficial," he said.

"Wearing these wristlets may not seem to benefit you, but in actual point of fact one's magic can be very difficult to channel," Dulcini said. "They act as a graduated license. You perform some small amount of duties for the league, and show us that you can be trusted, and we allow you access to more advanced levels of power. It's a win-win for everyone!"

"I see," Randall said. "And you would be the one in charge of this system? He who safeguards the deeper secrets?"

"But of course," Dulcini said.

"And Pavlov—"

"Guarding the gate with the others," Dulcini said.

"Good," Randall said. "Here I was afraid this was going to get messy."

He twisted his left hand—books from the shelves surrounding them exploded in every direction. Pages and letters and handwritten notes fluttered on the breeze. Randall disappeared in the explosion, reappearing in a shady corner where he knew he wouldn't be seen initially, and cast a hasty glamour over himself.

Dulcini's whole body was a mask of shock. Comically, a single book lay on the shelf still. Randall squinted at it—Mortimer Miles' Cryptid Compendium, it looked like. He moved his hand and yanked at the air. The heavy book swung forward and down. With a scrape like a mausoleum door opening, a part of the bookshelf swung open.

Dulcini got to his feet, turning around, pistol drawn. He was pointing at the air around him, muttering under his breath. Randall could feel the air boiling; could feel his magic being sucked away, little by little. Soon his glamour would fade, and all it would take was a little shimmer in the air and Dulcini's bullet would meet him head on.

There was no choice. Randall acted on instinct. The pistol swung up, he appeared next to it, snagged it, reappeared behind Dulcini, and pulled the trigger.

There was an explosion of sound.

Here one second, gone the next. A bullet wound like an exploded orange plastered the pile of books and paperwork on the ground with the League head's brains. Randall dropped the pistol, hands shaking, and carefully erected wards around the room.

A fat lot of good those would do against another few magicians; but Randall knew he was running on limited time. His plan had always been to draw the League's attention, and steal some of their rarest books... but this was skipping ahead about fifteen steps. He'd never intended on murder.

Wasn't his first, Randall thought, a flicker of annoyance in his chest. Somehow they kept getting easier...

He hurried down the dark passageway into the bookshelf. Clearly this was a hidden tunnel. Dulcini had said himself he guarded deep secrets. There were whispers on the street of old, dark magic hidden away in crumbling books and reliquaries.

A light greeted him as the only source of illumination. A bare, naked flickering bulb cast its hideous glow on shelves and shelves of intricate masks. Green glass inset their eyes; protuberant beaks stretched like monstrous noses from each. Randall recognized the old signs of a plague doctor mask. He knew there was something there... some hidden power. The air seemed to vibrate in the room around each mask.

Across the way, a gigantic steel door. He crossed over and knocked on it. Warded and spelled, no doubt; but a few flickers of the wrist and the wards shredded.

A squeal of metal. A flicker of panic rose up over him. There were raised voices coming from down the hallway... he stepped inside the vault. It was now or never, whatever this was in here...

A soft red glow from a lantern. On a brass plaque underneath, a latin transcription.

"Luna Cruor," he whispered, grabbing it.

He could feel it taking hold of him, then. That same oily feeling he got so many years ago, when he summoned them. The Ladies. Whatever this was in this lamp was something deeper. Something darker than he'd ever known before. It was a power to rival no other. He reached out to it with his own intuition, digging deeper, and began to feel it uncurl and unfold inside him. And as it reached the crescendo, as it filled him even further, he felt the world spin.

Stars. A blinding pain in his jaw. The cold feeling of the vault floor on his face and his elbows. The hard, digging elbow of the man who tackled him digging into his back. The shattering of glass, the spilling of some manufactured special oil. Crimson flames flickering up into the nonexistent breeze. The power of some shining evil staring down at the world from the center of the blackest cosmos possible, its single red eye piercing dimensions after dimension of space and time...

A Promethean flame burning hot in the atmosphere...

He awoke again in the study, next to Dulcini's dead body. Four men were standing over him. He gasped, sucked in a deep breath, skin shocked and face wet. Someone had thrown water on him. The moon outside the window was full and round, but the air was different.

Dark. Crimson. That same feeling of when the lamp had broken... He stared at the sphere in the sky and found the angry eye of some eternal blind God staring down at him. The moon hadn't been like this before the lantern broke...

He shook his head and tried to sit up, but his hands were shackled to the floor.

"Such a shame," one of the men said. Randall tried to focus—it was Pavlov. "We bring you in, try to give you the benefit of the doubt. And here you go and kill the one man that was on your side."

"We don't take kindly to traitors in our community," another man said.

"Murder. Robbery. Possible arson. Destruction of a priceless relic," Pavlov continued. "How many crimes can one man commit in a single night?"

"Let me go," Randall said, pleading. "This is all some kind of misunderstanding. He pulled the gun first—I was just trying to find some way to escape..."

"No," Pavlov said. "I liked your little trick earlier, back at the Orpheum. Very impressive. Illusion, I take it? Red dye, cornstarch, and powdered crestwort to make it boil... fishing wire on mock hands, and an underground fan mechanism to suck the mist back into your sleeves. An impressive work of pretend. However, we'll see how you like real magic. We're going to perform your little trick in here. But since I'm a kind man I'll give you sixty seconds to escape. We'll see what your solo act looks like."

Pavlov waved his hand. Two guillotines built themselves from nothing and stood, hanging at the ready in mid-air over each of Randall's wrists. They pulsed heat, and each blade was glowing red, as if just pulled from a forge...

"You could try to magic your way out," Pavlov said, "Then again. You do have those wristlets Dulcini was so fond of on your hands. But suffering's just a part of life, right? I mean, isn't that what you said? Do mind the after effects—the scorching on the wounds ensure the degradation of the tissue. No incantation that's ever existed can fix burnt flesh."

Pavlov turned over a timer glass on the table. The men laughed, and the door to the study closed behind them as they left Randall to his fate.

Sand slipped down the timer. Randall struggled and cursed against his bonds. He looked around for anything to help him. He could only see the back of Dulcini's exploded skull, the gleam of the double guillotines, and the bright red evil moon hanging outside.

He tried to draw on his inner strength—to probe the boundaries of the magical system, but there was nothing. It was like someone had turned his inner current down to nothing.

"Somebody help me," he said to the world, but nobody did, except for the moon, which stared down, watching. A horrible inky black feeling began to unfurl in his chest.

The sand slipped down, speck by speck, until it was over.

The blades snicked.

Blood flowed, and flesh seared. Randall shrieked—the awful darkness in his chest seemed to burn the atmosphere as it spewed from his mouth. There was no trick here to save himself. No sleight of hand to save him.

He screamed himself hoarse, smelling the horrid stench of human flesh. There was nothing left to live for, he knew. Even if he survived, he was a freak. There was no doing magic without hands anymore. He'd be one of those gimps ever after. Some helpless old fool who used to do parlor tricks, a literal waste of space.

He sat up with his stomach, tried to slide himself to his feet, and felt fatigue sear through him. If he pooled his magic, if he tried to tap into its internal forces he might be able to seal the wound, to reverse the charring, to barely heal himself, but he'd never done anything like it before. His trick at the Orpheum had been just that—a trick.

He focused and panted. The face of the stuffed Wendigo stared down at him, the light of the moon bouncing off its glazed porcelain eyes.

"Help me," he said, rambling, magic fitzing and fusing wildly through his veins, trying beyond all hopes to make sure he survived...

Something dark curled up in him in his self-inflicted healing coma, stretched its wings, and pushed. He saw it, then—floating above his handless body, an incorporeal being in the ephemeral wastelands overlooking the Black Hills.

The Old Manse atop the hill. A towering Victorian beauty. Woodlands everywhere. Something hidden ages ago, a long time past, digging itself up from a shallow grave… and in the shadows of the forest, the same dark shadow running, grunting, stinking, *prowling*. The evil eye of the moon staring down, perfuming the land with its horrid crimson fog.

A thump awakened him. Randall jerked, groggily shifted his head to the noise's origin. The window. Red-stained moonlight staring down, and a dark shape that moved closer to the glass. He blinked, shook his head, squinted… and what he saw sent a thrill of horror in his chest.

There was a monster at the window. The face of the thing, like some furred, man-faced buck, staring inside, its red eyes resonating with the darkness in Randall's very own soul, a black, oozing tongue dragging up the glass…

One of its taloned hands raised. With another thump, its prize knocked against the window. Pavlov's head dangling upside down from its newly exposed vertebrae.

Hot bile swam in his throat, and the creature smashed it through the glass, tossing it in at him. It rolled, spinning, dangling vertebrae oozing and dripping human juices, coming to a stop next to his face. Randall tried not to be sick.

It turned away from the window. He could hear men shrieking outside. He looked at his hands—his stumps, more like—ragged rotted black ends no good for anything.

He got to his feet slowly, stomach filled with regret and fear, and watched through the window at the carnage outside.

A silhouette rose in the night, unfolding itself on digilegs, antlers a crowning glory in the night. Razor-sharp talons flickered as it moved. It howled, darting after its prey…

The four men who did this to him became its victims. It moved like thunder; carving into them from the shadows as fireballs and other elemental forces failed to put it down. A cascade of hands and legs and pieces, chunks of skin and bone and organs flying through the air, and all the while a horrible shrieking scream of men terrified beyond reason...

"I did this," Randall said. He seemed to be babbling incoherently, blackened stumps held up to his face, eyes stretched in terror, a pall of red light streaming from the broken glass on him. "It was me. I did this. I killed these men."

And he slid to his bottom against the desk, wedged between a head and a body, sobbing, rocking back and forth as he babbled. The eyes of the stuffed Wendigo on the wall stared down at him glassily.

And just like that beast taxidermied on the wall. Randall would never age again…

Many Years Later

He lit from tree to tree, jumping gracefully, tattered edges of his tuxedo flapping in the breeze. His hands may have been missing, sure, but he'd been able to reroute the magic in other directions. Even if penmanship was beyond him nowadays.

He wore one of the plague masks, the green glass of the eyes glowing with its weird internal combustion, the filigreed Phoenix on its side a protective glyph. He was stalking his next mark, of course. There had been reports of people going missing in this area for months, and he had a strong suspicion it had to do with his old friend—the Wendigo. A little light recon wouldn't hurt.

He'd heard the sound of voices from a distance. He alighted on a bare patch of ground, and tuned in his mask with a click noise.

It was five people around a campfire. One of them was a man telling a story, with an eyepatch and a fedora on his head. It was a little hard to keep track of what he was saying. There was a half a second, however, where he blinked, and he was almost sure that the one-eyed man smiled directly at the tree he had hidden behind…

An explosion of undergrowth, and a razor-tipped arm from nowhere knocked him to the ground. The man in the tattered tuxedo nudged off his mask, gasping in air. The atmosphere stank like hot dog sweat, like rotten bodies lying in the sun…

The dead-eyed, leering face of the Wendigo stared down at him, teeth bared and tongue hanging. There was a moment, then, where Randall and the Wendigo appeared to see each other, eye to eye—a resonance between them—and then the sound of the one-eyed man laughing in the clearing ahead distracted the foul beast.

Randall rehitched his mask, struggled to his feet, and leaped, floating back into the trees.

He knew what it was capable of. He didn't have to stick around to know that the whole campfire was being dismembered, bit by bit, savaged and ravaged and filleted like so many playtoys…

One day, he thought, gliding from overhang to overhang. One day I'll put to rest the thing I brought to life. Even if it kills me…

CHAPTER 4:

BEAUTIFUL SUFFERING: A LAZARUS STONE STORY

A splitting ache in his head was what first seeped into his consciousness, a dull emptiness that seemed to go on forever. Flashes of memories came to him in spurts as he dove higher towards reality. He'd been thrown from his horse. There was something—some kind of smell, some huge darkness just out of sight, chasing him, crimson eyes staining the darkness. A strange-looking bird-creature, with glowing green eyes standing over him as he fell...

He snapped his eyes open and gasped. Well, one eye. The other eye was strapped closed, and the socket ached. He put a hand up to it, wincing, fingers feeling along the edges. Someone had wrapped gauze around it and the top of his head. With frantic fingers he traced along the edges, hoping beyond hope that what he thought had happened hadn't...

It was a futile effort, though. Whoever had wrapped him up had made damn sure the gauze was going to stay. Frustrated, he held the socket and sat up.

He was in a four-poster bed somewhere. A full crystal pitcher of water was on his bedside stand; a note, written by someone with little dexterity, was left on his bedside table. He grabbed it and held it up in front of his open eye.

"Wasn't much I could do to salvage the eye. Speaking purely from experience, missing body parts seems to be a hazard around these parts, but I'm sure you'll adapt. There's some food in the servant's quarters if you need a nosh before you leave. Please let yourself out. There's a dirt path back to town—you can take one of the horses in the stable, if you'd like. Just avoid wandering *back* into the forest. Wouldn't like to save you twice—don't think you have enough eyes to keep losing."

Signed with an inconsequential scribble. If he didn't know any better, it was like the damn thing was written by someone with little control over what was holding the pen. Lazarus put the note down. Well, that confirmed his fears. He got up, throwing off the covers. His whole body ached. He supposed getting thrown from a horse would do that to you. He limped from the bed, slugged back a glass of water, and grimaced. The nerve endings in his dry mouth came back to life and screamed. He drank another two glasses and then woozily dragged himself to a mirror on the opposite wall.

An iron-wrought frame with dragons dancing on it surrounded his face. He looked like shit. A huge purple bruise extended out and down the right side of his face. His hair was matted and tangled. Scratches, well on their way to healing, decked his torso. He clearly hadn't been bathed, which he had mixed feelings about. He supposed it was just enough he'd been dragged from the forest. He finally turned what was left of his gaze on his bandage. He touched it and again, the orbit ached deep in his skull. Wincing again, he used the mirror to trace the lines of the bandage back to where the knot looped around on itself. He pulled and yanked, carefully and slowly unrolling the gauze. When it got to the pad over where his eye used to be, he fingered the edge and hesitantly pulled. There was no pain from it—he was terrified he'd yank the badge off and a spill of inner minced organ meat, or perhaps brains, would spill out on the floor, as if the bandage was one big scab. He even imagined the tattered, empty remains of his eye would dangle, yo-yoing out to the ground, dripping blood.

"It won't be as bad as you think," he muttered to himself.

He pulled the bandage free, and immediately the ache retreated. His closed eyelid was all that greeted him, with some heavy purple mottling all around the socket. Bracing himself for even more pain, he slowly, carefully opened the lid.

Something in his brain split, then, like a thundercrack through the hemispheres of understanding, and he found the world awash in a spectral fire that consumed his attention.

Well, not the world. His reflection. Where one particularly long scratch was across his chest, there was a corona of crimson fire flickering transparently, like ghost flames. He raised his fingers to the wound—they, too, flickered at the edges. In fact—the whole of his reflection was awash in the crimson flames.

He looked at his hands in real life. The flames were still there. Focusing on them seemed to make the fire flicker faster. He held one hand out over the other, and could feel the flicker as a warm pulse.

He looked up at his reflection. The damaged eye glowed red, a spinning circle of energy inside it. It looked almost exactly like the eyes of whatever that thing had been in the forest…

He turned and looked at everything else. Small spectral patterns floated here and there—dust motes, perhaps, in muted blues and greens. The note on the bed had a muted, infinitesimal green haze, but it was nothing compared to the joy of the flames he saw flickering on his own body.

He ran through the house, filled with a renewed sense of energy, shirtless and manic. He paid no attention to any of the rooms, with their muted browns and blues, instead following the bright red warming hue of something flickering from the forest in the front windows.

He burst from the front doors. He felt younger than he'd ever felt in his entire life. The shadows of his past—the disappointments and sadness, tears and fears, all had melted away in this glorious new experience. His cheating wife and horrible life melted away in this new radiance. The woods around him were awash in bright beacons of ruby and crimson, separate hues flickering inside one another.

He ran towards the first beacon in the woods. It was an open, swirling vortex like in his eye. He looked into it, like looking into eternity, and he could see the machinations of a spindly ragged-haired creature, waiting in the snow for its tricks to bear fruition as it tormented children to death. There was no judgement here on morality; this was something extrasensory, a causal linkup between mankind and something far older than what Lazarus had ever experienced. He knew that, if they survived, they would be forever changed by their experience, like he was.

He ran to another portal. A hulking, stinking creature sped through a forest, in pursuit of its love, tearing apart anyone who would get in its way. Another portal—swirling ghosts descending on a young girl next to her dead parents. Yet another portal—everywhere he looked, these monstrous creatures were stalking humanity, teaching them lessons, and tainting them with the same crimson flame.

He turned, and found open portals all around him. He looked through each one—saw the process, the cycle of suffering. Learned the deepest anguish of mankind and how it could bring forth that eternal pyre, that new knowingness, that powerful light from beyond time and space. Anguish beget pain, and pain beget light. What a miracle—what a rebirth he had gone through! That suffering he'd experienced—it had allowed him this beautiful gift, this dark taint, and he knew he would do what he could to spread this dark joy to all that he met.

He looked up, at the Moon. It, too, was awash in flames, full and bright, beaming red like a corona. Something older than time stared from it out at him, something unknowable in its horror and something primally welcome. It was Home.

His right eye and the Moon locked gazes, flickering with eternal light.

"It's so beautiful," he said, laughing, as humanity was punished all around him through the various open portals. His hair buzzed in the static of the crimson, maddening fire roaring through his veins. "It's so goddamn beautiful!"

"Come," he heard, a whisper in his ear. "Come assist me. Come free me."

And he listened, rapture spreading over his face…

SUNDANCE IN THE MOONLIGHT

Illustration by Anton Tolstobrov

CHAPTER 5:

SUNDANCE IN THE MOONLIGHT

In a small clearing between the black pines that stretched their black and spindly fingers up into the dark sky, Grandfather sat with several of the young men around a fire. Between the trees, water could be seen, and along its moving surface, red light glittered and sparkled from the river's reflection of the blood moon above. The fire lit Grandfather's face from below, and made the words of his storytelling glow with ancient life. His gray hair was woven into two braids, decorated with feathers, and hanging down on either side of a face wrinkled by sun and time. He wore a magnificent vest with geometric designs of the sun, moon, and stars, set on a background of light blue. In his hand, he held a long wooden pipe, also decorated with feathers and bands of color. Grandfather was an old-timer, and the younger men around him were not dressed in such a tribal fashion. They wore jeans and band shirts, depicting other tribes that wielded guitars in battle, and whose strange music was carried across the air of the land by a mysterious box called the radio.

Even so, you could tell by traces here and there that the men who sat around Grandfather were Lakota Sioux. Some also wore their long hair in braids, or were bundled up in sweatshirts and blankets woven by the women, wrapped in the black, red, yellow, and white patterns of their people. As Grandfather passed the pipe around the circle, they puffed introspectively, inhaling the sweet, traditional smell of tobacco. Next to Grandfather sat Eric, his grandson. Eric was known as Gray Wolf among his friends because he had gleaned the wisdom of his grandfather from the myths and legends the Lakota Sioux elder told over. Gray Wolf was quiet and introspective, but every once in a while he would make a witty remark that had everyone laughing.

"And so," Grandfather began, "before there was anything in this world, before the river, and the pines, and the mountains, and the reservation, and Elvis, and white bread, and television…"

Grandfather's list drew a few chuckles from the crowd.

"…before all of this, there was nothing. The Great Spirit, *Wakan Tanka*, existed in a great emptiness, a great darkness, called *Han*. He was lonely, lonelier than a gambler who has just laid down a full house, and reached out to sweep in the chips, but sees that the four queens across from him have emptied every penny in his pocket. Isn't that right, Running Horse?"

Grandpa looked out across the circle to Phillip Smith, who was known for being a jokester and an avid poker player.

"It is so, Grandfather," Phillip agreed, and some of his younger brethren laughed.

"*Wakan Tanka* had to do something about this loneliness, so he did what anyone would do in that situation. No, he did not turn on the television, or head down to Steel Joe's for a cold beer. He created companions for himself. He gathered his energy together and formed *Inyan*, rock. Then he used *Inyan* to create *Maka*, earth. He was attracted to *Maka's* beauty, and so he mated with her, and from their union *Skan*, the sky, was born. *Skan* brought forth *Wi*, the sun. These four gods were powerful, but really, they were all still part of *Wakan Tanka*.

"These gods produced companions of their own: Moon, Wind, Falling star, and Thunderbird. They made these four companions to help in the building of this world. The four companions created more gods and spirits, like the Four Winds, Buffalo, and Whirlwind. They also created two-legged creatures that you may recognize: man and bear."

"Bear has four legs, Grandfather," Gray Wolf interjected.

"I am a storyteller, Gray Wolf, not a math teacher," Grandfather replied, and the crowd laughed.

"That is a story for another time, young son," Grandfather eventually conceded, gently patting Gray Wolf on the back. "They also created other aspects of the world that we live with every day: *Sicun*, thought, *Nagi*, death, *Niya*, life-breath, and *Nagila*, shadow. Remember however, that even though creation had turned into one big party, everything was still part of *Wakan Tanka*. Even you and I are part of the Great Spirit," Grandfather finished, taking a puff from the pipe before passing it around again.

Suddenly a blood-curdling scream pierced the night air, chilling everyone to the bone. Grandfather and the circle sat in silence as the fire crackled, and smoke curled upward from the pipe that rested in Phillip Running Horse's hands.

"Quickly!" Grandfather commanded, rising from his seat.

The young men stood and followed Grandpa as he walked off into the woods. Grandfather was an old-timer who lived and practiced the ways of the ancestors. In his prime, he could track a deer through the woods for three days on end, and return with fresh venison and a brand new vest. He could sneak up on a rabbit, and elude a hungry bear. He knew how to be one with nature, so surely Grandfather would find his way through the dark and locate the source of the scream. They young men followed behind him, clumsily breaking branches and crunching twigs underfoot, but Grandfather did not care. They were not hunting game that could be easily scared away; they were looking to find someone who sounded like a woman in distress.

Gray Wolf followed the young men, but he had spent much time in Grandfather's company, and learned the ways of hunting. He moved with stealth, poise, and quiet. Feeling the small knife strapped to his boot, he wondered if he was going to need it. He wondered if Grandfather were armed, and if the other young men carried knives or guns.

Suddenly the party emerged into a clearing by the water. There was Grandfather, kneeling by a sobbing woman curled up into a ball. The blood moon could be seen clearly in the night sky, sending red shafts of light to play over the world below, lose themselves in the dark woods, and dance along the river. The blood red tint of the world made the scene eerie in Gray Wolf's mind, and probably in the minds of everyone there, for the young men shifted about nervously. They looked around, startled by the sound of an owl or anything else that moved in the night.

"My child!" the woman screamed, before breaking down into incomprehensible sobbing.

Grandfather said nothing, asked nothing, but merely held his hand on the woman's back.

"My child," the woman sobbed again, this time pointing to the river.

Some of the young men began to dash towards the water.

"Wait!" Grandfather yelled, holding up his hand. "Do not go in yet. You will not be able to see the child anyway."

The young men were confused, but they respected Grandfather.

"What happened? Breathe! Breathe!" He asked and commanded the crying woman.

The woman sobbed and breathed deeply.

"A creature came from the water, and took my daughter. It dragged her back into the river. She is gone! Gone!" the woman burst out into a fresh cacophony of weeping.

Grandfather looked out toward the water.

"Do not bother going into the river," he said to the young men.

"Grandfather is right," said a young man named Jonathan Powers, also known as Soaring Eagle. "Even though the moon is out, it is still night. Even though it is summer, the water is cold. It moves swiftly, and when you are least expecting it, it will carry you away and smash you against the rocks."

At this assessment the screams of the woman rose.

"When we return to the reservation, we will notify the park rangers," suggested Phillip. "They will know where to look for the child," he concluded, avoiding the word *body*.

"Lift her. Carry her," Grandfather rose and commanded the young men.

Gray Wolf watched as a pair of the young men linked arms, forming a seat for the distraught woman. She did not fight them to remain by the lake, and indeed seemed to accept that the child would not be coming back. She sat, stone-faced in their arms, and sobbed occasionally.

The party made its way back to the campfire. Phillip doused the flames, which protested to being put out with a hiss, and Grandfather placed his pipe in a bag. The men walked through the woods to their cars and trucks. The woman was placed in the bed of Grandfather's truck, and her bearers stepped into the truck bed as well to support her emotionally and physically. Grandfather and Gray Wolf sat in the cabin of the truck, and Grandfather turned the key in the ignition.

"What has happened, Grandfather?" Gray Wolf asked.

Grandfather was silent as he turned onto the road and led the caravan of vehicles back to the reservation, their machine-eyes lighting up the dark red night ahead of them, piercing the shadows like swords of light.

"*Unktehi*," was all Grandfather said. Gray Wolf felt something inside of Grandfather that scared him away from asking more. There was a strange mix of fear, anger, and courage behind Grandfather's stoic face, swirling like the stormy pattern of a gemstone trapped inside of a rock.

Grandfather parked the truck in front of the woman's trailer. Her name was Raven Braid, and she was a single mother. Her husband had owned a tobacco store in town and was half-jokingly named Burning Ember, but he had died several years ago in a car accident; now her only child had just been swallowed up in the river. Grandfather and Gray Wolf got out of the cab, and they young men in back jumped down from the truck bed. One of them picked up Raven Braid and passed her down to the other young man before hopping down to the ground. They carried her into her trailer, as other cars pulled up around Grandfather's truck. The young men jumped out and made their way up to Grandfather, looking to help.

"Go home," Grandfather commanded, holding up his hand. "Gray Wolf, Robert, and James will stay with me here tonight, to guard Raven Braid from further harm."

The men shuffled, unsure of what to do until Phillip took the lead.

"I will go down to the Ranger Station right now," he said, hopping into his truck.

"Do not travel alone tonight!" Grandfather urged.

At this, another young man hopped into Phillip's car. They zipped off down the road, and the other young men said their goodbyes in hushed voices, and drove home.

Grandpa took Gray Wolf by the shoulder and steered him toward the trailer.

Inside, Gray Wolf admired the weaving work of Raven Braid. Having only her daughter and no husband, Raven Braid had more time than most to devote to her craft, which in this case, looked to be weaving. Incredible blankets were draped over the couches, hung up on the walls like tapestries, and draped from the ceiling. The whole room as a colorful universe of blacks, reds, whites, and yellows, set in geometric patterns against a sky of light blue, much like Grandfather's vest, which, come to think of it, was the handiwork of Raven Braid.

Grandfather set a hot kettle on the stove, and Robert and James placed Raven Braid on the couch, where she sat, staring off into space. They all sat in silence for some time, until Grandfather brought tea out for them to drink.

"Drink, my dear," he insisted, pressing a hot cup into Raven Braid's hands. She took the cup and dutifully took a few sips, staring into the space in front of her through the wisps of steam from the cup. They sat all that night, until they fell asleep one by one. Eventually Gray Wolf fell asleep as well, and when he awoke, he saw Raven Braid sleeping soundly, Robert and James passed out on the floor, and Grandfather staring out the window at the sunrise. It seemed that Grandfather had been up all night.

The next day, a tribal council was summoned, and the whole reservation sat in the town hall. This meeting was not like the gathering the night before. Instead of sitting in a circle, there were rows of chairs stretching from the front of the room to the back. No pipes were present here, only a few urns of coffee and some Danishes from the supermarket.

At the head of the people, the mayor sat at a long table, flanked on one side by a woman named Glittering Beads, and on the other side by Grandfather. On either side of Grandfather and Glittering Beads, more men and women sat at the table, six in total. Mayor Paul, or White Feather, was a good man, but Glittering Beads was a little more questionable. She was so named because she owned a large share in a casino about three hours away, and while some of the money was funneled into helping the community, Glittering Beads took long vacations away from the reservation, and it was rumored that she had a nice house in Florida by the ocean.

The room was filled with men and women of all ages, their arms crossed. Curiosity filled the air, and pity for Raven Braid's loss.

"Let us begin the meeting," White Feather began. "Grandfather, you have called for a tribal council meeting today. Many of the people in the reservation who are not part of the council have also come along to hear what you have to say."

Grandfather rose and the attention of everyone in the room focused. Many of the people respected Grandfather, for he was a living link to the way life used to be. While their own mothers and fathers had passed on, they still had Grandfather to remind them of the Lakota Sioux way. And yet, they were not prepared for what Grandfather was about to say.

"As many of you know already, last night Raven Braid's little girl was snatched up and taken into the river. Phillip volunteered to drive down to the Ranger Station, so they could begin to look for the girl. James, Robert, and my Grandson Gray Wolf, stayed with me at Raven Braid's trailer last night, in order to keep watch, and make sure she was okay. Now she is still at home, resting, and her mother Gentle Elk is watching over her. This will be tough for her."

There was a moment of silence, as everyone pondered Raven Braid's multiple losses, which had transpired in just a few brief years.

"But I am not here to tell you the details of what you already know," Grandfather continued. "I am here to tell you why this happened."

White Feather and the tribal elders leaned in with interest. Glittering Beads' gaudy and somewhat tacky costume-jewelry bracelets clinked together, and everyone in the room seemed to be holding their breath.

"For some number of years now, there has been a lot of pain on the reservation, in fact, ever since the arrival of the Americans. We know that already. How they brought guns, and alcohol, and disease with them, and forever changed our people. They carved up the land, and crisscrossed it with concrete roads, and buildings, and planted their flags everywhere they could. But that was many moons ago, many seasons ago. Who would want to sit and meditate about all that pain? Time comes and goes, and I am not here to complain about all of that."

"What is troubling you, then, Grandfather?" White Feather asked respectfully.

"I am talking about the more recent pain, the pain that many of us have felt within the last few years. I feel that the pain and suffering has increased in this new generation. How many women have experienced what Raven Braid experienced with her husband, losing him to an accident caused by fire water? How many of our children have tuned themselves out to the old way of life, and picked up drugs—I'm talking about hard drugs—and moved off the reservation to abandon their mothers and fathers and sisters and brothers to loneliness and the pain of missing them? We have lost touch with the way of the Great Spirit. We are sick inside." Grandfather's voice faltered and a tear fell from his eye.

"This is all stupid," Glittering Beads said with a wave of her hand. "Alcohol and drugs is a problem everywhere. And quite honestly, I don't see what the problem is," she continued. "And all this talk about the old way, and the ancestors, and the white devils...please, Grandfather. Sit down! Relax at home. Enjoy your pipe and your stories. Let the tribal council handle the affairs of the reservation."

"Let Grandfather speak," White Feather said, taking Glittering Beads by the arm and guiding her back down into her seat.

"Thank you, White Feather," Grandfather continued. "I believe that *it* has come to feed on our suffering. To feed on our pain."

Some of the Indians assembled began to shuffle nervously in their chairs, uncomfortable with what Grandfather might be approaching with his suggestion.

"What is that?" someone called out.

"The *Unktehi*," Grandfather whispered, so quietly that people in the back of the room could barely hear the old man. In any event, neighbors told their neighbors what Grandfather had said, until the whole room was ablaze in conversation.

"Enough!" yelled White Feather, standing and waving his arms. The talk died down after a few seconds.

"Grandfather," White Feather began, "there are some who may have disagreed with your assessment of the community," he said, nodding at Glittering Beads. "I myself see value in the points you raise. There have been problems...sadness, alcohol, drugs, and spiritual..." White Feather searched for the politically correct word, "...malaise. Things are not the way they used to be, perhaps. Even so, we must live, and work, and play in the modern world. Times have changed since the days of hunting with a bow and arrow. But this talk of the *Unktehi* takes it to a whole new level. A horned serpent climbing out of the river to snatch children...it's just a fairytale, Grandfather, meant to scare little children into going to bed."

"Why have you summoned us all here to tell us this," said one young man, his annoyance mirroring that of others in the room.

"The old man is off his rocker," another challenged.

"Please, hear me out!" Grandfather begged. The crowd quieted. They still respected him.

"The *Unktehi* feeds on sadness, and misery, and pain. It was awakened by the blood moon, and came to feast on our suffering."

"Whatever killed Raven Braid's baby, is surely something we can bring down with guns and knives," said one particularly burly young man, standing up and looking around for approval. Several heads nodded in agreement. "It's probably a big bear, or something," he suggested, throwing out his hands and looking at Grandfather.

"It is the *Unktehi*," Grandfather persisted. "And if you attempt to kill it with guns and knives, you will only make it angrier, and more powerful."

"Grandfather is right," a quiet voice spoke from the table of the elders. Everyone turned to see Hummingbird, an elderly woman seated two chairs away from White Feather. Hummingbird was even older than Grandfather, but she mostly stayed in her trailer, so people didn't really know her as well as they knew Grandfather. "It can only be the *Unktehi*. There is no bear that would climb out of the river, and return into the water carrying a child."

"And why not?" the burly young man persisted. "Bears fish in the water, don't they? They can swim just as well as any of us!"

"You are making a big mistake," spoke another soft voice from the crowd. People turned to see yet another elder, in his wheelchair, parked by one of the middle rows. "I remember that the *Unktehi* has come here before. It came in the days of my own grandfather, and in the days of my father as well. For many moons, it was not seen around these parts. But now I see it returns," spoke Sly Raccoon, a man so old that no one even knew his English name.

"Sly Raccoon, you can barely remember what you had for breakfast this morning," the burly young man disrespectfully said, knocking Raccoon's words to the floor.

"It was Danish," Raccoon smiled a toothless grin, holding up one of the Danishes from the coffee table.

The room burst out into a commotion of babbling noises.

"Quiet!" roared White Feather again. The crowd quieted down, but the burly young man stood up again.

"I say we just deal with this right now. Whether it's a bear, or the *Unktehi*, or Bigfoot, or the Boogeyman," he yelled. His very words seemed to swagger with bravado.

"Grab your guns and you knives, if you have any courage, and follow me!" So saying, he stormed out of the hall, followed by at least half a dozen strong looking young fellows.

Grandfather sat down, shaking his head.

Gray Wolf had been watching everything happen from his front row seat. He had ridden an emotional roller coaster during the whole conversation, watching Grandfather share his thoughts, get shut down and mocked, then supported by the other elders, and ultimately disrespected as the young men walked out of the room.

"This meeting is adjourned," White Feather called out, and the assembled crowd began to disband without much ceremony. White Feather walked over to Grandfather and put his hand on Grandfather's shoulder.

"Don't worry, Grandfather, they'll be okay. They're just headstrong boys. Blood runs hot in their veins."

"I am not just concerned for them," Grandfather shook his head. "I am concerned for all of us. They will antagonize the serpent and its ugly horned head will come slithering into the village to kill us all."

White Feather looked up in exasperation. He rubbed Grandfather's shoulder, gave it a squeeze, and walked away.

"What should we do?" Gray Wolf asked Grandfather.

"Wait and see what happens," Grandfather said simply.

Gray Wolf and Grandfather were sitting down to a meal of baked beans and hot dogs cut up into pieces when they heard the first screams. Grandfather continued to eat, but his hand shook a little as he lifted the spoon to his mouth.

"What was that, Grandfather?" Gray Wolf asked.

"As I expected," Grandfather said simply.

After the tribal council was adjourned, Gray Wolf and Grandfather had returned to his trailer to have dinner. The sun had set, and darkness permeated the reservation, punctuated by the light of the almost-full moon, now beginning to wane back down to blackness.

Grandfather took a few more bites of his dinner, and then put down his spoon.

A knock on the door made Gray Wolf jump.

"Also as I expected," Grandfather repeated, pushing his chair back and making his way to the trailer door.

"Grandfather, no!" Gray Wolf screamed.

Too late. Grandfather opened the door, and there was… White Feather. The mayor was holding a camping lantern, a worried look on his face. Behind him a large SUV growled in the night, and it looked to be filled with Indians on the inside.

"Grandfather, I…" the mayor began.

"No need to say anything," Grandfather replied, holding up his hand.

"What do you recommend we do?" The mayor asked.

"Go home. Wait. Tell stories of the Great Spirit, smoke a pipe, play some drums, chill out," Grandfather said with refreshing youthfulness. "There is no point in following the headstrong and hot-blooded warriors into the battle. If they will return, they will return."

The mayor bid Grandfather a good night, and climbed back into the SUV. He conversed with the Indians in the vehicle, and they drove off back towards the heart of the village.

Grandfather returned to the table, and he and Gray Wolf finished their dinner. Afterwards, they played checkers, and Grandfather told stories about the Great Spirit until Gray Wolf fell asleep on the couch.

The next morning, the mayor knocked on Grandfather's door again.

"They did not return last night Grandfather," he said.

Grandfather put on his vest and called for Gray Wolf. Sleepily, Gray Wolf got up from the couch and followed his grandfather and the mayor to the SUV. The trio hopped into the vehicle and began to drive down to the forest by the river. They parked by the trail that led down to the clearing where Grandfather often regaled the young men with stories around the campfire. The sight that greeted them there was horrific.

Blood was everywhere, in puddles on the ground, splashed on trees, and even dripping from the branches. *Why is the blood dripping from the branches?* Gray Wolf thought, looking up. He nearly vomited when he saw dismembered body parts strewn throughout the pines, like so many Christmas trees of death and destruction. In the background they could hear the river rolling timelessly along, concealing the horror hidden and lurking beneath its sparkling waters.

"Oh…" was all the mayor could say.

Grandfather knelt and began to wail out a song to commemorate the souls of the dead warriors. As he sang, more vehicles pulled up, and Indians made their way down to the clearing. Some of them vomited when they saw what had happened there, and others who knew the song that Grandfather was singing joined in his plaintive wail. Grandfather and the other elders stopped the chant, and a quiet stillness descended upon the clearing.

"Now do you believe me?" Grandfather rose and turned around to face everyone. "Guns and knives will not destroy the *Unktehi*. Guns and knives are weapons of sadness and misery. The *Unktehi* cannot be defeated with suffering and pain: it feeds on it."

"What then, must we do, Grandfather?" White Feather asked.

"We must do the Sundance. We must purify our souls and reconnect with the Great Spirit. That is the only way to drive away the *Unktehi*."

There was silence in the clearing.

"Lead the way, Grandfather," White Feather commanded.

Grandfather gathered the men of the village to the sweat lodge. Gray Wolf joined them as the men disrobed in the locker room that had been built next to the *Inipi*, or sweat lodge. The *Inipi* itself was built in the traditional way, with sixteen young willow trees that had been planted in a circle long ago, and pulled together in a dome and tightly covered with animal hides, so that no light could enter the dark space within.

In the center of the *Inipi* was a fire pit which represented the sun, and a small, crescent mound of dirt which represented the moon, encircling the glowing embers. These external signs of the cosmos, normally high above the earth, now sat within the inner world of the cosmos, the human womb, suggested by the dark enclave of the sweat lodge. The Indians who participated in the sweat ceremony would emerge reborn.

The men entered the *Inipi*, and Grandfather led the ceremony. They sat in a circle on sacred sage that had been gathered for the occasion. He chanted the old chants, his voice an echo of Grandfathers before him, going all the way back to the time of the Great Spirit. He smoked the ceremonial pipe, and passed it around the circle to cement the bond of the men participating in the ceremony. Grandfather had carefully selected rocks and dried them in the sun so they would be ready. Pouring water over the rocks, Grandfather reminded everyone that breathing in the heat would purify them, and they would emerge reborn.

The room grew hot, almost unbearably so for Gray Wolf. In the darkness, Grandfather led traditional drumming and singing, and the pitch-black *Inipi* filled with the song of the ancestors. Gray Wolf felt like his lungs were on fire, but he held on to Grandfather's voice as the sacred elder carried them through the ceremony.

During the ritual, the door of the *Inipi* was thrown open four times, to represent the four ages described by the Sacred White Buffalo. This action split the ceremony into four parts, and each part was a step in the healing process Grandfather hoped to achieve for the young men. Each phase also corresponded to a color and a direction on the sacred medicine wheel. The first stage corresponded to the color yellow and the East. It was a time of getting used to the darkness, the heat, and the enclosure of the womb-like *Inipi*. Next came a stage corresponding to red and the South, a stage of coming to terms with relationships and unsolved conflicts. After this came a stage corresponding to black and the West, a time for forgiving and embracing the self, and recognizing inner demons. Many of the men by this point were crying, wailing, and screaming, as the heat, darkness, and darkness within was confronted and filtered through their breathing and wailing. The final round was associated with white and the North. Grandfather guided everyone to think about giving thanks, appreciating Mother Earth, the universe, and the spirits of grandfathers and grandmothers before.

Grandfather stopped the chanting, and the door was thrown open one last time. The men emerged, reborn, crying, and mostly bare-skinned, like newborns coming into the world.

"Our impurities have been left behind in the *Inipi*," Grandfather assured them. "But the *Unktehi* is strong. We must do this ritual for four days."

By this time, the sun was high in sky, and Grandfather encouraged the men to go home, rest, and prepare their strength and energy for the next day. They repeated this ritual under Grandfather's guidance for three more days, and each time, Gray Wolf felt himself more strongly connected to the earth, the spirits, and the Great Spirit. He could feel that each time, their impurity and pain and suffering was left behind in the sweat lodge, as they emerged renewed and reborn. On the fourth day, after they emerged, Grandfather said it was time for the Sundance.

In the light of the moon, the whole reservation had gathered around the sacred sun-pole placed in the middle of the lawn in front of the town-hall lodge. Normally, the Sundance ritual was performed by strong and healthy young men as a rite of passage during the day, but Grandfather had called for the village elders to come forward and submit to the ancient ritual tonight. Grandfather and three other wizened old men stood on the lawn, their shirts removed, as Healing Song, the medicine man, took some of the flesh of their chest between his thumb and forefinger. He ran a very small but sharp knife over their skin, and thrust in a strong skewer of bone, roughly the size of a small pencil. These bone-hooks were attached to a long rope, which was fastened to the top of the sun pole. Gray Wolf noticed that Grandfather did not flinch as the hooks were placed in his flesh, and he wondered what it would be like when he was ready to do the Sundance.

The drumming and chanting started, and Grandfather and the other elders began the Sundance. They moved their limbs like trees waving in the sacred breeze of time, and they shuffled their feet to the stamping of the drum. Their objective would be to break loose from the rope which tethered them to the sun-pole. Gray Wolf was nervously wondering if Grandfather and the elders were up for this ritual, as old as they were, but the elders were strong and resolute in their sacred dance.

Suddenly a terrible scream was heard in the night, but it was not a human scream. Grandfather had warned the drummers and chanters not to stop their sacred song, despite whatever they might hear. They carried on, but the blood-curdling sound could be heard above the ancient wailing. Gray Wolf felt an immense shadow of sorrow and misery approaching, as if something were coming that could darken even the light of the sun.

Suddenly, an enormous horned lizard, bigger and longer than ten school buses, broke through the pines. Its tail flailed around behind it, smashing trees, and crashing down on trailers that meekly stood along its epic path of destruction. The beast had a terrible face, with red eyes that glowed like unholy embers. It charged right toward the assembled crowd of the reservation.

Men and women alike screamed and ran, but they could not run from the beast that dashed quickly toward their fear and misery. It grabbed people by the head and flailed them around, snapping necks and flinging decapitated corpses left and right. Its horns plowed right through people's chests and backs, and it wore the writhing corpses on top of its head like a living hat of human suffering. Its tail smashed the lodge, and its teeth clamped down onto everything it could.

The Unktehi.

Grandfather and the elders did not discontinue the Sundance, but most of the drumming and chanting had stopped, to be replaced by voices of panic and terror. The *Unktehi* feasted on sadness, fear, and negativity, and the dancers in their resolution must have been exuding an internal strength that repelled him, but it delighted in chomping off Glittering Beads' head. Her casino and greed had caused the people much misery, and even filled her own soul with bitterness.

Suddenly the beast turned toward the dancers, for it must have detected some faltering confidence on their part. It lumbered toward the dancers and the sacred sun-pole. One by one, it opened its massive jaws and swallowed the three dancers that had accompanied grandfather. Without a scream they were gone, the ropes that had once tethered them to the sacred ritual lying on the grass. The beast turned toward Grandfather.

Quick as an eagle dashing down to the river to snatch a fish, Gray Wolf grabbed the hatched at his side, which some instinct had told him to bring tonight. He hurled it at the *Unktehi*. The weapon was too small to do more than bounce off the beast's scales, but at least it grabbed its attention. It turned toward Gray Wolf, and Gray Wolf started to back up toward the trees, mesmerized by the glowing red coal-eyes of the beast.

Suddenly Gray Wolf found himself trapped between two trees. He tried to free himself, but he was stuck between the pines that *Unktehi* had ripped apart. The beast was drawing closer, opening its great, terrible jaws—

Then Grandfather broke free from the tether of the sun-pole. The bone hook was ripped from his flesh, and blood poured from the fresh wound, but Grandfather did not seem to care. Gray Wolf could barely believe what he was seeing as Grandfather ran towards the beast, and suddenly jumped up into the air. His arms became feathered wings, and he morphed into an enormous bird.

"*Wakiyan*," Gray Wolf whispered in awe. "The Great Thunderbird."

The *Unktehi* turned away from Gray Wolf to do battle with the massive bird.

The serpent snapped his jaws at the Thunderbird, which flapped its wings, backing up towards the lawn in front of the town hall, and luring the *Unktehi* away from the woods, out into the open. The horned lizard-beast took the bait, and moved out toward the grass. Suddenly the Thunderbird was upon the beast, pecking away with its enormous beak. The serpent's tail lashed out, hitting the wings of the great bird, and its teeth closed around one of the bird's talons, attempting to drag it down to earth.

But the *Unktehi* had drawn too close to the *Wakiyan*, and the Thunderbird plunged its beak into one of the serpent's glowing red eyes. The *Unktehi* let out a ferocious scream, a sound that felt like a popping balloon releasing a whoosh of stored up pain and misery. The *Unktehi* let go of the Thunderbird, and started limping its way to the woods, harried by the *Wakiyan*. The bird soared above the trees, and seemed to be following the lizard-beast below, which could be heard making its way through the pines, presumably back to the river. A great splash and a hiss was heard, and then all was quiet. The Thunderbird circled in the moonlit sky, and let out a piercing cry of victory before soaring upward into the starry blackness.

What happened that night became a legend among the survivors. The *Unktehi* had attempted to massacre the village, killing at least twenty men, women, and children. The next morning, Gray Wolf and a brave group of men followed an enormous swath of destruction among the pines down to the moving water of the river. The shore was stained with blood, but the *Unktehi* was nowhere to be found, and the sand and rocks indicated that it had slipped back into the river. Grandfather did not return. He had become the *Wakiyan,* the Thunderbird, and saved the reservation from the foul, evil beast. Gray Wolf knelt down by the shore and let out the victory song that Grandfather had taught him, waving his hatchet in the air.

Almost two decades later, in the dark forest, and under yet another blood-red moon, three men wearing mechanical-looking masks and garbed in black were chasing something in the dark, sanguine light. One of the masks looked like the head of a futuristic Phoenix, another like a cybernetic lotus-flower, and the third like a wolf bearing a metallic grin. The eyes in these masks glowed with a dim, blue light that suggested a digitized energy beneath. They were cold, terrifying, and carried only a vague suggestion of potential humanity underneath.

Two of the men began to lag behind, panting for breath, but the third member of their party pushed onward, pumping his arms and willing his legs to fly. Suddenly he came to a stop and his feet were precipitously close to the edge of a deep canyon. He looked up into the night sky and removed his mask, the one that appeared like a robot-wolf.

The young man was Eric Gray Wolf, and he cried out into the night.

"Grandfather, come back! Please come back!"

All that could be heard was the thunderous flapping of large wings, like invisible lightning splitting the heaven, and echoes indicating that the source of the noise was moving farther away into the distance.

CHAPTER 6:

SASQUATCH LOVE: AN A-HOLE STORY

He had never known what love was, not before Her, and once She came into his life, He'd never known happiness like her again. She was a broad-shouldered beauty—covered in thick, lustrous brown hair from her head to her feet, her pouty mouth and facial plate naked as her palms. Her teeth were like none He had ever seen before; strong and yellow and oh-so-sharp, like that of a bear's. He'd once seen her bite her way directly to the center of a maple tree. That took some jaw muscles, He knew, in that way that He thought, because anatomy was not something they taught Sasquatch, who were rarely, if ever, allowed in schools, public property, or public knowledge.

She was heaven-sent. Of course the Sasquatch didn't exactly have a word for heaven; they didn't have any words, come to think of it, other than pointing and grunting, and this was pretty effective seeing as there was two things a Sasquatch did in a forest: Put things in their mouth, or crapped. It was a simple life, the lives that these Sasquatch lived, and yet they were two of the happiest of their kind that had ever existed.

It was a meet-cute, really—He did not know the words for Meet-Cute, but understood the concept from watching a couple of squirrels squabble over a pile of acorns in a comical way. He had been craving some honey for the better part of a fortnight, and knew that there was one specific place in the Forest that he would find it. The angry, buzzing, flying crunchy-crunchies stored the stuff jealously in their gargantuan waxy hills in the middle of the Forest. It was guarded by their elite force of special bastards who ensured they chased away nearly every interloper who decided to swing by the clearing. Most of the other animals in the forest had already learned not to try and interfere—a cadre of death strikers would arise, angry wings buzzing, and chase them from the premises.

He had pondered how to crack their defenses, in that way that Sasquatch think. Without language, the thinking process is more of a picture of images sliding in and out of focus. There's also the speed issue. Most human beings, for instance, think things in a manner of one or two seconds, max. Sasquatch, on the other hand, take their time to ruminate.

On this particular day of craving honey He had perched himself on the edge of the clearing, staring out at the battlefield. A dead carcass of a deer was buzzing with the angry fiends' feeders. A series of mental images played themselves out in His head—various scenarios involving distractions, smoke, fire, animal attack, etc.

He was so intent on his planning, however, that He didn't notice Her. Her, swinging through the forest with all the grace of a winged bird, attached to a vine, swinging through once to grab the hive, and then dismounting and running like a wildebeest into the depths of the Forest while the winged crunchie-crunchies collectively buzzed in mid-air, confused.

By the time He had finished his planning, and his eyes caught up to tell Him what had transpired, the angry buzz-buzzes had amassed forces to chase after Her. Her beauty and grace was one thing—but in all His years, He'd never seen another one quite like himself. He had seen the sadistic honey-birthers swarm almost any creature in the forest to death before. An inkling of a thought came to Him, then—the only other one of his Kind, stung to death! It seemed a tragedy.

He bounded through the forest after the bees, panicked, and barely caught up to Her diving into the lake at the end of the shore, hive held firm under her arm. He paused, waiting for the splash of her resurfacing to breathe. A small reed bobbed up to the surface instead, with the blowing of water bubbles alongside it. He narrowed his apelike eyes at it carefully. He wasn't quite sure what was happening, really, but He knew that things usually didn't resurface so late.

Time passed. (Time is relative for the Sasquatch, to be sure, but time passed nonetheless.) Taking it as a lost cause, the angry crunchie-crunchies decided unanimously that it would be less hassle to rebuild from scratch, and they turned and flew back to their headquarters.

He had seen the results of not surfacing before. (Almost fell prey to it, once or twice, truth be told.) She was probably gone, gone forever. And all that honey would go to waste, too…

He waddled over to the shore nearest where She had entered the water, and then breathed in deep and plunged his head down under the water. Instead of a furry sodden lump, He saw Her, lips wrapped around the reed, staring at him with a bizarre expression on her face. (Because when you have seen no others of your kind before, and haven't socialized, then you really have no basis for comparison.)

Her eyes got wide. His eyes got wide. Her hand curled up and reached out like a rocket, (though of course he had no idea what those were,) and all He saw was black, and all he tasted was lakewater.

He woke up in a cave later, with a little fire going out in front of him. He was breathing; other movement in the cave indicated he wasn't alone.

Grunt, He heard, in a sultry tone.

He rolled over. She was there, ample of bosom and particularly lithe. She had a feminine odor to her—harsh and raw and rough and bloody. She bared her teeth at him, then cracked open the hive in half over a rock. She carefully slid one half over to him.

He reached for it with tentative fingers, then dragged it over to Himself. It was a good piece—dripping with honey, with a ton of the small wriggling larvae inside it.

They sat together, two Sasquatches against the world, backs up against the cave wall, eating honey and bee babies with their furry fingers, and when it was over and they'd both been satisfied She punched him in the face again and straddled him. Then They made love, or, as the noise they would make later on would indicate, '*ooka-ooka-ooka-unnnnhhhhhhhhhhhh.*'

He had never been so satisfied in his entire life.

They lived on in this way in mutual satisfaction. They would hunt together; they had erected their own little cave dwelling they decorated with various twigs and leaves. She had learned lots; clearly She was more intelligent than He, and it was a trial, but eventually He had learned a lot of her wily feminine tricks, such as using Her thumbs and crafting tools.

Together they learned how to get honey when they wanted. After some time, however, they also learned how to distract the terrifying humans and steal their picnic baskets. One or the other of them would hide in wait; the other would pointedly walk in a single direction in clear eyesight of the human beings. It was something that was quite popular—humans would try to pull out their little squares and snap bright lights at them, but if you moved fast enough it didn't really matter since they were practically harmless.

Nights were spent getting punched in the face and making sweet, sweet *ooka-ooka-ooka-unnnnnhhhhh*. His life had never been better.

And then one night, It came. The Lake in the Sky. A terrible storm had risen up, and was threatening a downpour. The moon was bright red and full, and the woods were filled with a horrible red mist. The other animals in the woods were terrified. Even She, the bravest of the two of them, grabbed and tugged at him to stay back in the cave.

Gale-force winds blew up and in, tearing down their decorations and scooping them from the cave. One of Her favorites was the empty beehive from when they had first met. The winds grabbed it, spun it around, and carried it off into the distance. Panicked, She ran after it.

That's when the Hole opened up. A swirling mass of bright red lights, its magnetism pulled at Her, and the winds lifted her up, Her hair blowing towards the portal. She grabbed onto the trees nearest her, gripping for a hold. Even He rushed out, grabbing leaves and stems to stay anchored on the ground.

He reached one furry hand up to her outstretched palm, but it was no use—she released her death grip on the tree to try and grab Him and that was all it took to lose her. The Hole and the winds gathered her up and took her away… and when She was gone, the Hole closed and the storm died out.

He would do anything to find Her again, He knew, and the love that had grown in his heart began to grow icy and cold… He screamed, so loudly that the trees themselves shuddered around him, beating His chest in frustration and anger.

THE SOUND OF ONE HAND CLAPPING

Illustration by Anton Tolstobrov

CHAPTER 7:

THE SOUND OF ONE HAND CLAPPING

"Addy-*chan*," *Okaasan* said, on one morning like any other, her beautiful face like a moon looming overhead. "We're going on a little trip."

"A trip?" Addy asked.

"We're going to see Mount Fuji," *Otousan* said, his smile wide. The creases around his eyes wrinkled when he spoke, and his eyes were wet and shining behind his glasses. "We'll have a beautiful picnic in the forest."

Addy was six years old; slim and petite, with long black hair to her waist, she looked like a porcelain doll compared to her parents. *Otousan*, her father, was a salaryman, gone for most of the week; *Okaasan*, her mother, was a housewife and Addy's best friend.

Addy was overjoyed at the idea of a picnic with the family. After all, *Otousan* was never home normally. (And how weird that he had been, she thought, in that idle way that young people have half-formed thoughts when they are learning the ways of the world.) The idea of a trip with all three of them together made her little heart skip with joy.

Okaasan dressed her up in the cutest outfit she had, and afterwards, they worked together to prepare the meal for their outing.

"Carefully, carefully," *Okaasan* said, showing her how to press the onigiri into the right shape, and how to layer it in the nori seaweed.

Soon they had three bento boxes all prepared—umeboshi, onigiri, nori salad, and some cold tonkatsu from the night before.

"Mustn't forget drinks," *Otousan* said in a chipper voice, holding an opaque bottle and some glasses.

He and *Okaasan* met glances, and paused, and then the moment passed.

Years afterward, Addy would remember this moment most of all.

They left and locked up the house after *Otousan* and *Okaasan* walked through it twice. Though they beamed and seemed happy, there was something to them, Addy knew. Something hidden, locked away inside that mask that everyone always wore.

Addy, who had not learned her hiragana yet, but was trying, noticed the paper plastered on the front door. It was bright red, with dark black hiragana and kanji scribbled all over it.

"Evic—" she started to sound out, but *Okaasan* grabbed her hand and gently steered her towards the vehicle.

They packed up the little SUV *Otousan* always drove. It was shiny and silver. The seats were comfortable and leatherbound, but *Okaasan* strapped her into a seat.

"We're going to take a long drive, Addy-*chan*, so we want to make sure you're extra comfortable," she said.

Addy nodded, and soon they were headed out, engine thrumming beneath her feet, the SUV driving on through their neighborhood and out of the city and into the lush green wilds of nature. Rice paddies and fields further out gave way to abandoned industrial pipes and fields; these broke way over time into a vast forest that seemed to swallow them alive.

Here and there Addy could see small shadows flit through the underbrush. The silence in the car was almost deafening. Usually *Otousan* would play the radio; usually *Okaasan* would sing. Instead, they were being quiet.

It was not at all the happy feeling that she had wanted, though again she was young and this feeling was not one she could not properly get across given her limited vocabulary. Instead she started to sing.

It was a silly little song—a riff off a popular koan her mother had taught her.
What is the sound of one hand clapping?
What is a bird with one wing flapping?
What is the question that none shall ask?
What is the servant without a task?
What is the moon when there is no light?
What is the day when there is no night?
What is the sound of a tree in the stream?
What is the dreamer when they have no dream?

Addy looked at *Okaasan* when she was finished singing. *Okaasan*'s knuckles were tight against the armrest of her chair. A single, strangled noise escaped her, and she fell silent again, shoulders shaking. Addy was not sure what was wrong, but the feeling that something was off in some fundamental way was thick in the core of her.

The trees in the woods near the car went on forever. Bored, Addy turned her attention to the passing scenery. Here and there, she had been seeing glimpses of white. When *Otousan* slowed the car to a stop to make a long, winding turn, she saw something in the woods.

It was a woman in a white kimono, face pale as maggots and dead eyes burning holes behind her long, scraggly head of ebony hair. Addy closed her eyes and shrieked. *Okaasan* turned around and shook her, to make sure she was okay, and by the time Addy opened her eyes again the SUV was speeding off and there was no one else around.

"Are you alright?" *Okaasan* asked.

"I saw a woman in white in the woods," Addy said.

"Just the *yurei* playing tricks," *Okaasan* said, smiling gently.

They parked sometime later. Mt Fuji was huge from here, a vast rise that stretched up into forever. Addy felt like if she tilted her head up enough she could see to the top, but it seemed impossible. There was too much mountain.

"And now we hike," *Otousan* said.

Addy could not see his eyes behind his glasses.

The three of them wandered through woods that got thicker and darker as they went. Finally, when they reached a wide enough clearing, Okaasan made a noise that seemed quiet enough but meant they should stop.

The three of them spread out a blanket, and spread out the food. They ate in a companionable silence, and Okaasan and Otousan kept stealing glances at each other.

"And now a drink for my special little girl," Otousan said.

It was peach ramune; her favorite. She guzzled it down greedily. The cool breeze stirred through the trees, and Okaasan started to hum her song, and before Addy knew what was happening she was sleepy.

"Come lay your head on my lap," Okaasan said, patting her thigh.

Addy crawled over and curled up, ebony hair spreading over her mother's leg, and before she knew it she was fast asleep.

When she woke up, nighttime had fallen. She had vague memories of her parents moving, but now panic thrilled through her system.

"*Okaasan?*" she called out tremulously, sitting up and rubbing her eyes.

The picnic basket was still there, and the blanket, and the empty baskets of food. Only now her parents were nowhere to be seen.

"*Okaasan?*" she called out again, getting to her feet. "*Otousan?*"

Giggles greeted her from the edges of the clearing. There was a shaft of bright light that pierced between two trees further on down the clearing, and she stumbled towards it, sense of panic in her chest rising.

The light was that of the moon and the sun, but before she could get a grip on it she saw it start to change. Holding her hands up to her eyes, she noticed the light darken, turn crimson. She would not know the word for this—lunar eclipse—for some amount of years to come.

Red ribbons were tied around trees here and there. It seemed to be a path beyond the trees, beckoning to her. Giggles just out of sight happened again, and she could sense things rustling in the undergrowth.

"Okaasan?" she called out again.

Something growled behind her, and a white shape moved in the side of her eyes. She turned and something with bright red eyes stared at her for a second from the darkness, before lunging. Twisting around, she shrieked and stumbled forward, holding onto the red ribbon for purchase, hair and tears streaming past her face.

"Okaasan!" she shrieked, running, and her voice echoed in the trees around her.

Whatever it was was gaining on her. Hyperventilating, arms pumping, Addy finally cleared the red ribbon when she tripped over a rock. Her knee hit the ground, and she cried out, shrieking and expecting to be eaten at any moment—

Nothing. She paused, breathed in deeply. There was a creaking from the boughs of the tree before her. She opened her eyes, only to find herself face to face with a familiar looking shoe suspended in midair.

She lifted her head. Just like Mt Fuji, she felt like she needed to lift her head all the way up to see, but she knew it was them. Otousan and Okaasan, pale and swinging from ropes, faces occluded and bulging. A strong breeze whipped through the clearing and the boughs shifted; her mother's hand slapped, once, against her own thigh.

She felt sick. She did not know what this was, why they looked wrong, but she knew *something* was wrong. Voices cackled from all around her, and as she turned she found herself surrounded by countless staring faces, eyes bulging, black scraggly hair streaming down their faces, white kimono sleeves hanging from their arms outstretched towards her.

She would never forget that smell—that smell of waste, of terror, of rot.

They drew closer still, surrounding her, and she shrunk down into herself under her mother's hanging feet, and she closed her eyes and screamed and screamed and screamed until strong arms wrapped themselves around her---

--and the strong arms shook her, again, years later, and Addy's eyes snapped open. The face of her uncle, *Oji* Tenzen, stared down at her, warm and full of caring.

"It's just another bad dream, Addy-*chan*," he whispered.

Addy's senses readjusted to her surroundings from her terrible nightmare. Here she was on her futon, quilt half-off, and shivering in the early morning breeze. *Oji* Tenzen was a warm presence, made all the more awkward by his closeness.

"Your room is a pigsty," he said. He wrinkled his nose. "And it smells in here."

"Get out!" Addy screamed, drawing the covers around her and kicking.

Oji Tenzen got to his feet on joints that popped, guffawed loudly when she slapped his back, and exited the room.

Addy was seventeen years old now, and she'd lived with *Oji* Tenzen since that fateful day so long ago. As she'd grown older her recollection of that day had faded into smears of memories half-occluded with time. Nightmares of the incident plagued her every sleep, however—nightmares of running, of burning eyes, of figures in white that stank of filth and rot...

...A single pale hand slapping a leg...

The shower washed away the grime of her night sweat, and when she dressed she felt almost like a new person again. She took the steps two at a time, and smelled the hot, fresh welcoming smell of rice and morning lotus soup.

"Let's talk about tonight," *Oji* Tenzen said, as they ate breakfast.

Addy stared at him from under her hair.

"You're willing to listen?" she asked.

"Of course," he said. "Your *Oji* is always willing to listen to his niece."

"I'm sorry to say this, but. Respectfully. I can't go to cram school anymore," she said.

Oji Tenzen sucked in a deep breath.

"But your college admissions—" he said.

Addy stared at him with baleful eyes.

"I won't do it," she said.

"Addy-*chan*," Oji whined. "Come now. Is there someone treating you poorly there?"

She shook her head.

"Is the coursework too hard, perhaps?"

She shook her head again.

"Ah," he said. "The delusions have started again."

She did not say anything, but stared down at her bowl in somber silence.

"The Yurei are not real," he said. "They are merely figments of your repressed trauma. If you would learn to control your mind, Addy-*chan*, then perhaps—"

Addy slammed her chopsticks down on the table.

"You don't understand what it's like," she said. Her voice was heated, and she was breathing hard. "It's not the same for you. Once night falls, they chase me. On the way home from cram school, they come. When the room is silent, they come. Creeping out of the shadows, with staring eyes—"

"Figments of an unfocused mind, Addy-*chan*," he said. "Listen. I'll let you quit cram school in a month. But only if you promise me that you'll practice meditation my way."

"Your way?" she asked.

"You know I spent some of my youth in a Monastery," he said. "I practiced the way of *Rinzai-oryo*. The Middle Way. The spirit of Zen."

"A bunch of old monks that know nothing and answer 'I don't know' when asked anything important," Addy said, sneering.

"I will not say that you are wrong," *Oji* Tenzen said. "There's a reason I left. So much of the training is quizzical. It requires one to understand how things really are. To pierce reality through absurdity, to understand the absurdity of reality. In all the texts the Buddha states that inexistence is existence, that up is down, down is up. At the end, once you have achieved awareness, you understand that you understand nothing at all. Perhaps I skipped a step too early and believed I discovered all there was to discover. Perhaps not. But it is the way it is."

"And you think this would be a good way to focus? To focus on the ridiculous? The nonsensical?"

"Are you not focusing on ridiculous things now?" *Oji* Tenzen asked, and Addy fell silent. "You are a seventeen year old girl. You have your whole future ahead of you. Yet you are focused on a past that will never change, stuck being haunted by your own delusions about something that never happened. When will you let go and accept that suffering is a part of existence? Your ticket in this life to happiness is understanding that it comes bundled with sorrow. For every joy there is a sadness, for every great triumph a callow fall. Acceptance is the only true way to move forward."

"Acceptance of what?" Addy asked. "That my parents were weak? That they didn't want to fight anymore? That they abandoned their only daughter to die instead of doing the hard work of fighting for another future, even when everything was collapsing around them? If I accept that I saw nothing that night, then that means there was nothing they did except accept their fate, and mine. But if I believe in what I saw—if I believe that they were tormented by the *Yurei*, by the *Onryo*, then doesn't that service their memories better? Should I dishonor them in such a way to make them accept death instead of hard work?"

"So you would choose to fight?" *Oji* Tenzen asked. "Fight for their memories? Fight for their honor?"

"Yes," Addy said.

"And yet you say this, but you wish to avoid cram school," *Oji* Tenzen said. "You wish to avoid confronting them. You choose the path of a warrior, and yet you shirk from combat."

The words rattled across the table and seemed to strike Addy where she sat. *Oji* Tenzen may have been a senile old fart, but he was a master rhetorician.

"But how can I fight them?" she asked.

"Diminish their power," Oji Tenzen said. "What do they seek?"

"To frighten me," Addy said.

"And how do they frighten you?"

"They appear before me, and they speak to me—" she said.

"Then how do you divorce them of their power?" he asked. "If they only appear to you, if they only speak to you, then how do you control their power?"

"I don't know," Addy admitted.

"If they allow themselves to be seen, they want to be seen. If they speak, they want to be heard. If you control your mind and focus on what's here, what's around you... if you block them away... then no longer will they have the power they desire to wield over you. Whether they are real or not is not the question. They want to be seen, and they want to be acknowledged. Real or not, ultimately we can't say... but the way forward is to treat them as if they are delusions in either case."

Something kindled in Addy's mind, a small flame of Enlightenment that rose up, and suddenly she saw her future: It lay not in pondering questions of what is or what is not, what was or what could have been; but the state of things, and how she could adapt to them.

And it was enough.

At all hours of the day they came to her, those terrible *Yurei*, with staring eyes and scraggly hair. She would ignore them. She would meditate on the imponderable nature of existence. There is no right or wrong answer, she would say, and she would read from *Oji* Tenzen's tattered old paperback copy of the *Blue Cliff Record*, tracing her delicate fingers over each chapter and verse in turn, considering the twisting nature of delusion in all its forms.

Her academics soared. No longer was she bound to walking home from cram school with friends and avoiding certain alleyways. No longer was she a victim. Addy had flickering notions left of her identity, and her role in the world, but still when asked would frequently say "I don't know who I am."

Was she a girl that saw ghosts? Was she simply suffering from a delusion? Questions like this arose and washed away in the stream of acceptance. She was seeing something. Her only recourse was to control herself, to control her mind, to ensure that she accepted the reality of her situation.

And things progressed happily. She would meditate, endlessly, and the nature of how things were as opposed to how they ought to be would flicker to her in waves of understanding. The Yurei appeared less and less; disheartened, they began to hover silently in the background.

And things began to get better for her, until one day Addy woke up, on the cusp of applying to several colleges, and realized that it had become a part of her identity.

And in the knowing of who she was, in the feeling of her identity as a static thing, Addy fell off the path again.

At eighteen years old, Addy had decided she wanted to join a monastery. The fighting had been intense between her and her uncle. Addy wanted to help others, she said, and so she would join and teach others the way which cannot be taught. *Oji* Tenzen would snarl at the futility of one thinking they can help others.

"True enlightenment can only come from within," he said. "It's a vainglorious quest to try to impart your personal wisdom on others."

"Are you not imparting your own wisdom upon me by forcing this decision?" Addy asked, and *Oji* Tenzen was struck silent.

Addy had won.

Oji Tenzen and Addy had driven miles and miles through Honshu, through remote rice paddies and forested fields northwards to the Shimokita Peninsula. Here, *Oji* Tenzen said, was the very same monastery he had joined as a youth. It was an isolated temple, dedicated to the way of Tendai Buddhism.

"You said you studied *Rinzai-oryo*," she said.

"Ah, but I did," he said, and Addy grew greatly confused.

"Then why are we going to Osorezan Bodaiji Temple?" she asked.

"Should there not be acceptance in your heart?" he asked.

To this Addy had nothing to say.

"I'll miss you greatly," *Oji* Tenzen said, later.

"Should you not accept my parting?" she asked, and there was a fire of arrogance in her tone.

"But should one not accept the suffering of passing from another's life? Your decision will cause a reaction no matter what it is," *Oji* Tenzen replied, for he was the wiser still.

They rode in a companionable silence along the twisting narrow highways, the lush foliage surrounding them growing higher and higher on the journey and passing away as they hit the coast.

Osorezan Bodaiji Temple. Located at the foot of the Mountain of Dread, it was a massive temple where blind priestesses passed messages on from the dead thrice yearly. The lake it surrounded was poisonous, and belched foul vapors at all times of the day. It was seen, by some of the ancient monks that had founded the Temple, as the gateway to hell. Few fish swam in its sulfurous shores, and memorials to the dead bedecked the landscape on all sides.

They parked the Jeep. It was a solemn looking sight from a distance. Impressive as all get out to the eyes, it was a massive spread of a temple that nearly swallowed the entire shoreline. *Jinzo* statues on every corner were beset with small cairns, gifts stacked atop them.

"Why are we here?" Addy asked.

"We confront a reality, and we make a decision," Oji Tenzen said. "See the women there? The *Itako*. The blind women hear the messages of the dead. They pass them on. Go to them. Ask them your questions. Allow yourself to see what you can about answers you may still have. Afterward, we will talk with the Head of the Sect."

Concerned, Addy turned to her uncle.

"Where will you be?" she asked, voice uncertain.

"Taking a dip in the sulfur springs," he said, stretching. "Your old *Oji* Tenzen is getting quite advanced in age. My joints need the heat and the minerals. You'll be fine."

Addy paused. As headstrong as she was, she still felt trepidation in her soul.

"I'm terrified," she said.

"Why?" he asked. "Have you not conquered your fear of the *Yurei* already?"

"Well, I thought so," Addy said. "The idea of accepting them as real frightens me."

"And in that, you have revealed your own choices," he said. "You have chosen to believe that they are not real, that they are only delusions in your mind's eye. Instead of suspending yourself between two ideas you have chosen that which you feel you ought to follow, and thus, you have lost the truth."

"But isn't that what you told me it was?" Addy asked.

"What right have I to foist my wisdom on you? I cannot claim the truth, as when we grasp it, it falls by the wayside."

And Oji Tenzen disappeared into the crowd.

Addy sighed, then turned and faced the direction of the temple. There was a group of temple-goers, all here for the festival. Here and there, floating quietly some distance away, if she relaxed her mind enough, she could see the *Yurei* hovering. Over cairns and *Jinzo* statues they swarmed en masse. Out in the waves they stood like statues, occasionally patrolling, lost on routes that they couldn't possibly understand.

She drew nearer one gathering. An *Itako* clutched a rosary to her bosom. Her eyes were rheumy and white, and her skin was mottled, wrinkled with age. The sulfur of the lake around her seemed to have seeped into her skin. She looked, perhaps, as if she had one foot in the grave already.

There were no *Yurei* around the woman. However, as soon as Addy set foot within the crowd surrounding her, the elderly woman shrieked and pointed.

"You!" she said, and the tourists gasped and parted.

"Me?" Addy asked.

"The girl who does not know," the old woman gasped. "She knows not her history, knows not the answer for which she has been seeking. She thinks she knows, and she grasps for the truth, only to have it slip between her fingers again and again. Come closer, child."

An older housewife in the crowd grabbed Addy by her shoulder and propelled her forward. The old woman grabbed her by the palm, thumb on her opposite hand twiddling with her rosary made of claws and bones and offerings.

"You think that the way forward is delusion," the *Itako* said. "How can one find the truth in the illusion of Maya? When we think we know the truth, that is when we are the farthest from its grasp. Ask your questions of the dead, girl."

"Why?" Addy asked. "Isn't that the point? I'm not supposed to know? That there are two explanations for each side of a story and that I have to keep both ideas fresh?"

The old woman cackled again, staring at the sky.

"There is one truth," she said. "Ask what you must."

"Why did they leave me?" Addy asked.

"They did not leave you," the old woman said. "Yet you were left."

"Who killed them?" she asked.

"Who can say?" the old woman asked. "Noone killed them, perhaps, and yet perhaps something did. Are you not sure yourself of what it is you see?"

Addy sighed.

"What was the point of talking to you?" she asked.

"Perhaps there was none," the old woman said. "Yet the dead answer the questions you ask regardless. I am merely the vessel for their words. They speak to you, through me, and if they are quixotic it is hardly the fault of this old woman, is it?"

"What should I do?" Addy asked. "Will I find the answers here?"

"You shall find the way, certainly, but answers? It depends," the old woman said.

"So what should I do?" Addy asked.

"Find the noise in the wind, the sun in the sky," the *Itako* said. "Find the Black Hills, that lay across the sea. There you will find your answer. You will find the state of being, the essence, the answers to which you have yearned for so long. Or perhaps you shan't."

And that kindle of understanding that had once flared so long ago reignited; Addy's mind was cleared, and she saw the meaning behind the woman's words.

Later, when *Oji* Tenzen wandered over and found her, eating takoyaki by a distant cairn, he looked at her and hesitantly asked a question.

"Have you found the answers you came for?" he asked.

"Perhaps," she said.

The two of them rode home in the Jeep together.

After much finagling, after much discussion, and a lot of heated, confusing debate, Addy found herself with a passport headed for America some few months later. Her English wasn't too bad—thanks to cram school, of course, which, from this far of a distance, she found herself impressed with. Yurei hid themselves in the overhead compartments and crawled from shadows, dead eyes staring at her, and she closed her eyes and tried not to feel like she was suspended 10,000 feet in the air over the ocean in a sardine can.

Her airplane seat she traded in for a bus; she felt the bumping and the crowding and the noisiness of the terminal even after they hit the highway, smooth blacktop snakes crawling forth over the Midwest American plains.

She fell asleep to the sound of someone beat-boxing, and woke up when it was night. Most of the other passengers were at various stages of sleep in one form or another. She checked the overhead LED ticker, and compared it to the schedule she had in her hands.

Sure enough, she was right on time. Only a few miles out from her stop…

The bus pulled in to a halt in front of a deserted convenience store. The forest around it had swallowed it alive; hanging tree branches skritched at its roof, and a lonely path led off into the bracken. Of course she'd only managed to obtain a hand-drawn map before she left, snagged from the *Itako*'s hasty directions at the temple. The moon hung high and full in the night sky, and in the sudden silence of the night Addy found herself feeling exposed.

She half-expected them, but found once she had touched down they were nowhere to be seen. The same old spectres at the edges of her vision, the Yurei that had haunted her since her childhood, had now seemed to make themselves scarce. And how odd was that? She wondered. Perhaps Yurei weren't allowed on this side of the ocean…

She trudged on into the bracken, flashlight in her hand and determination in her chest. Somewhere there was a temple, where she would be accepted. Here their way might reveal the truth to her. Whatever that elusive thing was.

It was a lonely trek, and she did not feel necessarily safe here on her own as a woman. Though she couldn't see them for once in her life, she nevertheless felt something in the air, a presence like heavy static all around her. It did not help that she was obscured by fog on all sides, a fog so dense that it illuminated all the trees around her.

For hours she seemed to wander, until she was too tired to continue. She sat herself down at a stump and took a deep breath, willing herself to meditate. She was only as safe as she allowed herself to be, after all. As she fell deeper and deeper into a trance, she found her perception of time fleeing; soon, she opened her eyes and found herself completely surrounded by a crimson mist that seemed to hover over the ground like soup.

She glanced up at the sky. A lunar eclipse, staining the moon red. Her dream came back to her of so long ago—that same blood moon, the dancing crimson fog around her, and finding her mother and father's hanging corpses, one hand slapping against naked thigh…

They began to move in the trees, then. Shadows at first, the same old Yurei she had grown to know. Soon, however, she realized that whatever this mist was, it was somehow acting as a vehicle for them. They had substance; they had form. Their hands gripped trees, and a foul stench rolled to her from where they taunted her in the trees beyond the clearing.

"You're not real," she said, closing her eyes, and taking a series of deep breaths.

She opened her eyes after a few deep breaths, and found a familiar sight. A woman in a white kimono, pale as maggots face staring at her, head cocked, malicious grin on her waxen face. Her hair danced, and her talons were out-stretched as she slid closer and closer over the forest floor. The Yurei's voice was that of her mother's, from so long ago:

"It's just the *yurei* playing tricks," the she-beast screeched, voice a cruel parody.

"You're not real," Addy screamed, slamming her eyes shut again. "You're not real, you're not real. None of this is real. This is all a delusion."

She felt the mists float over her face, felt the dark static presence of the Yurei as she had never felt it before. Knowing without knowing, Addy opened her eyes carefully, trembling with fear as she felt a single talon slide its way down from her eyebrow to her chin.

Addy opened her eyes. The woman in the white kimono's eyes were all she could see.

"Kyahahaha!" The woman in the white kimono laughed, and in her mouth were teeth like razor blades, and in her eyes was the despair of a life long lost and never retrieved.

There was a click and a sound of the wind blowing from the trees; the *Yurei* in front of her face howled, and a flash like a camera happened, and then she just blinked out. Flashes happened everywhere else around her; Addy could hardly believe her eyes, but was that the Yurei shrieking as they ran?

A dark figure stepped out from the shadows. A plague doctor's mask on his face hid him from view; beaked like an eagle, it was shiny silver and glittered in the light of the moon. Green orbs stared from its foreign eyes. Atop the figure's head a black top hat; on its body, a rather dusty tuxedo in need of some serious maintenance. Metal clad gauntlets, fingerless, raised to the mask and fumbled heavily with a switch, exposing his face with the rushing noise of a pneumatic tube.

The rather handsome gentleman underneath removed the top hat next, bowing deeply.

"How do you do?" he asked. "I'm terribly sorry to be so impolite, but you seem to be under the very fatal impression that those things aren't real. They are rather more real than any of us would like them to be, I'm afraid. Now come along. We've got some hunting to attend to!"

He lifted his fingerless gauntlet, embedded metal circles whirling, and a blinding white light shone forth, and in Addy's heart of hearts she found a fire had kindled again, that of Enlightenment.

TICKLE ME MAHAHA

Illustration by Anton Tolstobrov

CHAPTER 8:

TICKLE ME MAHAHA: AN A-HOLE STORY

Horror movie marathon during a blizzard. No better way to celebrate the parents being gone for the whole New Year's weekend. The old tube-tv's picture rolled in Liza and Alexander's room, and Alexander groaned in frustration.

"Get up and fix it," Liza whined, brown hair poking out of the covers from where she had burritoed herself in.

"You do it," Alexander whined. "I did it last time."

"I'm cold and I don't want to move," Liza's lump said.

They were twins, though you wouldn't know it to look at them. All of seven years old, the two were almost at that tricky age where they would wind up getting different bedrooms. It was not something they were looking forward to, although sometimes it was nice to not be in the same classroom together.

Stacey, their older sister, popped her head into the room. Stacey was nearly a decade and a half older than both of them, and back from college for the winter holidays.

"What's all the whining about?" Stacey asked.

"Alexander broke the TV and he won't get up and fix it," Liza said.

"Not true!" Alexander said, outraged.

"You should learn this pretty early, Alex, but girls are pretty much always right. Even when they're wrong," Stacey said. "It's not fair but it's how you keep them around."

She stepped into the room and looked at the TV, then knocked the side of it. The screen rolled again, stabilizing. An old black and white movie about some watery creature from the depths of the lagoon was playing. Stacey shook her head and turned it off.

"Hey," the twins said, in various versions of outrage.

"That stuff will rot your brain," Stacey said. "It's not really scary anyway. You know what is scary? When your well-travelled older sister tells you a story about real life monsters."

"I don't want to hear about your ex-boyfriend again," Liza said.

"Hellz no," Alexander said.

Stacey looked at the two of them, lips pursed for a moment, and then shook her head and sighed.

"I mean real monsters, you twin turds," she said. "As in spooks. Scary things. Creatures that go bump in the night!"

"There ain't no such thing as real monsters, Stacey," Liza said.

"Yeah, no monsters. Don't exist," Alexander said, backing his twin up… though he was secretly terrified at the thought. Liza was always the braver one.

"That's what you think," Stacey said. "You really think the parents would tell you about monsters when you're so young? You're not mature enough to handle something so scary."

"I'm mature," Alexander said, feelings hurt.

"This is just a trick," Liza said.

"Is it?' Stacey asked. "Don't you think I'd have something better to do on a Saturday night than come and bug you?"

Liza and Alexander locked gazes, and nodded. Stacey was often not very happy about spending time with them. Something clattered from the adjoining bathroom, and the toilet started its usual evening bubbling from windy pipes. Liza and Alexander were used to it; at least, Alexander pretended he was used to it. Liza seemed to have no problem with it, though the noise in the middle of the night made Alexander's skin crawl.

"Fine," Liza said impatiently. "Spill the beans. What's so scary?"

"Well, there are a lot of monsters out there," Stacey said. "But a lot of them are scared of the cold. So thankfully, a blizzard like this one protects us. Mostly."

"M-m-m-ostly?" Alexander asked.

"Quit trying to scare the baby over there," Liza said, though it sounded like her teeth were chattering.

"I'm not trying to scare you, I'm trying to warn you," Stacey said. "There's this thing that the native Alaskans had to deal with. They called it the Mahaha. It was a spirit of a frozen Inuit who had fallen into the water and drowned. They're not real smart, but the thing is, when you die, your fingernails and hair do NOT quit growing. So they stay frozen in the water, their hair dragging to their feet, their nails getting longer and longer and longer…"

"That's not so scary," Liza said. "If they ARE frozen, then they can't move."

"That's just their bodies, though," Stacey said. "Their corpses don't get up and move. Their spirits bond with the ice and snow. So when it gets cold, like it is now, their spirit can manifest into a new physical body. One with long, stringy hair, brittle from the ice and cold. Huge fingernails that drag along the ground behind them when they walk. Their skin is icy white, and their eyes are soulless, glowing red in the gloom. When Winter comes, they come. Looking for humans like YOU and YOU!"

Stacey swung her pointer finger to each of them in turn as she spoke.

"Why would they want to find humans?" Alexander asked, eyes riveted on his older sister.

"Yeah! Why?" Liza's voice chimed in, from the blanket burrito.

Stacey nodded over at Liza, who was creeping slowly out of her blanket fort unseen by Alexander.

"Their nails are perfect weapons of torture. They sneal up on their prey and…" Stacey said, fingers held out. She stood and stalked, step by step, to Alex. "They use them to tickle them to death!"

She launched herself on Alex, who screamed at first, terrified. Liza jumped. Soon, the both of them were laughing with a sense of dawning relief. Stacey picked herself back up and sat where she was before, sweeping her hair back behind her eyes.

"No, but really, the Mahaha sneaks up and tickles their prey until they are overcome by such intense giggling that they stop breathing… and then they *die*."

"That's so creepy!" Alexander said, shaking his head. "But how do you stop the Mahaha if it's tickling you?"

Stacey paused, thinking quickly. Liza rolled her eyes.

"You can trick them back into the water," Stacey said eventually. "If you push them into the water they'll drown, but for good this time."

Alexander sighed in relief.

"That's good to know!" he said.

Stacey got to her feet, checking her watch.

"Alrighty turds, time to get some sleep! Lights out in five minutes."

Stacey tucked them in, turning the TV off, and watching them from the doorway.

The toilet burbled in the next room again, the leaky ballcock in the top of the tank slowly replenishing water it slowly leaked.

"Goodnight Stacey," Alex said from the covers.

"Night Stacey, thanks for the good story."

"Night, kiddos." She looked at Alex, who was shivering, and a wave of sudden guilt passed over her. "Just remember, Alex. Push them in the water."

"Right, water," he whispered.

The howl of the raging snow storm outside whipped up against the glass window, lulling the both of them to a quick sleep.

Alexander opened his eyes again. It was clear that some time had passed, although how much Alexander wasn't sure. Outside the window, the snow was still falling. The TV screen was on, but there was only the national anthem playing and light dancing at the edge of the room. The toilet in the next room burbled and grunted to itself, again.

What had woken him up? He wondered. And then a slight squeaking, scraping sound greeted him from the walls...

"Nails," Alexander said to himself. "Sounds like nails!"

Alexander felt all the skin on the back of his neck rise at once.

"Liza?" he hissed, not willing to move. "Liza, do you hear that?"

The scraping continued again. He looked over to Liza's bed, and found that she'd burrowed herself entirely inside the covers, head down. Well, she was no use...

He breathed, and then like an action hero, kicked the covers off the bed and rolled off to the side. His knees ached where he landed on all fours, but like other kids his age, it hardly phased him. Another scrape, though, had him reach back up for the covers and wrap them around himself like a blanket.

He padded over to the window, fear shivering down his spine, and saw tree branches heavy with snow scraping the window.

"Whew," he said, and padded back to bed, turning the TV off again. "Stupid tree."

Still. He had a horrible feeling like something was staring directly at his back from the window. He could imagine it exactly like Stacey had said it—something with long, shaggy, brittle hair, nails that dragged behind it, red dead eyes and pale skin, and a horrible grin...

After some time passed, he fell into an uneasy slumber.

Were those... were those footsteps? And the scratching noise seemed to be getting louder... unmoving, barely breathing, Alex cracked open his eyes. There was something—a shadow or something, standing between their beds, illuminated by the moonlight reflecting off snow. It took one step closer, breathing heavily, and then another step...

71

"I don't want to be tickled to death," he breathed, under his breath. "Please leave me alone."

The scraping drew closer. Closer. Sweat was forming on his brow. He was burning up, but he knew his safest bet was to stay burrowed inside the covers. That terrible feeling of being stared at by something with dark intentions drew closer and closer… and suddenly he felt the covers ripped away.

He shuddered and screamed, but the cold nails were on his sides, tickling and tickling away. He jerked and screamed, rolling off the bed and away, panting and crawling on the ground on all fours to get away, but it was back again! Cold fingers stabbing into his sides…

The door slammed open, and a light came on.

"What the hell is going on in here?" Stacey asked.

"Mahaha," Alex cried, pitifully. "Mahaha!"

A familiar peal of laughter from behind him, then. Stacey did not look impressed. He turned and saw Liza standing at the edge of his bed, laughing.

"I'm gonna tickle you to death! Tickle tickle tickle!" she cackled.

"I hate you Liza. You're such an asshole," he said.

"Oh, shut your pie-hole. It was funny."

She crawled back into bed while Stacey came over to sort Alex out. Stacey hugged him and held him until his breathing became normal again, then tucked him back into bed.

"No more funny stuff tonight. Get some sleep," Stacey said, by the lights.

"I will," Liza said, voice twinkling as if innocent.

"Promise?" Stacey's voice was firm.

"I promise," Liza said, rolling her eyes and turning over in the covers again.

"I promise, too," Alex said.

And that seemed to be that, for the two of them fell into a deep slumber again… only for Alex to awaken, again, to the feeling of two hands crawling up his back.

"Knock it *off* Liza!" he muttered. "Leave me alone and go to sleep!"

As if in response, the fingers dug in deeper, and he squirmed, sighing in frustration as he turned.

"I said leave me alone," he said, and then gasped.

There it was, squatted over him, malicious leer on its muppet-like face, its sewer-water smell clear in this close of proximity. Its hair was a horrible snaggle of an unbrushed mess; its red eyes glowed at him, and it dug its unwieldy nails down into his sides again.

He squirmed and howled, trying to kick away and frog-crawling on his elbows away, flopping onto the floor. Over on Liza's bed, the lump of her encased in a burrito was lying prone. Had it already got her, Alex wondered?

"Please!" he screamed, between gasps. "Please! Go away and leave me alone!"

"Tickle! Must tickle!" it shrieked, voice like nails on a chalkboard, fingers digging in his sides.

There was a bang on the door, and it rattled in the frame.

"What's going on in there? Open the door! Open it right now!"

"Stacey," he panted. "Stacey, it's in here! The Mahaha is going to get me!"

"Alex, you locked the damn door," Stacey called. "Come unlock it now!"

Alex panted and struggled as the door shook in the frame. Unbothered, the Mahaha dug in, and Alex howled as he squirmed and kicked, knocking it backwards. He pulled himself to his feet and hit the bathroom, slamming the door behind him, back against it.

"Stacey!" he screamed. "Help me please. Please Stacey. I don't want to die!"

Something was scraping against the bathroom door. Alex tried not to hyperventilate. He could hear the sounds of his older sister rattling the door, trying in vain to get it to open.

"Liza!" he heard her scream. "Liza, come open this door. It's locked, Liza. Come unlock the damn door!"

Alex breathed in, breathed out. Thought back to what Stacey had said earlier, as the toilet tank bubbled in front of him…

"Fine!" the shriek voice called, laughing. "If you won't let me in, I'll take your sister instead."

"Liza, get out of there!" Alex screamed. "Liza, run! Now!"

And Stacey still rattling, banging in the background—"Open this goddamn door now!"

"Stacey, it's gonna get Liza! Help us!"

Alex stared at the toilet, hearing the scraping of nails.

"Come here, little one," the Mahaha's scratchy voice called, and it was distant. "I have something for you…"

"Liza, noooo!" Alex called. Thinking of her, he slammed open the door. At the noise, the Mahaha turned on the spot and grinned. Its long, curled nails dragged on tile floor as it made its way in, and Alex stumbled backwards, back hitting the toilet, hands held up to ward the thing away.

"Just wait a second," Alex said. "I'll let you tickle me to death if that's what you want, but there's something I have to show you."

"B-b-but it's in there. I mean, behind me." He scooted out of the way, and nodded at the closed toilet lid.

The Mahaha leaned down, staring. Alex lifted the lid, and it glared down.

Then he moved without thinking—kicking its knees out, and jumping from behind, elbow out, as if to suplex the thing. His elbow connected, and its long-nailed hands squirmed as Alex leaned with all of his weight on it.

There was a burbling noise, and Alex grinned.

"Stacey!" he called excitedly.

The Mahaha scrabbled for purchase, trying to breathe, as Stacey banged against the bedroom door, knocking into it with her full weight. It gave, and she collapsed against the bedroom floor, getting to her feet and drawing near to the bathroom.

"It's okay. I got it already, Stacey," Alex said, as it drew still. "I sent it back into the water, just like you said. Come see, come see!"

Stacey's hands shook as she gripped the bathroom wall.

"Alex," she whispered. "What have you done?"

"I did it! I killed the Mahaha for good," he said, triumphantly.

Stacey sank to her knees, sobbing, eyes wide.

Alex followed her horrified face down to where his hands were holding the thing in the water. Liza's hair floated in the water, and her pale hands hung limply over the sides.

And outside the window, the Mahaha peered in through evil eyes to witness the carnage. What use would a being such as it have with tickling? It wondered. Why, when its nails were so great for puncturing the eyes of its victim, to alter its sight? Why tickling? Why, when its nails could puncture the eardrums of its victims, to scramble their brains and make them unable to hear what was really said?

The Mahaha watched Alex drown his twin sister to death, cackling. It was only when it was over that it pulled its invisible, detachable nails from Alex's brain and eyes, and allowed him to see what he had truly done. The Mahaha breathed in the boy's sorrow; breathed in his pain; dragged a small smiley face in the bloody puddle in the bathroom with its eldritch power, and then cocked its head, as if listening.

An astral hole opened, yawning wide, and the Mahaha heard something from it… an echo, words quickly being whispered in the breeze…

It stepped inside, the screams of the terrified human boy like a sweet symphony to its ears, the whisper beckoning it to come, to join, to gather...

LAIR OF THE HODAG

Illustration by Anton Tolstobrov

CHAPTER 9:

LAIR OF THE HODAG

1896: Rhinelander, Wisconsin. Eugene Shephard's House.

It groaned and moaned; sobbed to itself, muttered, spoke obscenities into the glass that surrounded its trophy box. It had been talking for some manner of days now, and Eugene Shephard wasn't sure what to do.

Oh, the chloroform had worked, of a sort. That the thing fell unconscious and quit breathing—that was a mercy, to say the least. That it sprang back up, revitalizing itself, and began a nonsensical stream of babble was something entirely different. Even flaying it open and pulling out its organs didn't seem to do any damage to it. Within minutes of being mounted the scales began to twitch; its flesh crawled towards its jagged matching seams, and blood and ichor seemed to ooze and reknit over the wounds his carving knife had left. Stuffing and mounting it had seemed like the final end of any real flesh-and-blood creature, but yet here it was, a wire hanger and some electrodes up its ass, bemoaning its fate.

How could he have known he trapped a devil? It was all well and good to have a devil on display, a dead devil, at that, but had any devil in the Good Book ever sat and cried at its own fate?

His wife had nearly passed out when the thing in the glass asked for some water.

Eugene was a tall, pale man, with brown hair going-on-ginger and a sun-baked complexion that resulted in freckles all over his face. He sat in his library and considered, for some time, how he would handle this situation. He'd already sent his family away for the week. (His wife, bless her soul, had been nearly beside herself at the whole situation. The boys seemed less put-out, except for the fact he'd banished them. Even the housekeeper, after a quick instruction to send a message to the Mayor, had been dismissed for the week.)

There was a knock from the front door that echoed distantly to Eugene, and he took off in its direction, trying not to listen to the fresh new howls that had arose at the noise.

"Thank our Lord Almighty," Eugene said.

The Mayor looked a bit put-out; he took off his hat and shrugged off his coat. The weather was starting the first of the early frosts of autumn in the small northern town of Rhinelander, and the harvests were coming soon. A hunting trip in preparation for the long winter to come was what sparked this whole situation in the first place.

"Now Mr. Shephard, what is all this commotion about? Fritzi looked just like a ghost when she approached me."

"Ah, it's the creature I found, Mr. Mayor," Eugene said. "Well, there was two of 'em. The first one we blowed up with dynamite, and that seemed to do it. Few pickings, but one of the men got a good photo of it. I found the next one and thought I killed it with chloroform. Woke back up as I was field-dressing it and stuffing it for display."

A putrid moan from the other room floated in to them. The Mayor looked past Eugene, a horrified look on his face.

"Tell me you granted the beast a decent death, at least," he said.

"Ah, that's the thing, Mr. Mayor," Eugene said. "Clearly I woulda done the Christian thing and put it out of its misery. The ugly sonofabitch refuses to die, however."

"Refuses to die?" the Mayor asked, eyebrows huddled with confusion.

"I done everything but blown it up with dynamite and it still ain't done no good," Eugene said.

"Dear Lord," the Mayor said. "Well, you may as well take me in to see it."

The room smelled of skunk; of rotten death, of a snake's den or a lizard's shit. The light was all but non-existent, a few candles lit for the sake of bare-minimum visibility. Hunting trophies from years past floated in the gloom—an antlered head stuck out of one wall, and various tails were hung on display on what looked like a wooden plaque.

There, in the far corner, wires running in and out of it, lay the *thing*.

"The Hodag," the Mayor whispered.

It was scaly—a dark rich green, with a clubbed tail and spines that started on its neck and seemed to shrink as it approached the tail. Yet its face was strangely humanoid—large, expressive eyes blinked wide, with lids that shuddered. Horns criss-crossed on its head, and sharp canines jutted from the top of its mouth. It opened its mouth when it saw them, its lips forming words.

"Release me," it gurgled. "Please."

"No wonder there's only candles here, the thing is hideous," the Mayor said.

It sobbed behind the glass, shuddering at the words.

"It says light hurts its eyes, so I been trying to keep it dim in here," Eugene said. "I know the Museum people are supposed to be coming here soon. But I ain't got no idea how to tell 'em it's still moving around and talking. And you know how them educated types are. Real bleeding heart type folks."

"My God, they might try and say it's sentient and has rights!" the Mayor said. "Is that what you're saying?"

"Well, you said the words," Eugene said. "Look, as for me. I don't think none of this is right and it's getting to be a mess. I just want done with all this business already. Only the thing is, I can't get him dead. I'd rather just say the whole damn thing was a hoax and move on with it already. It ain't like there ain't a precedent for it on my behalf."

"But you can't just release the foul thing," the Mayor said.

It burst into a fresh wave of sobs and tears.

"Look, it ain't ideal. But we're in new territory here. I ain't never seen no animal that can talk, Mr. Mayor. This is Biblical stuff, I tell you."

"Biblical stuff, eh?" the Mayor said. He sighed, then crouched down and bent forward to the glass. He knocked on it, twice. The Hodag shuddered, blinking its bright wide eyes, and the Mayor cleared his throat. "Do you have a name?"

"Yes," it replied. "I am known to my people as He-Who-Stalks."

"Are you the one responsible for the missing farm-hounds?"

It blinked its eyes again.

"My brood needed nourishment," it burbled. "We live currently on the outskirts of your village. We come from another place, a sideways place, where grass grows purple and there is an endless swamp. We tried not to impede upon your village, but your men hunt the dwindling game in the forest and my brood grows larger every day. We could not reveal ourselves, so we took to taking that which we deemed unnecessary. You creatures are sentient yourselves; we deemed you too dangerous to hunt. Your own livestock are your food supplies. Taking them would only ensure more of our game was plucked from the forest. Yet your companion creatures, they seem to occupy little space and seemed to have little purpose."

"Those were pets and companions. Damn near members of the family," the Mayor said.

"Do we not all do what we must to survive?" the creature burbled. "Please, release me! I can feel the pain of hot metal burning me on the inside! I must go and check back in on my brood!"

"I heard that one of your kind attacked one of our hunters," the Mayor said.

"When cornered, we react to threats to our continued existence," it said. "Do not mistake self-defense for hostility. Please."

The Mayor passed a hand over his face in frustration, holding his eyes and tightening his grip as he got to his beard. He stood up straight again, and the creature wailed.

"I don't know what to do," Eugene said. "If we let him go, he may well go back to his family and tear through the whole town."

"Yet if he's not released, then this gets trickier than ever," the Mayor said. "The journos could get ahold of this and blow it out of proportion. Or his family could come looking for him."

"There's no way we could fight 'em off," Eugene said. "There ain't enough dynamite in the universe, and bullets don't stop 'em no ways."

"Good God, man, we're in a mess of a situation," the Mayor continued.

"Allow me to make a suggestion," the Hodag called.

The two men looked down at the horrid monster.

"We broker a treaty," the beast said. "A peace agreement. How long does your kind live?"

"The Bible states man lives no longer than 120 years," Eugene Shephard said.

"Then release me, and I will honor the pact between us. My brood and I will depart for our homelands. There we will stay for the length of time your kind lives. To ensure that none of your loved ones will fall prey to the advance of my species."

"And at the end of 120 years?" Eugene asked.

"My kind can return. Perhaps we can renegotiate the terms of our treaty at that point. Or perhaps, since you will no longer be alive, we will come back and devour those who live here."

"You ain't making a real compelling case on letting you out of here alive," Eugene said.

"I am merely informing you of the truth. Would you have me lie?"

"There's no way in hell that we could prepare for a whole batch of you," the Mayor said. "It's best we take a whole case of dynamite and blow up your brood right now."

"No!" the creature howled. "No! Fine. Release me. Allow my Brood and I to depart for the terms of our agreement. And I will tell you our weakness."

"Your weakness?" Eugene asked.

"You notice how our flesh is immortal?" the creature asked. "We have a natural lifespan, but violence and aggression are not ways we can die. Our flesh, our hide, it's our protection. There is a coating of certain chemicals that allow our cells to regenerate. Our wounds to reheal. Only one thing can disrupt this—the juice of a pulpy citrus fruit. There are chemical acids in it which we react poorly to."

"A lemon," the Mayor said. "By God. Go get a lemon, or some lemonade besides, would you?"

"I might have one or two in the pantry," Eugene said, absentmindedly.

"Well, go!" the Mayor snapped.

Eugene rushed off, and it was just the Mayor and the Hodag in the same room.

"You would use information learned during a peace treaty to destroy me?" the Hodag hissed.

"Or maybe just as a threat, for a bargaining chip," the Mayor said. "I don't like the idea of none of my citizens being snapped up by some gurgling swamp dragon. Nossir. So here's how this is gonna work. We don't kill you today, and when you come back—not until we're good and God-damn well dead—you be choosy about what you take. No humans. No livestock. And no dogs, by God."

"A shame," the Hodag said. "We consider the canine a delicacy. Given enough motivation, we could be convinced to dine on their flesh alone."

"Alright then," the Mayor said. "Dogs are fine, but be choosy! You only get the pure white ones. How's that for a delicacy?"

"Harsh, yet fair. And yet, at the same time, I feel perhaps this is a tad too restrictive for my family."

"The alternative is we kill your whole clutch in one go," the Mayor said. "I got plenty of housewives around here ready to make some lemonade."

"Fine," the Hodag hissed. "Just cut this damn wire out of me already!"

2016. Rhinelander, Wisconsin. Pat's Tavern Parking Lot.

Skye checked her reflection in the mirror. Wouldn't do to go in and look too out of place. She was a severely pretty woman, with high cheekbones and burnished copper skin. Her long, straight black hair—usually pleated—she'd allowed to hang free behind her head.

She thought about cover stories as she applied some lipstick. A natural shade, a little brownish, but it contrasted with her skin nicely, amplified her natural colors. Eyelashes—nice and long and beautiful. She batted them a few times. She was normally not one given to makeup, but this... this was a special situation.

She picked up the piles of newspaper on the seat next to her, sorting through the various articles she had clipped or printed out. "Mysterious Pet Napper Strikes Again!" "This small Wisconsin town has a canine serial killer?" Other clickbaity headlines in a post-tabloid world popped out of the pages at her. And of course, her prize. A tale of two missing children, still not found.

She had only thought about the case because the sheer level of disappearances boggled her mind. And to go from missing dogs to missing humans?

"You have a cat go missing at fourteen years old and now every missing dog is a devil waiting in the wings," the Head of her Department said, blonde curls swinging and voice filled with scorn. "We could be investigating people eaters and you're worried because a couple of pitbulls ran away?"

The fight had been intense, but Skye was entitled some time away now and again, and the two missing children had really sunk it home how bad this case could be. Besides, Skye argued, she was here to question some locals, understand some of the legends, and gather more information for her thesis. Skye was an anthropologist—knee deep in a low-residency graduate program, working on her doctorate for a very, how to put it... hands on program.

Weird, she thought. *Here I am. A woman in my mid-thirties. Grew up on the Rez. Never thought I'd be here.* Academic in one respect. Detective in another. The fact that she had dreamed of stalking these things as a little girl and now she was getting the occasional grant to chase them down, well. She'd heard of following your dreams, but there was a twinge of self-directed loathing that came with it, as if this were too much to ask of the universe. The voice of her mother haunted her in the back of her head—*you take everything for granted, you spoiled little shit, you're nothing and you'll always be nothing*—often played to tamper even the best of days with a little stone cold reality. Skye knew she might have been nothing, but the nothing she was was better than the nothing everyone else was. There was something to be said for a universe that didn't make sense. You didn't have to make sense, either.

She adjusted her bust, slid the newspaper articles back into their folder, and then finally walked out to the double-saloon doors. A native woman on the prowl, she thought. She'd dressed the part, stopping at a Drysdales some miles back. Red flannel button-up top, a push-up bra, short-short khakis that exposed a colored dream-catcher tattoo on her left thigh, a pair of worn hiking boots. She was redneck-gorgeous-native-american princess, today, some sweet Southern NDN who grew up around white people and was one of them, basic'lly.

She instantly got looks as she walked in. The smell of whiskey and cigarettes hit her, a thick miasma of human vice. It slid over her like a glove—the comfort here, the fitting in, the old days she spent out in the backwoods haunting divebars and making bad decisions with yet another hillbilly white man with a little dick, a fast car, and something to prove. It was not an unwelcome feeling—she had lots of good memories, lots of fun, lots of good times... but she was little more than just a notch on some cowboy's belt, another squaw he'd nailed good. She didn't love herself enough. She loved herself like she could have, like she knew how to, but even that fell short.

No direction, no goalposts, just endless nights of drinking and partying and sleeping around to kill the crushing weight of maturing too early. It was a wonder she hadn't been killed, she thought. The old her had not been trained at protecting herself—the old her had not had a knife in their boot, she thought, nor the skill to use it.

Still. She slid onto a stool with practiced ease and lifted her head, once, at the barkeep. He nodded at her, knuckle-deep in cutting up some fruit, and turned to her after a few minutes.

"Well ain't you pretty," he said. "How you doing today, darlin'?"

"Good," she said, faking a smile as much as she could. "Rum and Coke, if you got it."

He nodded and turned away, bustling some drinks. He was not an overtly aggressive man; rather, he was thick, soft around the edges. Bearded and seemed, somehow, sweet, in a way. He turned back around to her and passed her drink down the counter. His little beady eyes looked at her face for some time, before he nodded to himself.

"You're Lakota, ain't you?" he asked.

She nearly jumped out of her skin.

"Excuse me?" she asked.

"Lakota," he said. "My wife is. Similar complexion. Accent's the same. Just a guess, but the two of you may damn well be cousins."

"There are a lot of Lakota out there," Skye said, voice as close to neutral as she could be.

"Yeah, well," he said, and he seemed to reel himself back in. "What brings you all the way out to Rhinelander?"

"I'm here for my thesis," she said. "Anthropology work. I'm in the Doctoral program at Hallowtide University."

"'Zat so?" he asked. "What you looking into?"

"The pet disappearances, possibly the missing kids," she said. And here, her cover story floated to the surface of her lips almost automatically, a half-truth bundled in with some misdirection. "I have a hunch. I hear that there may be some occult practitioners that engage in animal sacrifice in the area and I'd like to learn more about their beliefs."

He looked at her, his face nearly inscrutable.

"You mean like some Satanists or something?" he asked.

"Or something," she said. "Researchers just look into things. We don't draw conclusions, we just gather information."

"Well, I'll tell you this," he began, but Skye was nearly bowled out of her chair by a woman shoving into the bar.

"Woohoo!" the woman slurred. She sloshed the remains of her mixed drink over the rim of its glass and onto the counter top. "Bradley, gimme another one!"

"I think you had enough Phyllis," he said.

"Yeah, well, water it down or something," she slurred. She turned and faced Skye, still uncomfortably close, her hips and thigh pressed into Skye's. She looked like one of the 700 Club members' wives, a bleached-blonde white woman with her hair in a messy beehive and lipstick so magenta it may as well have been pink. She had bright blue watery eyes that blinked, roving over Skye's face. "Oh, aren't you just the prettiest thing. What's your name, darling?"

"Mahpee," she said, stutteringly, "or Skye. However you'd like it."

"I'm Phyllis," the drunk woman said. "We don't get pretty girls like you roll into town often."

"Skye's an anthropologist," Bradley said, behind the bar. "She says she's here to investigate the missing dogs."

"Missing dogs!" Phyllis said, and she barked a laugh. "Ain't that a hoot! Just like the old legends."

"Ah, that crap again," Bradley said. "Those are tourist stories, Phyllis."

"They're true, though," she said. "I bet you ain't never heard of the Hodag, have ya?"

Skye shook her head no.

"Been about 120 years by now," she continued. "They say old Eugene Shephard, huckster and charlatan that he was, supposedly captured the first one. Rigged it up with wires and made it hoot and holler and scream. Only problem was, it was fake. Made of wood. He came out and confessed to everything. That's those ugly dinosaur looking statues everywhere in town. Times was tough in Rhinelander back in the day, and scheming seemed to be easier work than hauling wood or heading down to the shore."

Skye *had* seen one—a green, sparkly monster of a statue at a convenience store earlier—but thought perhaps there was a fascination with the Muppets or something that the town had that she was missing.

"So you're saying they don't exist," Skye said.

"'Course not," the bartender said. "It's supposed to be a talking lizard smellier than a sewer, whining about his appearance. Dynamite, chloroform, and lemons are supposed to be the only thing that stops it. Now don't that just sound like some kind of folk tale if you ever heard of it?"

"Of course," Skye said. Her pulse was quickening. "So how are the dogs connected?"

"They say they only eat white bulldogs," Phyllis said. "Good riddance, I say. Them things fart. Ugly dogs, mind. Very ugly."

"You've all been extremely helpful," Skye said, and knocked back her drink in one go. Steam seemed to pour out of her nose. Phyllis and the bartender both stared at her with wide eyes, but she slid away from the bar and back out into the bright light of day.

She checked in with her mentor after she'd found a cheap hotel to stay in. It was more of a fleabite lair than anything, but she needed a few hours of shut-eye and sleeping in the back of her pickup, as many memories as it brought, was not exactly high on her list of things she preferred.

"How's your vacation been? Sorting through much childhood trauma?" her interim mentor, Vanessa, had asked.

"I think I found something," Skye said. "There's rumors of a creature here—the hodag. Supposedly 120 years ago there was a man who faked a lizard creature that ate dogs."

"So you've stumbled onto a publicity stunt run by the Mayor," Vanessa said. "Congratulations, I can already see your Thesis denial."

Skye closed her eyes and counted to ten slowly.

"You're doing the counting thing, aren't you?" Vanessa asked.

"Must you be such a persistent thorn in my side?" Skye asked. "Can't you just once back me up on the work I find important?"

There was a silence that stretched for some time.

"Darling, if you didn't have me to resent and prove wrong, wouldn't you just resent yourself and try to prove yourself wrong?"

There was an eerie sort of sense to it that Skye wasn't a fan of.

"Can't you just ease up on the snark?" Skye asked, exasperated.

"I'm not a psychologist," Vanessa said. "I wouldn't be able to tell you left from right about ticks or DSM manuals. But if you think I don't know my way around keeping neuroses distracted, well. I'll tell you this, m'dear. If you think you're the only grad student with problems, you must have had your eyes closed the entire program."

"You really think this is mentally healthy?" Skye asked.

"Is there anything mentally healthy about the work we do?" Vanessa asked. "The truth is, I've got enough work on my own plate, let alone having to babysit each one of you and keep you motivated. My job isn't to heal you, Skye, and it's not to soothe your ego. My job is to keep you on the right track to provable research."

"I'm beginning to understand the sky high attrition rate in this program. What if I'm right, though?"

"Prove me wrong, then, Skye. In the meantime, if you get nothing from this trip, then it's likely you'll be relegated to teaching duty ever after. So you'd better find *something,* unless you want to grade papers the rest of your life."

Vanessa disconnected. She was harsh, but fair—normally their relationship was much better, but Vanessa had to take on all the work from when Skye's mentor had gotten himself blown up.

"Fuck you," Skye seethed, at the air.

She did not like the fact that she sat there and stewed and thought about driving off, away from the town. Away from this state. Down to the South, past the border, all the way down to Mexico to drink an endless slew of Margaritas on the coast and lose all sense of who she was.

A little tinkle noise came from her cellphone. It was a message from Vanessa.

I hear there are chupacabras down South this time of year. Should help with your thesis, if you're so inclined.

"What a bitch!" she said, and then she laughed, because there was nothing else to do but prove herself.

A nap, a quick shower, her comfy robe, and some complementary tea and she felt like a whole new person. She moved the furniture away from one wall of the room—hefting a dresser and a table with no small amount of back pain, watching bugs skitter away—and tacked the Rhinelander tourism map on the wall.

Twenty minutes and a refresh to her tea later, she was typing away on the laptop and had secured the locations of at least three missing pets via address and location of disappearance. These she mapped out with a ribbon and a tack, and then stepped back. Didn't seem to be much, but… when she put two extra tacks up for the missing kids, some kind of strange pattern was emerging…

"Housekeeping!" she heard, alongside a knock.

She put her tea down and opened the door idly. A young man—white, with an adam's apple pointed enough to put someone's eye out—stood agape in the entrance.

Skye turned her attention from the board to the man, eyes suspicious.

"Didn't you just bring me my tea?" she asked.

He gulped a few times, trying to avoid looking at where her robe cupped her breasts.

"Yes, ma'am," he said. "I do a lot around here, as it happens."

"You're here to straighten up? I just checked in six hours ago."

"Just doing my final rounds before I clock out, ma'am," he said, but he couldn't look her in the eye.

She sighed.

"Are you familiar with this area?" she asked. "Rhinelander as a whole, I mean."

He nodded.

"Born and bred here, ma'am," he said. "I'm a local boy."

"Have you heard about the missing pets?" she asked. "And the kids."

He nodded, looking curious.

"You don't think the two are related, do ya?"

"I'm not sure," she said.

"Had a cousin lose a dog down Abner Street," he said. He looked at the map, then the tacks. "You mind?"

She shook her head, and he grabbed a tack and, finger tracing a line, shoved a tack at another place. He stood back, and the two of them analyzed the map together.

"So what do you think?" she asked. "It seems to me there's a pattern. This area here seems to be around where the pets keep disappearing."

She held her hand over a bit of the map between the loose circle.

"That's Boom Lake," the young man said. "More or less. Right near Hodag Park."

"That's a bit on the nose," she said.

"You a detective, ma'am?" the boy asked.

She shook her head.

"Just a grad student," she said. "Chasing after legends. You think they're open this time of night? The park, I mean?"

"Probably not," he said. "But I know a back way in. We could paddle in from Duke's. They got a dock there. See, you just rent a boat—or borrow one, as the case may be—and you do a little U-turn around the Wisconsin. It feeds right into Boom Lake, and there's a dock there on the inside of the park."

"What's this we business?" Skye asked.

The young man grinned.

"How else you gonna get in there?" he asked.

"Might be easier to just rent a pair of fence cutters," she said, but she knew she would be grateful for the company. Even if the young man was a little too keen for her liking. "You have access to the kitchen still?"

He nodded.

"We're going to need a lot of lemons," she said.

Her new companion's name was Brent, as it happened, and Doyle's was his Uncle's boat rental service. Brent was in his mid-early-twenties—a bit naïve, but good-natured. Best of all, he knew how to navigate the river. And he wasn't offensive to look at, even if that was his most redeeming quality.

"Some ground rules," Skye announced, on the drive. "This is an academic excursion. My job is to secure any data I can about the missing pets, and the kids. There is a possibility we'll run into danger on the way. If you have any reservations about putting your life on the line, then I'd advise you back out now."

"What kind of schoolwork you doing?" he asked.

"I'm tracking the Hodag," she said. "Or, by my estimate, a clutch of them."

He looked at her, eyebrows nearly touching his hairline.

"Ma'am, that's just an urban legend. You have to know that."

"What did you think the lemons were for?"

"To be frank, ma'am, I thought you were a landlubber worried about scurvy in case we got blown off course. When a pretty lady tells me she wants food I usually drop everything I'm doing to make sure she has it."

Skye paused.

"You're very sweet, Brent, and I think someday you'll make a woman very, very happy. But I need you to understand that between us, this evening, there will be no romance. Not an inkling. You can look all you want at me. You can think whatever you want. But just know that there is no way anything you are thinking will happen will happen. Do you understand? This is not a romantic story about breaking and entering or a midnight clandestine boat ride with a pretty Injun girl. This is a story about a very dangerous situation we are entering together. I need you to focus on safety and on potential threats and not get distracted by anything else you would rather be focusing on. Do you understand?"

He gulped and nodded.

"Yes, ma'am," he said.

"Great," she said. "Are there any other questions you have for me?"

"Why are we stopping outside of this neighborhood?"

Headlights illuminated the outline of a doghouse in the back of a house, behind a chainlink fence.

"To get some bait," Skye said.

Brent gulped.

His nametag said Sparky, and after the initial chomp on Brent's fingers, he seemed rather pleased at the new midnight adventure. He wagged his tail gently in the backseat, sniffing everything new.

"A question, ma'am," Brent said. "You aren't the one stealing the dogs, are you?"

She shook her head.

"No," she said. "I think that... whatever a hodag might be... if they're water dwelling creatures, they have access to the water. Most of the kidnappings have been at places alongside the Wisconsin. I just have a very strong feeling that if we have something that they might like, then we'll be more likely to find them."

"You're not actually gonna feed Sparky to them, are you?"

"No," she said. They were turning into Doyle's. The outline of the docks from here was a hulking spectre glimmering off the water's edge. "I'll need you to paddle."

"Any particular reason?" Brent asked.

"Yes," she said. She hopped out of the car, then pulled what looked like a small truncheon out of the side of her boot. She clicked a button on it—it unfolded, snapping metal and pyrite wire unfolding and zipping, until soon it was very clear she was holding a bow in her hands.

"Where can I get one of those?" Brent asked.

"You can't," she said, shortly. "But I'm good enough with it for two or three people. You'll steer, I'll shoot. If it comes to that."

"You're very serious about your work, aren't you, ma'am?"

"Extremely," she said.

After some initial misgivings about how much rightful access Brent actually had to Doyle's Boats, they were in and floating down the Wisconsin on a midnight ferry. The sound of the paddle breaking water and the occasional whine and scratch of their newest party member made an interesting counterpoint against the sound of frogs and owls hooting in the trees. It was cold-bone chillingly cold, and Skye knew that, were she to fall into the water it would be an incredibly unpleasant experience.

The rowing itself was painfully slow.

"This could have gone a bit faster had we got a boat with a motor," Brent gasped, between strokes.

"They would have heard us coming," she said.

"Ma'am, I don't mean any offense by this, but I'm not even sure the Hodag are real. It's just a town legend. Everyone knows Shephard was a huckster, a cheat, a vandal. Always looking to make a quick dollar."

Skye said nothing. Sparky was wagging the little stub of a tail he had, peering over the edge of the boat and watching dark shapes splashing in and around their wake.

"Guess it shouldn't matter, then," she said. "If there's nothing to be found, then we'll chalk this off as some light exercise."

They lazily rounded two or three bends—Skye could see the vast darkness of Boom Lake and the luminescent flashes of Hodag Park's night lights glaring from here. But Sparky was growling—stub nose in the air, he'd seemed to catch sight or smell of something neither of the two humans could perceive.

"Stay on your toes," Skye muttered, drawing her bow.

The water around them bubbled and boiled; like alligators submerging from the bayou, the ugly faces of four giant lizards broke the surface of the water. Sky's fingers were already drawing back an arrow laced with lemon juice and she was milliseconds from letting fly when one of them opened its horrible toothy maw and blinked.

"I wouldn't try that," it said. "The moment you sink an arrow into my forehead, the other three and any of us we have waiting below the surface will flip your boat. And you'll be little more than chum left for the fish in the bay."

"They talk," Brent said, eyes wide. "They exist!"

"Of course we exist," the seeming leader of them said. "We'll escort your craft to our lair. Our leader will have to decide what to do with you. No funny moves."

"You don't want to take our weapons?" Skye asked.

"Metal can't harm us," the Hodag Leader said.

"But we have—OOF," Brent said, doubled over.

Skye gave him a Look. Brent had seen this kind of look many times before in his life— often after he'd opened his mouth and dropped what he'd assumed was common knowledge in front of someone for whom it wasn't common knowledge.

"We'll treat with your leader," Skye said. "But you have to promise us safe passage out afterward."

The leader burbled an unpleasant laugh. It sounded like swamp gas escaping a muddy bog.

"I can promise you safety between here and there," she said. "Anymore than that and it would be outright dishonest."

"At least we know," Skye said.

Their caravan floated down to Boom Lake, past Hodag Park, and into a small cave on the far side of the lake. Skye'd had some time to filter through her thoughts on all this. Her hunch was correct, on some level—the Hodag existed, and their lair was central here amongst the numerous aqueducts and watery passages of Rhinelander. This was something, at least. That she had dragged Brent here, to his presumable death, was not something that overly weighed on her subconscious.

She was formulating plans. She'd already stashed her bow in her backpack, surreptitiously checking on the stash of citrus they'd brought with them. The carved-open lemon she'd used to stain her arrow heads was laying right on the top—she squeezed it and, with a bit of disgust on her face, found her hand dripping with juice.

There were glowing lichens on the roof of the cave, but there was little visibility for human eyes. The Hodag began to hum amongst themselves as they drew closer to the subterranean shore, a rather pleasant song, and before she knew it she could smell the sewer-water smell of lizard shit. It was an awful stench—one she was familiar with in passing. In her undergrad she'd had a biology class with one of the few Doctors her university could afford to pay, a Herpetologist by trade. His classes usually always revolved around his favorite subject—the evolution of lizards. His room always smelled like this—some prehistoric dung smell.

"I can't see in the dark like you can," Skye said. "Do I have your permission to pull out my flashlight?"

There was a bubble of noise between the Hodag, before their leader spoke up.

"You may," it said.

Skye reached into her backpack with her other hand, squeezing the lemon, and feigning a struggle.

"Brent, it's buried down here," she said. "Can you help me grab it?"

"I would rather stay over here and not move, ma'am," Brent gulped.

Skye made her voice as sharp as possible.

"Brent. I need your help. Now."

Sensing somehow that she meant business, Brent nodded and clumsily padded over the boat's edge to the backpack. Skye grabbed one of his hands with her free hand and jerked him down so his ear was at mouth-level.

"Squeeze this and shut up," she whispered. "I'm gonna try to shove one of these halves in each of our pockets."

He nodded, shoving one hand in and making an effort to look like he was pulling. Instead, he grasped a lemon half and pulled it into his fist, then shoved it in his pocket.

"Hurry it up!" the Hodag Leader snarled.

"It's just really buried deep," Skye said.

She dove both hands in and, after some time had passed, retrieved the flashlight. She clicked it on after wiping her hand off on her pants, and aimed it into the bowels of the cave. What seemed like hundreds of lamplight eyes stared back at her. Hanging from the ceiling, bobbing in the water, and clinging to the walls in various piles foul-looking Hodag of every conceivable shape and size watched them, with an almost uncanny hunger on their faces.

"You go ahead," she said, to Brent. "Pick Sparky up, would you? I just have to finish setting up here."

Brent, gasping like a fish, grabbed the bulldog in his arms and walked with scattered steps onto the shore before him. The Hodag bobbing in the water padded onto shore in his wake, drool hanging from the sides of each jutting tusk.

"Ah, shit," Skye said, from the boat. She'd landed in the water.

The whole damn thing was capsizing. Their bag, their equipment, everything was sinking beneath the surface of the lake. Brent felt his balls crawl up into his throat, dragging everything he'd ever eaten with him up to the surface, and let out a whimper.

"How are we going to get back?" he asked.

"We might not," Skye said simply.

"Jesus Christ," Brent said.

The backpack bobbed in the current for a few moments more before it sank beneath the waves.

"Walk!" their lead captor snarled, and they did. Sparky whined the whole way.

They travelled through tunnel after tunnel, winding their way into the interior of a large vault. Hodag stopped and sniffed them as they passed, and eventually, they found the leader. He was sitting atop a pile of dog bones—an ugly green thing, massive tusks pointed. His hooktail was lewdly hanging out and down his side. Skye noticed a ragged tear down the middle of it.

"Humans," he said. "I have not seen your kind in many moons. Tell me, has the man known as Eugene Shephard died? Have his children and children's children died?"

"Yes," Brent said.

"Then our timing was perfect," the Hodag said. "I am He-Who-Stalks, and it was I who first treated with the Shephard and the Mayor. Our arrangement was that we are not to take any human lives. And yet. Here you are, amongst my clan. Weapons in your bag, I am told. Were you not warned of the uselessness of metal upon our flesh?"

"We all thought you were an urban legend," Brent said.

"And yet you have brought a sacrifice," He-Who-Stalks grunted. "A white canine. Bring him forth to me."

Brent held the dog in his arms. Both he and Sparky shook like leaves.

"He's a companion, sir," Brent said.

"Nevertheless, I assume you care more for your lives than for the lives of this lesser being?"

Brent looked around the room. Lamplight eyes and dripping tusks greeted him from every corner. He clutched the dog tighter. Sparky howled.

"Give him to me," Skye said.

Her eyes were glinting. Brent let the dog go, and Skye reached towards him to grab the dog. Her bosom touched his arm. It was just enough to make him almost not hear her say "When you see me make my move, run to the entrance of the cave and keep punching, then jump in the water."

Skye held Sparky in her arms, then walked carefully over to He-Who-Stalks.

"A gift, for the King of the Hodag," she said. "Ah, but first. An old custom from my people. Will you shake hands with me? I would be honored to shake hands with the King."

"I possess not hands," He-Who-Stalks said.

"If this is going to be an even cultural exchange then we need to try to accept each other's cultures," Skye said.

He-Who-Stalks deliberated, and then lifted an ugly stubbed foot in greeting. Skye grasped it, and He-Who-Stalks burbled, wriggling, trying to escape from her grip.

It was like he was made of butter. Scale and skin and flesh melted away as he howled. The stench was ungodly. Skye finally let go and reared back, open-hand slapping him across the jaw. It melted off. He roared, tongue lolling about in the air like some worm.

The rest of the Hodag were stunned. Skye took her chance—scooping up the dog and pulling Brent with her, she took off through the crowd of Hodag.

There was a piercing shriek from behind them—out of some darker, secluded passageway a huge reptile as large as a house was lumbering, gaining speed, anger in its veins. The floor shook underfoot beneath them as it stomped onwards.

"Momma Hodag," Brent gasped.

The she-lizard screeched again. As if her shriek broke the Hodag from their spell, they launched themselves at her and Brent. Skye reached out and punched one that came close, hand moving like a hot knife through grease. Brent windmilled through the crowd until he reached her, both fists flailing and melting as he went, and soon they were back to back.

"On three, we bolt to the water," Skye said.

"But they'll just crocodile roll us," Brent said.

"I sank the boat after I sliced each lemon into pieces," she said. "The backpack's a huge lemonade teabag. As soon as they sink into the water they're gone."

"How did you know this would work?" Brent asked, panting, lashing out and smashing through a Hodag's skull.

"I didn't," she said. "Three!"

They barreled through Hodag soldier after Hodag soldier. One lashed out and snagged Sky's leg; she howled, loudly, and reached around and slapped him. Its face melted with a snarl and a bubbling of flesh, rolling away to stamp its snout out, and she hissed as she moved on.

The Momma Hodag was in the back of the line, slowly but surely trumpeting their deaths, squashing smaller Hodag underfoot as she angrily snapped.

Progress was slower than they expected. The Hodag seemed countless in number. Even though they went down easy, Skye could feel the slickness of their vital fluids on her hands and the lemon in her pocket kept getting drier and drier. Soon, however, she and Brent limped to the shore. With a sigh of relief she slipped into the water. The open wound on her ankle seared, but she bobbed down and grabbed the bag of supplies and dragged it in their wake.

Sparky, God love him. He was doggy paddling. Brent was barely treading water. But, just like she predicted, the cave water had turned into one gigantic river lemonade. Hodag hissed as they touched the water, rearing back and waiting on shore, their knuckles hissing down to the pads of their webbed toes. They stood on the shore and cowered until Momma Hodag, unable to see, plunged through the crowd. Hodag were kicked into the water, bobbing and melting, some of them only half-succumbing.

A swarm of half-dead, angry reptiles on their tails. And then she herself, the Great Mother, jumped in. The waves from the shore splashed up and over them, one great big tidal wave. Skye barely had time to put a hand over Sparky's mouth and take half a breath before the tsunami wave hit them. Inertia spun her, shaking her ass over end, until she wasn't sure which way was up and the breath in her lungs was acid in her chest.

Sparky kicked away from her, paddling in a direction, and she followed his animal instinct and barely crested the surface as her lungs nearly collapsed. She gasped when she hit air, her head throbbing, and found herself surrounded by leering half-skulls. In the distance, Brent was screaming and waving at the Momma Hodag, who was laboriously trying to turn.

"What are you doing?" Skye called out.

"Saving your ass," he said. "Get out of here! Go!"

One half-dead lizard opened its mouth, snapping at her, and she hauled the backpack up and out of the water, smacking it on the cave water's surface in a lazy, dead-armed splash. Still, it did the trick—the Hodag screeched and backed up, but didn't appear to be any more damaged.

"Get out of—heaaagh—" Brent screamed.

The Momma Hodag bent down and snapped, like a snake. Skye saw Brent's legs kick in the air, suspended from between her teeth, and then watched as she gulped him down whole. Sky's stomach plummeted to her guts, and she turned away. The nearest area of shore seemed close enough—there was a bit down by the pier where she was sure she could scrabble up and over a rock ledge.

She headed for it, praying to the Ancestors and Grandfather that she would make it.

Nothing followed her. It was a minor miracle. As soon as she flopped onto the gravel of the shore she struggled to her feet. Her shoes had been lost somewhere back in the river. The boat was gone. Brent was gone. Her supplies were gone. All she had left was a couple of lemons and the leather backpack. Which would shrink really soon.

She cried there, where nobody could see her on the shore, and Sparky tried to lick her face, which only made her cry harder. After a solid five minutes of self-pity she climbed to her feet, dusted herself off, put Sparky in the backpack on her back, and then scrambled up over the rocky ledge, gasping by the time she made it up. Bedraggled, smelling like Atlantic tributary river refuse and lizard shit and Lemon Pledge, she stumbled into the nearest place that looked like it had people.

It was a diner. People stared at her like she was homeless, some vagabond off the street. She asked to use the phone, and called a taxi. One person said something about the wet dog in her backpack, but at the look on her face they quickly shut up.

When she made it back to the hotel, she sat on her bed. Sparky bowled out of the backpack and curled up on the soft covers. Skye grabbed him, staring quietly at the ceiling for some time before her hands and her subconscious slapped over to the phone on the side of the bed. She heard herself make the call; hanging behind her head, she found herself quietly watching over her own actions.

"Vanessa," she said. "I found them. The Hodag."

"Let me guess. You tried to stop them on your own, instead of scouting the location and calling for backup?"

Silence on the line, and then Skye's voice: "Fuck off, Vanessa."

"You know, I hate to put the screws in at a time like this, but you insisting on this rescuing bit is just endangering everyone involved."

"I said fuck off," Skye replied.

"Where are you, Skye?"

"My motel room."

"Stay in bed and rest," Vanessa said, and her voice was suddenly very soft. "I'll be there soon."

Vanessa disconnected the phone; Skye put it back in its cradle and sat up, slinking towards the shower room. She ran the water at full blast and hissed when the bite on her shin puckered and twisted.

Her advisor arrived-every bit the travelled woman of the world, with a pink beret and a matching women's suit that terminated in a skirt above stockings and high heels. Even her hair was in blonde ringlets. Her fingers each held an expensive looking ring. There was a T-shirt cannon on her back.

Skye said nothing, just cast her a baleful look and let her inside.

"So these things are weak to citrus," Vanessa said, sniffing her nose, and picking through spare pieces of lingerie here and there.

"Lemons seemed to be incredibly effective," Skye said, voice ragged. "Well, direct contact with lemons. Lemon juice, rather. Diluted by river water it only inflicts damage, but direct contact with actual juice dissolves their skin."

"About how many would you say were down there?"

"Close to five hundred," Skye murmured. "And one gigantic one. Size of a killer whale."

There was an uncanny fire that seemed to light in Vanessa's eyes then.

"So. I have this crazy idea." Vanessa put the T-shirt cannon on her shoulder, sighting it like a bazooka. "Hear me out—we fill it with lemons—"

"Every time with the T-shirt cannon," Skye moaned.

"Hey, it's a good idea in theory," Vanessa said.

"No," Skye said. "We're gonna need a couple of beer kegs—"

Doyle was compensated handsomely by Vanessa, and after a quick shouting session about the previous boat and his nephew they managed to rent a large houseboat.

They floated back to the caves, the motorized engine causing choppy waves. Vanessa and Skye each held what looked like a fire hose attached to handlebars; each of them was on board an ATV with a beer keg strapped to the back. Each of them in turn wore a bright yellow suit of armor which looked, at a close glance, as if it was made of very many lemon peels very carefully knitted and knotted together.

"Squirt with your left foot," Vanessa said. "Go with your right. Gearshift under the handlebar."

"Got it," Skye said.

Their engines turned on. Headlights flooded the darkness of the cave. The ATVs took off, skittering stones where they dropped into narrow surf, and zoomed up and over into the depths.

"Keep your eyes peeled," Skye said.

"I'm not seeing anything," Vanessa said, and then the ceiling fell on her.

A rock-colored Hodag dropped from the ceiling and landed on her back, claws clutching at the edge of the ATV. Vanessa screeched as it snapped at her, and her ATV took off. Skye aimed towards them, desperately pumping the pedal, but Vanessa was gone way too fast, her ATV jerking through stalagmites and rocky outcroppings.

The ATV's brakes screeched as it fishtailed into a wall, bouncing up and off in a different direction. The Hodag slapped into the rock and lost its grip, collapsing bonelessly and dissolving from a quick squirt as Skye caught up to it. Skye revved up and slid down to a stop where Vanessa was idling nearby.

"You okay?" she asked.

She nodded, and rearranged her hair. Snooty bitch hadn't even lost her beret…

"I thought you said there were like five hundred of these things," she said. "This place is empty."

"Maybe you scared them all off with your driving," Skye said, but they could both tell she wasn't sure if that was the case.

"Where'd they all go?" Vanessa asked.

"I don't know," Skye replied. "Let's keep looking."

They drove on, quiet in the gloom, headlights dimmed. Flashlights were cast everywhere—but there were no signs of anything. Just a stale smell of lizard tank.

After some time had passed, with no sight of anything, and a great feeling of unease in her chest, Skye found they were back at what she had considered was the Throne Room. She cast her flashlight over the whole of the cave, panning from left to right. There was a feeling of hollowness to the room; a feeling of an echoing cavern. At the far edge, right before she had determined there was going to be nothing in the room, she saw someone crumpled.

There was an odd feeling in her chest, but as she took off towards the pile of limbs she felt something that had been boiling hot in her chest unstick. An uncertain hope was floating to the top of her throat, only to be sucked back down and bleed acid when she saw his face.

He was shriveled. Oh, it was Brent, but his skin seemed somehow shrunken on his face, waxy and pale. She hopped off the ATV and bent down to him, lamplights casting over his form and making her cast shadows on the opposite wall.

"Brent," she said, shaking him.

She put two fingers to his jugular, and he stirred and coughed a wheeze that barely left his throat. His eyes blinked, rolled around lazily in his head.

"Holy fuck," he said.

"What happened?" Skye asked. "Are you alright?"

"Big Momma swallowed me alive," he said. "Man, that was fucked. I remember pissing myself, and then suddenly there was the cave around me again. I froze, and just acted dead. I guess. The lemon juice I had on me dissolved her from the inside. Anyway. They started speaking around each other again. Debating on whether or not they should try and eat me. One of them said it wasn't safe. Some of the other ones agreed. They squabbled back and forth about it, but eventually decided that we weren't worth the trouble to be eaten. Most of them left. Except for the deformed ones."

"Deformed ones?"

"They got half-melted. Their bodies wouldn't grow back. Including the King guy. They're back in there. I don't know how to say this, but they're doing something that's just. Since they can't mold themselves back, they're molding *together*..."

Skye blinked and turned back to Vanessa.

"You want to take him back to the ship?" she asked.

"We're going to have to talk about enrolling random citizens in your stupid acts," Vanessa said.

"Who's the pretty lady?" Brent asked.

"Vanessa Hargrave," Vanessa said, long nails extended. They shook. Vanessa tried not to let anyone see her shaking her hands free of slime afterward.

"We really have to get you back to the ship," Skye said.

"I'll be good for a little longer," he said, coughing. He slowly lifted himself to his feet, swaying. "Maybe I can help out a bit."

"You're too sick," Skye said. "You need to rest."

"Bullshit," he said, and coughed again. He held his ribs. "We're too far in this to back out now."

"Oh, let him tag along again. If he dies, it's less of a nuisance for us," Vanessa said. "Less paperwork, less annual checkups."

Skye shook her head.

"Hop on," she said.

"I'm guessing you guys brought back some firepower? Anything I can use?"

"Left the squirtguns back at the base," Vanessa snarked.

"We'll work something out," Skye said.

"How many are there, would you say?" Vanessa asked.

"Well, there *were* about a hundred of 'em," Brent said. "But now there's just one."

Vanessa and Skye's headlights panned over the atrium. Something didn't look right— didn't feel right here. There was an intricate webbing splayed here and there, bone and needlework and strung out veins. Here an eye sat perched on a piece of outcropping, there a bundle of nerves was.

Something massive breathed; the chamber itself, perhaps. Every tendon, nerve, bone quivered in the chamber. A hollow voice rang out to them.

"YOU… AGAIN…" the Hodag-thing called.

A gnarled, fleshy flower parted in the middle of the room, like an open jaw. A tongue lolled out, rolling, slopping wetly and fluidly against the ground in front of them. The King Hodag, He-Who-Stalks, was at the edge of the tongue—was *the* edge of the tongue, and his hateful eyes stared into Skye's own, body supported in the air by the gelatinized remnants of lesser Hodags' bodies.

"Howdy," Skye said.

"Good evening," Vanessa said. "I hear you're—"

The King Hodag appendage extended like a viper, snapping her up in a blink. It was so quick all that was left was her stupid pink beret on the seat of the ATV. Skye saw her headlights reflecting off of a bejeweled ringset on a hand as it slid into the thing's open maw. Then, with a rattle and a hiss, it struck again. This time, Skye was ready for it—she'd slammed the ATV into reverse, and Brent rolled into the dust. The Hodag King was after her, and snapping—she reversed out of the Atrium, back into the throne room, and hoped beyond hope that Brent had done the sensible thing and grabbed the other ATV.

There was a squeal, then, of tires thrumming and Brent too jumped out of the mouth of the Atrium and back into the throne-room, shredding dirt on the ATV. The King Hodag tongue snapped through the entrance, but could not fit—frustrated and angry, it roared, shaking the cavern. And then another pseudopod extruded through the entrance—a tentacle, looking like it was made of lesser Hodags.

"You juice 'em, I'll shoot 'em," Skye yelled, because she'd made sure they stopped for extra supplies on the way.

The fleshy tube squirted and spasmed: a group of Hodag oozed out in placental fluid, snarling and howling. Brent turned on the hose on one—it started to weaken, and an arrow with dynamite on the tip zipped into it. The explosion splattered it, rocking the foundations of the room. On and on they went—one after the other—more and more Hodag being birthed into the room, an almost endless stream, until there was the horrible smell of citrus and a pile of ichor nearly knee-deep that had built up.

"Running out of juice!" Brent said.

"Switch me!" Skye said.

Brent reversed, but a flying Hodag snatched him and barrel-rolled him, grabbing him by the throat and bashing him into the rocks as his ATV idled once it hit wall. Skye zipped an arrow out, and it struck true, but it was too late—there was no time to check on him. An avalance of more pieces, half-castrated Hodag with one leg and two unentangled themselves from the mess and quickly surrounded her.

She had her ankle-knife with her still—she withdrew it and stabbed that into her tank, and felt the pressure blast lemon juice all over her and her knife. A puddle soaked the whole ATV, dripping into a messy circle around it.

She hopped off the ATV, and gestured at them.

They flew at her—staggering now, just like her. One stab, a leap—a jumping slice overhead. Skye diced and stabbed and carved, calling on her survival against wild animals training the Academy had instilled in her. Hodag fell to pieces around her, until at last she was standing in a circle of guts and barely palpitating limbs, panting, almost falling to her knees.

An explosion—a wail, then, from the next room. The tendril melted—and on a wash of bile and body juice, on a wooden box top, Vanessa, T-shirt cannon extended over her shoulder, held the wriggling form of the King Hodag in her grime-spattered grip. She threw him to the ground between her and Skye.

"Please," he babbled. "Please. Leave me in peace. Your kind has done nothing to me but tear me, slice me, rip me. I'll return to where I came from."

"Skye, I believe I'll give you jurisdiction over this," Vanessa said.

Skye wiped her knife in lemon juice, and stabbed him in the eye, sinking it deep in until she hit his skull, and then further, into the meat of his brain. And then, as if he were mere liquid, he melted away.

"What a mess," Vanessa said.

"I would ask where you were hiding that, but I'm pretty sure I know."

Vanessa turned a sarcastic nod to her.

"Oh ha-ha. Our weapons contractor is in town, and I wanted a portable model. I'll have to introduce the two of you."

Skye said nothing—she'd gone over to where Brent had fallen. There was a smaller alcove behind him and the dead Hodag. Skye picked his body up and out of the way, gently putting him on the back of an ATV. Where he'd rolled there was an open area—something carved with clawprints, as if it was dug out. She bent down and fished around. Littered dog skulls were here—a pile of them, hidden away, as if in a trash bin.

Two pairs of children's shoes, too—and the bones attached to them.

The flannel-jacketed woman came into Pat's Tavern for the third time the same week.

"Kegs are out back," she said, motioning.

"Shame about them kids, but at least we found 'em," Bradley the bartender was saying. "What you think happened?"

"The Hodag." Phyllis, regular bar fly, knocked back a drink, smiling at the flannel-jacketed woman as she came up to the counter.

"That Hodag shit ain't real, Phyllis, I keep telling you."

"I need a shot," the flannel-jacketed woman said. "Tequila, vodka, I don't care. Just nothing that tastes citrusy."

Bradley nodded, dutifully turning and looking at his drinks.

"What about you, darling? What you think? Hodag—real or sham?"

The shot was extended over the table. Skye grabbed it and slammed it back, wincing and breathing.

"All myths have a basis in reality," she said, robotically.

Phyllis looked at her, and her face, then took her drink and ran off.

Skye went to sit down at a corner booth, where a huddled man, face like a gaunt skeleton, was clearly waiting for her.

"He looks like a boogeyman," Vanessa had told her. "Mind like a supervillain, though."

"Hey," the boogeyman said to her. He grinned. It was unsettling. "You Skye?"

"You Grimm?" she asked.

"That I am," he said. His breath smelled like pickled onions.

"Vanessa said we should meet. Talk shop."

Grimm nodded.

"I know you Academy girls like to do things with a bit of gravitas, but me and my Boss were looking for someone else to fill out the ranks. Vanessa says you do great field work, even if you have a tendency to cause huge messes."

"I try to avoid it."

"We encourage messes. Find them a bit healthy. Honestly—you don't seem cut out for academic life. It's not an insult—I just think you look like the kind of person that really wants to get things done." He tapped his nose. "You know what I mean?"

"I think I do," she said.

"You ever looking to get out there and quit the teaching, just give me a call. Or if you just need to blow something monstrous up."

He slid a business card over the table with two fingers, then fished the cherry out of his drink.

'S.C.A.R.E.D.' was in cursive on the front, and a number on the back. Skye picked it up and stared at it, flipping it over in her fingers, and when she looked up, he knocked back the rest of his drink, then got to his feet to leave.

She stared back down at the card again, thinking, thinking…

"Hey," she said, when he'd almost hit the door…

PART 2: LORE

CHAPTER 10:

BAILEY'S LAMENT

She coughed; stuttered; caught her voice and spoke directly into the microphone before her: a Yeti her older sister had bought for nearly a hundred dollars or more. Her blue eyes stared straight into the camera. She couldn't have been more than eighteen or nineteen at most—the room behind her replaced with a B-movie caricature of monsters, with her personalized logo, *Basement Bailey*, in the northeast quadrant.

"Hey all you Basement Dwellers," she said, smiling, tucking a black piece of fly-away hair back past her ear. She paused; here she would insert her usual intro logo. "My name is Bailey Nichole Flanagan. Or, as some of you might know me, Basement Bailey. I wanted to talk here today about something very personal to me. As some of you know, I'm kind of a shut-in, to be mild. My profile picture on Facebook is a freakin' turtle. That should tell you everything you need to know about me.

"I've had some of you ask some questions out of me. 'Bailey, where do you go to school?' 'Bailey, how do you have time to make all these videos?' 'Bailey, where is the best place to go for ribs in Oakland?'" She laughs at the last one, eyes twinkling like the stars behind her. "The truth is, I've been kind of enigmatic about answering questions that are too personal. And I know there's been a lot of radio silence since my six month hiatus started. The looming specter of questions you have regarding me and my life has finally become too overwhelming to ignore.

"I'm really torn, though. Am I obligated to talk about this? Where does my energy go when I step outside of my comfort zone? Am I wasting more precious spoons on you guys than I have to give? And ultimately, I realized that even if it's hard, I have to get it out.

"I've been gone because of therapy. I'll come back to my break in a bit, but. I want to talk to you about something personal first.

"I was diagnosed with agoraphobia from my therapist at 13. I dealt with it by making it part of my personality. And isn't that funny? The struggles we all face in life, sometimes we use them to identify with others. We use our personal demons to classify us. To guide us. To show us the way. We have these screaming little fiends inside us that tell us who we are and demand so much of our attention. It's like this personal anguish leads us on a quest or something. And we can become so preoccupied with how to make it shut up, how to deal with it, how to trap it away, that we don't think about how to kill it.

"Therapy's an intense process, and I avoided it for years. You have to accept that you have a problem first. You can't exactly kill a monster if you refuse to accept it exists, can you? You have to plant your feet and understand what the problem is and accept that you have it, and that you're flawed. For me, I had to accept the limitations I'd let my anxiety and agoraphobia place on my life. I didn't have a chance at a normal social life. I became a Basement Dweller, just like all of you. I took my fear and my anxiety and I let them wall me in to this little tiny apartment in my sister's basement. I let it tell me who I was and what I could be. But I'd be lying if I said I wasn't grateful for it, in some respects.

"I wouldn't be where I am without my agoraphobia. I wouldn't have over a hundred thousand Basement Dwellers just like me tuning in and peaking their ears for the latest creepypastas that the darkest depths of the web offer. I wouldn't have the social media following I have. I wouldn't have so many of you who understand who I am and where I come from. I think of every one of you as my personal friends and confidantes.

"But I realized that my agoraphobia was killing me. Leaving the house to go to school was torture after a few years, and about middle school I snapped and couldn't take it anymore. I've been homeschooled. I don't get much one-on-one interaction. I lost friends—lost the ability to have friends. I missed out on so many milestones, so many important pieces of life. I haven't even had a date, held hands, or kissed. And as ashamed as I am to say this…"

She paused, breathed in deep.

"I couldn't even attend my own mother's funeral."

Another beat, and she continued

"I'm thankful for my sister and my grandmother—I have such amazing people that care for me, that are willing to go out of their way to meet my needs, but a small question kept popping up in my head: what happens when they die? Would I survive? Would I never have the chances they had at life—never be able to go to college, never be able to move out and meet my wonderful other half, never be able to live as richly and deeply as they did?

"So I started to plant my feet and understand the good and bad sides of my disease. And as much fun as this journey has been, I think I needed the break to focus on who I am. Or who I could be. Who I want to be. My parents were able to afford a travelling therapist, and working with him has been amazing. I've been able to walk down the sidewalks… explore the neighborhood I live in. Just that little bit of freedom did so much for my self-confidence and my creativity.

"I'm still a work in progress. I'm still one of you—a Basement Dweller, one who skulks the skeezy depths of the deep web to find the most horrifying stories people are willing to share. But I think that expanding my search out of the basement could yield even greater horrors and thrills than I've ever found before. And for once in my life… I'm not afraid of that.

"So I've decided to journey out of my basement. Away from the web. Out into the wilderness. I want to see what's there—the good, the bad, the ugly, the infirm.

"The world we live in is painful. It's scary enough on its own, if you know where to look. And looking away from that pain—that's almost a crime. How can we let something go by us like life—so big, so terrible, so awful in its endless ingenuity and sheer human torment. How horrible that we let it go without documenting it, without acknowledging those every day terrors.

"So I want to encourage you—all of you Basement Dwellers, all you misshapen and mistreated, you anxious and terrified walled-in people. I am with you. Come on out to play. The world sure might be awful, but it's better to talk about how terrible it is with others.

"I've got some great friends to help me on my way. We're planning a trip to the Black Hills, out in South Dakota. Prepping early for our Halloween episode, and periodically uploading our progress as we go. I'll be leaving regular updates every week going forward, so don't forget to subscribe if you're interested in taking this journey with me. I'm looking forward to an even more terrifying part of my journey going forward."

And in the darkness of her basement, in the gloom of a dapple of sunlight that pierced, creeping, through a boarded-up window, she hit STOP on the audio recorder and the camera, sitting back, and wiping a little bit of dampness off of her right eye with the back of a hand.

"It's scary, but it's worth it," she breathed, to herself, but she didn't sound convinced.

CHAPTER 11:

THE BLACK HILLS

BEFORE

Bailey had bumped into him quite by accident, over the melons at the grocery store on an experimental journey into the great urban wilderness she called Oakland. He walked up to, stopped, and parroted something to some people he didn't know, and they all laughed, and Bailey couldn't take her eyes off him.

He had a voice like a Disney prince; blonde hair, blue eyes, and a fresh grin across his face. She'd never been to this store before, and yet there was *something* about him that made him stand out like a sore thumb.

She followed him all the way to the oatmeal aisle before she realized she was stalking him, and then recognition hit her like a ton of bricks.

"It's you," she finally said, shocking herself.

"It is me," he said, broad grin on his face. "Lester Falls."

They shook hands, and Bailey did everything she could not to squeal. Lester was a famed voice impressionist and theatrical actor that had his own vlog. He'd got his start on the Vine platform and moved onward from there when they ended it. He was witty, irreverent, and everything a girl could ever want. But she was pretty sure that he liked guys.

Pretty sure. Still, there was something about a face like his that made all your inhibitions fly out the window. Somehow or another, in his presence, you really felt like your dreams could come true.

"You look familiar too," he said, Disney Prince voice gleaming in the air. "Have you been to one of my shows?"

Bailey shook her head. "To be honest I haven't been out of my house in like a year. That's not even an exaggeration."

His eyes grew wide.

"It *is* you!" he crowed, and his pixie eyebrows rose.

Everyone in the store looked over at the two of them, a wash of faces staring, and Bailey felt the urge to slither back to her house like a Djinn that had been banished back to the underworld.

"You're Basement Bailey," he said, laughing. His blue eyes twinkled. "Holy crap, this is an honor and a half. I always wondered where you lived. I mean, Oakland? It's so big. You would have thought we'd bump into each before at some point."

"I wasn't kidding about the house thing," she said. "I'm actually fighting the urge to run away right now."

His face grew serious, and he placed a warm, perfectly manicured hand on her shoulder. She felt her body call out to his touch despite her best preservation instincts.

"Sounds like you need some help," he said. "Imagine it—we could team up together. Costar in each other's videos. Imagine the headlines—" and here he raised another hand, outlining an invisible header in the sky. "Lester Falls helps Basement Bailey out of the closet. It practically writes itself."

Her face crunched up in uncertainness.

"That seems like an awful lot of work," she said. "Look, I'm grateful for the offer and everything, but this is more progress than I ever thought I'd make before. And I've been on hiatus for six months anyway. Haven't had the motivation to come back to anything."

He nodded his head, face filled with understanding.

"I've been there. Trust me. I have a whole web series about it. You should really consider it though—me and a couple of other vloggers are going to film a couple of co-op Halloween specials out in the sticks. South Dakota—way out in the forest in the middle of nowhere. We'll do some camping, some hiking, and try to find some monsters."

"Who else?" she asked.

"Black Jack Vance and Missy Specter," he said. "You know, the horror King and Queen of Youtube. Basement Bailey crawling out of her hole to go on a ghost hunt with two of the Creep Kings and yours truly—that's almost too perfect of a setup. I can't imagine anything better."

Bailey nodded, struck with thought.

"I wonder what the odds were," she said.

"Pardon?" Lester asked.

"The odds of the one day I go outside and bump into you," she said.

"Happy coincidence, could be?" he asked.

"Just weird," she said. She paused. "Look, I don't believe in coincidences. I think everything happens to us for a reason. We get signs that tell us what to do. And this is too unlikely to be happenstance."

"Well," Lester began. "Look at it this way. The great outdoors is basically quiet and undisturbed. There's hardly any people there. It's like finding a basement abandoned in the middle of nowhere. You should be comfortable there, even if it's outdoors. Because correct me if I'm wrong. But you're more scared of people than you are the actual outdoors."

Bailey nodded.

"Yeah," she said. "It's scarier to face human beings than it is to face monsters."

"Sometimes," he said, nodding. "But I'll tell you this, Bailey. People like us, we need to stick together. Make a natural network. Collaborate and create. You get the picture, right?"

She nodded.

"It's about ingenuity, and sometimes ingenuity takes teamwork," Lester said. "How else can we stay fresh and relevant? Actors have to reinvent themself for every performance."

"You think I should start my vlog back up?" she asked.

"I think you'd be silly not to," Lester said. "May as well capitalize off all this while you're at it. Look. Make this next vlog series about your journey outwards. Away from your old comfort zones. It can inspire people. Make them get up off their butts and do something."

"Yeah," Bailey said. An old flicker of unease unfurled itself from her chest. "I just. I'm not sure how to arrange any of this. Not even sure if my grandmother or my sister will let me go."

Lester put his hand on her shoulder again, and spoke in his perfectly manicured voice.

"Listen, Bailey. You don't have to plan any of this out, alright? Me and Jack and Missy have been planning this together for months. Just pack yourself some supplies—basic camping kit. Bring some canned food, maybe a tent and a sleeping bag and a couple changes of clothes. And souvenir money. We're only gonna be gone for a weekend—three or four days, max. I will literally not take no for an answer."

Bailey's uncertainty broke into a hesitant smile. "Okay."

He looked relieved, then big-eyed as he patted his pockets. He pulled out a card, extending it with two fingers.

"Almost forgot! Take this. If you have ANY questions please give me a call."

She nodded.

He bent at the waist, in a theatrical bow. "Now if you'll excuse me. There is a very cute bag boy with an ass that won't stop screaming my name, and I want to make him call me Daddy. Ciao!"

And off he went, two fingers to his temple, disappearing into the crowded store.

Bailey stared down at the card in her hand, turning it over and over in her hands.

NOW:

That was what brought her here: lugging a huge suitcase filled with supplies behind her off the Greyhound, away from the entrance to Wall Drug, grunting as she pulled it up the steps to the adjacent parking lot. She found them all staring at their cellphones, leaning outside an old station wagon. It was a dull, rusted-looking red, with orange upholstery from the seventies by her best guess. All three of the others were dressed up per their internet personas. Black Jack Vance had dyed-blue hair, in messy dreads down to his shoulders. He was smoking a cigarette, and all of his piercings glittered in the sodium arc lamps. He looked dark and mysterious, with ebony skin and amber eyes. He was British, but touring the states. His channel—Black Jack's Found Footage—was extremely popular, as was an Alternate Reality Game series he'd uploaded to Youtube under a pseudonym. Brass Wasps was one of the scariest Youtube series Bailey had ever watched—helping solidify the mythology of the Lengthy Man that had sprung up, a monster all on its own that seemed to crawl its way from the internet and into real life. He had helped write and star in it.

Missy Specter was a little different. She, too, was buried in her phone. She had cherry red hair in a pixie cut, and her foundation was so pale it seemed to make her glow with a white light. Bailey was not given to comparing herself with other girls, but she couldn't help but be intimidated in some respects—Missy had a weird energy to her, some raw, boisterous sort of Southern charm that Bailey couldn't possibly hope to match. She drew killer, chilling art; some of the most terrifying pictures that could be found on the web were traced back to her. She did art tutorials on her channel, and helped design some of the character art for the SCP Foundation games—another creepy internet thing, the SCP Foundation stood for Secure, Contain, Protect. It was an open source alternate reality game mixed with a monster archive, sort of a collective creepypasta archive done in military speak. It was an impressive resume she had, and an even more impressive project to be attached to.

Then of course was her savior—Prince Charming himself, Lester Falls, also buried in his cell. He seemed to be scrolling mindlessly through his phone, gaze stuck to his screen as she drew closer. She had to get within two feet of him before he blinked and pulled himself away from its hypnotic embrace.

"Oh, hey!" he said, face breaking into a beaming smile. "Nice to see you, Bailey. How was the bus ride here?"

"Not short enough to want to climb back into another one," she said. "What's everybody up to?"

"Networking," Black Jack said, without looking up.

"I'm going over some of my recent edits," Missy said.

Lester looked a bit bashful, and breathed in.

"Honestly, just scrolling through Grindr," he said. "The Black Hills area is as about as dry as I am, and that's saying something. The nearest dude is 17 miles away and he looks like my uncle. And not one of my attractive ones, either."

Bailey laughed.

"You're a pervert," Black Jack said.

"As are all men," Lester countered, smile beatific. "Shall we pack and ride, people? The wonderful vistas and forests of South Dakota, in all their associated isolation, awaits."

"I guess," Missy drawled, and put her phone down.

"Whatever you say," Black Jack said.

"Introductions?" Bailey asked.

Lester's face broke into panic.

"Oh, yeah," he said. "Okay. Jack, Missy. This is Basement Bailey."

"Oh, the Creepypasta Creeper," Missy said. She smiled. "I dig it. Nice to meet you, lady."

She beamed, and clapped Bailey into a hug that smelled of honeysuckle.

"The elusive Bailey," Jack said, his accent rounded at the end. "Very nice to meet you. I've heard lots of good things."

He shook her hand.

"Road trip!" Lester crowed, and his voice echoed dully into the gloom.

They travelled west for about 80 miles on I90, travelling through Wasta and Wicksville and New Underwood, stopping for a quick lunch and a cigarette break in Rapid City when Jack complained about being cramped.

"I could use a break from driving anyway," Lester said.

They stopped at the Kathmandu Bistro; Bailey had never had Indian cuisine before, so it was a real experience and a half. She loved the thick, hearty lamb curry and chicken lollipop. Most of the seats were empty, and most of the customers that were there were absorbed in their food, so she hardly felt threatened.

Again, all of her friends were on their phones. Bailey wasn't sure what she was expecting, but a little more rapture with the scenery may have made her feel more at home. Still, they were friendly enough when she was able to get their attention. And the fact that they seemed to have few expectations for conversation made her feel weirdly comforted.

"So," she said. "Where are we heading first?"

"Mt. Rushmore," Lester said. "We get to see a couple of huge heads. I want to do one of those poses where it looks like I'm picking Washington's nose."

"Crazy Horse monument afterwards, because we have to make it fair," Missy said.

"Then we're heading north," Jack said. "We've got an interview scheduled with some of the staff at the Bullock Hotel in Deadwood. Supposed to be haunted. We've also booked ourselves some rooms there for the weekend. We can use it as a home-base, sorta thing. Somewhere to go between trips."

"Though we do have plans on camping for a night or two," Lester said. "Good to have backup plans in case it rains or something."

"Ugh, camping," Missy said. "If humans were made for the forest we would never have left the trees."

"I haven't been camping since I was a little girl," Bailey said. She felt the old darkness billowing up in her chest, and tried to stamp it back down again. "We should ask around and see about any weird stories anyone has about the area. We could investigate a real-life urban legend. That would be cool."

"Well, we can work out the details on the way," Lester said. "Oh, this chicken tikka is hitting me right where it counts."

"Right in the arse," Jack said.

Lester nodded.

"I can't help my perfect genetics and my perfectly round ass," he said. "I am how Mother Nature made me."

Bailey laughed, and when they were done, they all piled back into the station wagon and took off to the Southwest.

They entered the Black Hills, she could tell, when the forest grew up and around them, sprouting suddenly from the ground and swallowing the road alive. Ponderosa pines and other ancient trees towered in waves as the pavement gave way to more winding roads that went up and down hills and valleys.

There was an energy here, of course. She could feel it in her bones, down in the core of her. Some fundamental inner nature of the land itself. Everything seemed old, historied, textured. Some sort of permanence hung over the land itself, and as they drove on and on into the Black Hills she found herself fighting a slowly-growing, nagging sense of unease.

They hit Keystone; Missy had to pee, so they stopped in-town, and Bailey marveled at a goat she noticed bounding up a hill. White fuzzy things with black horns, they hopped around like demented rabbits in some respects.

The three of them not in the old convenience store stood in a circle near the van, facing the forest.

"Mountain goats," Lester said, in explanation.

"Does anyone else feel funny?" Bailey asked.

"The atmosphere's a bit thick," Jack said. "Humidity, prob'ly."

"I don't know," she said. "It's like the wind is alive or something."

"Living wind?" Lester asked. "You're sure it's not just your agoraphobia kicking in again?"

Bailey shrugged.

"Could be," she said, voice quiet. "I'm just... so, it's not always like this. But sometimes I stay indoors because the house 'feels' safe. And the outside feels... I don't know. Sometimes menacing. Sometimes stressful. Depends on the place. There aren't a lot of places that feel like home. Solid and stable and warm and comforting. Sometimes an area feels mad, or sad, or upset."

"Tha's half the fun of travelin', innit?" Jack asked. "Stepping outside of that stable rut. I feel like the energy of a place gets so stagnant sometimes. Seein' the same thing, day in, day out. Like to drive a man mad. Like there ain't nothin' fresh to squeeze outta the wind."

Lester looked back and forth at the two of them.

"I don't get it," he said, shrugging.

"Iss an emotional, sensation thing in the gut," Jack said. "Can't explain it, but people have tried. Is the spirit of the place, sort of thing. You're not crazy."

"My doctor seems to think otherwise," Bailey said.

"Yeah, well, he can go stuff it," Jack said. "Right up his bum."

And that seemed to be that. Missy came back and they piled in again, and in her chest Bailey felt the old hills speak softly and quietly to her, like an old wizened family member with plenty of vitality left. Almost like a grandfather. And she closed her eyes and tried to feel it; and before she knew what was happening she fell asleep.

She woke up when the van stopped. They were at the Memorial. The huge faces of the presidents stared down at them, eyes wide and unblinking. She imagined them opening their mouths to give her wisdom. Sandstone and desert in some areas; patchy grass in others. She climbed out of the van and saw something white leap up and away into the distance from a far hill.

"Mountain goat," Lester said again. "Man, look at the honker on that guy."

She got out and stretched, eyes bleary still from sleep. There seemed to be a figure paused at the base of the monument. Someone dark—but she blinked, tried to focus her eyes, and it was gone.

Lester got his snap of the nose-picking, and when they had sufficiently stared at the giant heads ("Not a lot to take in, issit?" Jack asked. "Just a coupla heads in a row") they departed again, road-bound.

"Crazy Horse Memorial next," Missy said.

"Of course," Jack said, voice riddled with sarcasm. "Can't wait to go out of our way to see another great bloody head on another mountain."

"Hey, it's a history thing. Not fair that we go and see these white guys and not stop and visit the Chief," she replied.

Jack opened his mouth to reply, then shrugged.

"When you put it that way," he said.

They went west, on the rickety 244, arcing southwards after a few miles and stopped at the Laughing Water restaurant. (Lester flashed a pass at the people manning the entry booth—Bailey wasn't sure what it was, exactly, but he seemed relieved that it worked.)

"Where is this face again?" Jack asked.

They parked and got out, and Missy scanned the horizon northwards.

"Over there," she said.

It was a half-submerged face inside a plateau. Giant cranes decked an abutment nearby. There was something almost sinister to it—as if it were waiting, slowly, to come out of the rock. Bailey knew that her feelings were sometimes accurate, and sometimes, she'd just been reading too many ghost stories. Even still. It was imposing.

"Oh wow, another face," Jack said, smarting off.

"For now," Missy said. "It's a big huge deal—all those rocks underneath are going to get blasted away, and when it's finished, the arm is supposed to be twenty feet long. It'll be nice to see it completed some day."

"We could pay for a tour up to the top," Lester said. "But it gets a little pricey."

"I don't think I budgeted that in," Bailey muttered.

She did not want to go closer. For some reason the mountain itself seemed… different. She was not sure what the feeling was, but there was something on the edge if she concentrated. A sort of unease. As if the rock itself wasn't happy—perhaps it was dreading another round of explosions, she thought, but wasn't that silly to impart some emotion to the land?

106

They went in and ate another quick bite—mostly sodas, but Jack had to try an Indian taco. It was almost unanimously decided to skip the trip to the museum.

"Didn't come here for history," Jack said. "Non-creepy history, that is. Though I'll give you this place is ripe for some writing, I'll tell you."

"Next stop—Bullock Hotel, the most haunted hotel in America. Or some other such nonsense," Lester said. "I'm just excited to get a look at the town of Deadwood. I loved that show."

"You have no taste with that pseudo-Shakespearean nonsense," Jack said.

Missy curled up her face.

"You only watch reality TV," she said.

"Yes, well, just because I'm a hypocrite don't mean I don't have a valid point," he said, and they all laughed.

The other three piled into the van, but Bailey stayed staring out at the distance, taking in the view.

"Onwards and upwards, Bailey," Lester called, from the driver's window.

Bailey, however, was entranced with the mountain. She looked down at a brochure she had picked up from the restaurant about the place.

"My lands are where my dead lie buried," she intoned.

The face of Crazy Horse stared off into the distance, taking in the whole of the Black Hills. Someone called her—she was not sure who—so she turned and made her way back to the van, and they left.

They headed North. Past Black Elk Peak, a towering mountain, through Hill City, through Silver City, north through Merritt, past Roubaix, and finally to Deadwood proper. Only took an hour or so—but Bailey could see they were arriving as the trees began to edge away, and a small city with a strip seemed to be carved from the woods themselves. The Bullock itself stood, almost too squat, less historic and grand than she seemed to be expecting. Of course, she thought, the picture we paint in our heads is always a little worse, a little better.

It was a squat three story castle, of sorts. Maybe castle wasn't the right word. It was made of architecture that grew like great stones out of the ground, with vast glass front windows, railings on the second and third floor. It seemed almost Victorian in design.

The other three had their camera phones out, clicking away. Missy did a selfie with the sign.

"Check-in, then," Lester said.

"Tour guide Barbie," Missy quipped, but he winked and smiled, undisturbed.

"Right this way," he said, voice suddenly feminine and demure. "Check-in is inside. Meanwhile, please keep all luggage inside the vehicle and lock the doors behind you. We don't want any stray mountain goats to steal our precious cargo."

"Precious cargo?" Jack asked.

"I don't know about you guys but I have like fifteen *very precious* butt plugs I intend on using before this trip is over with," Lester said. "Just so we're clear."

The Disney Prince with a secretly filthy mouth. Bailey loved it.

Check-in went quick enough. The four of them strained and struggled to get their things into the rickety elevator, and up to where they were staying on the second floor. The floors had a lavishly patterned aubergine carpet that creaked in places, and Missy and Bailey decided they would share a room.

"I just want to lay down and sleep forever," Missy moaned, dropping her stuff at the door.

Bailey nodded. Their room was nice—not too atmospheric, to be honest, but the walls were cream-colored, the floor had a nice brown patternwork stitch to it, and the bedspreads kinda reminded her of looking at a playing card.

"You think Jack's gonna be okay with Lester?" Missy asked.

"I think Lester is a dignified individual," Bailey said. "But the minute he brings a man back to the room is when things'll get tricky."

"Maybe Jack'll want to join in," Missy said thoughtfully. "Lester could take him to a whole new world…"

Bailey giggled at the image.

"Okay, enough polite backstabbing," Missy said. "Let's go to the bar already. Mama wants a drink."

The girls left together, and met the boys downstairs. The bar was located right inside the casino—great clouds of smoke hung low, and elderly people with more retirement pension than time left on their own clocks sat, almost lifeless, as they plunked penny after penny into the machines. The feeling was claustrophobic, and Bailey did her breathing exercises to help herself calm down. It helped, but not much—the air was too thick with vape smoke and nicotine, and the acetone smell of alcoholic drinks all around her.

"Where are we gonna go, then?" Jack asked Lester, when the girls arrived.

"What's up?" Missy asked.

"Management's not in until Monday," Lester called out over the noise around them.

Flashing lights and dials and vidscreens blared all around them. Bailey was trying hard not to hyperventilate. *Where would you go if you ran, you stupid idiot?* She asked herself. *Back up to your room? You think you'll be safer alone?*

"And?" Missy asked.

"Don't have permission to shoot a segment here," Lester said, voice as glum as it could be when raised. "They were very intent on that—said we'd have to get management's permission, and the guy in charge won't be back from *his* vacation until Monday. I guess Youtube fame doesn't net me Russell Crowe levels of access."

"You really should have set this up in advance," Missy said.

"Yeah, sure," Lester said. "Let me see, how would that go… 'Ah, yes, my name is Lester Falls and I make six second streaming videos online and have a lot of likes and subscribes on Youtube. Can you please give me unlimited access to film in your location and also please don't charge me?' "

"You just thought we could come here and make it work?" Jack asked.

"I thought if it did work it would be a bonus?" Lester asked, shrugging his shoulders. "We were going camping anyway—figured we'd get scarier stuff out there. And honestly—usually my charms work better in person. I'm pretty sure the lady in charge is a lesbian. Or needs a better hairstylist."

Bailey was *really trying hard* not to panic, and her friends arguing did not seem to be helping. She closed her eyes—tried not to feel like she was spinning, caught in some vertiginous whirlwind of anxiety pulling her into an ooze in the ground. She focused on centering herself… drawing energy from the earth beneath her feet, breathing in deep and taming that wild nature within, *pulling* with all her might—and an unfamiliar voice popped in to the conversation.

"'ey, look, we have got a celebrity here," a man's voice said. It was deep, fluted, almost singsong in its melody, and instantly soothing.

She opened her eyes, and saw him. A young man about her age—black gleaming hair plaited into a braid down his back, chestnut colored skin and cheekbones that stuck out like handlebars. Oh, he was handsome—looked like he was chiseled from stone, with dark smoky eyes that seemed somehow ethereal. He was smoking a big fat cigar, and had his arm around Lester's shoulder. He was, however, a whole head taller than Lester.

Lester was, for once, completely quiet. He looked as if he had been transfixed—as if he were a moth staring upwards into a bright porch light.

"How ya doing?" the native man asked. He reached forward for everyone's hands. "Man, I seen all of youse guys on the Internet. This some kind of Youtube reunion?"

"Sorta," Jack said.

"I heard you saying you was looking to film something somewheres," he said.

Lester nodded, mouth open, practically drooling.

"Name's Devin Quick Bear," the young man said. "I'm native to these areas." He guffawed at his own pun, then took another puff off the cigar. He exhaled through his nose, absolutely coating Lester's face. Bailey could smell a powerful cloud of musk come with it— not just burning tobacco, but some intensely masculine, nearly overpowering scent. It was— almost like a natural man's sweat, but twice as powerful.

The others introduced themselves.

"We're, uh, looking for a place to film something spooky," Lester said, voice shaking.

Devin squeezed Lester's shoulder, in an almost overly-familiar way.

"Then I'm the man you need," he said, and winked. "I heard word there's an abandoned cemetery out to the South of here. Way out in the middle of the woods. Hails all the way back to the pioneer days, you see. Nice setting for something spooky, don'tcha think?"

Jack and Missy looked at Bailey.

"I vote we go," Lester said, quickly. "Devin, would you be so kind as to be our tour guide?"

"Absolutely," he said. "Would do me some good to get out. I didn't have much else planned except blowing half my check, and making some campfire in the woods seems like a more productive way to spend my time. We could stop and get something to drink and something to grill. Have a gay old time of it."

He looked right at Lester when he said it, who seemed to almost faint.

"You want to help me pack my bags up in my room?" Lester asked. "I'm not sure what to bring out to the woods. Total tourist and a city boy." He giggled.

"Dear God," Jack muttered, *sotto voce*.

"Yeah, let's go," Devin said. "Get a head start, right?"

Devin squashed the remains of his horrible cigar in an ashtray, and the two made their way out of the casino, Devin's arm never leaving the other young man's shoulders.

"At least let me get my stuff—" Jack began, but they turned the corner and disappeared. "Guess I won't get my shit together until later."

"You think they're really packing?" Bailey asked, voice optimistic.

"Packing something," Missy said.

There was a general store down the way: Bailey and Missy stopped and got some camping supplies—basic foodstuffs, really, and some quicklite wood, lighters, flashlights, the whole getup. The return to their room to pack was quicker than expected. Bailey caught sight of Jack sitting on the floor in the hallway, looking dejected.

"Still in there?" Missy called out.

"I can hear 'em from 'ere," Jack said, despondent. "I don't know who's doing what but someone's either really good or really bad. Sounds like a couple of mountain goats going at it." He held his head in his hands and groaned.

"Good luck," Bailey called out, and the girls entered their room again.

"We'll really be out in the middle of nowhere, and near a cemetery, to boot," Missy said. "I don't know how you're feeling but I'm getting a little creepy shudders about all this."

"I think it's cute," Bailey said.

"I don't mean Lester and his random tricks, I just mean hot-footing it to the woods. An abandoned cemetery, too. Sounds like an axe murder urban legend waiting to happen."

"You don't think you'll get some inspiration there?" Bailey asked.

"Hell no," Missy said. "I get plenty of inspiration at the bottom of a bong at home and staring out my dining room window. I can't work outside my house. I mean—I figured this would help in some kind of way, and I think some cross-promotion would help boost my numbers—but I think you're going a little whole hog on this 'outside-means-inspiration' business. It's really easy to buy into the nonsense men try and tell you. They don't know what it's like to be women."

Bailey nodded.

"That's true," she said.

"I don't even think it's that weird that you're a shut-in," Missy said. "Any woman with half a lick of sense would be, especially in a big city with all these creeps hanging around. A city street is an avenue of transportation for a man but sexual harassment avenue for a woman. Men get the protection of being considered masculine and aggressive. Maybe not all of them—and don't repeat I said that—but I mean, if you were a mugger, who would you go after first in our group?"

"Probably me," Bailey said. "Or you."

"Exactly. Women wear more jewelry. We're not taught how to fight and be rough. No wonder we hide away from everyone. Think of the famous female hermits throughout history—Emily Dickinson, Emily Bronte, Harper Lee, Greta Garbo. They all wanted to be left alone. I know Lester has these visions he wants to pursue, but honestly, sometimes, you need to be a hermit. Sometimes socialization is more dangerous for women than men. It's a lot of endangering yourself. Vulnerability. You have to protect your energy."

"Yeah," Bailey said. "But I think I just let it win too much. If I never let myself leave when I was uncomfortable I wouldn't have gone on this trip. And it's been pretty good so far."

"So far," Missy said. "I'm not trying to be a bitch but 'so far' will only get you so far."

And that seemed to be that, for they continued packing in silence. Bailey wondered, briefly, about Missy's ideas. They sounded good enough. But still. Bailey wasn't fighting her agoraphobia because of her (admittedly male) therapist, or because Lester had told her it was a good idea. It was her fight. As much as it scared her she knew she was going to have to face it, head-on, and it wouldn't get any better unless she reached out and tried to make it better. It may not have meant much to anyone else, but it meant the world to her, and she knew she'd do anything to face the demon of isolation one on one and take it down. By force, if necessary.

CHAPTER 12:

STORY TIME AT SETTLER'S END

They departed as the sun was setting through the distant trees; nighttime was coming over Deadwood, and it was all Bailey could do to stay calm. Lester and Devin had met them back at the van, looking freshly showered and a little too perky.

"It's called Settler's End," Devin said, once it was decided Missy would drive. "A little old place tucked away in the woods down south. You wouldn't know it was there if you wasn't looking for it."

"Good thing we have you," Lester said.

"I know, right?" Devin asked, grinning.

They headed South-bound; past ghost towns and roundabouts and crooked roads.

"A thought occurs," Lester said. "Bailey, have you done any research on this area?"

"A little before we left," she said. "You know my thing is creepypasta and cryptids. There's rumors of a goatman that wanders the woods. I didn't find much on it, though. More like a few abbreviated entries in old online forms. Probably written by high school kids."

Jack looked over at Devin.

"What you think?" he asked. "You eva heard such a thing?"

"We have stories sometimes," he said. "The moon comes out, it gets all big and bright, and sometimes. The Elders like to say things haunt the woods around here. Heard some stories about little devil people that haunt certain areas and chase people away. A goatman sounds new to me, but…"

He cut himself off, mouth pursed. It was a new look for him—pensive, rather than cheery. Bailey wasn't quite sure how she liked it.

"I'm Lakota," he said. "We don't talk about such things at night. So I won't say a whole lot. Except. Our Elders are kind of set in their ways and they don't always read up on the things they ought to. So sometimes they're superstitious. But. I have heard of… ah, well, shapechangers."

"Shapechangers?" Bailey asked.

"That's not their name," he said. "They're men—usually another tribe. Someone not a part of the Community. They embrace the Dark. Hunt during the full moon. They change their form."

Something thumped off a back window, and the five of them in the car jumped.

"Maybe I just hit a bird," Missy said, voice optimistic.

"Probably just a branch from a low-hanging tree limb. Better not to talk about it," Devin said. "They're smart, and sometimes they know their own names. And sometimes they're called when we say their names."

Bailey could feel her forehead flush with heat.

"We brought marshmallows," she said, more to distract herself than anything. "We can get a nice campfire going and cook some dinner."

"Haven't had a cookout in a long time," Jack said. "Sounds fun."

Missy, in the driver's seat, drove onwards through winding roads and trails, Devin occasionally telling her where to turn. After some time passed, Devin called out to take a left and they turned at a sharp angle to the highway, entering a dirt road that veered off into the undergrowth.

"Drive real slow through here, it winds like a snake," Devin said.

Bailey's eyes were arrested on the road ahead. Two dirt wells carved themselves into a gravel path before them, studded with rocks and weeds in the middle. Under-used and abandoned hardly seemed like accurate words—destitution and corruption from centuries and civilizations long-past was the feeling. Well-worn trails at least meant there could have been other humans around, if things went sour… And here Bailey seemed a little impressed with herself. Given a choice between classifying Unknown People or Monsters for scariest she would have said Unknown People hands-down a year before. But now that she was out here in this dark place her phobia seemed to have flipped itself. She wasn't quite sure she could call it progress, but it was certainly something.

The land itself seemed foreign and unused to human touch. She could sense a curiousness about it, from the trees. Some outside interest, some weird, ancient understanding that this place was not a place humans often tread. It wondered what they were doing there, in their dirty growling engine.

Finally the trees parted after some time—there was a small stagnant-looking pond on the right, with trees that crawled from beneath the water, dead stumps raised like outstretched bony hands. Opposite it, there was a flat clearing with rocks, tombstones, crosses made of wood, and rusted-looking fence here and there. A mess of broken gravel and pavement was their new parking lot. At the far end was an all-but-destroyed wooden structure next to a path off into the woods. It looked like a death trap, like some turn of the colonial-era two-story schoolhouse. A metal cross hung upside down from its first floor peak.

They parked in the gravel, then got out and stretched. Frogs croaked from the pond. Trees beyond it seemed to crowd over the water, a viridian fringe of hanging moss and pine needles. There was no telling in this kind of darkness how far the pond went.

"Great, no reception," Missy said, staring at her phone. She reluctantly slid it into her pocket.

"This is a lovely place for a shoot," Jack said, unpacking his cameras. "We could all sit around a campfire. Tell some scary stories. Have someone hide in the woods to jump out and scare us."

"So why do they call it Settler's End?" Bailey asked.

"You have GOT to wait until I hit record to start," Jack said. He fumbled around with some equipment, then hit a button. "There, okay. Go on. Ask the question again, Bailey."

She wet her lips with her tongue and asked again. "Why is this place called Settler's End?"

"It was a pioneer cemetery," Devin said. "Back during the gold rush, when the lands and the treaties were basically proven to be worthless, the white man moved in to Lakota lands and started stealing as many plots as they could. They were searching for gold in the hills. This was one of those little mock-up shacks in the area. It was a church and kind of a school.

But you know schoolhouses were different then, they were all different grades pushed together in one class. Times were different, though if you watch the news maybe you start to think maybe not so much has changed.

"Well, settlers started dying. They needed a place to bury them. Here they lie. Wish there was more to it but that's about it. Used to be a pretty popular place until most of the locals dried up in the forties. Now it's just a place. Sometimes people come back to visit, sometimes not."

"Have you heard of any paranormal activity in the area?" Jack asked.

"They say that sometimes people hear wailing in the woods," Devin said. "But there's lots of wildlife in the area. I ain't no expert but this place sure gets under your skin."

"I feel like the land is sad," Bailey said.

Everyone turned to look at her. She felt embarrassed; blinded, too, by the bright camera light.

"I'm just saying it's sad," she said. "The whole history of the place. The land itself is holy land for the Lakota and it was stolen and then the energy they put into it is just gone now. And now the land doesn't know what it is anymore. I just get the sense that it's mourning, unsure of what it needs to be."

"Deep," Lester said.

"I had no idea you were such a philosopher," Missy said.

Bailey shrugged.

"Just a feeling," she said.

"Well, it can be a resting place for the night. We can build a campfire and make it into a nice place for a visit," Lester said. "Let's give it a reason to be happy again, am I right?"

Devin smiled.

"Sounds like a good plan to me," he said.

"Then it's settled," Lester said.

And so they worked together to build up a fire. Missy and Bailey went to find stones; Lester and Devin and Jack went to find wood. They made a strong circle with stones smooth and sharp, heavy and light. Twigs were stacked underneath bigger hunks of deadwood. A couple of false starts and some muttering from Devin later, they had a nice little fire going, with Bailey and Devin taking turns as firekeeper.

"I used to go on campouts a lot when I was younger," Bailey said, at Jack's inquisitive eyebrow.

Fire tending was a sacred job. Bailey remembered days from when she was younger—out at the lake's edge, watching the brown water lap the shore, listening to the owls hoot in the cedars and hearing and smelling the sizzle of fresh meat on an open charcoal grill. Sometimes they would just make a fire in the evening, burning citronella sticks whole to keep mosquitoes away. Her father taught her how to handle the fire—taught her how to watch the embers, see where they tampered off, see how the wood was going to catch. She may have been a recluse for most of her life but the great outdoors still spoke to her.

Hot dogs went on sticks first. Hot grease and fat dripped into the fire and flickered up, staining the night air with black smoke and delicious smells.

"I got a ghost story," Jack said. "Missy, hold the camera."

She grunted and grabbed it, then panned it on him.

"Okay, so this one's a little basic," he said. He ran a hand through his dreads, puffed them up as he thought, then slid them backwards over his head. "So you know I do the bits about Brass Wasps. We talk about the Lengthy Man. Well, there's something else to that story. It's not just made up."

"BS," Lester said.

113

"I'm not lyin'," Jack said. "Honest to God. Swear on the Queen Mum. Brass Wasps ain't real, but there was some weird stuff that started happening when we was filming. Er, but first. I guess I gotta talk about Tulpas, don't I? You familiar with Tulpas?"

"Yeah," Bailey said. She tried not to show anything on her face. "A Tulpa is a thoughtform—like an artificial mind construct. Sort of a phantom hallucination a person can create through willpower. After a long enough time of being imagined they'll appear before the summoner. Almost like a willed form of schizophrenia."

"There's different theories—all highly experimental, of course—" Jack said. "I'll get back to that though. I first started noticing people talking about seeing the Lengthy Man in their own homes a few years into filming Brass Wasps. The internet being what it is, I was a bit skeptical. People like to gleam a little bit of internet fame for themselves and coopt something that's in the public domain. But this was different. People started saying they was getting strange disappearances in their neighborhoods. Weird knocks on the door at night. Looking at old footage they ain't seen before and seeing Him there, standing and leering with his blank white face and staring eyes. Hands all stretched and grasping. I seen a couple of 'em, but you have to understand, I was thick in the middle of Brass Wasps. If there really was a Lengthy Man hanging around and haunting folks, you'd think he woulda bothered me at some point. For all I knew he was a big fat nothing—a zero on the reality scale, some scary myth we tell ourselves to jump a little in the dark and feel better about our lives.

"It started with the lights, though," Jack continued. "My best mate—with me on the project since forever, a Spaniard named Antonio. He was my buddy. He usually dressed up like the Lengthy Man in our videos. He had this knobby sorta frame that really fit the aesthetic. Easy costume, too, just a black suit with some white hose for the head. We worked together on Brass Wasps since the beginning. Well, about three years in, he comes to me one night. I'll never forget that night—his eyes were shining. We were standing under streetlights—sodium arc lamps, the yellow puddling kind, and there was something about his eyes—they were just gleaming when he spoke to me. Maybe it was the angle. It was like there was this thin sheen of tears in his brown eyes, and that light was just bouncing off of 'em. It looked like the eyes that a deer had—tense, frightened, hollow. As if at any moment the deer will bound away to escape danger, and even it doesn't know what it's going to do.

"'I seen some lights last night,' he tells me. His voice, too, his voice was raw and scratchy, tired like he hadn't slept any. 'I watched 'em come in through the window,' he says to me. 'And at first I thought they was just car lights—headlights from the road or something. But then they started moving up the wall. You'd think if it was actual headlights they'd stop at some point—but they rose up, crawling, spinning round each other, floating up the wall and up to the ceiling. They danced there, on the ceiling,' he says to me. 'All night. There wasn't nothing reflecting them. Shouldn't have been there.' '

"I didn't think too much of it at the time. Didn't look like something he couldn't have taken care of with a full night's sleep and some strong coffee. I thought maybe he'd just got a little something extra with his kush this time and it wouldn't be anything I had to deal with. But he came in the next day to the shoot—told me the same thing. 'I was up all night watching 'em,' he says to me. 'They started spinning when they noticed I was watching them.'

"Well, me, I'm getting concerned. I keep thinking maybe all this horror movie shooting might be getting to be a bit much. I was having some girlfriend problems at the time, so it seemed like it would be better overall for me to just wrap up shooting for a week or two and go back to everything after some time off. Antonio would get some rest, I could patch things up with the Missus. We could restock on film and maybe go over some editing in the meantime. Good for everyone involved.

"Antonio seemed to like the idea. He seemed tired to me, a little paler than usual. Black circles under his eyes. I told him to rest up and if he didn't quit seeing the lights to maybe take a trip to the doctor. He nodded and told me he'd keep in touch. Well, that was the last I saw of him."

"What?" Lester asked, and leaned forward.

"I heard from his mother about a week later," Jack said. "She said she'd found him one morning, eyes rheumy and gray, staring up at the ceiling. There were no lights on—he wasn't breathing. She seemed heartbroken. After the funeral, I volunteered to clean his room. He had a bunch of old papers he'd written and scribbled things on. Pen, pencil, crayon, whatever was handy nearby. I wasn't sure what to do at this point. Some of the scribbles looked weird important—we're talking manifestos, babblings, rantings. A lot of it story ideas for Brass Wasps. I checked in on his computer—doing what friends do best and clearing the weird porn before his family found it—and found a lot of bookmarks on Tulpas. On thoughtforms. On Brass Wasps. The nearest I can piece together, from what a few of his private Facebook posts were, was that he was leaving a trail for someone to follow who maybe had seen what he'd seen. It started with the lights. Soon enough he couldn't be in the same room with a mirror without seeing the Lengthy Man standing over his shoulder, just standing there, and static screaming in his ears. At night he would look out the window and see him—LM, staring and scratching at the paned glass. The last journal entry is dated the day before he died. It just said 'tonight, I think he's going to enter my bedroom. I don't feel safe.' As far as I'm aware that was the last thing he'd ever typed."

"Bullshit," Devin said.

"On God," Jack said.

"Do you think the Lengthy Man got him?" Lester asked.

Jack shook his head.

"Maybe he went insane. Maybe there was something else there—something else lying under the surface of his brain waiting to leap out. Maybe. One of the other people on the cast—Margo—she thinks it was a Tulpa or something that took that form to terrify him to death. I mean. If the Lengthy Man were real he would have gotten everyone who worked on the series by now, you'd reckon," he said.

"Would he?" Bailey asked. "I mean, think about it. You think he might have been a Tulpa—but wouldn't that make him your child, in some respects? Don't people only know about him because of your show, Brass Wasps? If he kills you then doesn't that cut off access to everyone else he could haunt?"

There was a silence then, in the woods, between them all.

"Well, I don't know about all that," Jack said.

Someone laughed to break the tension.

"You almost had me going there for a minute," Lester said. "You're good at this pseudo-narrative, is-it-real or is-it-not business."

"'S a true story" Jack protested, voice whining.

"It sure scared the hell out of me," Devin said. "And trust me, I know scary."

"What about you, Missy?" Lester asked. "Any scary stories from you?"

Missy blinked and thought about it.

"Did I tell you all about the cursed painting?" she asked.

"Nooooo," Lester said, voice fascinated. "Do tell."

"My Mom bought it on Ebay for us," she said. "She knew I liked spooky artwork. The listing said it was haunted—said that it changed and moved on occasion. I never would have fallen for such an obvious scam myself, of course, but Mom eats that kinda stuff up. Like candy. Anyway, she orders it and it arrives and she surprises me with it after dinner."

115

"What did it look like?" Jack asked.

"The weirdest, most mournful painting of a small child," she said. "He was practically crying when we unwrapped it the first morning. The kid in the painting, I mean. You know those hyper-realistic, gross-out closeups they do in kids' cartoons, like on someone's bad acne or something ugly. Imagine something like that, but it's a Precious Moments doll face. Big wide eyes, trembling chin, dimples, and curly blonde hair. Like the Gerber baby had hit ten years old and was seriously on the cusp of throwing a huge tantrum. It was ugly, but it had a certain style to it. The artwork felt very animated, and the piece had a lot of energy to it. You could almost feel the kid moving in the frame. Without thinking overly much on it, I hung it in the living room over the mantel-piece. This was the same room, incidentally, as my gold fish."

"That was a weird right turn," Lester said.

"Not as weird as you think," she replied. "I didn't think much about it, other than how weird and weirdly out of place this picture was for my house. But the next morning I noticed two things. Number 1: the painting. It had changed. The little boy was no longer sad looking. I stared at it, baffled and astonished. There seemed to be no way to make that happen without it being some optical illusion. Maybe, I thought, I'd just viewed the painting in a different light and the expression I had mistaken for sadness was really this unplaceable expression of emotion. It was not until after I found my goldfish dead that I would place the look—that of something or someone satisfied, in some fundamental way, darkly satisfied and humorous about it, eyebrow and lip curled up in an almost Machiavellian-subtle Mona Lisa smile."

"What did you do?" Bailey asked.

"What else could I do?" she asked. "Fish funeral. It wasn't a huge loss since I'd only won him at the fair that summer, but I'd grown pretty attached to the little idiot. He was just floating in his tank, pale belly facing the sky, fins unmoving. We played Green Sleeves and sent him off to the sewer pipe in the sky. C'est la vie, little fishy. I have to say, though, I was a little bit suspicious of the painting from that point forward."

"Did you tell your Mom?" Devin asked.

Missy shook her head.

"What would I say? Mom, the little boy in the painting killed my fish. I mean, she bought it because it was haunted, so it wasn't like she wouldn't have believed me. I think it was that I didn't want to believe my own senses."

"So what happened next?"

"The painting would change every day," Missy said. "Every day some new presentation. Sometimes the little boy would stare out from the painting, sometimes he'd be farther back and facing away. It was aggravating, because I was never sure how I was going to find it. Some days it might be cool outside and he'd be gone—just an empty landscape, a black nothingness that mocked me. Other days, he'd get angry and stare out of the frame inside the house. He was just a staring eyeball at that point, red-rimmed, horrible veins bursting in and out of his staring eye. I took some pictures of it, but they never seemed to come out. Physical film—the film would come out underexposed or overexposed. Digital film, or cellphone camera—the image would get all blurry. I was ninety percent convinced that I was either going insane or that there was an actual spirit inside the damn thing.

"Then it started messing with my cat," she said. "His name was Jezzie. A big tubby fatso, some huge tabby we found as a trash gremlin some time back. He was never comfortable in the same room as that painting. A few times I walked into the room and found him staring at the mantelpiece, yowling, insensible. Wouldn't respond to me except to hiss. Like he was terrified. I was too scared to pick him up, but if I opened a door he would run, tail between his legs, out of the room. And he'd never had that problem before with the room. I knew something had to be done, but Mom had paid quite a bit of money for the painting, and if I were to do something like sell it the likely scenario was she'd kick me out."

"You at least talked to her after you saw how Jezzie was acting, right?" Bailey asked.

Missy nodded.

"She pooh-poohed my concerns. Told me I was seeing things. Every day I'd point out how the painting would change, and she'd look at it and not see anything different. I thought maybe I was going crazy after a while. But I noticed that something had changed in Mom, too. She would sit around the house and stare at things, with this vacant look on her face. A few weeks in, she started finding weird stuff all over the house. Odd, half-finished notes that seemed to come from nowhere, dishes in the fridge. I would come home and find that she was sitting with her purse in her hands and looking quite seriously in the distance, a look of confusion on her face. It always gave me a shudder. When I shook her and asked her what was wrong she wouldn't say much, just that she'd found another bizarre message."

"So then what happened?" Lester asked.

"I talked to a friend at school about it. She got concerned with me. Really concerned. Told me she was going to come over and help me sort things out. She brought this little device. Plugged it into the wall. It lit up and started blaring. She got a serious look on her face and rushed me out of the house. Rushed my Mom out of the house. Went and got the cat, then told me to leave the doors open.

"Turns out it was a carbon monoxide leak the whole time. She called the fire crew in and some safety inspectors. I guess when I hung the painting up over the mantelpiece the hangers we'd used pierced an outlet gas line from the fireplace setup we had."

"Oh, creepy," Devin said. "That's terrifying. and I know terrifying."

"It took us a few months to heal up. Thankfully it didn't do too much damage. I guess the high-def digital camera was able to pick up the air currents when I tried to take a picture. And the film I was using for analog—I'd picked up infrared. Infrared film warps when exposed to carbon monoxide."

"A real Scooby doo mystery solved," Lester said.

They cracked out the marshmallows, passing them one by one and shivering a bit in the gloom. After some time of silence, Lester opened his mouth again.

"Okay, I thought about it. My turn.

"Now that sounds interesting," Devin said.

"Okay. I got one," Lester said. "It's called the 11 Mile game. They say that, when you really, really, ridiculously want something. You can take a long drive through the woods to get it. But you have to be really sure you want it, right? If you waver in your resolve, you'll get terminated. Whatever's waiting in the woods—the people who came before you, who fell off the road, the path, whatever... they're waiting to pull you down with them."

"I've heard about that one before," Bailey said. "It's a pretty famous Creepypasta."

"Yeah, well, mine's a little different," Lester said. "I actually did it."

Bailey sat up.

"What?" she asked.

Lester nodded.

"In that old rustbucket station wagon over there," he said. "Look. I don't know about you guys. But I wanted this. This fame. It was all I could ever think of, ever since I was a kid. I started trying in high school—started taking drama classes, training my voice, watching as much TV as I could and recording myself. Then Vine came out. I made a few, and everyone in class was really supportive, but they just weren't catching on, you know. So I figured I needed some help."

"Tha's cheatin'," Jack said.

"Might be, but if you fail, the punishment is death and/or eternal torment, so I figured no risk, no reward, am I right?"

Devin grinned at Lester.

"I like the way you think," he said.

Lester preened, and then continued.

"So the rules say you have to think about what you want. There are a number of obstacles on the way that will impact your ability to pay attention. Well, I found my direction, gassed up, and made myself a checklist of do's and don'ts. I wasn't gonna let any ghosts from beyond come and grab me, that was for sure. So they say—no radio, don't roll your windows down, don't turn around, no matter what you hear. Don't exceed thirty miles an hour. And whatever you do, do not attempt to leave the vehicle.

"So I start my drive in the forest. Beautiful redwood forest all around me. The rules say that you have to find the right road. Whatever you want, you'll find signs for the right road. And sure enough, after a few miles, I found it. A big old star ornament stuck on a tree right on a narrow gravel pathway. I turned down it, and soon found the sky was dark. A vast, shining array of stars greeted me. The air in the car was colder, somehow. All in line with the rules, of course. I reached down and fidgeted with the heating.

"Second mile forward. I was watching my odometer. Hit something—a pothole, I think. The car nearly jerked off the road. I realized there were twists and turns coming up, and kept my eyes focused on the road before me. This was a big, curvy stretch, no fence on the sides. Rocks, tree limbs, everything you can think of in the way. Directions say this is near about appropriate. Drove on and on, barely taking my eyes off the road to watch the odometer. It clicked over, and I could feel the air drop in temperature, again.

"The gravel turned to a dirt road. This felt like off-road stuff, and me in this big old station wagon. There were. I don't know how to describe this, but there were shadows moving in the trees. Real nail-biting, unnerving stuff, if I'm being honest. The road would widen, shorten, thin, turn around a bend and disappear almost entirely. I kept on trucking, though.

"About the fourth mile. Temp gets colder. I start to feel like. I don't know. This sense of paranoia? Like someone's trying to whisper something I can barely hear in my ears. More dirt road. More of my hands clutching at ten and two and considering I may not have made the best decision at this point. I mean, dirt road at night? But they say you basically die if you turn back. I wasn't ready to get lost forever in the forest so on I went.

"The clearing parted in the fifth mile on the driver's side. The moon hung overhead—crimson and round, seeming to stare down over a vast crystalline lake. The instructions are extremely clear here about not looking to your left at the lake. They say something will pull you in, drown you. I kept on going. Now, I should mention. This whole time. There's this bright red light so powerful on the road it's all I can do to keep myself from looking.

"Sixth mile. Headlights started flickering as soon as the clearing closed up again. No more moonlight casting serial killer vibes on the road, just me in my mother's beat up POS about to have fuse problems. I'm getting terrified at this point. This is really starting to become real, right? It's too much to handle in some respects. But still. Car's getting even colder. And that was when my radio turned on.

"A nice, polite voice started narrating a news cast. 'Falls family found dead.' I don't want to go into it, but it was basically a very detailed description of an entire family murdered. *Mine.* The instructions mentioned something about your greatest fears. Well, reading it's one thing and hearing it's another entirely.

"Seventh mile, juking and weaving in the dark. I start to hear this heavy breathing, and then I notice something's breathing in my ear. I try to keep my eyes on the road—I don't turn around, don't even blink, just stare ahead. All these dark figures in the trees started appearing. They start cauterwauling, all these shadows. I was terrified, and as soon as I heard whatever was in the car with me start screaming in my ear I screamed myself. I just kept screaming, gasping in deep breaths and screaming myself ragged until I finally lost my breath and realized the shadows all around me had disappeared. The odometer clicked over.

"Eighth mile in. Headlights start going again. Road gets rougher, somehow. Sharp valleys and narrow turns. I hazard a look into my rearview mirror. Whatever was there was gone... but I could see them filtering out of the trees behind me. Shadows upon shadows, all human shaped, arms outstretched, walking slowly. My headlights flickered off a few times. I braked to a stop. Would wait until they were almost on me, then kept going once the headlights flicked back on. My steering wheel was like ice—no amount of heat blasting from my vents was helping.

"Ninth mile. I wanted to stop and breathe. This was too much. Time felt like it had dilated, like it had stretched out in some fundamental way. I could see them coming ahead from the trees, piling out like a horde. And then my car engine stopped.

"They were cracking at the windshields. One by one, swinging, hitting, stomping. I could hear them babbling. Screaming. My eyes were closed, here. I didn't think I'd survive if I opened my eyes. Later on, I would re-read the instructions and find myself thanking my lucky stars I did close my eyes. I revved the engine back on, eyes closed, and then peeled off. I could hear thumps—when I finally opened my eyes, I swerved at the last minute to hit another curve that jumped out of nowhere. They were still shrieking in the back. This whole sequence must have repeated two or three times. I think I pissed myself somewhere in the middle.

"Finally. I hit another clearing about the 10th mile mark. Off in the distance, through the rear view window, the shadows had stopped moving. They were watching me as I drove. Even the ones further ahead in the trees. My breath was coming out like fog. I could feel my fingers freezing around the steering wheel. Off in the distance, there was some bright red light. I felt a sigh of relief. Almost there... almost there...

"But there was something the instructions said about that red light. I couldn't remember it. It flickered up and blazed ahead of me. I could feel it in my bones, scorching me. The steering wheel started boiling. The car stalled. I tried to turn it on, tried stomping on the brakes, but it started pulling me, and the car with it. The shadows had gone. All there was was this yawning hellmouth open before me, and I could do nothing but scream as it sucked me in.

"I managed to close my eyes—some kind of preservation instinct, I think—but the air started to feel heavy all around me. I could hear cackling. The sound of whips. Gunshots. I peeked a few times—and shrieked. My mind must have blanked out what I saw. But again, that self-preservation instinct kicked in and my eyes shut themselves after moments. It must have been only half a minute, according to the instructions... but it felt like an eternity. Like I was being punished. Like I was watching thousands of people suffer...

"Sometimes at night, I can still hear the unearthly noises. And I wake up from horrible dreams... horrible dreams of open, yawning holes in the sky, vortexes that spin like the universe itself is screaming at me, and something's whispering in my ear..."

He stared off in the distance, shoulder shaking, and in the sudden quiet—his usual theatrical embellishment was gone, and only a small whisper had started coming from him about halfway through, as if he were forcing the words out.

"Well, did you get what you were after?" Jack asked.

Lester jumped, as if he was noticing the world around him again.

119

"Well, I found myself on the road I started on, that same stupid star ornament on the tree. I fish-tailed into a three point turn and took off. When I got home, one of my Vines had gone viral. I don't know what happened. I guess I did the ritual right."

"Oh man. Heebie-jeebies. And I should know heebie-jeebies," Devin said.

"Okay, Bailey," Lester said, and the old jovial mask came back up. "We all told our story. You tell us one."

Bailey nodded, considered it, thought better of it… and then decided to talk about it. Even if she'd have to omit some things.

"I haven't told anyone else this," she said. "But I know what the root cause of my agoraphobia is."

Lester quirked an eyebrow.

"Do tell," he said.

"My Dad," she said, shortly. "It was a long time ago. I was maybe ten years old. We had gone on a father-daughter camping trip, just the two of us. I think he wanted a boy—he was always teaching me stuff about the outdoors. How to watch for birds, how to start fires, how to prepare a campsite. Survival stuff. He was a prepper. So little trips out to the lake were things we did more than anything else.

"Well, the final camping trip we went on together started like any other camping trip. We were gonna be gone for a weekend. It was just any other summer weekend. Weather an awful lot like this. Nice and sunny, but cool. Low humidity. We were gonna fish and he was going to try to teach me how to frog-gig. It's when you use a little mini trident. You get a sack, or a pillowcase, or something you don't mind frogs peeing in. And a halogen flashlight. You basically follow the sounds of the frogs croaking. When you see them, you stun them with the flashlight, then a quick stab and you pop them into the bag. It was kinda fun as a kid. That Friday he'd taught me the basics. We spent a couple of hours that evening down at the fishing hole—this little inlet where a river trickled into the lake. It was like bullfrog paradise. We must have gotten five or six big fat ones."

"What on earth would you do with bullfrogs?" Lester asked.

"Eat 'em," Missy said. "Clearly."

Bailey nodded.

"We had a midnight frog feast. Dad showed me how to fillet them and prepare them. They're pretty good, if you clean out the organs and focus on the meat. Otherwise you're just eating a bunch of bugs, you know. So anyway. On Friday night we heard it at first. It was a little sound, at first. A far-off bleat."

Devin's face became pensive.

"Then closer and closer. Soon, we found ourselves surrounded by the campfire while something we couldn't see bleated like a sheep or something at us. And the stench—my God, it was everywhere. Thick, cloying. Like rotten skunk on the side of a highway that's been sitting there, moist and wet, during a hot humid rain. After a while, though, Dad kept the fire up and it retreated. He told me it was probably nothing but an owl and told me not to worry about it.

"But I saw it the next day," Bailey continued. "It was a little flash of white leaping through the forest. Jumping, bleating. But it wasn't moving right. It was on its hind-legs. Stalking through the area. It was shaped almost like a man. I told Dad about it, and this time, he decided he would do something about it. I don't know why we didn't go home. To this day I don't know why we didn't go home. I guess you couldn't really trust your ten-year old when it came to them seeing a monster.

"Well, the stench came back as night dragged on, and Dad made me get in the tent and stay in it. He said he'd take care of whatever it was. All I heard was it bleating-laughing, almost. And Dad screaming. Oh, he screamed. Screamed and screamed. And what was worse-when it stopped. When the screaming quit. I looked outside, peeked through the flap. Something with square pupils was staring in at me through the slit. It laughed—sounded like a person, almost. And its breath came in to the tent, and I almost passed out.

"I ran back to my sleeping bag and tucked my head into it, wrapping myself like a little burrito. I didn't come out until the morning. And when I did. I saw Dad. Flies had gotten to him overnight. The frog-gig had been used on him—was shoved down his throat and through the other end, staking him to the ground like he was a bullfrog, on his knees and looking ready to jump away. Blood had trickled down from his mouth, and his eyes were staring straight ahead. Unblinking. I tried to touch him—tried to move him, but I'd seen what we did with the frogs the night before. It looked like a punishment to me. I didn't know what else to do but scream and cry.

"I was stuck in that campground for another day with my father's dead body," she said.

Lester's mouth was open. Missy looked ill. Jack's eyes were wide.

"I'm so sorry to hear about that," Jack said. "But that's the most metal story I've ever heard."

"I'm not finished," Bailey said. "I wasn't found until Monday. I guess Dad hadn't thought to charge the phone—I couldn't find where we parked the car. I didn't want to leave the camp. I was in uncharted territory, but I knew enough about survival to fend for myself. I caught a few fish, some frogs early in the morning. Started a fire to keep warm. I tried to cover Dad's body with his sleeping bag, but it wouldn't stay where I sat it. I tried to avoid looking at it. Thinking about it. Well, finally my saviors came and grabbed me.

"It was an old couple. They lived out in the woods, they said, and they were looking for a new daughter. I was so young—I had no idea what to do, if I could trust them or not. But what else could I do? I went with them back to their cabin. And it was a cabin, some log-cabin styled one room little hut with dirt floors. I remember it just like it happened yesterday. They had an old black and white TV with an antenna and all they got in was Beverly Hillbillies. They made me work for them during the day. I did their dishes and did the cooking. At night they made me sleep in a cage. Sometimes... the old man would come in at night, and he'd... he'd."

Missy sat down next to her, holding her shoulders and hugging her. There were tears in Bailey's eyes, great emotion in her voice as she struggled to continue.

"I was lucky," Bailey continued. "About a week in, the cops came. I was back at Mom's house within forty-eight hours. It was a big deal. They sealed the records in the court cases to protect my identity. I had to see a therapist for it."

"Holy shit," Lester said. "It's amazing you even survived."

"It sounds almost unbelievable," Jack said.

"I know," Bailey said. "The therapist didn't believe me, about the monster or the people that took me in. I guess they found my father washed up in the river somewhere. The police did a kit on me. There was DNA evidence of someone of unknown origin. The police assumption was something had happened between Dad and me—the sexual abuse—and I fought him off and he fell in the water and drowned. But I know different. That's not how it happened and I know it. I haven't been able to really trust people again. Mom and Grandma and everyone were so happy to find me alive and safe after ten days of going missing that they bent over backwards to make me feel comfortable. I guess being obsessed with stories of things in the woods and not being able to trust were just part and parcel of it."

"Geez," Lester said, whistling. "That was a heavy load of emotional baggage to get off your chest."

"It's a shame none of them believed you," Devin said. "Because I've got a story I think you'll find interesting."

He leaned forward, and began to tell his tale.

CHAPTER 13:

DEVIN'S TALE

I was a Rez boy born and bred. My ancestors were birthed from the earth into the Black Hills. It was our sacred spot; our sacred soil. Over time more and more whitepeople snapped it up. Laws and regulations meant to protect us got struck down. There was a goldrush and more and more of this forest surrounding us was parceled up and divided. You should know the history, even if you don't.

That's kind of the point of Crazy Horse. It's a pipe dream—who knows when they'll finish it. We have to rely on the white man to fund it still. Thankfully a lot of guilty people know what their ancestors did. They keep donating and donating. Maybe in another fifty years we'll get an arm carved out of the rock. Maybe.

Look, I know all this was ancient past. But it still impacts us to this day. Rez life is awful. Our people weren't made to be all squished up together with nothing to do. We used to be a part of the environment—living off what the land freely provided. But the colonialists—they carved and tore up what was there, what was natural. They took what they wanted—didn't give back. They didn't speak with the Grandfather, the Great Mystery, the *Wakan Tanka* and listen to his cries.

I only bring up this ancient history because deep in our bones the rez men know. We Lakota have to grin and bear it every time we see a football team with one of our people as their mascots or see a white guy talking about his latest startup scheme to clean the oceans. Must be nice to have the resources or the time to think about this stuff. Benefits are there and they're great, but we're a weak people. We know it. The land knows it. The waters know it. The heavens and earth, they know it. Even *they* know it.

They are the shadows. They're things that live here with us. It's hard to talk about them. This is not typical Lakota speak. This is an older sort of Medicine. A dark kind.

Grandfather is not kind. He is generous, but he is not kind. If he were kind he would smite the ones who did us wrong. But he sees all. He waits and watches. He gives and he takes. It's part of a balance—the way the wheel spins.

What you have to know is that in the old days there were shadows and the shadows lived. And they didn't like us. Not us Lakota, nossir. We worshipped Grandfather and the shadows were born opposite him. Some say on the dark side of the moon. Some say in the places the sun shines not. All I know about it is what I was told.

In the olden days. We men were enslaved by darkness. We lived deep in the earth under the whip of the shadows. The shadows are as old as the dirt down below. But Iktomi the trickster was not happy with the shadows. He came in the form of a Wolf. He dug deep down into our mud caverns and convinced us that we would love it on the surface. In time our people rose from the ground—escaped the shadows that enslaved us—and we emerged into the forest. This forest. The Black Hills. This sacred land was where our people escaped the shadows. And that's why Crazy Horse and his men Ghost-danced.

But we were slaughtered. That great slaughter caused a rift. It was not known to me or many other Lakota but there were of our people those so aggrieved by centuries of degradation by these colonialists that they would do anything for revenge. And the shadows that used to keep us in chains, the ones that waited in the woods, the ones that the sunlight chased, they were eager to do what they could to help. Because vengeance and bloodlust is what they feed on, these dark things.

So some of our people went and took the Bad Medicine. They turned away from Grandfather and the Great Mystery. They spoke with that-which-lurked. And they forged pacts with these shadows. Their rites were strange and arcane. They were no longer the children of the sun and the lands and the Black Hills. They were children of the moon, and when it hung fat and pregnant in the sky more shadows slurched forth.

I only know all this because I seen one of them. The shape-changers. I won't say their name. They move like Iktomi the trickster—changing their form at will. I have seen owls with sneakers on. I have heard of people whose property gets vandalized. Heard from people who have had strange weapons and such stuck in their vehicles. For years all us Lakota kids heard these stories. 'Stay out of the woods,' we were told. 'The shadows will gobble you up. And don't leave the house when the moon turns crimson red.'

So me, a Rez boy, I was a badass with a huge chip on my shoulder. I wanted to show these punks what for. I was not afraid of shadows. So I secretly scoffed at the elders when they gave us their warnings. I had not let my rotten stepfather beat me black and blue to fall down and weep when some puff of air that was too frightened of the sun would come around.

I got my chance when they started after my neighbor Mary. Mary was a kind young woman, but she was very innocent in some respects and very, very sheltered. Her father was a drunk—an NDN preacher that had adopted the white man's religion. He beat his own wife, and everyone knew it. Except for Mary, it seemed.

Mary didn't have to deal with what was going on at home all the time. She was getting an education off the Rez. Every day she would wait at the bus stop at the far edge of the dirt road—past the dogs and the despair. Her mother would always dress her in white. It wasn't traditional garb, but it was what she liked. She was beautiful, like a little weaved doll. Her father was protective of her.

I never trusted him. I think every guy's come to blows with him in the Rez once or twice. Myself included. He was a rat bastard, a real dog. I would spit on him if I cared to waste the body fluid. Yet as mean as a snake as he was to his wife, he treated Mary like she was made of glass. It was real weird—watching it happen. They spoke rumors over it.

Well these Dakota came by. We assumed they were Dakota. They took the same bus. They lived out in the woods by themselves. A real weird bunch. They were Rez boys, tried and true, but there was something *off* about them. I couldn't tell you what it was. They stank like axel grease and bad nightmares—that sweat smell you wake up with when you've been tossing and turning all night in your sleep, haunted by things in your mind. They were wild boys—hooting and hollering at women and treating 'em with no respect. There were three of them boys, all about the same age, one year apart, and they lived with their grandmother. Nobody'd seen her before. There was talk amongst the elders. That she had been sighted once—a beauty, but blind as a bat and walked like she was made of glass. She was the head of their little group. Family was called… ah, well. Don't want to bring that up. There are sayings about it. You don't go calling things after dark.

Well, the boys had started to harass Mary. As spoiled backwoods boys are wont to do. Well, Mary put up with it, but she didn't like it. Had a real temper like her father. Snapped at 'em, snarled at 'em. Told 'em to go fuck themselves. It seemed to work at first, but, perhaps seeing how feisty she was triggered something in the middle boy. His name was D. We'll just call him that, since there's not much fear in it.

D starts to take a liking to Mary. He gets closer to her. Trying to be her friend. To shape up and impress her. Greasing his hair back, dressing clean, taking Bible classes and whatnot. I could tell, though, that there was something in his eyes when he looked at her. Some kinda gleam. Some kinda weird undercurrent in his face. He was trying *hard* to be good, and nobody who knew them boys knew it would wind up good in the end.

School dance comes around—some kind of early Winter prom I guess—and Mary winds up relenting and she goes to the dance with D. Halfway through the night the two of them disappear. Mary shows back up, and D is gone. Mary's crying, her dress is torn, her lip is busted and she's bleeding and she's just making these horrible sobbing noises. I guess something had happened—we all figured we knew what went on. D was waiting like it was some kind of fucked up game. He goes to get her to let her guard down and he takes advantage of her. That was the story as she told it, or at least that was the story as it was passed around.

Well, Mary's Dad finds out and leaves his house with a shotgun. He's ready to blast this little piece of Dakota bastard off the face of the earth. He manages to track him down two towns over in a bar, smoking and drinking and bragging about what he done over a game of billiards. Word has it Mary's Dad cracked a pool cue over his head and dragged him out of the bar unconscious.

Nobody knows *exactly* what happened next, but the long and short of it was that D went missing. Nobody ever seen him again after that. No body, no body parts, no hide nor hair of him. It was like Mary's Dad had flung him from the face of the earth and tossed him directly into the sun. Rumors swung around about it. Some people said that D had been murdered, strangled to death, and that Mary's Dad had tossed him into the lake.

No matter what happened, because ultimately nobody knew, Mary moved out of her parent's house, in with her Grandmother in another city. So now it was just an angry abusive possibly murderer with his beaten wife as my neighbor.

It was about three days after Mary left that D's Grandmother came to the Rez. She was escorted by her two remaining grandsons, and her eyes were so white they were practically boiled eggs. They walked her right up to Mary's house and that old woman proceeded to beat that front door down with her cane.

Mary's Dad swung open the door and roared at her. The two strapping grandsons—hellions, the both of 'em—stepped forward. Attacking D with a pool cue was one thing, but taking on two of his brothers face to face with an old woman in front of him seemed too much. Especially in-town, with the neighbors watching. Mary's Dad stood down.

"Where's D?" the old woman demanded. "Tell me where you put his body."

"I don't know where your little piece of dog shit went," he said, but of course I'm paraphrasing.

"You give me his body and I forget about all this," she said. "We just need his body."

He shook his head at her.

"I don't know where he went," he said. "I dropped him off in an alleyway near a hospital after I was done having a little chat with him. Did you hear tell what he done with my Mary?"

"That ain't no excuse for killing no one," she said. "If that deserved death, you'd have been dead three times over and I'm not miscounting."

All the color drained out of Mary's Dad's face, and he seemed to shrink.

"I don't know where he is," he said, again.

"Then on your own head be it," she said. "You have seven days to tell me where his body is."

"Or?" he asked.

She turned around and slid a forefinger over her throat, then gripped her boys on the arm.

"Let's go," she said.

And off she crawled back to the tin can she lived in out in the woods.

That was the first day. That night, we all heard the sounds as the soon as the moon came out from behind the clouds. Pittering, pattering feet. Laughs and heckles. Everyone locked their door, closed their windows. They knew the kind of Medicine that a woman with her eyes could throw. Merely making eye contact ensured that you could be infected with it, too. The whole Rez was in a state of shock.

The second night they found footprints on the soil.

The third night we all saw claw marks on the siding of their house. Hoots and hollers and the wailing of cats seemed to come through our windows.

The fourth night the dogs outside were murdered.

The fifth night, the dogs came back, voices high and yipping. Gash marks blew out their tires.

The sixth night, Mary's mother went screaming out into the night. Nobody ever seen her again.

And the seventh night. I decided I would do what I could to help. I was not afraid of these things. My older sister told me in hushed whispers what they were, and I felt a strong urge to face them one on one. I was drawn to the idea of them—like some weird power coursing through my veins, making its way through my teeth and up into my spine. I wanted to face them.

I lay in wait from dusk until the evening, hiding myself in the hedges on their property. Imagine my surprise when I saw them—the shadows. They were shaped like wolves, like Iktomi from the legends, but they walked funny. They loped forward, with powerful bounds, and they would speak to each other, deep guttural words and sounds. My heart seemed to want to pound right out of my chest. They had golden eyes, gleaming with crimson from the moon overhead.

I shook in my hedges. The sight of them, and the feel of the Bad Medicine from the two of them was enough to make me sick. I bent over and lost my lunch, and they caught sight of me. All my instinct at fighting had gone—I wanted to run. Started to, getting to my knees and starting to sprint, but I could feel their footprints behind me, the ground pulsing with their steps, and before I knowed what was happening they got me."

"They got you?" Bailey asked.

Devin nodded.

"Dragged me away," he said. "I woke up strung up next to Mary's Dad in the blind woman's house in the woods. Bad medicine was all over the place. A giant cauldron against one wall smoked. They were charring something in the room. I wasn't too sure myself. I was trussed up with my wrists in the air, dangling. I saw them use a knife and plunge it into Mary's Dad's neck, catch his blood in a goblet, heard him screaming."

"How did you get away?" Lester asked.

"I didn't," Devin said. "They gave me a choice. They said I could stay quiet and they would teach me their Medicine, and I would run with them. Or I could suffer the same fate Mary's Dad did."

"So what choice did you make?" Lester asked, voice shaky.

Devin smiled, teeth extremely white.

"What choice do you think I made?" he asked, and lunged.

CHAPTER 14:

THE GOATMAN COMETH

Lester shrieked, and Devin laughed as he tickled him in the ribs.

"Jesus!" Lester said. "That's not. Fucking. Funny!"

Jack's face was a riot of tears and mirth.

"Oh, Devin, you've got to stick with the crew," he said. "That was perfect, man. We got all of that on film."

"Great," Devin said. "That was a really good plan."

"A plan?" Lester shrieked.

Bailey laughed.

Jack and Missy wanted to explore some of the ruined schoolhouse, and Devin and Lester wanted some alone time, so Bailey was left by herself stirring the fire.

It was not a good place to be by herself. Mentally, she thought, though God knew it was probably not safe to be out here all alone. Missy's earlier diatribe about the perils of womanhood was not something Bailey thought about often, but here it came back to her on the rushing of wind through the trees and the crackling of pine and oak branches as the fire popped.

Bailey was not superstitious by far and large. Superstition was for old wives and people who had never seen anything. She was beyond that—at a point in her life where she knew that literally anything could happen, at any time, at any place, at any moment, for no reason other than the universe wanted to give her a big fat middle finger. If she could control her environment, she knew, she could control to an extent what came in and out of it. The little basement room back at her sister's brownstone in Oakland was her safe little fortress. She knew she would retreat back there at some point—it was only a matter of time—but she also knew that she needed air. She needed new energy. She needed the feeling of seeing new sights, new sounds, new people. A long-hidden ennui had suffused her being after years and years of her only connection being through a bright, streaming LCD monitor. And though she was satisfied, in a way… living a half-life in that little coffin of a room, she also knew that there was more to the world than she was letting herself have.

She was conscious of the impacts of no exercise. She was terrified of the idea of being a female version of a neckbeard, forever living at home. She was no Emily Dickinson—she was not Bronte, cloistered away like a nun. This was the internet age. There were no scullery maids or picturesque views of New England to sweeten her creative spirit. She knew that in this slice of the present everyone was plugged in to this vast labyrinthine thing that spread over the world. Humanity was a hivemind—a chaotic hivemind, sure, but a hivemind anyway. When people got sick they logged onto the internet to see what they needed to do. When people needed to book appointments, they logged in and sent out an email. Communicate without seeing someone? A thousand ways to do that on the internet. It was almost like telepathy. Hell, if she wanted, she could login and order groceries… summon a car… It was almost like they were living in the future and everyone who participated was in danger of losing some vital connection with the Earth itself.

That was why she needed out of her self-induced prison. She knew that places had a feeling—knew that they breathed and lived on their own. She knew, too, that there was no way to touch that ephemeral feeling without being there. Something about the air itself, some vital energy in its background, needed to be experienced. It was part of some bigger cycle she had only intuited herself, some movement of energy, some exploration of place and person and living thing and nurturer. The world could only experience itself by interaction with that which walked across it.

It was a crazy thought, but it seemed harmless enough, so she hadn't thought to bring it up to her therapist. It was a belief, nonsensical perhaps, that made her want to go out and combat the paranoia that kept her locked up. It wouldn't do her any good to divest herself of it. It was one of those self-imposed little daydreams, some delusion.

She wondered how much one could learn if they listened to that gut feeling. She stirred the fire, watching the flames go down, and thought about the past again. A forest was one thing. A campground and a cemetery another. Of all the places she had thought to visit, some place like this—an old campsite, a place where the dead were literally waiting in the ground to her left, some mere feet away, set her nerves and made her clench her teeth now that she was alone. She knew she would likely be safe, but she wondered—fighting against that sealed feeling she had locked away so long ago in that attic apartment—if her father would have survived had he listened to the earth groan around them, like she had.

She knew that there was a tang in the air whenever the *thing* had drawn closer, all those years ago, and the thinking of it made her shudder. If her father had sensed that tang, that pull at his consciousness, would he still have survived?

The cool chill air of a South Dakota westerly breeze blew in across Bailey's neck, and she drew closer to the embers. She was stuck on the horns of a dilemma. The logs had burnt out to white coals, ash, with only a little bit of burnable wood left to power what flickering gouts came up here and there. She was out of wood—out of fuel. She could either sit here by the flames and watch her protection die out—for in her head the fire seemed safe enough, seemed light and bright enough to chase away any ideas Devin had put in her head about shadows and other things that slurched and yipped in the night—or she could trek out and find something, anything, to burn that would bring her protection back.

Here there was no grandmother to protect her and keep her safe, no yappy older sister, face in a constant purse of disapproval, forcing an impermeable divide between them. Here she was alone. Her friends were here, but they weren't with her, were they?

She breathed in and out. The flames were going to die either way. For now it was a matter of whether she wanted to be a sitting duck, or have some kind of control over her own life. She rose to her feet, brushing off her knees, stretching out limbs and toes that had fallen asleep as she crouched, eyes piercing the horizon for some dried enough bracken to keep the flame going. She could follow either set of friends—Jack and Missy were gone towards the schoolhouse, Devin and Lester off in the woods. There was no way she was going to put nails or two-by-fours in the fire, and as much as she wanted to give the boys some privacy she knew that the best place to find fallen branches would be further in the trees.

She headed off, cellphone in hand, its flash illuminating the ground at her feet and keeping her from tripping on mossy rocks and small bits of tangled undergrowth. There were no real footpaths here, like there were in some nature preserves she'd been to. Here it was wild, untamed. Devin and Lester had moved through the rushes and the stinging plants without harming anything.

A fallen-over tree looked dried and withered. Thanking her lucky stars, she maneuvered herself over to it and started breaking branches off it with her bare hands, feet on the trunk and heaving with all of her strength to snap them. After she'd gathered a decent enough pile, she stopped. Something was pulling at her, telling her to be quiet and listen.

She paused and tilted her head, moved her hair back behind her ears. The wind blew through the trees, and with it, the slight small muffled sound of moans came to her. Well, it *could have* been moans—from this far off, it was too muffled for her to understand what, exactly, she was listening to. But she had a bizarre feeling in her stomach. She was being told to run—run far, far away. And yet, she knew that if something had happened to one of her friends, she couldn't just leave them here.

A thick thrill of adventure came over her. Mixed with a rational voice.

"It's probably just the boys," she said quietly to herself. "They're having fun out here and nothing's wrong and you've spooked yourself the fuck out thinking about the past. Get a grip, grab the wood, and go back to the fire."

But still. An aching, nagging sense of responsibility rose up in her chest. She knew that if something had gone wrong and she did nothing, it would be another chapter in her history wherein she was a prisoner of her fate. She did not want to feel this isolated feeling any longer—no longer wanted to wallow in her suffering, to allow others to wallow in their own. Slowly, she creeped forward through the trees and found herself stepping ever-so-slowly through undergrowth and weeds until she found herself at the far edge of a barrier of trees surrounding another clearing.

Here she could hear them louder, the moans, and they sounded agonizing. It sounded like Lester. Knowing that she was probably just interrupting them, she dared not draw any closer. Still, though. She wasn't too knowledgeable about how all... *that*... functioned, but it didn't sound like Lester was enjoying himself, much if at all.

She was met with a horrible smell. It smelled like rotten mildew, like piss and shit, like stinking mattresses and the bottom of swamps dug up. Her intuition was telling her that this way lay danger; and if Lester was in the thick of it, well, she knew she would have to interfere.

She stepped forward. Closer. There was movement in the clearing, but it was almost too hard to see. Moonlight barely pierced the branches interlocked overhead.

"Hello?" Bailey called out, voice trembling in the breeze.

"Go... away..." she heard. It was an odd sound—a noise, a shaking sound, halfway between a throat growl and Devin's voice.

"Bailey?" Lester called, and he sounded like he was five years old and trying desperately to find his Mommy.

Bailey aimed her phone into the clearing, and clicked the brightest flash on a picture. What she saw, illuminated for half a second, stuck in her chest and made a scream want to rip out of her throat. She knew what she was seeing, even as her conscious mind struggled to process it—a sort of shock, she knew, one she was very familiar with.

For there was Lester, legs bent double over his head, eyes watering with pain and blood pooling from scratches on his face. What loomed over him was a horrible shaggy beast, with a white coat and elongated proportions, claws for hands, some tumescent snake-like thing disappearing in and out of the young man grunting below. Horns decked its head, and it groaned and bleated as it thrust.

"Bailey," she heard, in the dark. It was Lester. His eyes glittered in the light of the moon. "Run."

There was a horrible mumbling from him then—the sound of him babbling, babbling the words 'No, no, no, no, no' and a sickening gasp, as if for air. A crunch in the dark, and then no more noise, except for the horrible harsh bark of what sounded like a goat.

White hot panic rose in her throat, and she turned and ran back in the direction she thought she came from. Small trees whipped up from the ground around her to slap her in the thighs—branches she hadn't seen before loomed from the gloom to catch her hair and snag her. A few times she fell—always hearing the bleating and the rustling of the branches behind her. She found herself breaking through the treeline in an unfamiliar area—it was the other side of the broken down schoolhouse.

She banged with all her might on the closest door, body-slamming it, and it gave. She spilled inside, then turned around and surveyed the room around her. A huge looking bureau sat against the wall—she dragged it over, fingernails snagging and breaking, and felt something in her shoulders give. She screamed, using her arms to lock on and leaning backwards with all of her weight to knock the bureau over.

It was solid—heavy. It slammed to the ground in front of the door. Pausing momentarily for breath, she took in the other sights around her. A set of stairs on the opposite side of the room led up and away. She booked it up them, feeling the creak of the wooden beams beneath her feet.

Jack was fucking Missy in an abandoned room upstairs. Bailey wanted to laugh for a split second—was that what this was? And here Bailey was without anybody but a horny goat after her. Missy saw her first, sitting up and slapping Jack in the chest to stop.

"Bailey?" Missy asked. She sat up, pulling away, trying to cover herself. "What's wrong?"

"There's something out in the woods—" she babbled, turning and locking the door.

"I told you we shouldn't have left her alone," Missy said.

"No, you don't understand," Bailey said. She turned around and started pacing, grabbing around for something heavy on the table. She found an iron poker. "It was a goatman. The one they talk about here. There's legends of it. It was the same kind of thing that got my Dad."

"Bailey, honey, you're bonkers," Jack said, zipping himself up.

"It got Lester," Bailey practically shrieked, turning around and wielding the poker. "I'm not crazy!"

"Bailey, just calm down," Missy said. "We're here for you but we need you to put down the weapon."

There was a loud *CRASH* from downstairs, and a loud whooping bleat.

"That's *him!*" Bailey hissed.

Even Jack and Missy stared at each other before heading directly for the table to grab something else. Jack had a knife; Missy some kind of stool.

"I'll watch the door," he said. "You two hide. If whoever's after your tries to burst in through here, I'll do my best to gut him. Take any chance you can to run." He sighed and shook his head. "I don't want to die here."

The boards creaked outside the second floor landing. Breath was hushed in everyone's throats. The onwards creep and click of hooves on wood came closer and closer, and Jack hid himself to the left of the door.

"Remember what I said," Jack mouthed to them, from his hidden alcove.

The door slammed open. A wave of hot stink rushed out to greet them, and there it crouched, gleaming and proud, horrible erection hanging and covered in blood. Gore clung to its body here and there. Its eyes seemed to gleam crimson, and its elongated limbs swayed.

"I can smell you," the goat-thing said. "You smell almost as good as Mary. As Lester. I wonder how good you'll feel when I rip off your head and fuck it?"

Jack came from the side and slammed into the goat, who bleated in pain. The two of them struggled against the wall. Jack slammed the Goatman into the side of the door, and before she knew what happened the two had fallen, grappling with each other and punching and slashing wildly. Bailey grabbed Missy's hand, and the two of them hopped over the struggling tangle of limbs and booked it into the hallway.

Jack screamed. Bailey did not turn around, but Missy did—and she, too, let out a low and miserable wail. Bailey did the only thing she could think of—she headed up the next stairs to the tiny alcove of a belltower. These ones crawled up and around, in a tight series of concentric squares, until she was able to crawl, breathless, onto the roof. The tops of the trees greeted her eyesight. She wanted to do something—thought, perhaps, about grabbing onto one of the limbs and trying carefully to crawl in them, but it had been far too long since she'd scaled any trees at all. Her only hope was that whatever it was—and she had a strong, strong suspicion it was Devin—would think she'd done the smart thing and ran down to the ground floor.

She waited, breathless, trying not to make noise as she hyperventilated. But soon she heard pounding on the steps, and the goatman stepped forward from the belltower and met her on the roof.

"You knew right away," he said, voice croaking. "Didn't you? You've seen my kind before."

"Go away and leave me alone!" she said, holding out the poker.

He bleated in laughter. His eyes were red like the moon overhead, full and bright.

"I told you the story," he said. "I couldn't have made it more obvious if I'd tried. I wasn't going to kill Lester, but you really gave me no choice. One lonely little gay boy in the woods gets raped and everyone thinks it's been too long and he's making up stories. Witnesses, though? Those have to be taken care of. That's the way my people walk."

He stepped closer to her.

"I promise," he said. "I'll be a lot more gentle with you than I was with Jack and Missy. You might even enjoy it if you close your eyes. Of course, I'll beat you if you keep them closed."

Something swung, then, from the branches behind her. A wash of noxious fumes assaulted Bailey's nose, and she saw something blurry and furred drop in front of her. It looked like some kind of large ape—though it was bigger than Bailey had ever seen. It rushed forwards towards Devin, grabbing him with both hands. He bleated and scratched back at it, and soon the whirling struggle fell off the roof.

Bailey scrabbled to the side and looked down. The two were continuing to fight! She knew that whatever this smelly ape was, it was her savior, and it was now or never. She ran back to the belltower steps, and took the first flight down.

She was stopped short by the scene of carnage in front of her. A caped man in a bird mask was crouched down, staring intently at a pile of gore that Bailey realized was the splattered remains of Jack and Missy. With a sick feeling in her gut, Bailey sank to her knees, grabbing the wall to stop from falling and rushing forward past the new bizarre creature before her. She ran down another set of steps to the ground floor, peeking through the shattered remains of boarded-up windows at the fight happening before her.

The goatman and the ape were fighting, huge fists and talons smashing into one another. Bailey wasn't sure what to do—that weirdo on the steps above looked somehow even more frightening than the two monsters out front. A knot of anxiety bubbled up in her chest. She was literally stuck between a rock and a hard place. If she rushed out the door there was a chance that both monsters could grab her, but down here?

A voice curled up in her ear, and a touch of something metal against the lower side of her back froze her in place. She struggled to turn, and screamed.

The thing in the bird mask, eyes glowing with green flames, stared down at her. The gauntlet on its hand was spinning, but seemed to terminate abruptly at the wrists. It had no hands!

"Don't move," the hooded figure said, the words hissing through the mask like exhalations. The flickering green flames in its eyes had her in its grip, like she was hypnotized. "Move, and you're dead. Look outside."

"What are you going to do to me?" Bailey asked.

"Throw you out to those things out there if you keep talking," the voice hissed.

The ape-thing and the creature that was Devin rolled across the ground. Devin grabbed it by its shoulders, slamming its head into the ground, and sat up, long talons gleaming in the moonlight.

"You think you can take me on?" he screamed, and swiped.

Bailey looked away. Her savior was screaming… she could feel something in her chest, hot and raw, squirming...

"Shit," her captor said. Its green burning eyes turned to her, burning like flickering incandescence. "Stay here. Don't move. I'll come back for you."

He stepped forward and pushed against the door. He phased out, then, like he never existed at all, and she soon saw him reappear in front of the door.

She blinked, astonished.

He raised his gauntleted hand and the engravings on it glowed, setting in action a spinning motion. From the treeline, another hooded figure jumped down and landed, gleaming bow drawn, the metallic head of a nocked arrow pointed directly at the Goat-thing. Another hooded figure appeared, drawing two wickedly curved blades from holsters near its boots. They seemed to be aiming forward. Yet another hooded figure appeared—it slapped a hand against its breast, and a series of unfolded machinery expanded on and out from its robes, unfolding into what looked like a very complex humming laser beam. The four hooded figures were positioned in exactly a diamond formation, Bailey thought.

"Step away from the Sasquatch," the laser-beam wielder said.

Devin tossed his head back and roared into the night sky. Sleeping birds and bats flew from their nearby roosts, flapping into the night sky and away from danger. Bailey heard a 'ziiiip' noise, and suddenly where Devin's throat had been was now an arrow.

The monster slapped at the new breathing tube, clawing at it and snapping in half. Blood gushed from the wound, but it seemed to heal a moment later.

"Onto Plan B, then," the hooded figure with the bow said, shrugging.

The hooded figure with twin blades ran up and slashed, from down to up, right shoulder drawing the weapon upward, and Devin jumped back just in time to avoid being cut. The beast slashed forward, and the figure's other blade flew up and parried the talons away.

A pair of fingered claws slapped against the window pane in the door Bailey was staring out of, melting into a human index and middle finger before sliding down the pane. The Devin-creature held onto its paw, a startled noise coming out at first, before he struck out with a fist and slammed the figure with the blades backwards. It leaned in for one more severe strike, but a pulse of light poured forth through the air, sizzling as it hit flesh. Devin howled, choking. The figure with the blades rolled away to safety.

"It's time," the one without hands called out. Symbols flashed and glowed on the stump device on his wrists—too quick for Bailey to register—and then before she knew what was happening a concussive blast of pressure knocked the Goat-thing off its feet and onto its ass.

It seemed like each of its limbs was plastered to the ground, and glowing lines were wrapped around it. The hooded figure with the blades stepped forward and, with one quick movement, sliced Devin's head clean off its shoulders.

"Good riddance to bad trash," the laser beam figure said, and slapped his chest. His machinery folded itself back up, sticking on the ends. He sighed and started to fiddle with it.

"She'll be okay once I patch her up a bit," the one with the bow said, bent down on her knees and checking the barely-stirring... Sasquatch? Was that what the laser beam guy was saying?

Bailey clamped her hand over her mouth. Her friends were dead upstairs, and now the only one around her that wasn't a cultist or some other sort of freak had just been beheaded. Panic flew in her chest.

It did not help when the hooded man with the glowing eyes reappeared behind her, the cold metal of his stump wrists touching her, paralyzing her, yet again.

Bailey, despite herself, screamed. There was a hiss of air and a pinprick in her neck.

"Are you scared?" it asked. "Because we are."

And then Bailey remembered nothing but falling...

S.C.A.R.E.D.

ILLUSTRATION BY ANDREW PAPPAS

CHAPTER 15:

S.C.A.R.E.D.

Bailey awoke burrito-wrapped in a set of soft burgundy sheets in a four-poster bed to a throbbing in her skull and a scream in her throat. A hot knot of guilt sat waiting for her in her chest, and as the memories bobbed to the liquid surface of her mind she felt them unfolding slowly, one by one, little flowers of memory and pain that she knew she would never be able to forget.

Her friends, dead. Devin, beheaded. A group of—for all intents and purposes, *cultists*, had surrounded her. She'd passed out at some point. Exhaustion? Adrenaline? There was a small, insistent needling feeling at the back of her neck. She slid her hand up and around the knot. It felt like an insect bite. She'd never had an injection before on her neck—was that what it was? What were they going to do to her?

She quietly listened all around her. No noise, but muffled movement in the next room. She wasn't tied up or anything—a mercy, that, though she was in unfamiliar clothing. Clean clothing, at that. She'd tripped and fell in mud and undergrowth and probably blood at some point the night before. Whoever had taken her in was interested in keeping her healthy, at least.

A thousand and one possibilities entered her mind. Were they cultists? Were they kidnappers? Random people who just happened to be friends with a giant forest ape? That seemed the most unlikely of all.

She calmed her breathing, slowed down her mind, and focused on the world around her. There was a thrumming in the air and in the wood of the room she was in. She could feel whatever energy was here in the background. It was electric, static, humming, high-paced. It was the energy of a collective. High-energy people, with serious tasks to be done. She detected no malice in her vicinity. There was no acrid tang of a place that had grown resentful through abandonment. This place felt worn, lived-in, a place that had seen its fair share of use.

A monastery? She wondered. She opened her eyes. The four-poster bed was far too gaudy and sumptuous for a monastery. Unless she was some sort of virgin sacrifice, of course, and they were saving the best accommodations for their prized guest...

Still, the energy felt safe. She could sense something—something old, ancient, hidden, some wizened knowledge cloistered away by the rest of the building at its core. She had felt dark energy like that before—safe and contained. It was always walled-away rooms, old places where tragedies had been boxed up, boarded-up, and nailed-over. A restless sigh from rattling lungs and something that used to be friendly once that had lost all joy.

She did not dare focus on that energy. Wherever she was now, her only chance at escaping was to be on her toes. Obedient, compliant, whatever she had to do to make these people feel like she wasn't a threat anymore. And when she got her chance she'd hightail it away from here. Wherever *here* was.

She got to her feet, parting the curtains on the bed and toeing the ground first. Hardwood floors, immaculately taken care of. She scanned the room she was in. Against one wall, an oaken bureau, looking like it was from the turn of the previous century. Against another wall—a vanity, the mirror stained and frosted over from years of use. Here and there dust sat in corners untouched by any human hands. With a little bit of shock, she noticed that whoever had taken her had also grabbed her bag. And her friends' bags. These were piled in a corner in the far side of the room, next to a window.

The window was nailed shut. Beyond it, she could see a gorgeous dawn rising over a vast swathe of coniferous pines, an evergreen forest that was nondescript and empty of any familiar markers. If she managed to slip away, at least she would have the cover of the woods. But she thought again of Devin, of Lester's timid moans, of the snapping noise of his neck breaking, and she turned away from the window and drew the curtain.

Her friends' bags stared at her. How conscientious of them, she thought. Whoever had abducted her at least had the courtesy to bring her stuff with her. She crouched down and sorted through her suitcase. Most of her stuff was in here, but there were tell-tale signs that their stuff had all been gone through.

Searching for weapons, Bailey thought, which is what her plan had been in the first place. She knew there was a curling iron in her bag, or at least in Missy's bag, and emptying both of those out on the floor showed nothing remotely stabby, pokey, or burny left. The cell phones were gone, as were the chargers. Par for the course.

They'd thought this through then. Whatever this was. Of course, it was a likelihood that they were good guys. They had, after all, showed up when her friends were being eviscerated. Maybe they'd just got there too late? That forest ape sure seemed intent on taking Devin down... And anybody would be just as nervous as Bailey herself was. Maybe they were just protecting their own asses from someone who'd just seen her friends all die. That could cause even the most level-headed of people to snap, she thought.

Still. She grabbed a wire-lined bra and tested out its tensile strength. It stretched, the wire remaining obstinately strong. She snapped it again, like a belt, and then balled it up and shoved it in the surprisingly deep pockets of the pajamas they'd dressed her in. Worst case scenario she could use it to strangle someone in the hall, then slip away.

Someone had left slippers by the door. Bailey slowly tried them on. Only a little too big. They might be a liability if she had to run... but still. The floor was cold, and it wouldn't do to look like she was rubbing their hospitality in their face...

The door to the room opened easily and, mercifully, quietly. It opened into a hallway. Electric sconces, looking like old gas lamps, lit the dark hallway like small nightlights. Doors extended on in every direction. A light and some voices compelled her to turn to her left and see where her captors were. She tried to move as quietly as possible, tiptoeing and crouching against one wall.

There was a recliner right at the opening of the next room, where the hallway opened into a massive sitting room. The chair was old, luxuriously pleated and emerald. It also managed to provide her plenty of cover. From the angle she was at she could see three figures seated around a coffee table. A giant taxidermied grizzly was mounted in one corner; a grand piano was near it.

A man, a woman, and… Bailey's hands went to her nose. The other thing—the ape. Its odor was present even over here, on the other side of the room.

The ape grunted. It was massive—nearly seven feet tall, and hunched over while the woman picked up implements and worked on its back.

There was a snag, and the ape squirmed and growled.

"Sassy, quit being a baby!" the woman said. She was not wearing a head piece or a plague mask; rather, she was a severe-faced native woman with long, black pleated hair. She wore a white button-up blouse and a pair of jeans. Bailey could not see her feet from her vantage point. "If you don't let me stitch this up you're gonna be in even worse pain in the long run!"

"It'll be alright, you big gorilla," the man said. He was seated, legs crossed, in an armchair some ways away, staring into the fireplace, a morning cocktail in his... were those prosthetic hands? His voice was exuberant, greased at the edges, sounding a bit like a theatre performer, or perhaps a circus barker. "You did very, very good, Miss Sassy. Took care of that nasty Satyr, yes you did."

"It was more of a team effort," the woman said. She pulled the ape by its shoulder back to her. "Stop moving away, you're making this harder than it has to be."

"I think our girl did some fine work," the man said. "We should take her out to eat or something as a reward. Shave her down and dress her in a fine gown, get her a mani and a pedi. A night on the town with all of us as a team. It'd be brilliant."

"You're drunk," the woman said.

"Yes, well, there's nothing like liquor to erase the sight of the vivisected from one's mind," the man said. "I'm about to top this one up, would you like a Mimosa while I'm up?"

"I'm kinda busy," she said, holding up a needle. "I need to stay sober."

"I'm so glad I have someone as responsible as you on the team," the man said. "Makes it easier to delegate."

"I wish you would at least wait until the evening before you start drinking."

"It's always five somewhere, my dear," he said. "When do you think our little survivor will wake up?"

"No idea," the woman said. "I'll go check on her when I'm done here."

"Not many people go toe to toe with a Satyr and live to tell the tale," the man said. His prosthetic hands clamped and unclamped as he shook and mixed drinks. "I'll tell you, she's got something in her. Something brilliant. Brilliantly peculiar."

"You just have a soft spot for strays," the woman said.

"Perhaps," he said. "You know me, I've got a good nose for these kind of things."

"You're a regular Bosley. You're a Charles Xavier. You're a great Zordon," the woman said. She threaded another needle and started to hook it through flesh. "Okay, Sassy, almost done—" but suddenly the ape shrieked so loudly the glasses rattled. Bailey, shocked, jumped backwards from her hiding spot and banged into a cutlery cabinet.

The man and the woman both looked over at her.

"You're awake," the man said.

Bailey looked up from where she was sprawled on the floor.

"I'd offer you a hand, but I'm afraid I have none to give," he said, and his prosthetic clamper snapped once or twice.

She scrabbled to her feet.

"Okay," she said. "Level with me. Are you guys kidnappers or cultists?"

"Oh, the masks," the man said. "And your friends. Oh, I'm so terribly sorry, there must be some confusion here. My name is Randall Erickson."

"Bailey," Bailey replied.

"These two lovely ladies behind me are Mahpee and Sassy. Mahpee, you fat gorilla, say hi."

The human woman snorted.

"Fuck off, you pig," she said. "He's not normally like this. Only when he drinks."

"But I drink all the time," he said.

"I was trying to be nice but we really should have an intervention sometime soon," Mahpee said. "Sassy, say hi to Bailey. This is our new friend. We rescued her last night."

Sassy snorted, stretched, and lumbered to her feet. The stench of her fur was like a thick, feminine musk that swallowed Bailey alive. Bailey felt like a small animal in the eyes of some huge predator, and shrank back against one wall as the creature approached.

Gently, tenderly, Sassy's arms scooped her up and she felt a wet set of lips plant a very gorilla-like kiss on her forehead. She was sat back down even more gingerly.

"Oh my god," Bailey said.

Sassy lumbered with footsteps that shook the living room back over to Mahpee and assumed the stitching position again.

"Sassy's our dear friend and teammate," Randall said. "She's sort of the strong arm of the law. This is probably implied by her name, but she's a Sasquatch."

"Who are you people?" Bailey asked.

"We're part of a very special team," Randall said. "We're called S.C.A.R.E.D. It's an acronym—Society for Cryptozoological Analytical Research and Enigmatic Discernment."

"We're still arguing about that one," Mahpee said.

"Not much of an argument, is there? I'm the Boss."

"Yeah, well, as your underling, I have an obligation to tell you when I think things can be done better. I think it'd be better like 'Society for Closing Astral Rips and Eliminating Despair."

"Yes but that won't win any research grants," he said. "It's a bit arcane, don't you think? What's your opinion? Which one tells you more?"

"Well," Bailey said uncertainly. "Since I don't know what you do here then I don't know. What do you do?"

"We—" and here Randall paused. A dour look rose over his face. "We close astral rips and try to eliminate human despair. Okay, so I see it, but I still think it's lacking."

"Maybe start at the beginning," Bailey said.

"Long story short," Randall said. "You're standing in the former League of Magicians headquarters. Back in the day it was an illusionist's guild hall. To make an incredibly long story short, after making some hard decisions earlier in life I found myself face to face with a rather bizarre creature. A cryptid—a fabled monster whose existence is all but unknown and whispered amongst the tongues of men who are considered unreliable. Unfortunately for me, I was unable to sleep off the effects of my encounter, or write it off as some drunken hallucination. My hands were missing, as you can see."

Two prosthetic grippers spun on their axis.

"I decided I would do my darndest to study them. Soon, I found myself stumbling on a secret. Cryptids are so rarely seen because they are. How to put this? Interdimensional creatures. They come here from far away places that are overlaid with our own. They are drawn to human despair, human suffering, and certain astrological events—blood moons, for instance—allow them to pierce between the layers of reality and come tumbling through."

"Is that what Devin was?" Bailey asked.

"Devin?"

"The goat guy," Bailey said. "You sliced his head off. He was our friend until he turned."

"I don't think he was ever your friend," Randall said. "I have only fringe accounts, but shape-changers are definitely cryptids. They work a little different than most, but the blood moon allows them to access their true abilities. He seemed to be a Satyr. Nasty buggers, them. Greeks told tales of Satyrs—their monstrous lusts, their pining for human sex. They're not always dangerous, but it seems he was blooded and had done this a time or two before."

"Shit," Bailey mouthed, sotto voce. She gestured at the great ape in the room. "So is that what she is? A cryptid?"

"A Sasquatch, yes. Travelled here from far away, but she seems to be quite harmless. My studies are an ongoing struggle and we're collecting lots of data constantly. I use this mansion and our technology as research headquarters. We aren't quite the squeaky clean image of respectability as some of our team would like, however."

"I still think we need to make our focus on prevention instead of after-the-fact," Mahpee said, voice arced on the end. It seemed this was a conversation they'd had many times before.

"Are you saying my friends could have survived if you stepped in earlier?" Bailey asked.

"That's debatable," Randall said. "Cryptids are dangerous creatures, and the number of people who study them—ourselves, and ourselves alone, practically—are in limited supply. If we stepped in and overestimated our abilities, I would have dead teammates. Then any future issues could potentially become worse. We're a private operation here. Limited funds, even more limited staff. And I'm quite protective of my team. Given the same situation, wouldn't you make the same decision?"

Bailey thought about this for a moment.

"Yeah," she said. "But—my friends—"

She thought of Lester, whose only crime was looking for love and who had pulled her away from her dark quiet cave of seclusion. She thought of Jack, of Missy, of the times they had shared together, the sights they had seen, the stories they had shared.

The ache started in her chest and moved into her stomach, pulsating and dark. She was familiar with it—this feeling of loss, of someone never waking up, of someone never again being able to smile, at someone passing beyond the veil and just leaving! Somewhere.

Bailey fell to her knees, sobbing. Randall looked down at her, some strange, unknown emotion filling his face.

"Would you like to see them?" he asked.

"Randall!" Mahpee's voice was harsh, sharp, reaching across the room like a dagger.

"It won't be pleasant, but there may be some closure in it," he said. "We left their belongings with you. We have an incinerator on-site, in the second stratum of the basement. In case of bad accidents. It wouldn't do for the authorities to witness any of the attacks. Widespread knowledge of the deaths has a sort of way of attracting attention to them, and it builds up, causing more sightings. So it's best we just clean up the mess and pretend that whoever it was disappeared into the night."

Bailey considered this, grief raw in her chest.

"Show me," she said. "I need to see."

There was some sense of satisfaction in his eyes, then. She didn't know him well enough to know, but it was approval.

CHAPTER 16:

THE COMPOUND

There was an elevator at the far end of the hallway. It was one of those turn of the century style contraptions; a rickety clanking paternoster with a spring-folded door that looked, more than anything, like a freight elevator.

"You're sure, then?" Randall asked, voice serious.

Bailey nodded, unable to meet his eyes.

"Then down we go," he said.

The Victorian trappings of the house quickly faded away as the freight elevator made its creaking descent. Lower and lower—the walls stained in some areas with fluids she was not a fan of. She could feel her hair whipping up, wanting to stand on its ends from the updraft. After some time, a loud fan kicked on.

"Decontamination," Randall said. "Might want to hold your breath."

Steam blasted inwards at them. Bailey coughed.

"Just a concentrated vapor. Think e-cigarette juice made from white sage," Randall bellowed, over the noise.

They hit the ground floor, and the freight door retracted on its own.

"The true inner workings of S.C.A.R.E.D.," Randall said.

It was a huge compound that looked, more than anything, like a gigantic warehouse. She stepped inside and looked all around. Beat-up old cars, huge set displays, and other assorted minutiae was stacked here and there in gigantic piles. The smell of axel grease and old machinery came to her, alongside the smell of dust.

"A recent addition," Randall said. "It was the eighties and I was going through a Howard Hughes phase, convinced my only means for peace would be to live my life down here secluded from all people and things that crawl in the night. So I created this fabulous bunker. Unfortunately, there is a formula which dictates who can adequately live the sort of recluse fantasy I was after and I did not do the math. Most of my fortune had been drained just excavating the place." He paused. "And paying hush money to the survivors."

"Survivors?"

"Well, the workers I'd hired accidentally woke something up," Randall said. "Something as old as this place itself. Another Cryptid, I'm assuming. Thankfully I was able to capture it—no small feat—and subdue it. Its inanimate form is that of an egg. I'll have to show you sometime."

"You still have it?" Bailey asked.

"Well, it's not like I knew what to do with it," he said. "I can't exactly call the EPA, now can I?"

"So you just hold these things down here?" she asked.

"No, no, no," he said. "Back to my story. I realized at the end of it all, once we got the bloodstains out, that I'd basically made myself a large underground garage. I figured that digging a big enough hole wouldn't save me from the monsters, so the only sane thing to do would be to study them and see what would save me from them. Hence, S.C.A.R.E.D. was born. More or less. There were some bumps and hitches and questionable decision-making on my end here and there. But here we are."

"I can only imagine," Bailey said.

"Yes, well, onwards," he said, and tilted his head away from the garage. "The morgue is down this a-ways. Thankfully, I didn't have to have this portion installed. The League of Magicians had an incinerator down here already. It was trivial to revamp the space and outfit it with a few dissection tables and a walk-in freezer. Upgrading the furnace to a crematorium did make the contractors give me a few funny looks, but thankfully, that was what the crematorium was for."

Bailey turned to look at him, a piercing glare on her face.

"Ah, yes, a little gallows humor," he said. "When you've seen as many people die as I have, you start to lose your sensitivity about it. Forgive me my faux pas. Humor is one way to smother to death the violently nagging sensation that life is a cruel and meaningless joke played on you and you alone. Could you get the door? The passcode is 666. Oh, don't look at me like that, it's easy to remember. I keep asking Grim to put some kind of ID card in, on account of the old clip-clops—" and here his fingers buzzed and snapped. "But it's not really high on his list of priorities."

Bailey punched the number in, and the door buzzed loudly.

They walked inside.

There was a young man in there—older than Bailey, but much younger than Randall. He was all long limbs and bizarre, practically skeletal face. He had a headset made of complicated gadgets on his head and was looking through a magnified lens at, to Bailey's horror, the severed head of the Satyr she'd known in life as Devin.

"How apropos," Randall said. "Bailey, meet Grimm."

"Hey," the young man said. His teeth were crooked where he grinned. "Glad to see you're awake. Don't mind me. Just doing a few experiments on this sucker before we incinerate it. Watch, I think I almost triangulated the frequency we need to revert the transformation."

He waved a baton over the head. It buzzed, and the muscles in the face started to churn. Like liquid snakes under the skin were burrowing themselves in the flesh, the fur fell away and soon enough, the face reverted to that of Devin. The rocking motions of the head from its muscular contortions caused it to roll, one final loping slide, and before she knew it Devin's eyes stared straight at Bailey's.

Bailey couldn't help herself. Her gorge rose like a rocket and everything she'd eaten in the past twenty four hours started to come up. She turned to a nearby wastebin and held her hands over her mouth but before she knew it she was violently ill.

"A few manners, perhaps," Randall said.

"Ah, yeah, sorry," he said. "Forgot you mighta known this guy, right?"

She heard a loud 'thump' and turned to see him walking with another metal wastebin over to the far edge of the room. He sat the wastebin on the ground, turned a giant wheel, and a huge grate at the far end of the room opened. He chucked the contents of the wastebin inside. They hit the metal inside with a splat noise. He closed the giant grate again, then flipped a switch on. Bailey watched, unblinking, as flames began to lick up at the edges of the window.

"Show me my friends," she said.

"Darling, you've already lost your lunch, are you sure you don't need a lie down?" Randall asked.

Bailey felt something in her heart crack.

"Look," she said. "I'm not your darling. I'm a woman, and I might have my problems, but I've seen a lot. Yeah, maybe that—"and here she gestured at the wastebin filled with her earlier endeavor. "—happened. But I've seen way worse in my life. I need to see my friends. I need to know what happened to them."

Grimm nodded without saying much more, and walked to the far end of the room. He punched in another passcode, and then a blast of cold air greeted Bailey.

"Come in," he said.

She walked to the threshold, staring at her hands, and then stepped across and looked up.

Someone had arranged them to at least look like they were sleeping. Faces and toes were sticking out from under blue surgical sheets. Grimm stood at the edge of the walk-in, a silent specter. Bailey walked around each of the slabs, fingers touching the edges of the marble, lifting here and there to stroke hair or pat on sternums. She tried not to notice how Lester's neck was bruised and twisted, how a neckbone jutted from broken skin, mottled purple from his last mistake. She tried not to feel how Missy's sternum sagged, how the sheets clung to exposed viscera, how Jack's normally cocoa skin was now pale and purple.

She made figure eights around them all slowly, one step after another, as if a nun making her daily prayer walk, and after she'd done this three times for each slab she stopped at the far end.

"You can lock up now, I'm finished," she said, and walked out. She did not look back.

Her hair was in her eyes, and her head was down. Her fingers twitched at her sides. Randall and Grimm locked eyes with each other. When Grimm locked up the walk-in, she nodded her head once, then walked over to the furnace at the far end of the room. She stared inside the window for some time, quietly.

"And you're sure that he won't come back?" she asked.

"Not when he's ashes," Grimm said. "Or headless, besides."

"Good. I'd like to sit here for a bit, if you don't mind."

Grimm dragged her a chair, throwing worried glances at Randall, and Bailey sat down in it, line of sight directly on the flames. From the side, he could see her eyes gleaming, bouncing the flames back off of them.

An hour passed. Randall rang someone for coffee. The three of them sat there until the incinerator died down.

"How do I turn it on again?" she asked.

"I don't think—" Grimm started, but Randall held a prosthetic clapper over his mouth.

"Show her," Randall said.

Grimm nodded, scurrying over and showing Bailey which knob to press and what time to put it on.

"Just like an easy bake oven," she said, and there was something in her voice that chilled the other men to the bone.

She sat there again for another hour, two, three. When the flames died down this time, she got up and faced the men again. Her hair was in her face, occluding her eyes.

"Thank you," she said. She brushed her hair back over her face. There was a single tear that had drizzled its way down to her chin. Her face was dried, almost burnt red, but her eyes glowed with something almost dangerous. "Show me."

"Show you what?" Grimm asked.

"Show me how to kill those things," she said.

The furnace erupted behind her, one final hurrah.

CHAPTER 17:

TRICKS OF THE TRADE

"Perhaps it's best for some sleep, wouldn't you think?" Randall said. "Got a lot to cover, and today's been a pretty big day. Don't want to have to explain anything twice. Spoils my appetite."

Bailey nodded, and they walked as a group back to the elevator in the basement.

She fell asleep after staring at the canopy of her four-poster for hours. The fabric seemed to be a million pieces, individual fibers the lot of them, and she wondered if there weren't a way to reach in and pluck a single strand out—to collapse the whole thing at once.

She did not dream—a mercy for her when she awoke. There were memories enough inside her head, in the blank spaces when she closed her eyes.

The smell of something pungent carried to her; her stomach's loud, insistent growling was the only thing that caused her to finally move. She wasn't sure how she felt to be honest—there was a numb shock in her, a dreaded silence and a feeling of something at the edges of her consciousness. The old pull of depression tugged at her bellybutton, drawing her back to the safety of her covers. It fought with the red specter of death that haunted her heart. It was not sadness-not yet, because there hadn't been enough time to even understand what was or wasn't real. It was only certainty, certainty mixed with ire. This was no normal ire—it was the bilious black hatred of countless alchemical texts that yearned with a solid hate to utterly, savagely destroy all whom had done this monstrous act. And still, confusion—a bright blue cloud, a swarm of insistent yippings at her that something had been done, that there was no more need for her anger because the punishment had already happened.

Her stomach growled again, and soon she stumbled to her feet, off and away towards the sound of noise some corridors down.

She burst through a set of double doors to a large dining room. Faces turned towards her, quiet conversations coming to a stop. Mounted heads of various creatures decked the oaken walls, staring down at the lot of them as if some macabre hunting trophy display. Bailey wouldn't be surprised if it was, knowing some of them as briefly as she had.

Everyone she'd seen so far in the compound was seated at the long table. Randall was at the head, hunched over a sippy straw. Sky and Sassy sat at his left side. Across from them, Grimm and an unknown girl were seated together. She looked—well, Bailey wasn't sure how to say it. Asian. She had long, black hair down to her shoulders. Bailey hadn't done a count, but this was the amount of cloaked people she'd seen the other night.

"So this rounds out the crew?" Bailey asked. "Staff breakfast?"

"We've got one or two on away missions," Randall said. "This'll be a good start, though. Everyone, this is Bailey."

A chorus of greetings back.

"I haven't met her yet," the unknown girl said. She got up, came around the table, and wrapped Bailey in a giant hug. Bailey could feel herself shrink down. Body contact, this close? Somehow that was more terrifying than anything she'd seen in the past forty-eight hours.

The girl withdrew her arms. "I'm Addy."

"Bailey," she said, extending her hand.

They shook, and Bailey knew it was as awkward as she'd ever been in her life. Still, Addy seemed friendly enough; and Bailey got invited to sit next to her, which she gladly took over sitting next to the considerably smelly bulk of Sassy.

"What are we eating?" Bailey asked.

Two double doors that led away into an anterior kitchen swung open, and a gnarled-looking old woman with a considerable hunch limped her way into the room, a covered platter in one outstretched hand. She was so old, however, and so gnarled, that she seemed very nearly a living troll, with skin the color of a chestnut. Her hair was pale yellow, and her big, swollen eyes put one in mind of some Disney-esque caricature of a witch.

"Ah, Barbary," Randall said. "What's to be this morning's course?"

"Leftovers from last night," she cackled. "Goat curry!"

Bailey felt her stomach churn. She thought about last night—hadn't she been standing near the incinerator, watching his bones turn into ash?

"That was a tasteless joke last night, and it's even more tasteless this morning. As I'm sure this dish will be."

"You handless pile of garbage," Barbary shrieked. She tossed the plate in front of him with some force, causing his glasses to shake but ultimately settle back down. "Go wipe your own ass!"

"I wish I had fingers, if only so I can purge this pig-slop you call cooking. Perhaps it'll taste better the second time around."

"It's a wonder your wife left you, you charming old ponce."

Barbary slammed her way back into the kitchen.

"Someone want to do the honors?" Randall asked, pinching his clopper sadly.

Sky bent over and lifted the lid. A huge ceramic serving platter of what looked like the worst gruel known to mankind sat and burbled like a gray swamp.

"Miss Barbary," Randall called out. "Can you please bring out the revolver? I'd rather shoot myself than eat this. Some butter and salt will work if you'd rather watch me die painfully."

Bailey looked over at Addy.

"They recently went through a rather difficult breakup," Addy whispered.

"Randall and *her*?" Bailey asked.

"She's not always like this," Addy said. "Barbary's a *rusalka*. Normally she could win a beauty contest, and her cooking used to be divine. But ever since they had a falling out it's been gruel and cruel jokes. It's a real Dr. Jekyl/Mrs. Hyde thing."

"What did they fight over?"

"You didn't hear this from me, but I heard that he watched the latest episode of Gilmore Girls without her."

"That bastard," Bailey said.

Addy shrugged and nodded, as if to say, he should have known.

"He won't apologize, either," Addy said. "Won't even admit that it was a dick thing to do."

Bailey shook her head. Somehow getting lost in the little things helped. What it helped, she wasn't sure. A little inkling of a suspicion in her heart told her it was mostly an act—that sort of dramatic flair people can have at first, a dazzling first impression. Randall struck her as a showsman. How else could you sign people up to be expendable soldiers in a war against the unknown?

After breakfast, Randall, Grimm, and Addy walked with Bailey down to the basement elevator again.

"We'll start your training today, though a good portion of this program is going to be merely educational for the first week or so. I need you sharp—no, perhaps sharper—than you've ever been before. Do you have any experience with weaponry?"

"Uh," Bailey said.

The elevator sage-vapor washed over them.

"I'll take that as a no. Martial arts training?"

"I was a yellow belt in karate," she said. "In third grade."

"Have you practiced since then?"

Another puff of vapor washed over them.

"I'll take that as a no. We'll have you work with Eric when he comes back. Unless, of course, you're more inclined to learn from Grimm or I. We each have our own unique means of combat, I'm afraid. Alright, then. Any survival skills?"

"I could probably live in the woods near a river for a week before I drowned myself out of boredom."

"Alright, then. Anything else?"

"Ah—" she said. "Well. No, no not really."

"Nothing unique about you that stands out? No hidden techniques, no certificates, former employment skills? At this point we'd even take on a cook if Barbary doesn't get over herself."

"I'm pretty good on the computer," Bailey said. "Also. Gosh, I don't even know why I'm saying this, it's gonna sound so stupid. I guess it's not stupid in a world where goatmen exist. I can sort of. Feel out the earth. The energy of a place."

"Is that so?" Randall asked. His eyes seemed to flash. "You and I and Eric will need to put our heads together and do some experimenting at some point. Well, you've heard the basics of what we do. Onto the nuts and bolts. A tour of the Warehouse proper, I suppose I should say. You are interested in the pursuit and study of these creatures, as you indicated last night?"

"If you'll tell me how to kill them, then yes," she said.

"A bit bloodthirsty, are you? Can't say I disapprove. Though I wonder if perhaps your enthusiasm may be something to watch going forward. Hmmm."

The elevator clanked to a stop, and the four of them stepped into the Warehouse. Their first stop was a wire-cage area, filled with gadgets, a vast computer screen, and tools of nearly every size hung with no apparent sense behind their arrangement.

"This is my office," Grimm said.

"This place is a mess," Randall said. He made a face at the far wall. "Good lord, what on earth is that nailed to your corkboard?"

Grimm grinned, then took two huge steps to the wall. He pulled something out—Bailey saw dull iron and then watched in horror as he twirled the thing on it in a circle, like an olive impaled on some sort of giant plastic drink sword. Sparkling glitter puffed from the thing's desiccated wings. A tiny face with an even tinier tongue hung out like a dry mini-raisin.

"Is that a fairy?" Bailey asked.

"Pixies, to be precise," Randall said. "And, deadly nuisance that they are, this is still a macabre display, Grimm. Don't you have some kind of glass box or dehydrator you can use?"

"Don't want to stink it up," Grimm said. "I had to get this stuff dried, and honestly. This seemed like the best way to do it. I tested some of the powder out already on a few of the smaller ones. Seems to work."

"What powder?" Addy asked.

"Grimm has this asinine idea that pixie dust will paralyze most cryptids," Randall said.

"And pixie dust is?" Bailey asked.

"It's like moths and butterflies," Grimm said. "Look. Their wings have these delicate scales—so delicate it resembles a powder—that assists with lift and, well, whatever other functions a pixie's biology has. I know for sure that it can cause a sedative effect on human beings. Pixies, despite their size, are pretty much left alone by other predators and cryptids. My theory was that there was a Cryptid-specific toxin on their wings that assisted them being kept alive in whatever weird ecosystem they come from. So, the basic goal is we capture and kill a few pixies, grind up their wings, and see what their powder does when applied to cryptids, for instance."

"As confident as you are, you have to understand that this is a dangerous and foolhardy endeavor," Randall said. "You know how bloodthirsty these things are. If their powder worked like you claim it does, they'd dominate the foodchain. They're agile, intelligent, have digits, language, and a fierceness that's quite frightening. The ability to paralyze bigger cryptids would make them kings. Instead, they spend their time in trees and darting about."

"Well, when this works out the way I know it will, you'll owe me a big fat apology," Grimm said. "And a pay-raise. Five extra dollars an hour."

"Deal," Randall said. "Let's make our way to the Zoo, please."

They walked further on. This part of the Warehouse stank. Cages upon cages, aquariums upon aquariums. Everywhere they walked there was something new staring out of a cage or an enclosure at them. Some glittering bit of eye, something with too many teeth, too much nails, or a tendency to literally fade into the shadows…

"This is our Zoology Lab. One part museum, one part living zoo, one part scientific experiment. I got the stray hair to capture some of the less aggressive cryptids and house them here some years ago. Well, we started with the dangerous ones, too, at first. Lost quite a few men during that series of debacles. Figured it wasn't worth the hassle for live captures on ones deemed a threat after so many times of trying, so now we just get the fluffy bunnies. So to speak."

A big fat rabbit, albino with red eyes, was staring at Bailey. There was something about it that compelled her to draw closer to it. She reached a hesitant hand out, an incessant voice in her head screaming 'PET THE RABBIT,' and before she had reached her second knuckle through the gates a hand on her elbow pulled her hand out of the way. She turned and found Addy pulling at her.

"It almost got you," she said, pointing.

Bailey turned back around. Where before there was a beautiful white rabbit, now a toad-like thing, as if a rabbit whose fur had cankered away stood in its place. Goblinoid skin, cankered and sore and raw-looking, green as mildew met her gaze, alongside cat-slit eyes. It opened its mouth, and a small snapping tongue clamped at the bars. It hissed as it hit the metal.

"What on earth is that?"

"Grimm calls it 'Bunnicula,' but it's a vampiric mole hare."

"It sure looks like a mole," Bailey said.

"It has a short-range glamour and usually tricks its prey into thinking it's an easy meal. Very nasty things. One little nip and you would have been infected."

"What, it would make me into a vampire?"

"No, no," Addy said. "You'd get MPV if your body didn't fight it off. Mole Papilloma Virus. Your skin would basically look like its skin, give or take the color."

"Ugh," Bailey said. "And this is one of the less-dangerous ones?"

"Yup," Grimm said. "Keep your arms and legs inside the car at all times, ladies and gentlemen."

"What about Sassy?" Bailey asked. "She doesn't seem threatening."

"We have a couple of cute ones here and there," Randall said. "Sassy in particular is one of the good ones. She's very kind. Not driven by base instinct, and not particularly malevolent. There's a five-legged dog around here somewhere, but he sort of comes and goes as he pleases."

"We call him Spot," Grimm said. "As in, can you spot him? Where'd that wet spot come from? You can't keep him in a cage, he just sort of blinks through it and out the other side."

"What about your wife?" Bailey asked.

"Barbary is what she is, and I shan't say a word against her. But honestly, that she-devil confounds me at times."

"You shouldn't have watched her show," Addy said.

"Yes, well, she told me I could!"

"What were the words she said?"

"She said 'Go ahead, I don't care.' And crossed her arms over her chest."

Bailey shook her head.

"That was a trap," she said.

"I know that now," Randall hissed, peevishly. "Shall we continue on with our work? We still have equipment fitting to get to."

Bailey nodded, and they continued on.

The hallway was lined with masks on every side—terrible-looking bird masks, hanging from hooks, with old-school rubber-and-trenchcoat suits.

"So what's with the masks?" Bailey asked.

"Plague doctor's masks," Randall said. "Originally, the Plague Mask was used to deter the smell of sickness. Medieval physicans believed that bad odors carried sickness with them—when the Black Plague took Europe by storm in the 14th century, it wiped out a good fifty percent of the populace. Roving physicians dedicated to treating the ill outfitted themselves with these masks. They stuffed the beaklike protuberances with heavy spices, pleasing scents, to avoid the smell of the dead."

"Why do you have them here?"

"Think of them as a historical archive," he said. "This Mansion was the former head of the League of Magicians. Early operations usually required some similar gear."

At the end of the hallway was a door, with another punch-code password. Grimm entered some numbers and the overhead lights flickered on. More vapor hissed down from the doorway as they entered. This room was made of mirrors and silver metal. A row of eight costumes hung in rows on each wall. Cybernetic plague masks, with emblems emblazoned on each one, stared out at nothing. These were the suits, then.

"Addy, could you take our new friend's measurements?" Grimm asked.

She nodded, and pulled some measuring tape from a toolbox in the far corner. Bailey posed as Addy asked her to.

"So what are these suits for?" Bailey asked.

Grimm grinned.

"We updated a lot of the older, more ceremonial stuff. Here, look."

He pulled down a mask with a wolf emblem from the wall. Before her eyes he twisted and pulled at parts of the mask. The front mouth-piece came off, then the eye compartments opened.

"Just gonna go over this a bit at a time," he said. "This is the glossary stuff, really. So here we have detachable mouth-piece. I hate putting it all here, but it's interchangeable in case any parts get knocked off. And the connections are done with interlocking earth magnets. That sucker ain't flying off your mask for nobody. Note here the beak. This is a three-in-one compartment. Here we have an air filter—a stench filter, really. Think of it like an emergency respirator. Some of these cryptids stink. And it's not just a stink, it can have an adverse reaction on the human nervous or respiratory system. You know. Fungal spores, mold, the like. Behind that is the two-part emitter. It has two settings—one is a basic clicker setting. Consider it like echolocation. Its calculations connect to the HUD in your lenses up top and it can help you react quicker to Pulses of Crimson."

"Pulses of Crimson?"

"An energy source—sort of halfway between a wave and a frequency. It's similar to electricity, from a biological and etheric standpoint. What I'm saying is. It's kind of like a chi pulse, or a cryptid detector. There's theories and such."

"It's despair," Randall said. "Despair is a. Ah, what's the word? A putrid force emanating from all A-Holes."

"He means Astral Rips," Addy whispered, from her hemline.

Bailey nodded.

"Human suffering causes Despair to leak from them. It's like a pheromone–a drug, a lifeblood. Human suffering is like the sweetest of candies to the more malevolent cryptids. Despair is what they're made of—what pours forth from an Astral Rip. And you know what they say. Misery loves company. The more Pulses of Crimson—the more Despair comes from someone, the more likely they are to be a target."

"Now would probably be a good time to tangent into her past," Grimm said.

"Oh," Addy said. She got back to her feet and dusted her hands and knees off. "We've been watching you for some time."

"Oh?" Bailey asked. "Like, my channel?"

"More or less," Addy said.

"We have a system that can track Despair," Randall said.

"Pulses of Crimson," Grimm said, voice pointed.

Randall rolled his eyes.

"You've been on our radar for a while. Your obsession with details on Cryptids is something we've never seen before. Your little podcast or whatever is quite a hit around here. We heard your last video—saw some of the comments, and where you said you'd be going for your next trip. We've had Eric—Gray Wolf, perhaps, I should say—following you since you hit South Dakota's border."

"Did he know? Did any of you know about Devin?"

"No," Randall said. "We just wanted to protect you, and this place can be Cryptid Headquarters sometimes. I had a suspicion about you, and it turned out to be right. Don't be alarmed when I say this, but I believe you are a Beacon."

"A Beacon?"

"There's no proof behind that," Grimm said. "She wouldn't have survived to this age if she were."

"We can analyze her," Randall said. "Right here and now."

"Woah," she said. "I'm right here you guys. Explain to me what a beacon is."

"Beacons are. The perpetually unlucky. Birthed under a cursed star, they are destined from their youth to have a hard life. One filled with accidents, untimeliness, and despair. Tell me, how was your childhood?"

"My Dad died when I was younger," Bailey said. "I've been housebound ever since."

"And how did he die?"

Bailey bit her lip.

"It was something like Devin," she said. "One of those creatures."

"That's exactly what I thought," Randall said. "Oh, you poor girl. You hid away from the public because you could sense it wasn't safe. Am I right?"

"The earth talked to me," she replied. "Places spoke to me. I could tell where I would be safe, where I wouldn't be."

"And yet another cloistered orphan has been delivered into my graspless grasp," Randall said, staring heavenwards. "I knew there was something special about you. We'll just have to get you trained up, then. Alter your fate."

"Excuse me," Grimm said. "I'm about done with this nonsense in my lab. Are we gonna continue the lecture on keeping her safe, or are we going to get another astrology lesson?"

Randall pursed his lips and tilted his head in deference.

"By all means, continue," he said.

Grimm nodded, bushy eyebrows furrowed, and then continued dismantling a helmet.

"Okay. Where were we... Stink filter, and the Despair Emitter. Third thing—you click the Despair Emitter over and it becomes a two-wave radio communication uplink. The third click lets you talk through your mouthpiece. The fourth click is the Cryptid Caller, which is sort of the opposite of your echolocation. Lets you try and communicate with them. Useful for a ton of stuff, especially distraction during battle. All of that is connected to a lenticular HUD that overlays your Blood Moon lenses. The lenses have a special light filter that allows you to more easily see both Astral Rips and Cryptids, as they are not often revealed without the Blood Moon being present. The faceplate itself is made of titanium and is for all intents and purposes invulnerable to bullets. We have a unified cryptid database based on the old classic Mortimer Miles' piece we call the Cryptid Compendium—it's one part AI battle analysis program, one part upload link. It takes in data from the battle around you, and interfaces with your suit and the neural network in your helmet to provide more effective strategy. It gives you a bit of an edge in battle, is what I'm saying—makes you more lithe, more capable of movement. This uplink also allows you to modify power supply to any technical add-ons or parts of your suit."

"This sounds really sophisticated," Bailey said. "Like piloting a Gundam or something."

"Just a batmobile inside a bat-mask," Grimm said. "You'll get the hang of it sooner or later. The suits—well, there's a lot of them. It just depends on your specialties. And since we don't know what your combat ability is likely to be, the most we can do is get you some basic protection for now."

"I think I have an idea," Randall said. "Bailey, my dear. Take me to it."

"What?" she asked.

He gazed at her with intensity in his manic eyes.

"Take me to it. Without me telling you what it is, I need you to take me to it. Right now."

"How can I take you to something if I don't know what that thing is?"

"Consider it a test of your survival skills," he said. "The ancient mystics called this ability to sense things 'dowsing,' though I believe your ability is a bit more advanced than finding water. Take me to the most important thing in this building. You have five minutes."

Bailey blinked. Her chest was pounding. She closed her eyes. Addy and Grimm were protesting behind her; behind her eyes the noise of them faded to static, faded away, and soon all she could feel was the vast emptiness of the room around her and the thrumming, humming pulse of the Thing.

It was big. Powerful. Celestial, practically, she thought. She opened her eyes—she could feel where it was, could see the trail practically extending in front of her as she took off into a run. She heard voices behind her as she turned a corner, then another one. A flight of stairs behind a door extended her down into the darkness of yet another sub-basement below. She took off down step after creaky step, using her mind to see.

Lights flashed behind her—green and blue pulses like headlights illuminating the mildew-stained brick around her as her teammates clambered after her. She passed down and around, another tight circle in a long hallway, and when she finally got to the end she put both hands on the metal vault door.

She panted, catching her breath. Whatever it was behind here was calling to her, calling to her in drum beats, pounding louder and louder. There was a sound at her shoulder, and she turned in the gloom.

Randall's beaked mask stared at her. She could see his eyes through his lenses, see his clompers as they reached out to the vault door. Another hiss and a rush of sage-vapor; the creaking of the deadbolts opening one by one was practically torturous.

"You've passed, Bailey," Randall said. "This is It."

"It's vile," she said. "I don't trust it."

"As well you shouldn't," he said. "This is the source of our power—The Lantern."

It was wired up in a Tesla Coil, crimson energy pulsing from its glass panes like mist spraying from the shore. The energy was being drawn up through the coil, spinning as it went on and away into some higher part of the building.

"What is it?" she asked.

"Light collected from a full Lunar Eclipse. Of course there's more to it—more in it. But this is the source of my power. The arcane might I off-handedly wield. You, not knowing what it was, led me to it. Which makes me believe you are the one to follow in my path."

"And what path is that?" Bailey asked.

"The path of the Magician," Randall said. "Or rather, yours would be the Shaman. Perhaps."

"And what does that mean?"

"That means in the darkest of nights you'll always know the way," Randall said.

And wasn't it a curious thing, Bailey thought, feeling the evilness of this thing washing against her skin. Was this not the same crimson specter that hung over her, burning her from inside as she watched her tormentor's remains turn ablaze? Was this not something she, too, could call from—some vast effective anger, some unfiltered spring that could wind its way around her fingers and ensnarl her enemies in its embrace?

And she turned, after some time of watching its crimson flames churn, though it was not without some struggle.

WENDIGO/WHEREDIGO?

ILLUSTRATION BY ANDREW PAPPAS

CHAPTER 18:

WHEREDIGO?

Bailey met Eric—Gray Wolf—that evening, leaning over Addy at the banquet hall. He was tall—handsome—and utterly mysterious, with bronze skin and short-cropped black hair. Of everyone he spoke the lowest and the least. He seemed to be on familiar, if not friendly terms with everyone, and introduced himself shortly after everyone ate.

"Nice to finally meet face to face," he said to Bailey. "I watched you and your friends for some number of days. I grew very fond of you all. I'm sorry to hear about what happened."

Bailey nodded. The old ache in her chest throbbed. Her friends were something she hadn't forgotten about, but in the swirl of everything new and shiny she felt a hint of remorse that she hadn't been thinking about them. What would their families do? She wondered. Who could she even tell? Would they even believe her? She knew her sister wouldn't. Her sister would just lock her up in an insane asylum and tell her to get off the internet.

Eric scanned her. His soulful eyes were like black orbs analyzing everything about her. And yet, there was a softness to his gaze.

"What can you do?" he asked her, after a few moments.

Bailey thought on this for some time.

"I'm good with computers," she said.

"She's great at Dowsing," Randall said. "She says she can listen to the earth beneath her feet."

Eric nodded.

"Your training begins after dinner," he said. "Eat enough to energize you, but not enough to slow you down. We'll suit up, you and I, and head out into the woods."

Bailey felt a small sense of trepidation bloom.

"Already?" she asked.

"I did tell her the first week would be primarily educational," Randall said.

"I happen to believe, as my Grandfather did before me, that the best education is hands-on. What use is theory if she's not acclimated to danger?"

"No direct skirmishes," Randall snapped. "Nothing dangerous. She's a very useful find, and I'll not see you get her eaten on her first night out."

"No battles today," Eric said. He turned to Bailey. "My primary talent is tracking. I was taught how to move through blades of grass like a serpent by my grandfather, and blend into a crowd, or even nature itself. The nature of my training—and this phase of your training, going forward—is going to be that of intel gathering. We move as specters, silently slipping in and out of precarious situations. When we find a creature, we mark its location, analyze it for any potential weaknesses, upload the information we find to the central algorithm, and withdraw. We do not engage. Do you understand?"

Bailey felt a part of her insides twist up and recoil, snapping, like a snake.

"The whole point of this is to kill those things," she said, and her own hostility surprised her.

"We have a process in place for a reason," Eric said. "We all have our talents and strengths. That's part of what makes this team work. We each have our own part to play."

Bailey closed her eyes and nodded, and then, after a moment of steady breathing, nodded. She could see the sense in it, even if she didn't like it.

"Good," the older man said. "Suit up and meet me by the old willow at the front of the building when you're done."

And then he was off, shrinking around the corner like a flittering shadow.

"He knows what he's talking about," Addy said to her. "If anyone can teach you tracking, it's him."

Bailey nodded, but she wasn't happy.

An unpleasant half hour later, (fitting into her temporary plague suit after dinner required a bit of talcum powder and a lot of praying,) she was nearly ready.

"Look at her," Grimm said. "Our little girl, all grown."

Skye nodded with approval.

"Here," she said. "This is not yours, but for now, it's the only one we have available. But it served very useful in its time."

She reverentially handed a mask over. It had the visage of a straight-beaked bird on it, a small icon on the side.

Skye and Grimm looked at her with a certain sense of satisfaction, and then one of them broke the silence.

"Okay. Eric's waiting," Skye said, after a moment or two.

Bailey nodded and turned. It felt almost like the two of them were looking through her, past her, and at someone else…

She was finally outdoors, for the first time in what felt like forever. The smell of the forest outside the mansion was thick and heavy—rotted plant growth, the smell of fertilizer wafting from the drooping rose bushes. The faintly estrogen-heavy musk of Sassy's presence in the past twenty-four hours was a mere piquant spritz in the breeze.

Eric was there where he said he'd be, helmet tucked under one arm, leaning against the towering willow's trunk and picking his nails. He seemed to be staring off into the horizon. From where they were situated, it looked like the Manor was on a sheer cliff's edge overlooking a rolling valley of evergreen forest that was shaped like a giant bowl. Far, far off, Bailey could see what looked like carven pathways into the ground, and a winding car trail that zigzagged erratically through this particular part of the Hills.

"You ready?" he asked, at her footfalls.

She grunted out a yes, taken slightly aback that he'd heard her. She had been trying to sneak up on him, too…

"Randall told me you can Dowse," Eric said, when she drew level with him.

"He asked me to find something important, and I did," Bailey said.

Eric nodded, continuing to look at the forest in silence for some time.

"I use physical tracks," he said. "Physical tells. Droppings, bent branches, tracks. I think I've found the leavings of an old, old foe, and his handiwork. I could probably track him myself, but consider this a training exercise. I'll bring us to where I found his tracks. You can take us from there."

Bailey nodded, uncertainty on her face. She said nothing; neither did Eric. He did not seem to be one who felt the need to fill silences. Bailey was not, either. They stared at the horizon for some time.

"These are the Black Hills," Eric said, pointing out at the ocean of trees before them. "One part, at least. This embankment we're on looks high up, but there's a gentle path by that root. We can make it down by foot. It's about six hundred yards to the spot I found. How good are you at hiking?"

"Well, I *was* a shut-in," she said. "Most of my exercise was from my desk to the fridge."

Eric said nothing, and Bailey blushed at watching her attempt at humor splatter against the brick wall of his personality.

"The Moon is ill-positioned," he said.

She looked up at it. Was it waxing, waning? She wasn't sure. It was a thin half-wedge.

"Is that bad?"

Eric said nothing.

"It is," he said. "Come. Move quietly. Walk on your in-step. Let not the wind know of your passing."

And he took off in a light jog to the edge, near a root, and turned onto an unseen footpath and down below.

"Jesus," Bailey said, leaning forward and jogging after him.

She was rather hoping that killing Cryptids had less running, if she were being honest with herself…

The old man with the eyepatch had not had anything to do in some time. He spent his days lazing around, listening to the sounds of the creatures in the forest, shuffling around aimlessly, occasionally driving to the edges of the state. As if he were a firefly, he was drawn to suffering, but it sure seemed in short supply as of late…

A sense of ennui had settled over him. The ins and outs of existence were boring after all this time alive. The modern world held no thrills or surprises, save the occasional blood moon, or his stumbling over a rip in the world. He had heard the whisper, so long ago, tell him to bide his time. How many years had that been now? Time seemed to pass in an inordinately dull fashion.

He'd had a big lunch, so he had passed out in his truck, amidst the refuse. His blood sugar was off—he knew it was something he needed to get checked, but what was the point? It wasn't as if anything could touch him, really…

The warm sunlight soaked him to his bones, and when it became too much he sat up and belched, staring out the grimed window, knocking food wrappers into the floorboard and anticipating another boring stretch of a day.

But then a voice in his ear was whispering sweet nothings to him. He jerked straight in his seat to attention, a gnarled, wizened old man, graying hair frizzed and matted. The inside of his truck was near rusted out, with the leather seat cushions patchy and mildewed from time—he'd gotten it some years back, when he was... well, not much younger, but had less aches and pains. It was nowhere near as fulfilling as a horse, of course. What he wouldn't give for a reliable horse! he thought, but of course the whisper had promised him that when the time had come, and he had fulfilled his end, that it would provide him everything he could possibly desire.

He felt the whisper of its words tickling him—felt the phantom of its presence hovering over his skull. At times before he had felt it, deep inside him, deep inside his skull, its venomous invisible tongue licking the lobes of his brainstem. Oh, what pleasure it had brought, this invisible Whisper, the one who sat beyond the sky yet slithered tight around his torso.

"Lazarussssss," the whisper rasped, the ancient, thirsty beast that it was.

"After all this time! Whatever you wish," he said, voice exultant. His gaze roiled in his skull as he surrendered to its embrace. What began as a solid mist of pressure against his face soon turned into sharp nails raking, the feeling of his cheek being lanced by a serrated, sharp blade. He could feel his nerve endings screaming at him and he moaned in terror and pleasure intermingled.

"The time draws near, my dear devoted Lazarus," the whisper continued. "The time is nearly at hand. Have you awoken him? The Wendigo?"

"He sleeps, but he is yet upon the land."

"Excellent," the whisper rasped. "You must retrieve for me *that object*. I will tell you what to do next. Let me guide your hand, oh beloved child. Let me kiss you, and make you feel better."

Lazarus' eyepatch glowed with a crimson light as the presence sunk its fingers into his brain. He sat back and shuddered, moaning, feeling fireworks alight in his mind. A mental image bloomed up before him—the old Magician's Headquarters, a mansion on a hill—the horrible, putrid beast he shared a kinship with, the axeman to his usual hunts for the Whisper. He saw a lamp in his mind's eye—its glow, the same repulsive one as the wound that glowed under his eyepatch.

"*That object!*" the whisper hissed. "Go to your brother. Lie in wait. I will tell you what to do when the time is right."

"Yes, my lady," he groaned.

His eyepatch strobed.

They were at a clearing, on a footpath. Bailey could smell lakewater nearby. Huge gouges in a tree were carved into its bulk, the wounds seeming to bleed. A foul pile of excrement was no longer steaming, but what looked remarkably like a human hand's skeletal system, minus flesh, was reaching forth from the pile. Ligaments and tendons apparently went straight through a cryptid digestive track.

"Too much fiber," Bailey said, in the silence.

Eric turned his head and looked at her with a blank expression that seemed to be judging her. She wanted to crawl in a hole and die.

"Here is where you take over," he said.

She nodded her head, and leaned back against an old oak. She closed her eyes. Breathed in, breathed out. Felt her awareness extend beyond the confines of her body, past the sticky sweat and talcum powder strapping her into latex, past the close rebreather of the mask. The earth beneath her feet called to her, in a soothing voice, but mingled with that was some befoulment.

Of course it was—here were its droppings. She could sense in them something of its energy—a besmirching of the surroundings, and the horror of the frightened human. Like a fragile butterfly, she felt the leftover human energy battering against the unholiness that surrounded it. She reached in with her mind—tried to crack it open—and felt something give, minutely. A feeling of gratitude towards her, and then the butterfly had flittered, whatever that little bit of consciousness was.

Now there was only she and Eric's comforting, if stoic energy and the crimson stain in her mind's eye. She followed it—seeing landmarks here and there, rushing onwards past the crimson road, swirling down and down and down beneath her and deep into the belly of the ground. Whatever they were tracking was there—under the earth, hidden away, deep deep down below. She could feel it stir at the presence of her mind, and she withdrew, snapping back into awareness of her own body with a jolt.

She sat up and gasped. Eric looked down at her with concern.

"Good nap?" he asked, mouth twisted into a smirk.

"I found it," she said. "It's somewhere nearby, but below us. Deep, deep below."

"Can you still feel it?" he asked.

She nodded, hesitantly.

"It'll get stronger as we get closer," she said.

Eric nodded at her.

"Lead the way," he said, gesturing.

They arrived, finally, after what seemed like an hour and too many breaks for Bailey's tired legs. It was an old mineshaft entrance, cordoned off beyond National Park regalia. Posted signs warned people to stay out. 'Falling danger' in big letters was posted. 'No Public Entry!' in another.

Eric had checked in on his locator, and mapped the coordinates out.

"Yeah, summon the team," he said, after finding the right frequency. "We're at the old Mineshaft near Beaver trail. I saw fresh fewmets on my way here. Likely Wendigo. Yes. Yeah. No, I don't think it's a good idea either, not enough clearance. Might be faster if you take the van through the Park. Right. Okay. Are we benching Baby Bird? Is that right. Okay."

He turned off the communicator and turned to Bailey.

"And now we wait," he said.

"That's it?" she asked.

He nodded.

"That's pretty much it. Our job is done here."

"What do we do next?" she asked.

"Wait for the team to arrive."

"Is that it? What was all that Baby Bird stuff?"

Eric said nothing, but checked a few of his settings on the mask. After a few moments of expectant silence, he finally spoke.

"You're Baby Bird. You're benched. When they bring the van around, you get to keep watch over it. Leave the murdering to us for the day, Baby Bird."

"That's hardly fair," she said. "Can't you guys give me a gun or something?"

"Do you know how to handle a firearm?"

"I'm at Platinum rank on Call of Duty Black Ops."

It was not an answer, and she knew it wasn't an answer. Yet another flat balloon of a joke slowly deflating in the silence between them.

To her surprise, Eric cracked a grin at her.

"We should play sometime. When work's not so busy."

I guess every brick wall has a crack in it somewhere, Bailey thought to herself.

The Van arrived finally, after fifteen minutes. It was white, and had flowers painted on it. Bailey pursed her lips at it. As a basement dweller, she'd watched a ton of television. (What else was there to do in her free time?) A flower van seemed the single most conspicuous sign she could think of. Randall rolled down a window and extended a clomper in what she assumed was a 'come hither' motion.

She and Eric walked to the back of the van. The doors opened and they climbed in, very carefully. Skye and Randall were in the front seats, and Grimm was in the back.

"No Sassy," Bailey said, with some relief. "And no Addy."

"Sassy tends to get claustrophobic," Skye said. "Bringing her into a Mineshaft would ensure we'd all get buried alive when she hulks out and knocks out a supporting structure."

"Addy's watching Sassy," Randall said. "Girl's night, I suppose."

"So what's our battle plan?" Eric asked.

Grimm grinned, and turned to the wall. There was a big computer monitor there, with a fold-out keyboard. Apparently this functioned as part of their mobile design.

"I looked up a schematics of the Mineshaft. We'll be using that as a guide, but it's old, possibly outdated. We'll need you on point, Eric. We brought some torches, too. Fumes ought to cause the flames to flicker blue when we get closer."

Eric nodded, and said nothing further.

Grimm looked at Bailey.

"Eric told you your job already, right?" he asked.

Bailey blinked a few times.

"I get to guard the van," she said, voice dismayed. A stray idea bobbed its way up into her mind. How long had she been with these people now? Was this really where she wanted to be, what she wanted to do? All she could feel was a burning in her chest, though—a bilious hatred for the horrid thing down in the depths of the earth.

"You've seen how tricky these battles can get," Randall said. "You have no weaponry and little training. You're lucky you survived your skirmish with your departed friend the other day. This is a kindness we're giving to you."

She nodded, and stayed quiet.

"I need everyone to give me a wide berth when we make contact," Grimm said. "I've got a concentrated version of the Pixie wing powder. I'd like to use it to see if we can't partially immobilize him."

"Wagering a lot on that, aren't we?" Randall asked.

"It's not that we don't trust your work," Skye said. "But Grimm. This might be a dangerous idea. Surely we can try and immobilize him first, and then try the powder."

"This is the safest way," Grimm said. "How many other lives have we lost? We have to do something to make this easier on ourselves. Just trust me, please."

162

Bailey spoke up, then.

"Have you tried tranquilizer darts?" she asked.

Grimm blinked at her.

"Of course," he said. "Most Cryptids have a neurological system that runs differently than ours. Some of them are compatible with our biology, and others are changed. I'm assuming it's divergent evolution. Anyway. This guy we're tracking down. The Wendigo. Not a good candidate for tranquilization. We've studied some younger specimens—the hide is too thick for normal horse tranquilizers. And of course, when you do get a big enough gauge, it just makes it angrier."

Bailey made a face.

"Figures," she said.

"Are we ready, then?" Eric asked. "The night threatens to close in."

The four of them nodded, and Bailey sat back, feeling, if she were being honest, a bit left out.

"There's a radio if you get bored," Grimm said. "And I left a hardbound copy of Mortimer Miles' Cryptid Compendium if you're interested in boning up on future encounters."

"What do I do if you don't come back?" Bailey asked.

"We will," Randall said. He paused thoughtfully. "Well, we usually do. I would suggest that you drive the van back to the Manor and consider a new path in life."

"Right," she said.

"Hey," Grimm said, his skeleton face looming. "This powder I've made is the real deal. We'll come back. We've done this quite a few times before."

And then even he left, slamming the back doors on the way out. She watched the four of them through the window; they casually walked over to the Mineshaft entrance, lighting torches outside of it. It looked like someone had pried off some old loose boards at its entrance. After some quiet discussion she didn't hear, they nodded and set off, Eric in the lead, plague masks on their heads.

She sighed, and sat back against the van window, her head touching the glass. The effort from her jog seemed to drain her; she found herself falling asleep in the heat, and when she woke up with a start, covered in sweat from nightmares about goats that turned into her father, she found an old man with gray hair had pulled up beside the van in his truck.

He hadn't seen her yet—no way to, really. The angle she was at let her see his reflection in his side view mirror. Granted, she couldn't see much of him, but he looked deranged. He would cock his head, eyes lolling, and at times it looked as if he was arguing with someone. She didn't see anyone else in the truck, though...

Carefully she slid from the back of the van and into the driver's seat. She was careful not to touch any of the knobs, wipers, gizmos, or doo-dads. From this angle she could see he was alone. And then, to her horror, he turned his gaze and his single showing eye (the other eyepatched) looked beyond her and seemingly into her soul. The old man grinned, white teeth like tiny skulls in his mouth, and immediately Bailey felt everything in her stomach drop to her knees.

She looked around the van with terror suddenly. Weapon, weapon. Surely a team of monster bounty hunters would carry something she could protect herself with... She scrabbled through piles of paperwork, opening the glovebox with the hurry of someone who knew her life was in danger, and up-ended old pizza boxes as she scrabbled back into the back of the van. Was there *nothing* here? She wanted to scream...

And then she heard a sound that made her blood run cold. *Someone knocking on the window politely.*

She turned and looked at the window. He was there, grinning and leering, eyepatch seeming to glow around the sides.

"Hello, beautiful," he said. His voice was dull outside of the glass. "I was interested in buying a flower."

He lifted his eyepatch and Bailey saw something stare back at her, some swirling vortex of energy that seemed to rip at her consciousness, and she could feel her hand raise and unlock the door on her own. She screamed inside her head, but she was transfixed. She railed against this power—this hypnosis, this crimson allure, and barely managed to pull her face away. She staggered, like a zombie, out of the van's side door, limping her way away from him, to the trees…

She tripped on pavement, sprawling, and lay there stunned on her side.

"Help me," she squeaked, to a nearby oak, and then lay still. Her body was betraying her.

Old boots—cowboy boots, tarnished and polished and leatherworked, ancient relics from an era long past walked up in her eyesight. The old man went to his knees, and one calloused, grimy hand reached out to her, caressing her cheek.

Something flew from the trees, something small and person-shaped, but she couldn't see it. The old man was knocked back, grunting, but soon she heard a struggle and saw a crimson flash and then whatever had tried to help her was now no more. His hand gripped her hair as he loomed over her paralyzed body. He yanked her hair by the roots, turning her gaze to his own.

"Such a beautiful creature," he said. "A shame. Not often the small ones awaken themselves to defend those of your kind. You have something special about you… something we detest. You'll just have to go with your friends, I suppose."

He pulled back his eyepatch, and again that glowing vortex spun and entranced her. She could feel her mind opening up, free, being scanned and infiltrated and controlled, and the old man's careful, hysterical drawl whispered into her ear again.

"I just need a beautiful flower from a beautiful woman," he said. "There are some gorgeous Cave Bonnets that grow only in the dark. I have heard there's some deep in the mineshafts below. Would you be a doll and go get one for me?"

Bailey felt the sense of it in her soul, and she nodded.

"Of course," she said dreamily. Her body picked itself up and she walked, slowly and carefully, padding over the grass to the mineshaft in her view. She could feel the darkness of it rise up and around her on all sides, swallowing her whole, and behind her she saw crimson flashes, one after another—could hear the rumbling of stone falling, falling, falling, and the little hallway of light she had seen before was now nothing more than a wall of blackness sealing her in tightly.

"Bring it to me," it whispered in his ear, outside the mine.

Lazarus grinned, shuffling back to his truck, and slid inside. Away in the distance he had a meeting to get to…

CHAPTER 19:

THE BELLY OF THE BEAST

Darkness enclosed Bailey on all sides; little cracks of light shone in through the rubble behind her, but other than that she had no bearing. What had Grimm said about her helmet? Wasn't there some kind of tracking device on it? Surely they had thought of infrared… But that was a moot point. She'd taken her helmet off in the van, and hadn't had time to suit up again. Come to think of it, hadn't she seen the rest of them enter with torches? Other than the smell of sulfur she couldn't see any trace of them. Hell, she couldn't even see her hand in front of her face.

"Shit," she hissed. Her voice echoed in the gloom. She supposed she was in a large cavern. She patted her pockets. Normally she'd have a lighter for just such a situation, but of course it had been taken during all the initial confusion and she'd never thought to ask for it back.

The crazy man outside had wanted something from her, but it was all a blur. She hadn't known what she was after coming in here. Something about flowers? She'd felt a strange compulsion when the man had spoken to her, like she was someone else listening to something very important very far away…

What was it her Dad would say? Sit still and focus on your breathing.

She nodded her head and closed her eyes, inhaling through her nose. It smelled of mildew and musk, of animal waste, of rocks and minerals and mud… and something putrid…

She was inside a cave, but was that really any different than being stuck in her basement? She could deal with enclosed environments. There weren't any people here, after all. Just a thick, rotted, mildew smell—the smell of mud and wet rain, mixed with a greasy, old copper smell. And something spoiled just on the fringe of her nose...

"Where are my friends?" she whispered to herself.

An image of Missy, Jack, and Lester popped up in her mind's eye. Dead on a slab. Heads wrenched backwards, eyes open and unblinking. That could be her, she knew, if she didn't find the people she was with.

And yet. Another horrible thought bloomed up in the midst of all this. She didn't have a light. Should she wait here? She had read about mineshafts in a book somewhere. They had switchbacks, u-turns, carbon monoxide. Dead ends. Deep elevator shafts cut miles into the earth sometimes. If she made one false step somewhere, she could potentially plunge directly down into a shaft. Break a leg, and bleed out. Nobody to save her.

Crazy man out front. Wendigo, presumably inside somewhere. Rubble over the entrance that was nigh inescapable. Literally trapped between a rock and a hard place. If she had known what awaited her outside her basement apartment was her friends dying and a literal escalation of danger, she would never have made the decision to come out here.

But that wasn't true, and she knew it. She knew she would try and try and try again. To try and push herself. Leaving her basement hadn't exposed her to new danger, it didn't create new problems. It awakened her. There was something in her, Randall had said.

She heard his voice in her thoughts: "Be brilliant!"

And as soon as she heard it, she felt her way over to a small alcove of rock and sat down, closing her eyes and feeling the cave wall against her back. She saw in her mind's eye, and felt in her heart:

Her new friends were deep down below her somewhere. There was a line she could tug between them and herself. Something was pulsating down there beneath them, where they were, and they were tracking it with them like mud on their shoes. She would be safe if she proceeded cautiously. She recoiled her consciousness backwards, nearly mentally tripping over something she'd totally missed before.

There was something evil in the same room as her.

She opened her eyes again, scanning the darkness desperately. There was a presence at the far end of the cave-mouth, where she had seen the glow catch from her friends. A putrid wash of stink rose up to meet her. Two glowing red eyes in the gloom peered beyond her, to the cave rubble at the entrance. And she felt the floor shake ever-so-steadily as the lumbering quake of the thing plodded closer and closer to the shafts of light.

She held her breath as she watched it. Tried to shrink herself down. She'd tucked herself away in a place away from the sunlight; that was luck itself, she calculated, unless there was more to her gift than she knew. She could see its horrid fanged face as it approached the rubble, saw its shadow with elongated antlers. Watched its sharp talons feel for weaknesses in the rubble.

It bent over, sniffing the rocks intently, snuffling an awful snuffle, elongated neck unsettlingly snakelike. Something in her heart told her to get up as quietly as possible, to run the opposite direction of this thing. Even if the opposite direction would be deeper into its lair. She got to her feet, sliding up against the cave wall. She tried not to breathe, not to make a sound. Tried not to click on any of her gear. She inched slowly up, trying not to kick rocks or gravel that had fallen beneath her where she sat.

She was almost all the way up—almost in the running position—and she heard it turn. Its red eyes stared at her, unblinking. Surely, she thought, and here she felt wet urine puddle down the side of her suit leg. Surely it can't see me.

And then it sprang at her, and she pitched forward. Fell right between its legs, felt it slam into where she was against the wall and groan, dazed. She felt a large thump as it fell to the ground, shrieking and caterwauling, and she kicked rocks to get to her feet and into a running position. And then she was off, off into the dark twisting and turning spiral of the mineshaft and praying that her intuition was correct…

The inside of the Mansion was quiet. Almost too quiet. If Lazarus hadn't had the dear sweet voice of the Whisper in his ears, he wouldn't have believed it was this easy to get inside. He'd driven his truck around the park, and past a sign that said 'private property' he'd driven off-road, where a freshly mudded track had clearly come from. A garage door was left open. More fortuitousness. There was a spritz of spray when he entered—a mist that burned his lungs and stank, so horribly he nearly could not drive further; but the Whisper hissed in his ear and he floored it, revving past the entryway and over the barrier, coming to a crashing halt.

He was here! This was the place in his vision that housed the relic he had been sent him to find. But where were the people? He was in a large, nearly empty garage. Off to one side, he could see an assortment of cages.

"Are you lost?" he heard, echoing oddly.

He looked all around him. The voice had come to him from high overhead somewhere.

"What ill manners, to ask a question before introducing yourself," he called, trying to be genial. "Why don't you come out and say hello?"

There was silence, then. He took a step forward. The voice called out again.

"I asked you a question." It was a woman's voice—young, foolhardy. Filled with arrogance. He hated her instantly. Lazarus just abhorred rude women.

"And I gave you my terms," he said. "I'll have to show my own way around, I suppose."

"You have until the count of three to get back in your truck," the young woman's voice came again. He couldn't place it—couldn't trace her. It echoed from every corner of the gargantuan warehouse. "Once I hit zero, if you're not in your vehicle, I'll put out your other eye. Three."

Lazarus raised an eyebrow, and stepped another foot forward.

"Two."

Another step.

"One. Final warning."

He lifted his boot and took one last step. A flurry of movement from his right side—he turned, and with nearly inhuman speed caught a throwing star between his fingers, millimeters from his regular eye.

"Clever," he said, and then the world turned upside down. He'd been so focused on the throwing star he hadn't seen her descend upon him like a winged creature, leaping and planting a foot in his sternum. The inertia from the distance she came from took the wind from his sails, hit him so hard he flipped right over onto his stomach. He groaned; the whisper ranted and railed in his ear, and then he felt a weight on his back.

Dark hair blotted out everything he could see, and he felt his hands being tied together around his back.

"And just because I don't like to tell lies," she said.

She wrenched his head back by his greasy hair. He watched as her throwing knife came closer and closer. He wriggled against her grip, screamed, moaned, shrieked. Begged to a God he had long ago abandoned.

"You can't do this," he said, panting.

"I can," she hissed, another whisper in his ear. "Now understand that I'm choosing not to."

The blade withdrew again. His eyesight was safe. For now.

He breathed out a gasp he hadn't known he was holding.

"You might think I'm overreacting a bit," the young woman hissed in his ear. "But there's a sasquatch asleep upstairs that's had a pretty rough weekend and by God if you wake her up you'll wish you were blind so you can't see what we're going to do to you."

He struggled against his bonds, and groaned. His left eye watered, phantom pains making the socket throb.

"I'm just lost," he said. "Lost and afraid and I can barely see, and you want to steal the eyesight from an old man? I'm just lost."

"A lost person doesn't gun it into a secret base with a truck and walk around like he owns the place."

"I was looking for the ranger cabin," he said. "There was something in the forest—something big and frightening."

Addy punched him in the kidney. He groaned. A throb of excruciating pain wore through him.

"I saw you that night, you sick freak," she said. "You sitting at that campfire. Watching and laughing, taunting those poor people as the Wendigo ate them. Randall said not to engage—said you were a talent, a rogue agent, someone who mingled with these evil things. I don't know what you are and I don't give a fuck. But anyone that can survive being in the Wendigo's vicinity and live to walk around isn't trustworthy in my book."

Lazarus quit struggling, and his body went limp.

"Are you going to kill me?" he asked, voice meek.

"I'm not sure yet," Addy said.

"Well, you'd better make up your mind before I make it up for you," he growled. "Because when I get out of this situation you'll wish you took my eye when you had the chance."

Addy punched him in the gut again, for good measure.

They had descended down to the fifth shaft. Unlike the previous two, this one had been shored up—there was room to stand up straight, and walk around. Their torches flickered, casting strange, wavering lights over wooden beams here and there, but as of now there had been no change.

"Anybody else worried?" Skye asked quietly.

"Immensely," Randall said.

"This whole place smells of Wendigo," Eric muttered.

"Sensors are overloaded," Grimm said to himself. He took a few paces into the middle of the room. "This should be it. I don't understand—"

His torch caught and burned blue. He stopped, and looked back at the rest of the team.

"Bullseye," he said. "Stand back a bit."

The blue light was flickering quietly and dimly, and he paced around the exterior of the room, deliberately taking two steps at a time. At the back circumference of the rounded room, the torch showed a passageway that had just been hidden from their pooled light. Beyond it, responding, perhaps, to the presence of people, something flickered in the gloom, some kind of fluorescent red.

Grimm walked towards it, torch dimming and burning a bright blue ember. The passageway turned, sharply, and when he stepped around it there it was.

The portal glimmered before his eyes, a radiant crimson.

"I made contact," he called.

Randall stepped forward, torch hovering politely six inches out from about elbow height to the ground, and it burned a bright blue as he crossed the mid-point of the chamber. He disappeared beyond the rest of the group, and took his place near Grimm.

"I know how that works, but it always catches me off guard," Grimm said, pointing at the hovering torch.

"We're standing in front of a gate to another dimension and you tell me this is what you're worried about," Randall said.

The portal shimmered in the open air of the cave. Weird rock formations on all sides of the cavern were bathed in its glow.

"Twenty bucks says this A-hole is why the mine was sealed off in the first place," Grimm said.

"Decades," Randall breathed. "Decades I have looked for this particular entrance. For the Wendigo's lair. How was I to know it was so close to home?"

He lifted one of his mechanical gauntlets to the portal, the gauntlet's rings shifting on their own, and began a series of intonations. The edges of the portal started rippling—Grimm could feel the weight of the air around him churning…

A burst of noise from the main chamber, then. Grimm and Randall jumped.

"Guys," Skye's voice called. "Come back this-a way. *NOW.*"

Grimm and Randall slunk back around the bend in the passage and peered into the main chamber. Bailey was there, panting, holding her knees.

"Where'd your helmet go?" Grimm snapped.

"There was a man—an eyepatch—something about flowers. The Wendigo is coming!" she panted.

"Catch your breath and speak clearly," Skye said.

Bailey gritted her teeth and glared at them.

"I don't know how much fucking clearer I can get," she said, eyes wide. "The Wendigo has been chasing me all the way down here. I managed to double back and confuse it a few passageways back, but it's pissed and looks hungry."

"Battle positions," Skye said. "Bag 'em and tag 'em."

"Remember, don't kill it!" Grimm said. "Not right away, at least."

Everyone scrambled into far corners of the room. Randall dragged Bailey back to the passageway that led to the portal. She looked down at his lack of hands. All nubbins, he was. How was her shirt being tugged, again? She blinked.

"Stay here," he commanded her.

"There was a man, with an eyepatch, and he made me come in," she said. "He said something. I don't know, my memory's all weird. The mineshaft entrance is collapsed."

Randall nodded.

"Stay hidden and quiet," he said, holding a wrist end up to his mouth, and seemed to float, wraithlike, back down the passage.

Imagine a circle. That's the whole fifth shaft chamber. Inside the circle are four pillars supporting the roof. These pillars are set up at approximately six feet from the north, west, east, and south of the room, and they divide the room into roughly four sectors, or quadrants. Near the north of the room is the passageway to the portal, where Bailey lay hidden. Near the south pillar was the shaft she had come from.

Behind each pillar the four battle-ready members of S.C.A.R.E.D. stood and readied themselves. Skye and Randall hid in the east and west, Eric in the south, and Grimm up north. It did not take long after their positions for the putrid stench of the thing to come wafting in to greet them. Their torches, hung up on the walls and illuminating the surroundings, immediately burnt blue.

It snuffled in, angry and pounding, visible dent on its forehead. Parts of its brain seemed to ooze out from behind its eye socket. It snuffled, antlers brushing the ceiling, and snarled as an arrow spun from the side and over its shoulder. Another zipline snaked its way out—some sort of telescopic device that criss-crossed it in the other direction. It made to cut them down when Eric made his move, dashing between its legs and hooking, bola-like, two lassos around each ankle. More and more lines snapped out from the dark, embedding themselves in the walls of the chamber, and before long the Wendigo was seemingly immobile, thrashing and screeching, its hands and arms bound and its bulk stuck standing upright in the center chamber.

"Make it quick," Randall cried. "Then we pull the neck-height line."

Grimm moved forward, unclasping a sachet on his belt. A handful of glittering powder was in his hand, and he stood as close as he dared as the Wendigo swiped at him in futility.

"Nighty night, friend," Grimm said, puckering his lips and blowing.

The dust shimmered in the breeze, falling over the Wendigo's face like snow in a globe. It fell still, seemingly transfixed, though its muscles twitched here and again.

"Haha!" Grimm crowed. Boldness made him draw nearer to the creature. He slapped it right in the stomach, as if a car dealer. "Nothing a little engineering can't hand-urgck!"

Its taloned hand reached out to grab him, and snagged him by the neck. Cables were snapping from where it had been immobilized, and with a casual downward smash into the floor Grimm shrieked and stopped moving. His legs had been broken; white bits of bones showed when the Wendigo picked him up again and, like an infant peeling a banana, its right hand snapped off his arms at the shoulders. He was going into shock—his mouth an open O as he was suspended in the air and his eyes rolling.

Afterwards, Randall had a moment where he remembered helping his grandmother hull snap-peas...

She'd blindfolded him, to take his sight, even if temporarily, but Lazarus could see even through the eyepatch and the fabric. One of his hidden talents. Everything was just a little misty and red, like a thermal vision outline around his surroundings. It was a bit like a sonar, he'd always thought, and he'd never wondered why he needed it...

"How much longer are you going to subject me to this?" Lazarus asked. "I believe this is considered kidnapping and bodily harm."

Addy flipped him off, cellphone to her ear, but only half-heartedly. She did not consider him capable of seeing through the metal of his cell, or his blindfold. It was a weakness.

He was upright, strapped into a chair in a cell, arms and hands bound behind his back, slumped backward, face staring up at the ceiling. He could move his neck, but at great pains—she was great at ropeplay, he thought idly. He felt like a calf that had been trussed up at a rodeo.

The smell of animal shit was all around him. The Whisper had gone quiet some time back—it was still here, of course, he could feel its presence. But it had withdrawn. Perhaps this was a test, Lazarus thought.

"I'll give you everything in my wallet if you let me go," Lazarus said, slipping into the clueless old man role he'd come so far with.

"If you don't quit talking I'm going to take your tongue," Addy said, outside the cell. She was pacing back and forth, her shoes on the cement floor making the oddest sullen thumps. Frustrated, she tried to call the team again; Lazarus could hear the numbers she was dialing, but the phone rang and rang and rang and still got no answer.

Lazarus knew she was distracted. And he knew he was tied up with a bunch of other common cryptids. But what was that she'd said about a sasquatch sleeping earlier?

He saw her hang up and sigh, frustrated. She started dialing again. How pretty she was, this little bird of a girl. Dangerous and precious all in one. He knew he would have a good time getting to know her, if only he could get the damn blindfold off...

He wriggled, twisting in the chair. There was a little lump on the back of the headrest, something squareish and plastic, he assumed, simply from scalp feel alone. He wriggled up to it, cursing her for her attentiveness to knotwork. This blindfold wasn't going to come off without a struggle, that was for sure.

A distraction. He needed to distract her. Sleeping sasquatch. The smell of animal crap all around him made him think, and without warning her in the slightest he took a deep inhale, then shrieked as loud as he could and shoved with his body weight against the chair, tipping it backwards. She saw him just as he started to tip, slowly, and for a moment she looked shocked as he was suspended at the inertia point halfway between falling back upright and slamming over, and with a thunderous crash and a blinding white scream of pain in his head he felt the blindfold loosen and his skull hit ground.

He considered his new worldview from the ground as the animals all around him— beautiful creatures that they were—began to hoot and squawk and holler. Oh, excellent, excellent.

"You're going to stay there like that," she called out to him.

"I didn't mean to," he said. "I'm sorry. I'm just an old man. Judging by the smell of this place, you all seem to track monsters, don't you?"

"Monsters don't exist, save scum like you," she replied.

He coughed. It was a ragged cough; tubercular and pained, one that he'd had for nearly fifty years. It did not sound good. It was stealing his body from him, this cough—part of what The Whisper had said to him would be healed once he'd done its bidding.

"I'm sorry," he gasped, coughing again. "When I'm laying down like this, I start to have trouble breathing. I'm sorry for making noise. I was scared earlier. I'm just a half-blind old man and I can't see. I'm petrified."

There was a silence between them for some time, and then, with a reluctant sigh from her, he heard the cell door open. Animals shrieked all around them. He felt the world move and shift. Somehow or another she was lifting his bulk—that tiny little girl moving his big old body around. And then he thought of his age, how old he was. How his bones creaked in his flesh, how tiny and gnarled he had become. He was weightless, except for the Whisper on his shoulders...

He could see again, around the edges of the blindfold. What's more, the eyepatch was slipping. The woman had locked the door again, and now she'd drawn a chair up and was sitting opposite him.

"Let's talk turkey," she said. "I think that's the phrase, at least. Why are you here?"

"I told you, I got lost—"

She pulled her knife out again, tossing it in the air.

"You can't see it, but right now I have my knife out. You lie to me one more time and I take your tongue. And you know I'm not kidding."

He looked at her, looked into her eyes, saw her intention. And he laughed, letting the veil drop, a wicked and tubercular laugh with a wet groan at the end.

"You want to know why I'm here? The moon," he howled. "The bloody crimson moon brought me here. Not the blood moon you're thinking of—that ominous portent of lunar fascination, dear Diana who sat high in the clouds and informed our myths. There is a moon, my dear, beyond the moon—one in opposite polarity and gravitational shift from our planet, so that it is constantly hidden from our sight. It has neither weight nor heft, yet it is the cause of our maladies. All of our maladies. We birthed it, long ago, our planet did—it was ripped from its bloody womb, and set in the sky by the shadows that walked here. A red tide of a place, where all of one's greatest dreams can be granted.

"Despair is driven to the crimson moon because it knows it must find its home there, there in the land where all exists, and all can exist. Despair must be transmuted—can be transmuted, desires to be transmuted, desires to escape from this mortal coil. The acts we perform are that of a blessing, dear, one where we liberate humans from the dread and the despair they feel on a daily basis. They are drawn back to that moon hanging high in the sky, where they can become something lovely, something which helps others, so they too can give the gift of eliminating despair."

As his words wrapped around her consciousness, a crimson flash came from under the eyepatch, and with a loud careening noise something off in the cages, in the distance, made a noise. It was just enough to distract her—he wriggled his head, shaking it vigorously, and the eyepatch fell down and away.

Her eyes met his when she looked back, and his right eye went up in flames. All Addy could see was a tunnel, a spinning vortex in the flickering fire…

"I'm just a hapless wanderer," he said, voice steady. "You've accidentally bound me. What a happy mistake. You're going to remove my restraints and show me where your greatest treasure is as an apology for the unpleasantness."

Addy struggled to make a decision, leaned forward in her chair, and stopped herself.

"What… what are you doing?" she asked, shaking her head.

"Simply telling you what you know to be true," he said. "Now. Remove my restraints, won't you? I'm not a bad guy. You deserve to treat me. After all, you threatened to take my eye."

Addy blinked, shook her head. Got to her feet and dragged her chair away.

"Whatever you're doing won't work on me," she said, out of sight.

"Clever girl," he called, to her retreating back.

Time passed. She made another call. Sighing with frustration, she slammed the phone down.

"Oh, hey. You should go back upstairs and get some rest, Sassy," she said. "I've got this under control."

Soft grunts in response. The Sasquatch had been awakened, then.

He heard something lumbering. A feminine musk washed over through the bars, and he knew that what he had waited for had arrived.

A dark shadow loomed into view, bending down and snuffling and staring in through the cell bars; a she-squatch, judging by the ridiculous bow in her hair. At the sight of Lazarus something rippled over her fur. Her hackles rose, and she growled, deep and low at him.

"What a precious specimen," he said, voice smooth like caramel. He willed his power to reach out, to enrapture her, to wrap his mind around hers…

"Oh shit, I forgot! Don't look at him, Sassy," Addy cried, running up to her and trying to drag her away.

But it was too late. The fur settled, and her face became slack. Well, slacker than normal, Lazarus supposed.

"Do be a lamb and help me out of here," he said to the she-squatch, eye blazing.

Sassy's plodding steps shook the ground as she moved closer to his cell bars. Addy was hanging on her, pulling at her arm, trying to move her gaze, shake her head, *something*, but Sassy's arm swung out, once, and Addy was knocked backwards into a nearby wall of cages stacked on top of one another. She did not move, but some of the smaller creatures slithered out and around her, escaping their prisons and squawking for their freedom.

"Perfect," Lazarus said, as his cell door was pried open. The metal squealed. "Absolutely perfect."

The battle was tense in the fifth mineshaft chamber, and Bailey could only hear what was happening.

Behind her, Bailey heard rustling, heard the laughing voices of what sounded like small children. She turned. She had hardly had time to consider the portal. And wasn't that strange, she thought to herself… portals are something we only tell ourselves exist in games, in fairytales, in books and movies, aren't they? She had no idea what it was, had never been shown one, and yet here she was face to face with one and there was no doubt in her chest about its properties.

Small flickering things pulled themselves from it, laughing and twittering. They hovered around her—little blue things with sharp teeth and glittering wings, and buzzed out and down the passageway. Someone, a man, had shrieked—the Wendigo was screaming…

She snuck out behind the pixies, perching behind the rock shelf that separated rooms, and watched. The torches had been extinguished in the scuffle. Flashes of red, green, and blue lights were dazzling all over the inside of the chamber. People were yelling orders at one another, and then before she knew what was happening an explosion of light! She shielded her eyes with one hand, squinting through her fingers.

What looked like a sharp knife on the end of a chain snagged around the Wendigo's antlers. It struggled and yanked, clawing at the air. Bailey thought she saw Eric holding on to the chain, and heard someone say: "Now!"

An arrow struck through the beast's stomach and pierced its back, and then exploded. A wash of gore and inner viscera spooled to the ground. It bellowed, grabbing onto itself in pain. Scooping what it could of its inner organs in its hands, it half-crawled, half-scooted along the ground of the chamber and began to retreat to higher ground.

"Someone check on Grimm!" she heard.

But the laughter was drawing nearer. The pixie wings glittered as they returned. They were dragging an immobilized lump. Bailey found herself shocked as the whole floating caravan drew nearer. Grimm was in their arms, eyes closed, unbreathing, just a stump of a torso and broken legs dangling obscenely as the flying blue demons dragged him further into the passageway.

"Stop them!" she heard Randall's voice call.

She spread her arms out like a barrier, tried to swat at them, but they dove out of reach, laughing and twirling, swooping back down like hummingbirds to grab what they had dropped and drag it between her legs. Despite herself Bailey watched as Grimm's remains were carried, ever closer, to the portal.

The vortex shimmered in the air. The blue creatures began to dance and cavort amongst themselves, and, pleased with their work, sang a merry song as they tossed Grimm up into the air and switched limbs.

"Ground us down when we were dead
Ripped off our wings and popped our head
Stuck us to a board with nails
Believed his plan would never fail
A fool no wiser than arm's reach
We'll take him back and there we'll feast.
We hope that you enjoyed our song.

But now we fear we're here too long!
Away we'll go to munch and crunch
And have ourselves a tasty lunch."

And, bowing, they began to drag Grimm through the shimmering air. Bailey felt herself being shoved to the side by something hard and metal. Randall pushed himself into the passageway, holding up his gauntlets and muttering. They were shaped like torpedos—completely fingerless, though there were strange, arcane symbols engraved on rings that wrapped their way around. Soon, the letters on the gauntlet glowed; the portal rippled, and the pixies shrieked and double-timed, their tiny wings flapping.

"What's going on?" Bailey shrieked, over the noise.

"I've got to close this rip before more of them come streaming through," Randall cried, and began muttering again. Sweat was pouring from his forehead.

"But what about Grimm?" she asked.

"He took his gamble and it was ill-advised," Randall said. "There's no more we can do. He knew the risks." And again with the incantations.

"But we have to at least bury him," she said.

"There's nothing we can do, you stupid girl!" Randall snarled, holding up his second gauntlet.

The last bit of Grimm's shoes, dangling oddly, were being sucked through the portal.

"It can't end like this," Bailey said.

And she made a decision, running and grabbing his leg and leaping *into* the portal…

Addy was being dragged by one hand.

"Sassy," she cried. Her voice was a whimper. She felt like a small cloth doll being dragged around by an angry toddler. "Wake up, come on. You're better than this."

The she-squatch's left fist bashed through the last layer of the vault door. She gripped it, then pulled and, chest flexing, the sasquatch roared as the metal whined and gave. Lazarus stood far, far away, watching as the metal door was bent backwards.

"Thank you ever so much for your hospitality," he said, to the two of them, and stepped forward.

The lamp flickered crimson there before him. The whisper's wheezing rasp was back again in his ear, and they both crowed together as he held the prize aloft in his hands. An eternally flickering flame burned inside its glass case…

Addy watched the man's face, one of horrible greed and terror as the glow consumed him. She could see it, as the flames flickered, as his face changed from that of an old man's to a skull's, an illusion caused by the strobe, and as if feeling her gaze, his evil eye sockets locked on her own.

"Thank you," he said. Tears trickled down his face. "Thank you. Words cannot express how much this means to me. But I'd like to pay you back, my dear. What was that old saying? An eye for an eye, a tooth for a tooth? Don't recognize the phrase? Perhaps something a little more familiar to your culture, then. I wonder, can you tell me what the sound of one hand clapping is?"

She stared at him, and she suddenly felt nine years old again, and she saw it—the thing she had been trying not to see, the horrid thing perched on his shoulder. It was an eye, its pupil like a goat's, and it leered at her, long tongue dangling.

Sassy's grip on her hand was getting tighter and tighter.

"Sassy," Addy pleaded.

There was a snap, then, in her bone and wrist and marrow, and Addy felt the shock and the exhaustion take her away.

The last thing she saw before she passed out was the old man with the lamp and the foul thing on his shoulder staring down at her.

There was no way to describe where Bailey had been; what she had seen; what she had smelled. The feeling of it rushed around her like a wind tunnel. Countless kaleidoscopic visuals had assaulted her, sensory details on all side until she'd cleared her head and found herself free-falling. She was in a shaft, weightless, descending down and down and down and somewhere in the middle of all this the gravity realigned and flipped. She was soaring upwards, wind battering at her hair. The walls around her oozed like blood, like she was in some vast uterine lining.

The pixies were ahead of her, singing songs and laughing and making mirth. She willed herself forward, trying to grab at Grimm's foot again, yearning to go quicker, to be more aerodynamic, and then, she could feel herself take off with a fresh burst and she stretched forward and—

Damnit, she said to herself. Nothing but shoelace, and it was hardly enough for a grip, but she felt something on her fingers, and when she looked again she saw them glowing brightly. She willed herself upwards, faster and faster, wind around her propelling her, the walls themselves beating in time with her breaths—

Her hand glowed as she grabbed him by his ankle, and she yanked as hard as she could. Her hands fell off the slick leather of his boots, and she felt one of his legs give a horrible squelch and fall off, spinning knee over ankle into the void below. She blinked, looked back up again. Something else was dangling there, something spectral and white, and before she knew what she was doing she reached up, hand glowing, and yanked.

There was a horrible feeling of traction, and for a moment the pixies and Bailey were in a tug of war, and then with a pop noise she felt herself falling. The pixies sped away, Grimm's other leg dangling, and she heard someone's voice in her ear as she continued soaring.

She looked down at her hands and looked up. Grimm was there, floating and white, staring at her with, she assumed, the same shocked expression on his face as she had on hers.

They stayed like that for about a second before gravity reversed itself again and they fell, plunging, downward and downward, the chamber walls oozing and spiraling around them, down and down and down and—

"Jesus," Bailey heard, when she could hear again.

She sat up. Beside her, a shimmering white form sat up, rubbing its head.

"Ow," Grimm's voice said, floating over the open air like an echo.

Skye was staring at the two of them; to her right, Randall was standing, gauntlets outstretched and rings glowing, spinning. There was a sizzling noise as the portal sealed up behind them.

"Grimm?" Skye asked.

He blinked and sat up, floating over the cavern floor.

"Why's everything feel so funny?" he asked.

"Because you're hovering two feet off the floor," Bailey said.

Randall bent down, staring at him. He passed a gauntlet through the shimmering form of him.

"I do believe you're not entirely corporeal," Randall muttered.

"What does that mean?" Grimm asked.

Bailey sat and tried to remember—tried to find memories, words, that could explain what she had been doing, that explained where she was, that explained Grimm. But nothing could come out of her mouth.

"I reached and tried to grab your leg," she muttered eventually. "It fell off."

Grimm looked down. His legs were intact, as thin and translucent as they were.

"Whatever happened to the Wendigo?" Grimm asked. "Did the pixie powder work?"

"Afraid it just pissed him off," Skye said. "He ran away. He's probably dying somewhere as we speak."

"A partial victory," Randall said. "Owing to its wounds, it ought not to survive the night, though we'll need to find its body and dispose of it before anyone asks any questions. And Grimm. I'm sorry to say you will not be getting a pay raise. But, at least we've confirmed two things here: Bailey is a shaman, of some power. And A-holes work as an entrance and an exit, for those gifted enough."

There was a silence, then, punctuated by Skye coughing into her sleeve.

"Yes, I heard it, can we please grow up," Randall said.

A click of static on the comms, then.

"The entryway is clear," Eric said. "Wendigo clawed some of the rubble open, by the looks of it. There's bloodstains and stench everywhere. But guys. You need to come out here and see this."

"See what?" Randall snapped.

"Get up here as quick as you can. Addy left a distress message with the van."

Skye slung one of Bailey's shoulders over her own and the two of them followed behind the floating majesty of Randall's stride and ahead of the bobbing spectre of Grimm behind them. It was only five minutes of silence, but the longer it went on, the worse it felt. Until at last the dusk and starlight beamed in through the front entryway, past the stony maw of the cavern.

The four of them met Eric outside, and stared at the night-time horizon.

Skye gasped.

"It's beautiful," Bailey said, because there was no other word for it.

Crimson sparks of light, Astral Holes ripping themselves open all over the sky. An endless procession of them seemingly twinkling like an entire galaxy of constellations in the evening air…

LEGIONS

Illustration by Anton Tolstobrov

178

PART 3: LEGIONS

CHAPTER 20:

BATHED IN BLOOD

Lazarus whistled a jaunty tune as the truck bounced over crevices and cracks in the road. The windows were down, the dusk had just set, and there was a fire in his heart that didn't seem like it wanted to stop. Old trash, whipped by the breeze, flew out the window and away behind him like a trail as he travelled.

His prize sat on the seat next to him, wrapped up in a seatbelt for safety. A delicately glowing old-style iron-wrought lantern, with glass panes. Inside it, flickering gently, was a flame that burned red. He had shuttered it for now—knowing beyond a doubt that it was going to stay lit, but trying not to draw any attention to himself before he got to where he was going.

"A little further," he heard, in his ear.

"The forest is starting to disappear," he said.

"I know. What purpose has this if we come too close to those hunters?"

"A fair point," he said, to nothing and no one.

Forests bled away to highways and plains, valleys that went on and around and caused the asphalt highway to dip and turn with them. Sandstone mountains, bereft of greenery, raised their peaks to the sky, as if trying to hail something from the stars. The greenery gave way to desert; scorched yellow and bled-out scrubby foliage overtook the land. Large crags arched and grew. Mountain terrain, Lazarus knew.

"As much as I bitch about missing my horse, this trip would have taken forever on it," he muttered. The conveniences of the modern day were something he could be enamored with, if only he let himself let go.

Minutes passed; even larger canyons and valleys sprang up and around him.

"There," the Whisper said.

He pulled over, driving his truck off-road and into a channel cut between rocks. He winced as the axles squeaked and whined, and when the channel became too narrow for the truck to fit in any further, he put it in park. Dust and dry dirt from where his tires had kicked up earth blew around him as he swung his pack around his shoulders. He unbelted the lantern, attaching it to the other side of his leather holster. He reached down with his left hand and grabbed his gun by the grip, withdrawing it gently. Runes were carved over the surface. He slid it back into the holster, and headed out through the canyon.

Colt on his hip, lantern blazing by his side. Knapsack on his back. Just like the good old days.

"How much further?" he asked.

"Climb to the tallest peak," the whisper clamored, practically vibrating.

Lazarus nodded, trudging ahead. This was his trip, he knew, his trip to take and make; this journey towards absolution. Canyons opened up and splintered on the path he was on. The whisper oozed into his ear which direction to take, and soon he found his way and, ensuring his knapsack was on his back securely, began a steep upwards climb, panting and wheezing as he went.

His bones ached beneath his flesh. His stringy, greasy hair slapped in his face. The wind was bitter, smelling of old minerals and salt, of baking clay setting after a full day of South Dakota sun. At one point the steep path wound around. There was a lip, barely enough room for his heels to grab on the ledge, and it did not look sturdy at all. But trust was a big part of it, he knew. He gathered in his breath, then slid across the narrow ledge. His wizened frame was light and airy; he found he could cling, like a gecko, to the outcroppings and he would stick. Natural preservation instinct? Some new power granted him by the whisper? He wasn't sure—it seemed too subtle to be anything other than sheer luck, he supposed.

He took it as a sign that his intentions were blessed by existence.

Once past the ledge, the path grew steep again, and he bent forward on it, doubled-up against the wind. Down below, off the side, he could see the canyon floor from tens, perhaps twenties of feet high. If he fell off somewhere, there was little chance in hell he'd survive in a way that wasn't painful.

Finally, the path evened out. There was a notch in this crag, a somewhat flat space about ten yards in to the peak.

"Here," the whisper said.

It was a perfect place to start a fire—the old remains of a prior abandoned campsite greeted him, a ring of rocks and ash. How many times had a whisper driven someone out here? he wondered. And was their whisper like his? Was their whisper some speech from beyond the stars, from some shadow world? What was it like to have that whisper be simply the joy of freedom?

In many ways, Lazarus felt himself confined. The whisper had been his friend, his dearest companion, but now that he was finally here, finally achieving that task he had been assigned, would it stay? What would his life look like, given he accomplished his wish? The whisper had told him of greater deeds still yet to be done, but the implications were that he could wish for what he wanted. His transmutation, his prize for his tasks, for assisting in the grand rite, that was his for the asking. And he wondered what he would ask for. Oblivion, perhaps? A freedom from the multitudinous dramas and aches that this life, this body provided for him. Or perhaps he'd ask for a house, somewhere, a nice cottage, and a good horse.

It was no matter. All that mattered was that he accomplish his task. He peered out into the night sky; constellations were coming out. Off in the distance, he could see the frail lampposts of highway here and again barely holding off the gloom, miniature from this distance. He bent down to the ashpit in front of him, and rifled around in his knapsack. He'd been instructed to bring fuel for the fire. Just a small spark would work, given the blaze was consistent.

He stacked the wood he'd brought, snapping up some dry bracken around him on the small plateau, and clicked his flint over it. A tiny spark blazed and caught. He held his hands around it, nurturing it, breathing gently, if asthmatically, over it, coaxing it out. It spluttered, and died. He tried again, and again, the merciless winds battering against him.

The whisper oozed into his ear, and he had a solution. He flipped up his eyepatch, and stared at the assembled wood. There was a red flash—a small fountain of flame erupted from the assembled wood, and soon the rest of it caught.

"Wish you would have taught me that one sooner," he said. "I was struggling with lighting a smoke just the other day."

The whisper remained silent, pensive.

Lazarus sat, knees aching, on an old log someone had used as a bench. He stretched and popped his lower back, then pulled his boots off and warmed his toes by the light of the fire. He sat in silence, for some time.

"*Make your move*," the whisper said.

"I will, I will," he said. He breathed in deeply, unhooking the lantern on his belt and sitting it down next to him. He unshuttered the flame, staring at it intently.

"All of that, just for you," he muttered to it.

"*Do it now!*" the whisper hissed.

"We must savor this moment," Lazarus said. "I've waited a long time for this. You have too, no doubt. Maybe longer than me. But give an old man his little pleasures."

"*You will have all the pleasures you desire, once the deed is done,*" the whisper said, and its tone was almost... what was that, frantic?

Lazarus lifted the lantern in his hands, staring in at the flame. It was an odd flame, this one—none of that refraction of light nonsense. It was like a small portal, spewing licks of liquid thought, mercurial and twisting, fountaining in on itself.

He considered, for just a moment, tossing it over the edge of the cliff he was on. It would fall to the canyon ground below, shatter, into a million pieces. It would be done with. The whisper would drive him mad, no doubt, but it would end this. Of course, he considered, he could toss himself over the edge as well. End his own pain and suffering. His thread would be done.

He held it aloft, facing the edge. The wind battered at his weather-chapped, aged face. He knew the scars on his own cheeks could be traced like the canyons below.

"*What are you doing?*" the whisper hissed.

"Thinking," he said, and nothing else.

There was a paranoid energy to the whisper; he could feel its fright percolating on his shoulder. This was erratic behavior, Lazarus knew, but wasn't that why the whisper had come to him? Some deranged old man who'd seen things nobody else should have seen, who could see things beyond what any normal person could see.

What was he trying to accomplish here? he asked himself. Was this what he wanted? Didn't he just want freedom from it? Freedom from what he'd seen? Freedom from this long isolation? He didn't want to be a mad man, some hermit on a mountain babbling to himself about the old times.

But isn't that just it? the whisper asked. *Don't you want everyone else to see what you've seen? Don't you want to help heal this world, help transmute it? Don't you want others to taste that suffering you yourself have tasted so often in this life?*

It was for only a second that he considered taking the selfless route, leaping off with the lantern, but instead, crowding out the anxious shriek of the whisper in his head, he finally turned and smashed the lantern into the fire.

The fire flickered and blazed up. Crimson crawled forth, little dancing echoes of energy that reached ever-upwards on the breeze. He could feel his eye activate, a surge of power zapping around in his skull. A feeling of rapture like none he'd ever experienced bloomed up within him, and he laughed from the sheer joy of it.

He sat back down on the log, then withdrew his gun. The markings glowed in the light of the fire. He dug in his knapsack. The etchings had been one part of the equation; there was a ritual for this, he knew. The original had a blade, a scepter, a club, going far, far back to the time before man could even wield a pen. Perhaps once there had been a crimson fire imbued into a quill, he thought, and the words it wrote burned like poison and created incantations on vellum...

He had gun oil in his knapsack. He got that and a cotton rag embroidered with more symbols, and began the ritual of cleansing. A salt scrub. He smooshed the white paste into every crack and groove. It wouldn't do for there to be any extraneous energy left over on the hull. He scrubbed and wiped it away, using linseed oil now to polish it. The dull steel of his colt twinkled in the light of the fire.

Then, with reverence, he held the Colt in both hands, palms up like an offering, and placed it deep into the heart of the flames, wondering at how his hands were not burned at all. There was a flicker, a catch, and the runes began to glow upon its casing. A bright light pulsed forth from them, and with a snapping sound like that of branches crackling, the revolver began an even brighter glow.

He plunged one hand in again, grabbing it by the hilt. The red aura of power followed it, angry little flames flickering around the muzzle and circuitously wrapping themselves around the insignias on the weapon.

He spun the chamber, holding it out at eye level, and loaded it carefully. Six bullets in it. He spun the chamber again, then shut it. This would be easier, he knew, if only he had both of his eyes back...

He aimed at the moon. Squeezed off a shot. Like a firework, the bullet spun and exploded, mid-air. Something dark, with flapping wings, unfurled itself out and soared into the distance. He grinned at it. Aimed at the next canyon, let fire. Another bullet zipped, exploding into a shower of crimson light. Something dark and furred reached forward, long sharp talons tearing and scrabbling at the ground as it pulled itself forth from the earth.

"Beautiful," Lazarus said. Hadn't he seen a cartoon like this once? An orange-bearded cowboy with a bad attitude. He fired the four other shots at random, one over each shoulder forwards and backwards. The wind picked up, and his hair slapped at him.

"Come to me, children of the moon!" he shrieked, with glee. "Come to me and feast upon the beautiful suffering of this plane!"

He reached down to his belt, scrabbled with it. A leather pouch, filled with ammunition, splashed to the ground and bullets went bouncing everywhere. It was enough lead to stop an army. He bent down, knees aching, and reloaded, snatching what he could in his frail fingers.

He let off six more shots near him, at the peak. The holes they opened in the void bubbled and meshed together; and with a crow of exhilaration he felt the whisper detach itself from his shoulder and flap over.

It became visible. A white mask made of pearl, eyeholes filled with the same substance, with spikes like a crown upon it, merging with the massive spinning portal. Beyond it, a form at first like a scrabbling spider came clawing forward, pale limbs windmilling and scurrying backwards, until it affixed the mask to its face and stood. The mask gave it some human resemblance. It rose to two limbs like its feet, turning, its bizarre conglomeration of limbs extending to both sides of its body. A glare of white light, and its right arm went down, leaving echoes of itself that were itself—the left arm going up, and leaving two similar clones. The six arms of it glistened in the light of the portal, and a shimmering vine exploded from the Mask and downwards, wrapping some regal clothing around it.

Lazarus' mouth dropped open. The figure before him had pale skin and a white crystal dress that hung like a chandelier. Six arms akimbo, bedecked with glittering diamond patterns seemingly carved into its flesh, and two legs striding majestically forward in crystalline high heels. She dwarfed him, this giant.

"My children," the Whisper called out. Its eyes could not be seen behind the mask, yet it looked directly at Lazarus as it spoke. Its many arms moved gracefully with its words, making different gestures. "Gather before me, oh Children! Come to me!"

Furred things clawed their loping way up the sides of the plateau. Flapping things alighted on the ground. More and more tears were opening themselves up around them; Lazarus turned and, with an exultant cry, re-chambered more bullets and began shooting more and more.

"It's beautiful," Lazarus said, looking at what he had wrought. "So goddamn beautiful!"

CHAPTER 21:

DEBRIEFING

Grimm lost his body—the base was destroyed—and now this, this ethereal fireworks show in the night sky...

"I suppose when it rains, it pours," Randall said. "Let us go back and assess the damage."

Everyone packed in and Skye drove, tires squealing as she took hairpin turns back to the base.

"Look at it," Eric said, voice shaking.

Their hidden Compound entryway into the hideout was destroyed—barriers busted and all. They slowly drove over the debris left from the break-in. Bailey bounced back and forth in the seat as they hit bumps. When they found debris too big to drive past, they parked the van where it was. Eric started clearing a path.

The rest of the team walked in past him, into the garage, a numb silence encompassing them all. A sage mist blew out at them, but it was feeble—damage had been done to the outlet pipes.

"Dear Lord," Randall said.

The cryptid cages at the Zoo had been upended. A few of the less-dangerous cryptids scurried here and there; there were clear signs of a struggle. Most of the tech hanging on the wall previously had been torn down and demolished.

"My stuff!" Grimm said, voice distraught, and bent over it. His hands passed through everything. "That's... that's not fair."

Nobody made a joke. They had been struck, at home. A dark cloud hung over everyone.

Skye and Bailey found the other girls upstairs. Sassy was shivering, shuddering, groaning to herself in a corner, intent on repenting for her sins. Addy had bound her own hand up in some gauze, inexpertly. Skye came over to her, unwrapping the fabric and wincing at the wound.

"We'll have to set this," she said. "Maybe see if we can salvage some serum from upstairs."

"Are you okay?" Bailey asked, walking up to the Sasquatch.

Bailey placed a hand on her shoulder, gently, and felt her quiver.

"She's mad at herself," Addy breathed. She was barely conscious. "The eyepatch guy— he was able to control her, to manipulate her. He almost got me, but I've had a lot more practice at watching my thoughts."

Sassy squirmed away from the touch, hunkering down.

"It's not your fault," Bailey said to her. She reached forward, embracing her in a hug. "He got me too."

Bailey couldn't see the sasquatch's face, but she could feel her back-muscles relax.

Randall blew into the room shortly afterwards. His battle gauntlets had been replaced by the pinchers, again.

"So what, exactly, happened? R&D is a wreck. It's like a petting zoo down there."

"Get out," Skye said. "She needs time to rest."

"I need answers," Randall snapped.

Addy sat up weakly, wincing. "It was that eyepatch guy, from before. I had him under my thumb, and he managed to mind control Sassy somehow."

"He did the same thing to me in the van," Bailey said, voice defensive.

"Curious," Randall said. "What was he after?"

"He got the lantern," Addy said.

There was a look on Randall's face then, like he'd bitten into a sour lemon.

"Two steps forward, fifteen back," he muttered. "That may just explain the fireworks show in the distance."

"Was that what you had me track down?" Bailey asked. "Before?"

Randall looked at her steadily.

"Yes."

"What is it?" Bailey asked.

"Something very important," he said. "Skye. I'll summon Barbary and we can handle Addy and Sassy's wounds. You and Bailey need to go, right now. Talk to her about what we discussed."

Skye turned and regarded him for a moment before speaking.

"Are you sure this is the right time for all this?"

"There is no better time. She needs to be able to control her ability. The sooner, the better. Go. Now. We'll clean up, see what supplies we can salvage, try and corral some of this mess up."

"Where are we going?" Bailey asked.

"More training," Skye said.

Skye walked with her to the library. It smelled of dust and old vanilla; the energy was clean and clear. Bailey could feel the untold stories in the books yearning for her fingers to trace the ink left behind.

Skye sat her down in a comfortable seat at an oaken table, and then came around the other side. Soon, they were looking at each other. Bailey had never spent time alone with Skye before. The woman was older than her, but not by much—but Bailey knew that the years Skye had on her were lived years, years spent seeing things Bailey had never hoped to experience.

"How did you get into the portal?" Skye asked.

Bailey considered this.

"I just did. I knew I probably could, and I jumped."

Skye nodded.

"And did you know you were closing it from the inside?"

Bailey blinked.

"No. No, not at all. All I remember was thinking 'I have to grab Grimm.' "

Skye nodded.

"What do you remember about the inside of it?"

Bailey thought on this.

"Not much," she said. "I remember falling, and flying—grabbing Grimm's leg, his leg falling off. The rest of it's a blur. A big knot all tangled up inside my head. I honestly don't know. I do remember thinking I had a killer headache at the time. When I came back."

Skye nodded.

"I'm an anthropologist by trade, and I study folktales, folklore, and non-traditional beliefs. I say this to say I only know this because of my studies. I'm not some mystic; I was never taught the medicine path, but I have studied my people's folk tales, and tales from other cultures, and I've read and seen things working with Randall that, frankly, I never would have if I stayed in academia, though I admit my program was a bit advanced. I do know that, on occasion, there are healers who rise up. The old school catch-all word is shaman, but there are some people who want to pigeonhole that term to Siberia for very valid reasons, but that's beside the point. You've had a calling. When shamans—healers—mystics—receive a call to service, they answer it. They are travellers between worlds, between this world and the other side. Typically, they retrieve souls who have been lost on the other side. Randall believes, and I'm starting to believe it, now, that you're one of these."

"This is all a bit much," Bailey replied. "I just got here. I can do some stuff if I focus, but I mean. Can't anybody, if they try? Isn't it normal?"

"It can be," Skye said. "Normal is such a Western concept of thinking, though. Like there's some status quo, some statistical reality that composes a delicate balance, that makes this world feel and sound correct. There's no such thing as normal. You can't measure it on an individual basis. You don't judge a fish by if it climbs a tree. You can't judge a dog by the eloquence of its speech. Normal is a parameter designated and set by each person in each culture on an individual basis. And if you let this term and these abilities other yourself, instead of embracing them, you're just cutting your arm off to spite your face."

Bailey stared at her.

"Look, I have a GED and took some online classes at community college," Bailey said. "You're talking way over my head."

"Don't cut yourself off from your talents," Skye said, and her voice was gentle. "Let me tell you a story about another spirit-worker like you."

And Bailey sat back, listening.

CHAPTER 22:

A SHAMAN'S TALE

This was in the olden times, when the weird pale men with muskets had not yet colonized the great Earth, and many of our people grew terrified of what howled in the darkness outside of their little huts. It's a story about strength, about will, about what the soul is made of.

In those days, there was born a man named Weak River. Weak River was called this because his mother was ill when she had him—she was of the Bear Clan, a mighty warrior bride of some renown herself, and it was a shame when she was brought so low. Weak River was different than many others in his clan—he and his twin sister were born under fated skies, under a starry constellation that meant they would be destined to do great things.

He was named Weak River because he himself was sickly when born. The midwife did not believe him to last longer than nine days, and his sister, Strong Waters, seemed to have the most life of the two of them, as if she had taken all of her mother's strength for herself in the womb. Yet, despite the midwife's pessimistic outlook, the great Wakan Tanka saw fit that Weak River would survive.

He did not bloom; that was not his path. He did, however, grow steadily in the way that children do. He was always small, however, and had some little quirks here and there that made him different than the others. While Strong Waters grew and flourished, becoming headstrong and independent, her Elders teaching her the way of the warrior, as most in the Bear clan did at that time, Weak River instead flourished doing the work of the women. Yet still, he had his odd mannerisms.

For one, he would talk to everything, as soon as he could talk. It was our way to show respect to our animal brothers, but Weak River sat amongst the flowers and sang to the honeybees. He could often be found lazing by the river, one hand swimming in and out, brushing the fish that swam by and asking them for news of the weather.

He was odd, but there was a place for him. The village Elder often conversed with him when something foul was happening, and he would get this stern look in his eyes and then ask yet another animal what was happening. This advice was useful more often than it was not; and soon Weak River found himself feared and respected for his wisdom.

Yet despite their differences Weak River and Strong Waters found themselves close as could be. Strong Waters often challenged others who would bully Weak River for his flaws. In this way, they lived a relatively peaceful youth.

But time passed on, and the Bear Clan heard echoes of a horrible Beast coming from the east. Two vast serpents who travelled together, intertwined around one another, nigh inseparable, who swam up from the ocean.

It was at about this time that Weak River found himself coming down with an awful sickness. It was well-known in those times, yet those who suffered it often died very quickly and painlessly, passing away in the night of an awful fever.

Weak River, weak as he was, nevertheless fought the infection. In his sleep, his sister would find him reclined, on his back, shadows dancing oddly around the fire. His eyes would shine red as he peered at her in the darkness, and often she found small animals had curled their way up next to his ear.

On the seventh day of his sickness, Weak River requested Strong Waters go and fetch him a specific flower. In those days, a trip into the woods was something to be feared—nature was both friend and foe, and if one did not respect it fully, one would be sure to derive nothing but destruction from its wake.

Nevertheless, whatever Weak River asked for, Strong Waters retrieved. Flower from a hawthorn, six sparrow feathers, and finally, gruesomely, the fat from a bear. These Strong Waters went to get herself—her adventures are complex, a totally separate story, really… but eventually, over time, she slew a fearsome Grizzly on her lonesome and returned to the tribe a Warrior of some skill.

The ingredients gathered, Weak River instructed her on how to mix them. She was shocked.

"You mean to tell me you sent me to make a medicine arrow?" she asked.

"Yes," Weak River replied. "Weasel visited me and told me that the scaled beasts from the deep draw ever closer to our lands. This fight in here is mine. That fight out there is yours."

"But how can I fight, knowing you're ill like this?" she asked.

His eyes blazed crimson, and the shadows grew ever-darker around him.

"I will win my struggle," he said. "As shall you."

And his eyes closed, and he slept.

Every day she checked on him. He was still sleeping, eyes closed, barely breathing. He would awaken and drink some broth every now and again, but then dove back into slumber. Meanwhile, Strong Waters heard word that some strange serpents had come slithering into the nearby forest. Whole herds of deer and clutches of bear had been devoured, only their bones left behind. The people of the Bear Clan knew it for a sign—they would be attacked next.

Strong Waters went to Weak River, and he opened his eyes to her.

"Feed me to the Serpent," he said. "When it comes, it shall swallow me whole. Pierce its heart, beneath the ribcage. There is said to be a great glittering red gem deep in its stomach. I will reveal this to you, and I shall rip it open where your medicine arrow pierces."

"But you are too weak," she said.

"Sister, I am strong, as are you. But as you move in sunlight, so I move in shadow. Do as I say, and the village may be spared."

And she understood the knowledge he had gained, in his time in the Underworld; and so she dragged him to where the woods were said to have been empty.

The carcasses of many bear and deer dotted the clearing, and a smell of something rotten permeated the air. There were egg shells nearby—the serpents had been mating. Strong Waters lay Weak River down in the grass, and he lay curled up like a child, so small and petite he was.

She went and hid in the boughs of a nearby tree, and soon Weak River began to sing.

"Unktehi, Unkcekhula, you scaled beasts
Climbing forth from the waters.
As you were birthed in water,
So too shall you be drowned by it."

As if these words were a magic spell, the snakes boiled and roared up from the ground, massive and frightening. The female, Unkcekhula, she struck first—snapping him up and swallowing him whole. Strong Waters watched, tears brimming from her eyes, as she saw her brother's body squirm down into the belly of the snake, but when she looked closer, she saw where his finger had bulged part of the snake's stomach out.

It was her sign. She sighted her arrow—and then with a *snickt* it tore through the air and pierced right through its stomach. It howled, bleeding black, and she watched as the shaft moved upward, carving the snake in half. Its mate, terrified, slithered away in fear.

Soon, Strong Waters watched as Weak River tore himself free from the snake. He was holding the hands of others—those who had been swallowed, and he kept pulling and pulling and pulling. More and more victims came squirming out, gasping in deep breaths of air.

Soon the clearing was thick with people, and the Unkcekhula squirmed, half-dead. Strong Waters notched a second bow, but Weak River held up a hand to her.

"Long have you devoured," he said. "And long may you suffer. Go back, back to the East—and where you lay your bones, may you never drink water again."

And off it shrieked, slithering and bleeding, and where its blood fell, the grass was eaten. And where it finally collapsed, its huge body sprawling and corroding the ground, the desert grew up in its place… and we call that the Badlands.

Bailey sat back when Skye was finished.

"So what happened to him?" she asked. "That doesn't sound like what happened to me."

"Ah, but that's where we dive deeper," Skye said. "Weak River lived as a respected healer from that point forth. He and his sister died on the same day, both as Elders of the village."

"I still don't see—"

"Normal snakes eat people and dissolve them," Skye said. "The glittering red gem—that sounds to me like a portal. You notice how Weak River kept pulling people out? My theory is the Unk Cekhula kept reserve food supplies in a pocket-world, tucked them away for later through a rip in her stomach. He literally dove into a cryptid, found a portal, and saved people from it."

Bailey sat back, eyes wide.

"So you're saying that's the power I have?"

"Maybe not exactly," Skye said. "But think about it. You were haunted when you were younger, by a cryptid that murdered your father. You can speak to the world around you. You have great wounds upon your psyche, and you yourself have dove into a portal to help heal someone."

Bailey shook her head.

"I don't know," she said. "I just don't know. This seems like an awful lot to handle. A lot to take on."

"Nobody's saying you have to push yourself right now," Skye said. "But you needed to hear this. It's vital you learn to control what's happening."

"It's just… so much, though," Bailey said. "Who am I trying to protect? Who am I trying to comfort? All I have in my chest is hatred for those things. I'm not some savior. I haven't been trying to keep everyone from harm."

"But haven't you?" Skye asked. "Think about your show."

Bailey blinked, shook her head.

"What are you saying?" she asked.

"Haven't you had a tribe you've been protecting? Not everyone can gather the audience you have. You have a certainty with which you speak, a power to your words, Bailey. You have told the people who watch your show two things: Number 1: Monsters exist. Number 2: It's okay to be scared of them and stay inside."

Bailey shook her head.

"But if I hadn't stepped outside—I mean, living in a basement, staying indoors. It's no way to live life, is it? Haven't I hurt so many of these people? Isn't that what my psychiatrist said? It's unhealthy to be scared of things that… that… don't… exist…"

"How many lives do you think you've saved, Bailey?" Skye asked.

"None," she said, and now she was sobbing. Memories of her dead father, memories of her dead friends. Memories of all the people she'd ever let down in her life came rushing back to her in a blur. All she could see was eaten faces, twisted-off heads. Monsters, stinking and horrific, haunted her mind's eye.

"That's not true," Skye said. "I want you to see something. There was a reason we were keeping tabs on you, Bailey. I want you to look at this list we compiled."

She handed Bailey a stack of paper.

"You've made nearly 1200 videos in the lifetime of your channel," Skye said. "Of these, 89% of the advice on cryptids you've given people has rung true. We did the math. The information you gleaned, just from examining the evidence, was as factual as it could be, given you had no interaction in the field. That's more than just guesswork. That's more than just a gut hunch. You were able to look past the fake and somehow pierce deep into the heart of the truth that this world really lives in. *You've done nothing but good with your gifts your whole life.*"

Bailey looked at the paperwork, rifled through it mindlessly.

"But why me?" she asked.

Skye shrugged.

"We can be damaged, or we can adapt," Skye said. A serious look entered her face. "And now that you know—really know, truly and honestly know—you can choose to continue the good work you've done or not."

Skye grabbed a ceremonial drum from a display, and sat it right before Bailey. There was a circle on it, a circle of crows, inked right on the leather stretching across the wooden frame.

"This is a ceremonial drum my people use. Drumming, beating, music—it's an ecstatic bit of power raising. It's a way of altering your mental state. It was said that Weak River used to drum himself into the Other World, during the later parts of his life."

"What should I do?" Bailey asked.

"Find out for yourself what's going on," Skye said. "And then do what you do best. Tell us what you see—tell us what you feel."

And she got up and left, shutting the door gently behind her.

RHYTHM OF THE DARK

Illustration by Anton Tolstobrov

CHAPTER 23:

RHYTHM OF THE DARK

How would this go, if she had her old camera on her? Bailey sat and looked into the mirror before her, watching her reflection. She still looked like the old pale basement dweller she'd considered herself; perhaps a bit leaner, a bit more trim than she had been before she left her house. What would all her fans think of her, she wondered, knowing about what she was?

And what did it matter, anyway? she thought. May as well bounce some thoughts off the audience. Monologuing like she had, in so many of her videos, had helped her talk through her problems.

She pulled out her phone, leaned it carefully on a large dusty book, and pressed RECORD.

"Dear Creeps," she said out loud. "This is Bailey, signing in for a new video. I just wanted to talk today about life. About the real world. I've been out and about in it now—getting a first-hand look at everything I'd only viewed before through a computer screen. Isn't half the joy of the unknown the fact that when we read about it—really dive in deep, we know it's at arm's length? I don't really know what I'm trying to get at here.

"Joseph Campbell says that Myths are an outward expression of our inward struggles. He argues that our psychological growth is simply the human story being told over and over again. The transformation of humankind from some base state to an advanced one is the primary factor in all sorts of fables and legends. Some heroes face outer struggles. Some heroes face inner struggles. So often, one must conquer their fears—both external and internal—before they can face the darkness head on.

"And what are we but players on a stage, as Shakespeare so eloquently put it. I guess what I'm asking is. What would you do in this same situation? How did you face down your fears? How did you feel about overcoming your own personal obstacles in your life? What would it take to really make you feel like the hero of your own story?

"Is this Imposter syndrome? This feeling that other people see something in you, something great. But all you can see is a pile of flaws, bricks in a rubble heap, a mess that's going to take years to reassemble?

"I know what my path is. It's much clearer to me than it has been for most of my life. I see the way forward, but it's studded with setbacks and snags and danger. Do I rush ahead, knowing the jeopardy I put myself in? Or do I keep myself safe? Slink back to my basement and hide away again, turn back from the people that need me the most?

"Thanks for listening, Fellow Creepers."

With a wan smile, she reached out and pressed the 'off' button, then sat and stared at herself.

"There is no path back," she said to herself.

She picked up the drum, sitting it in her lap, and then on impulse, lightly hit the surface. It made a hollow noise—a soothing noise, a deeply baritone whumph of noise that sent shivers down her spine. There was something physical in the act—she tried her fingers, tatting out a quick beat, trying to feel the sound of the drum and understand its intricacies.

She paused, then used the heel of her palm. *Thooom,* went the drum. She paused again, could feel a timer, a beat in her chest somewhere between the inside and outside of her core that was drawing her forward. Beat, pause, beat, pause, beat, pause.

Faster, then. Two beats. *Thoom thoom*, pause. *Thoom thoom*, pause. *Thoom thoom*, pause. Thoom thoom thoom, pause. Three beats, now, and she could feel her consciousness begin to unfold, the ego lying down in her brain and disconnecting, the various gadgetry that kept her skeptic-mind docile in her skull unlocking and expanding outwards like a satellite unfolding, and she felt the petals of an invisible flower peel back from the center of her skull, right in her sinus cavity.

Faster and faster—dum dum dum dum, pause, dum dum dum dum, pause, elbows jerking, the whole of her joining in this ecstatic dance. She could feel herself being twisted inside her body, her consciousness spiraling out with the reverberation of the drum, and before she knew it she was watching her hands move on their own and then she blinked and she was out, soaring upwards as her body carried on sending the beat into space.

There were two parts of her now—and wasn't that a bizarre sensation, she thought, feeling the acrid pull of her living corpse. The notes here floated as she floated, swirling around her and creating a vacuum, ripping space and time open for her in its own special way, and she plunged headfirst into the hole that floated in space, waiting just for her...

A reconnection, then, with the past version of her soul—the memories subtly aligning of this place before, but transiently, like half-remembered shadows clicking back into place. The walls pulsed like guts, again, as if she were sliding down an infinite birthing channel, and she saw a blinding blue light sear her vision as she drew closer to the end.

The constellations swam before her, and she struggled to open her eyes. She saw something from a distance—the Badlands, canyons and valleys spreading themselves out as far as they could. If she looked, she could see the winding of the Unkcekhula as its death throes twisted in the gloom, but then her vision shifted.

There was a man, near a campfire, with an eyepatch over one eye and a gun in its holster. She could see the torment flicker in him—a writhing crimson fountain nearly as bright as the campfire next to him. She could see the lantern's pieces glimmering in the flames, and saw the various shadowed things that crawled and creeped as they slunk their horrible way through the canyons and valleys.

Then her soul pulled and jumped; her vision flickered, and she turned her eyesight ever so gently, and there she beheld something so vastly white and prismatic she couldn't begin to fathom it. It gleamed brighter than the stars, except where it had eyes, and these were white spaces that threateningly vacuumed at her thoughts, compelling her to come closer...

Some gut preservation instinct kicked in, however, for she could feel her whole self fall back and away, diving back the way she came. Those unseeing eyes in a mask never lost her sight, though—the brightest of inlaid diamonds encrusted over what felt like a galaxy of darkness that swam eternally behind the nonexistent gaze of something so inhuman she hardly had words to describe the sensation.

It was like being watched by something primal—a planet itself in the sky, like laying on your back and looking up into the night sky and feeling the pull of the cosmos compel you to just let go of gravity and float, ever onwards, into the stars.

And then she felt a strong push and a pull; she was being shaken, and with the blink of an eye she jerked back and gasped, nearly shrieking.

Eric's face stared at her. She breathed in and nearly screamed, exhaling air through her nose like steam, and blinked. She was back in the library again…

"What are you doing with that?" Eric asked, snagging the drum from her clenched hands.

Bailey's head still swam. She could see the gaze of infinity behind her eyelids when she closed her eyes, rubbing them with the still tender palms of her hand.

"Skye handed it to me," she babbled. "Said I could try to use it to see, or something…"

Eric's gaze softened somewhat.

"You've been in here for about half an hour by yourself," he said. "Come on, we're having a briefing in the conference room. Randall says attendance is mandatory."

Bailey nodded, stumbling to her feet, grabbed her cellphone and followed him down the hallway.

All the while, she thought of the blank gaze of eternity in her mind's eye…

CHAPTER 24:

THE CRIMSON PULSE

Bailey and Eric came into the conference room. The air was expectant—Bailey had the feeling that they had been waiting on her for some time. Someone had delivered some food to the table, but it looked like cheese that had gone entirely off and sausages made from sawdust. Bailey poked a bit at an arrangement of fruit. The grape she touched collapsed, wetly. She grimaced at it.

"Finally arrived, have you?" Randall asked, voice peevish.

"I found her asleep in the library," Eric said.

Bailey opened her mouth to defend herself, but Randall cleared his throat before she began.

"After some minor cleanup, and some backseat driving—" Randall turned a resentful, half-baleful glare at the floating spectre of Grimm on the other side of the table "—We've managed to pinpoint the exact number and coordinates of Astral Holes that have opened up."

"What's the good news?" Skye asked.

"The good news is we know what's happening," Grimm cut in. "At least, quantitatively. There are approximately five dozen A-holes that have opened up permanently in the Badlands. Thankfully, it's a relatively remote location, so the chances of civilian casualties are reduced."

"And the bad news?" Eric asked, voice sarcastic.

"There are about five dozen A-holes letting creepy critters out in the Badlands. And there's some heavy, heavy Crimson Pulse coming from a specific location somewhere in the middle," Grimm said.

"I thought I saw something like that—" Bailey began.

Randall turned his heavy-lidded gaze on her.

"Dear, this is a bit of an emergency, so perhaps you can wait a bit," he said. "I don't mean this in a bad way, but the grown-ups are talking."

Bailey sat back and grimaced. The injustice of it—Randall thought she was so brilliant, did he, but when she had something to say… She could feel something flare up in her chest.

"What are our clean-up options?" Skye asked.

"I would normally whip something fancy up, but having no physical body at the moment sort of ties my hands, so to speak," Grimm said. "Pulling all this information up and trying to get a guy with no hands born in another century entirely to type exactly what you want was bad enough. Having to micromanage any engineering would make me want to just kill myself. Again."

"Addy says the intruder was after the lantern," Randall said. "That lantern is extremely important. I dare say it's a part of me at this point. I'm not unfamiliar with the man—but I dare not trust him. His plans are likely sinister, in the extreme. The high amount of Despair he's summoned puts me in mind of, well, an old case, to be sure."

"My hypothesis is that the existence of all these smaller portals has to do with the big mass of Crimson Pulse," Grimm said, and his ghostly fingers pointed at a specific spot on a printout. "Taking each of those portals down with a team of… what, two or three people that can actually affect those? It would be a game of attrition. No sooner would we have two down than another two would spring back up. It'd be like the worst game of whack-a-mole ever."

Bailey thought about what she'd seen in her vision. If that big mass of Crimson Pulse had to do with that… thing, she had witnessed…

"Guys," she said.

"Not now, dear," Randall said. "Our primary objective is threefold. Number one: we need to do what we can to find the Lantern. There is a chance the eyepatched man knows how to take advantage of its power. Removing that energy source from his grasp is paramount. Secondly: we must disable the eyepatched man. He should be considered extremely dangerous. His abilities thus far have included mind control, to a greater or lesser extent, and an ability to manipulate Suffering—manifesting these Portals all over like he no doubt has. Thirdly: The odds are good he has summoned something extremely dangerous. This would be the large mass of Suffering we've detected on the radars."

"Crimson Pulse," Grimm muttered.

Randall rolled his eyes theatrically and continued.

"The working theory is that the Eyepatched Man has summoned whatever dark beast he has, and it is through its power that this cluster event has occurred. Putting an end to the big cluster should, theoretically, shut down the other portals."

"What if the events aren't linked?" Skye asked.

"Then we deal with it when we come to that," Randall said. "Remove the head, and the snake lays still. Is that not all battles, to one extent or another?"

"Guys," Bailey said again. "I really think you should listen to what I have to say."

Everyone ignored her.

"Combat suits and gear up, everyone," Randall said. "Sage bombs, if we have some left. Addy, I know exactly how you're feeling right now, but if you could be a lamb and get Sassy ready."

"There's some C4 in the morgue," Grimm called out.

Skye stared at him.

"What?" he asked. "It was my secret stash. For emergencies."

Everyone was getting up from the table, including Randall, and still! Nobody listened to Bailey. Yeah, she thought, maybe she did fuck up a little during that last battle… But to be infantilized like this?

"Randall, I tried some of that drumming out," she said quietly.

He turned and looked at her.

"Oh good, then you're the party Bard now, you can keep our spirits up."

He floated out of the room, and she followed him, grabbing onto his cloak as he turned a corner.

"Look, you can't keep treating me like I'm some child," she said.

Randall looked down at where her hand had tugged at his clothing, quirked an eyebrow, and then turned again to follow everyone else.

"Look, you say I'm brilliant, and that I'm special, and sit Skye down to teach me a lesson about being a fucking Shaman, and then you turn around and treat me like a kid. I just don't know what you want from me!"

Randall held his clompers out, and grabbed her by the shoulders. He stared directly at her face, looking down his nose at her, and spoke in what she supposed was supposed to be his 'patient father' voice.

"Darling, you are very brilliant, and very special, but in certain ways, and of those none of them are appropriate for what we're up against. Throwing you into this battle or relying on your untrained skills at this point would be tantamount to suicide for all or any of us. Now if you'll excuse me, I need you to stay here and watch the Compound with Grimm."

"Excuse me?" Grimm's head appeared in the hallway from a plain bit of wallpaper, seeming to sprout from the wall like a bizarre fixture. "I'm not staying here, not for this. Fat chance anything else can hurt me now. Besides, you guys need some extra eyes, at least, right?"

Randall sighed, exhausted.

"Yes, fine," he snarled. "Everybody gear up. It's a family fucking outing. Just leave the compound unattended, won't you?"

"There's still your wife," Bailey said.

"Between me and you, I wouldn't doubt if Barbary didn't invite the Eyepatched man inside herself and make him some coffee," Randall snarled.

A wizened, gnarled old hand stuck out from a nearby doorway, middle-finger extended. The sound of sinkwater running, clacking dishes, and cursing came from deep inside.

"You'll all be the death of me," Randall grumbled, as he turned back towards the equipment room. "But you're staying in the van, Bailey. And don't give me any excuses about some old man hypnotizing you this time, please."

"I'll try to avoid it," she said. "But I think I saw something, earlier..."

Randall had just walked onwards, then. Bailey shook her head and sighed.

CHAPTER 25:

GEAR UP AND ROLL OUT

The carriage house was a stand-apart garage, some distance away from the Manor proper, and Bailey followed the team as they made their way over. Luggage, supplies, and equipment floated out as if being held by man-sized ants—Bailey blinked as Randall seemingly conducted equipment from the house to the garage, his nubs performing an acrobatic performance.

Bailey slid in past a pair of walking pants and peeked around the garage. Two cars—one a hearse, another an old-school van that looked like it came right from the sixties. The hearse itself was pretty nondescript, inasmuch as any hearse could be, she considered. The van, however—it was an old-school travelling VW, with a bright orange retractable canvas top, replete with a flap, and the acronym 'S.C.A.R.E.D.' on the side. She briefly wondered what had happened to the vehicle she and her friends had been driving in. Someone would have found it somewhere, surely...

Bailey watched Sassy drop an apple and grumble as it rolled under the hearse. Addy squealed in the passenger seat as, axels whining, Sassy bent and lifted the whole thing from the back end and grabbed her apple, gently sitting the vehicle back down.

"Be mindful of the suspension, dear," Randall's voice said, somewhere outside.

Eric was trying his best to avoid all flying luggage, shirt sleeves up and checking the tires and fluids. Grimm was poking halfway through the front windshield, dictating specifics to Eric.

"I can't see what you're talking about," Eric said.

"Hold on," Grimm said, voice echoing oddly, and he ducked a little deeper. His already-echoey voice rose up through the engine. "Here, I checked it, the belt looks fine. But we'll have to do something about this gunk buildup." He floated back up and hovered over the engine, seemingly laying on his stomach, legs arced over his translucent back. Bailey watched him as he bobbed.

"You okay?" she asked.

"Still getting the hang of this ethereal nonsense," he said. "I can make myself lighter and sort of will myself up, so the same principal should apply, in theory, to the reverse. Only I can't quite seem to make myself heavy enough to interact with anything physical."

Eric gave him a distrustful glance, and bent back down to the engine.

"Bailey, I heard you like shooters," Grimm said. "I learned a trick or two from them."

He straightened himself up, then landed, lightly, on the approximate left and right shoulders of Eric. Eric did not seem to notice, head stuck in the engine. Grimm started to squat down over his head, teabagging him.

Bailey let out a giggle, and at the noise Eric's voice bounced out from the metallic hood.

"Is Grimm mocking me?" he asked.

"Umm," Bailey said.

Eric raised his head, and there was a moment, in both him and Grimm's eyes, when Grimm's ethereal crotch passed through Eric's head. There was a zap sort of noise, and their eyes both dilated.

Grimm immediately shot over to the other side of the room, careful to avoid touching anyone else and holding his hands over his crotch. Eric rubbed at the back of his head, knuckles white on the tool he was clutching in his right hand.

"Did something happ—" Bailey began.

"I don't want to talk about it," they both said, in stereo. They locked eyes across the room, then quickly avoided each other's gaze.

"I'm gonna go, uh, see if the foundation is good," Grimm muttered, and zipped through the ceiling.

Eric stared at the tool in his hand, and a woozy look had come over his face.

"Are you okay?" Bailey asked.

"I… I think I'm good," he said. His voice had a bizarre relaxed quality to it. "I think I need a cigarette."

And off he slunk, staggering, to the outside.

"Woah, open flame, okay," she heard Skye's voice say. "Meanwhile I have a backpack filled with C4. Yeah, just stay far over there."

Skye charged into the garage, holding the backpack out at arm's length, then gently deposited it in the back of the van, with the air of someone throwing a dirty diaper in the bin.

"Grimm!" she shouted.

His head popped out from a rafter.

"You rang?"

"You care to explain the schematics I found in your locker?"

"No," he said, and his head disappeared.

"What's all this 'In case I'm betrayed' business?" Skye snapped.

He floated down to her, and his shoulders were bowed.

"Look, have you ever been married, Skye?" he asked.

She cut him a look that made him quiver.

"It's just like an emergency bundle I have stashed," he said, voice carefully greased to be as soothing as possible. "Just in case things ever got weird squirrely and I had to leave."

"There's a big difference between a nest egg and individually named explosives for each of our rooms while we sleep," she said.

"Yes, well, you've got to be prepared for every situation, don't you?" he asked. "Look, we have our own morgue and crematorium. Randall has access to all sorts of weird eldritch stuff that can make you disappear forever. If things ever went sour, tell me you haven't thought of how you'd escape."

Skye paused.

"Well, I'd just call the government and rat the whole operation out," she said. "Honestly, I get what you're saying, but explosives?"

"You use the tools you have?" he said, voice questioning.

Eric stumbled back in, eyes bleary, and yawned. At the sight of him, Grimm disappeared into the ceiling again.

"This isn't over," Skye said, to the roof.

"Have we figured out the driving situation?" Eric asked.

Addy rolled down the window on the hearse.

"I've got shotgun," she said. She held up her bandaged wrist. "You know I would never in a million years pass up the opportunity to drive, but I'm not sure I'm in the best shape for this just yet."

"Just what we need, more people without hands," Skye said. "Okay. Cripples and women with me. I'm driving the hearse. You good with the van, Eric?"

He nodded.

"I checked the oil, tire pressure, made sure everything's good to go for a roadtrip," he said.

"There's a bag of explosives in the back of the van," Skye said. "And I'm not sure if we'll have the room for Sassy."

"Great," Eric said. "Me and Sassy on a roadtrip."

"And Grimm," Skye said. "He's on my shit list. I don't want to look at him right now."

Eric opened his mouth to say something, but then shut it again.

"Got it," he said, trying to keep his face neutral.

Randall fluttered into the garage.

"Are we good to go?" he asked. "Driving arrangements been all sorted?"

"Heavy weapons in the van," Eric said. "Sassy, explosives, most of the equipment. And Grimm."

"Excellent idea," Randall said. "If there was another seat, I'd be tempted to ride along. Have a boy's outing."

"We can clean out some of the cargo, move it to the hearse," Eric said hopefully. "Or swap Sassy out."

"I actually need to talk to Randall," Bailey said.

Everyone looked at her.

"It's important," she said.

Randall gave her an appraising look, and then nodded.

"Alright then. Let's all load up!"

He flapped his clompers against one another, and everyone finished sorting themselves. Bailey slid in the back seat of the hearse, buckling herself and Randall in. She heard van doors slamming on the opposite side, and the hearse pulled out.

"Wait!" Addy shrieked suddenly.

Skye slammed on the brakes with a screech.

"What is it now?" Randall snapped.

Addy was fishing around in the glovebox, and pulled out something.

"I was at the novelty shop over off Pine the other day. You know, they sell incense and hookahs and all that. Look what I picked up."

She turned and flashed it to Randall and Bailey. It was an elaborate bumper sticker, with the words 'I Break for Bigfoot' on it, with a little silhouette of a sasquatch. She shuffled through them again, and brought out another one: "My Sasquatch can kick your Dad's Ass."

"How amusing," Randall said, voice dry.

"I also took a gamble with this one," she said. She held it out. "Got it custom made a few weeks back."

Team Shaman was emblazoned on it. Bailey felt something in her heart bob.

"Okay, need to get out and put these on," Addy said.

"The black paint and tinted windows are to avoid letting the world know we have a Sasquatch," Randall said, voice loud in an attempt to penetrate the open car door.

"Yeah, and the head hatch in the roof sure helps hide it," Skye said. "I had to convince someone we were transporting muppets down the highway the other week."

Randall cut her a glance.

"Touché," he sighed.

"I think they're cute," Bailey said.

"You don't think the Team Shaman one's a bit, I don't know, stalkerish?" Skye asked.

Bailey shrugged.

"I just witnessed Eric literally give Grimm head, nothing's too weird for me at this point," she said.

Addy got back in and slammed the door.

"We're good now," she said.

"Then let's get this show on the road!" Randall crowed.

Skye gunned it.

ROAD TO PERDITION

llustration by Anton Tolstobrov

CHAPTER 26:

ROAD TO PERDITION

"Are we going to talk about what happened?" Grimm asked, from the passenger seat.

"We have a gigantic monkey and a pile of explosives in the backseat," Eric said. "I need to concentrate."

Grimm said nothing, just stuck his head through the passenger side window and made a face at the hearse travelling side-by-side on the highway.

"Ook," Sassy said, in the backseat.

"I know, I know, I'll open the hatch here in a minute," Eric said, voice soothing.

Skye narrowed her eyes at Grimm's leering face.

"If he had a physical body I would knock him in the teeth with the sideview mirror," she said.

"You can't let the boys beat us," Addy said.

"We're supposed to be driving incognito!" Randall said.

"We're in a big black hearse next to a hippie van on the highway," Skye said. "If there weren't some antics between us, people would suspect something worse."

Randall sat back in the seat, head reclined against the rest, staring at the ceiling, possibly beyond.

"Perhaps," he said quietly, "I am not as brilliant as I imagine I am. Why else would I surround myself with these lunatics?"

Bailey looked over at the other vehicle. She couldn't see Sassy, but Grimm's face had been replaced by a very pale, very translucent set of cheeks.

"A full moon," Bailey said.

Randall craned his head over, and then shook his head and closed his eyes.

"Bailey," he said, voice theatrical. "You appear to be the most sane amongst us today. Please, attempt to distract me from my electronics expert showing the world his ghostly ass."

Finally! Bailey thought.

"I've been trying to tell you this most of the afternoon," she said. "Skye gave me her drum, and I drummed myself into a trance."

He cracked an eye open, looking her up and down.

"Oh? Anything interesting beyond that?"

"I saw where the lantern was," she said. "The eyepatched man has it. He broke it—right in a flame. His gun was glowing, and there was something else there. Something—well, I don't know how to describe it."

"I really wish you'd said something earlier," Randall muttered.

Bailey couldn't help herself. The words crawled right out of her throat.

"I tried to, but you've been treating me like a kid all day!"

"How else should I treat you, Bailey? We ask of you a simple task—keep your ass planted in the van. Watch it. Then you stumble into the middle of a delicate operation, dragging the creature with you, and throw everything to pieces."

"I—that's unfair. That eyepatch man—he did something to me."

"You're going to have to work on your powers more if you can't stand up to a simple glamor, dear," he said.

The hearse jolted forward, gaining in speed.

"Randall, can you just shut up and be nice for once?" Skye asked. "This is why you can't keep good help around. We risk our lives every day for you, for less than minimum wage—"

"And room and board, you're forgetting room and board," Randall said. "And insurance."

"Just be nice. For once. Bailey doesn't deserve the vitriol level you're at. She's a greenhorn. Fresh meat."

"Look, I try to make sure everyone's doing their best," Randall said. "Sometimes that means criticism."

"Yeah, well, some of us like to think of you as a father figure," Addy said. "You could do to be nicer on occasion. The rest of us learned how to deal with it, but honestly."

Something about Addy's words seemed to trigger him, for he seemed to visibly relax.

"We're a family," he said, as if reciting something someone said to him long ago, and he nodded. "Alright. Bailey. I want to apologize. It's not often that we encounter others like ourselves—human agents, I mean. It's not something I told you about, and it's not something I trained you for. I apologize for leaving you unguarded and unprotected. Your assistance in retrieving Grimm was invaluable, so I guess I could do to be a little less harsh."

Bailey recognized that it was as close to a real apology as she'd ever get.

"Who was he?" she asked.

"If the eyepatched man you saw in your vision, and the one that approached you are the same, then I wager a guess it's a talent I'm well familiar with."

"He was the guy you and I saw slaughter that group of kids," Addy said.

"Ah, him," Randall said. "His name is Lazarus Stone. He's very old, but very powerful in his own right. I've never been quite sure what his goals are, but it seems he's made his move. Bailey, you said he'd broken the lantern in a fire?"

She nodded.

"The Invocation of Arsha'kamal," he muttered. "A very old magick, very dark. Seems he's had some helpers whisper things to him. It's a Sumerian rite—a call to the underworld. An object of great power is used as a sacrifice. The sacrifice itself imbues the power of what was given up into the tool you wield. It's a way of transferring power from one item to another. Often used as a precursor to higher-level evocations."

"Evocations?" Bailey asked.

"Summoning magick," Randall said. "I don't think someone like Lazarus would have access to a full magician's toolkit, or half the knowledge I inherited, but using the Invocation with—what, did you say his gun was glowing?"

Bailey nodded.

"He's used the lantern's power, then, and took it for his own." He sighed. "This isn't good."

"What was in the Lantern?" Bailey asked.

Randall was quiet for a moment, lost in thought, and then spoke quietly, seeming to stare at his hands for some time.

"I've already told you a bit about it, but it's Despair. Suffering. The same viscous, intangible red ethereum we power our gear and technology with. We were using it as a source sample—the specifics of it elude me, but Grimm and I worked together to make it so that energy sources like that could be used with technology. It was years' worth of work. Thankfully, we have all the data source information recorded, and can possibly restructure it from the data we gathered, minus my Sc—well, we can restructure most of it."

"That sounded like a bunch of nonsense to me," Bailey said.

"Aren't you a millennial?" he asked. "Shouldn't you get all this?"

"I guess I skipped fundamentals of magickal technology when I was holed up in my house for most of my life," Bailey said, voice an arch imitation of Randall's.

"I felt the air scorch on that one," Skye said.

"Give me some skin for that burn," Addy said.

Bailey reached forward and high-fived her.

"Yes, well, put more simply. It's... a Scar. When the light of the blood moon descends upon us mere mortals, when our Despair becomes too much, it can crystallize, of sorts. Condense. Our most intense and passionate suffering can ignite upon the astral, producing a dense cluster of energy. This is the semi-physical remains of our worst events."

"Despair so thick it leaves a residue," Addy said, voice idle. She peered out the window, staring. The horizon was changing—forests were clearing, trees disappearing, and more craterous land was building up and up and up. "Hey, guys. Do you see that?"

Bailey looked out where she was looking. There were flickers, here and again, like the air was growing thick.

"What is it?" she asked.

"Randall," Addy said, and her voice was panicked. "I'm trying to focus, but I see them. The *Yurei*."

"Stay vigilant," Randall said, and his voice was kind and fatherly. "Remember. They're real, and they can hurt you... but you can hurt them back."

"Right," Addy said.

"There's something else," Bailey said. "I think I saw something near him. Near Lazarus. It was. I can't describe it, it was like when the sun shines directly into a mirror, that eye glare. But whatever it was, I know Lazarus was working with it, or for it, or. I don't know. It seemed to have something to do with the other things."

Skye flipped a switch on the console.

"Breaker breaker, we have contact," she said.

The soft sounds of psychedelic music poured out from the CB.

"The ice caps are melting," Bailey heard.

"Is that Tiny Tim?" Randall asked. "I thought I killed him in the eighties."

Eric's monotone voice broke through the haunting falsetto.

"Grimm found an old eight track," Eric said.

Grimm's voice cut in.

"I'm learning how to manipulate physical objects," Grimm said, voice excited.

"Please stay out of my personal space," Eric said to him.

"You should see Sassy grooving to the beat," Grimm crowed.

"Guess that explains the back end," Skye said.

The van was rocking and jerking, back wheels catching air. A sharp turn made the wind rip one of the bumper stickers off.

211

"Sassy, there are explosives back there," Eric said, and then they fell silent.

"Oh yes, perfect consummate professionals we are," Randall said.

The tinny voice of Tiny Tim floated through the CB: "You could be driving along the highway. You could be there, by your TV set. It doesn't matter where you are. I want you to think about the ice caps, how they're melting, how they're coming down, how all the cities are sinking into the sea…"

And then Bailey heard Addy shriek; felt the world twist, turn, bend, spin, felt her stomach knot up and watched, horrified as everything went in slow motion—

CHAPTER 27:

BATTLE IN THE BADLANDS

It was the woman in white that did it—the standing, staring, black tangle of waterlogged hair, the outstretched arm, pale and mottled-green. She was standing there in the road, and Addy saw her, saw her even clearer than Grimm, and Addy reached over and yanked the steering wheel from Skye, accidentally causing them to fishtail—

And there in the van, Grimm flipping them off, trying and failing to grab onto his seatbelt as the hearse next to them skidded, knocking into their airborn back end and sending them twisting, falling, rolling and spinning into a dead man's curve, screeching off the road in a shower of sparks where metal hit concrete.

Bailey watched all this in slow motion, watching equipment fly. Skye slammed on the brakes and they spun out. Her heart was beating in her chest, louder and louder…

Something was burning. There was a gasoline stench in the air. Bailey's head was a fog—and here she found herself unsure of where or what she was, slightly adrift between here and there. It was almost like she could feel herself hovering over her own body… some astral double floating above the wreckage…

"Girls!" she heard someone hiss, in her ear.

Someone was shaking her by the shoulder—someone with hard, metal pincers extended in a grasping maneuver. Her arm burned so bad she found herself wriggling free, but the pincers held her ever-tighter.

"Addy! Skye!" Randall hissed. "Don't move! Look!"

He waved a clomper towards the back end of the hearse, and Bailey, making great pains not to move more than she needed to, turned her head. Immediately, she felt a hot drip of urine bleed itself out into her suit-pants.

The canyon floor was floating below them, gently moving back and forth… as if the hearse they were in was precariously balanced on the edge of the highway. Bailey traced her surroundings with wide eyes, looking carefully to see out the sides of the window. And wasn't that precious, she thought, fear completely taking control. Look how the barrier on the side of the highway's peeled back, like it's made of rubber… and why do I feel like I'm being sucked towards the back windshield?

It was like she was on a roller coaster, she imagined, and they were going to do the big dip, only they'd never come back up…

"What are we going to do?" Bailey asked.

"Float," Randall said, bowing his head and chanting.

The hearse was halfway over the edge, rocking ever-so-slightly.

On the other side of the highway, dust settled from where the van had rolled over completely. Plumes of great gray smoke curled menacingly into the sky, reaching out and seeming to stroke heaven. The hippie van was on its side, the engine sparking and throwing flames, the ash from the brush that had caught fire falling like snow.

Noone seemed to move…

"Nobody move!" Randall snapped.

"I'm not moving!" Addy cried.

"Randall, you better have a plan for this," Skye said, staring, stricken, through the back mirror.

"I'm trying to focus," he said.

Bailey closed her eyes… reached her mind out, feeling herself snap out of body, floating over to the van. It was smoking. She looked inside, and saw Sassy had hit her head on the window and cracked it. She was breathing. Still, she looked like she needed a jolt, or something. Bailey knelt down next to her, tried to touch her shoulder, but nothing… and Bailey did the only thing she could think of. She knelt and called out to her ear, as loudly as she could: "SASSY!"

The Sasquatch practically jumped, startled, and sniffed…

There was a whining creak of metal from the van, and soon, the back door exploded. Sassy dragged herself out, hauling the backpack filled with C4 in one hand and Eric in the other. She sat both gingerly on the ground, then bounded over to the far edge of the road.

The hearse was hanging, slowly, ponderously over the edge of the highway. The fall was a good ten or twelve feet of narrow scrub and canyon wall. With a tremendous shriek of metal and a belabored 'Ook' noise, Sassy heaved and pulled the hearse backwards, back up onto the road, and then… once it was safe and sound, she ripped the driver's side door open.

Skye came first, coughing and wheezing, beating against Sassy's furry chest. Addy was pulled out gently, like a little doll, and slung carefully against Sassy's breast. The back doors popped open, and with wide eyes and bleeding faces Randall and Bailey slid out to their knees.

Off alone, on the side of the highway, Grimm's ghost was sticking halfway from the pavement, ass-up.

Everyone was alive, and not the worse for wear, as it turned out. Everyone did a finger and toe check. The van was doused after a quick mumbled invocation from Randall. Bailey, who had sworn she was halfway dead, decided that she would stay in the hearse, thank you very much. She did not speak about what she had done—mostly because, well. What was the point?

A slow dusk was descending, the sun setting in the sky and staining the horizon in ochres, oranges, and crimson.

"The odds are good this was intentional," Randall called to the gathered crew, wind whipping at his face. "As we draw nearer to this Massive A-Hole odds are likely that luck will not be on our side. You've probably wondered why deaths tend to be gruesome and deliberately vengeful when cryptids are involved. Why no simple claw marks, you may wonder? The truth of the matter is, probability grows exponentially more and more unlikely as we approach a Portal. The most horrible of outcomes is statistically more guaranteed."

Eric, Addy, and Skye all looked at him, their faces livid. Sassy was picking her nose.

"You never told us," Skye said, voice accusing. "Did you know, Grimm?"

His guilty-looking emaciated face stared at the ground.

"Your suits have Quantum Stabilizers," Randall said. "These guarantee a relatively normal margin of error in the event of an unlikely outcome. In essence, it's a field that counteracts the unlikely probability singularity that occurs in the midst of an A-Hole. Unfortunately, we've never gone up against something like this before. As we draw nearer to the Mass Event at the center of this, our odds of survival will drop. This is a statistical likelihood. Unless you have an indirect means of doing so, you are advised not to entangle yourself within a three hundred foot radius of the Mass Event. Are we understood?"

They all nodded.

"We may not make it back," Randall said. "I want to let you all know how much of an honor and a privilege it has been to boss you around. Onwards!"

And he turned, cape fluttering majestically.

Addy felt guilt well up inside her, guilt so thick and heavy that she thought it would make her vomit. Of course, the nausea could have been the Serum—a quick-acting mitochondrial boost, an isolated healing factor they were still working on. Her wrist was already feeling better of a sort, though the stabbing, throbbing, pins and needles sensation she'd been feeling all afternoon hadn't tapered off any. Her stomach ached. She thought, again, of the woman in white…

Years ago, when she was just a girl, the woman in white haunted her every step. That particular *Yurei* had stalked Addy all her life. The woman in white had tormented her endlessly, the seeming leader of a precession of more monstrous looking invisible fiends.

Addy's near constant exposure to this had blessed her with an innate sense of direction, like a compass, towards highly infested areas—she could see the air breathe before her, calling to her, beckoning her. Randall and she had trained and trained and trained this gift, honed it down to within an exacting science. Now there was only a quick muttering of some Mantras and she could feel it rise up in her, that second sight, staining the air with its invisible, etheric texture, swirling like crimson motes in the atmosphere.

It was too much tonight. Something loomed large here—something that felt familiar, something that felt—somehow—so big and vast that it was throwing off her radar entirely. She'd seen the yokai sprinting here and there—the ones that had not yet shown themselves, the hidden ones, with one leg coiled like a snake, and a single eye, and a long, leering tongue as they flapped and cavorted with one another. Old men's severed heads, tongues dragging them like slugs paddling in canoes, swam up from the ground in piles of unearthed mud. Addy tried her hardest not to scream, not to flash her *ginunting* and waste her energy here as some drew tantalizingly, fearfully close to her ankles.

The yokai, the yurei, they were heading somewhere. As the group trudged over the next ridge, the sound of the commotion was growing louder. Addy saw a pickup—*the pickup she'd seen drive into the compound*—parked about half a mile forward. They stopped on a narrow plateau. The curve they were standing on rose up into the air about twenty feet from canyon floor, and peering over the side was an unpleasant sensation in the pit of the stomach.

A foetid smell of cryptid began to wash over them, a cloying reek…

"Helmets on," Randall said.

"These readings are ridiculous—never seen anything like this," Skye commented.

"If only, if only," Grimm said. "That is a classic truck, I'll tell you what. You know, I wonder if I couldn't hop in that sucker and hotwire it. Run the guy over mys—URGH."

Sassy's hands slapped where his head was, cutting him off. Everyone chuckled, even Addy... except that she froze where she was, because there was something... She shuddered. Something ice cold, something ice cold that licked her right ankle from the heel up to about her calf.

"Randall," she said quietly, and then the world flipped over. She felt her wrist pop, hard, as she fell, and her tailbone screamed at her as she was pulled over to the side of the narrow outcropping they were on. She tried to fight with her heels, to dig in like a baseball player with treads, but there was something wrapped around her ankle, as if… as if… Her gaze slid down to where she was being dragged, and she screamed…

All inner thoughts died away as she beheld the monstrosity's tongue wrapped around her extremity, drawing her ever-closer to its open, gaping maw at the edge of the ledge…

It was a cloud of dust that took her away. Eric had blinked—just the once—and saw her fall, being snapped and pulled back like someone had wrapped a towline around her legs. He made to do a quick-release with his chain mechanism, to try and give her something else to grab onto, but as soon as he fired he heard a loud shriek as a putrid, moss-colored Jackalope herd bounced in between them, turning and charging straight for the group—

It was massive—pale and yellow, like maggots fed on banana peels, its single eyeball open, serrated teeth rotating beneath it, some massive mouth big enough to swallow a bear whole. It was flapping, flying, its open maw a catcher's net for its prize.

Addy's combat training kicked in and her survival instinct caused her to reach out with her right hand and stab a ginunting right into the rocky clay floor. She flipped over onto her stomach as she held on, the sharp knife glinting, and felt her ankles being pulled, ever tighter behind her. And then Eric's axe-chain soared out above her, landing neatly where her injured left hand was scrabbling at the dirt.

It cleanly separated her hand from her wrist.

She screamed, watching the hand fly into the air, second ginunting glinting iridescent in the moonlight—

It was a battle royale, on a suspended plateau in mid-air, where a fall was certain death anywhere you turned. Madness and chaos erupted. Portals were opening everywhere—closing and reappearing again. Monstrous centipedes ten foot long crawled forth, hissing pincers clacking. A flock of deranged, scaly bats the size of hawks dive-bombed them. Jackalopes ran like lemmings alongside the ridge, knocking people over and launching themselves to their doom...

Sassy picked creatures up and tossed them over the edge, attempting to clear a path. Eric was dangling from the other side of the ridge, axe-chain holding strong, kicking things in the face as they flapped nearer. Randall shot spell after spell—whizzing streaks of light, iridescent cannonballs that exploded, flames and icicles exploding at alternate times. Skye shot arrow after arrow, and watched an errant fireball of Randall's meet her arrow's shaft and catch it ablaze. She watched, wondering, as it soared towards the far side of the ridge, where Addy was struggling—

--and Addy watched her hand tumble directly into the Yokai's staring eye, ginunting's point sticking in its iris, but barely seeming to cause a scratch.

It howled, tearducts flowing, trying to wriggle, but a flaming arrow dinged off the ginunting's handle, embedding it further with a splosh of green vitae. The flaming arrow arced up into the sky, and landed with a heavy thud on the thing's extended tongue, pinning it to a stable part of the ridge a mere six inches from Addy's ankle.

Green ichor seeped from the wound in the monster's eye, and it collapsed, wings giving out. Addy screamed, trying in vain to grab onto Eric's chain, but the thing's tongue was still wrapped around her ankle... She turned and, feeling the strain in her hips, tried to roll the tongue onto Eric's axe, which had just started to come loose... and her leg gave out, and she fell, gravity pulling her towards the edge... hand grasping for leverage...

And then the tongue caught on where the arrow had embedded it into the rock, and she breathed, hyperventilating, as she pulled herself up, cutting away the thick, ropy monster flesh with a knife...

Eric walked his way back up the chain, praising his luck, putting one hand on the ridge and heaving himself up. He'd lost a boot to one of those devil bats. Someone was screaming, something about regrouping and pressing onward—and where did Grimm go?

A portal appeared, and something squat and grotesque dragged itself out. All Eric could see was a dark, coarse mass of hair and long, spindly nails—and before he'd known what was happening, it screamed and rushed at him. It was the size of a dwarf, and the sound it made was awful: "Mahahaha!" as it laughed.

Eric held up his chain, deflecting its attacks one by one, but lost the advantage and was forced back into the middle of the plateau.

Eric's back hit Skye's—and one of things' nails detached, launching itself at him in the blink of an eye. Eric dodged and it sank deep into Skye's shoulder, causing one of her shots to go wild. She grabbed the wound and cursed.

"Skye," Eric said, grabbing her.

She turned on him, and then her face froze. She pulled another arrow, taut, and aimed it at Eric's forehead.

"Why are there two of you?" she asked.

"What?" the Mahaha asked, grinning. It was… it was using Eric's voice! "What did you do to her?" it asked.

Skye's knuckles were white.

"Tell me something only the real Eric would know," she said. "Both of you."

"I've always loved you," the Mahaha said.

Skye looked at it, keeping the arrow on Eric, and then slid her eyes over to him.

"And? What do you say to that?"

"My favorite character in Zombies is Nixon, and one time we got really drunk and you played as Fidel Castro."

Skye moved the arrow over, and then let it rip. The Mahaha burst into flames, the smell of charcoaled hair burning in the air as it shrieked, wildly…

"How'd you know?" Eric asked.

"One time you came into my bedroom and told me that, and I quote, my dirty panty hose smells like Cheese Puffs. No man in his right mind would say that to a woman he was in love with."

The Mahaha screamed, rolling over the edge…

Bailey was sitting in the hearse. Night was coming on. She'd seen no headlights come behind her. But this long stretch of road was nice and empty and quiet and, she felt, somehow serene, despite the horrible knot of anxiety that had sat in her chest for some time. Stress had come down on her like a flying elephant plopping down on a power line, if the power line was her last nerve. She drummed her fingers on the dash, over and over again.

Of course, it was nice and quiet outside. That was good. Great, even. But it also meant she was finding herself sleepy…

Grimm's face was right in front of hers when she opened her eyes.

"Bailey!" he cried.

Bailey jumped back in her seat, eyes wide.

"What?" she asked.

"It's a slaughterhouse out there," he said. "There were too many of them. I came back to find you."

"What do you want me to do about it?" Bailey asked.

Grimm blinked.

"I was just gonna hide here with you!" he said.

"Is it that bad?" she asked.

Grimm's face was paler than usual, it seemed.

"Worse than you can imagine," he said.

Bailey's fingers drummed on the dash, rhythmically…

They had drawn together now—Addy's wrist had been cauterized, and she fought through the surge of pain with a renewed anger that boiled in her body. The five of them moved like a tank—Sassy in front, smashing open new pathways, tossing creatures over ledges and using anything (cryptid or other) she could pick up as a weapon. Randall stayed in the middle, deploying his Neural Network on things that approached them from above. Skye took leftmost flank, nailing things from a distance, and Eric took rightmost flank, clearing out anything that got close. Addy stayed in the back, wounded as she was, as their spotter, slicing and carving what she could with impunity.

They'd made it off the ridge, and down to a ground-level area. The only problem was it allowed them no way to break ranks and flee. This was, as all of them had reckoned, a suicide mission by now. On the top of a far ridge, Randall could see a flickering crimson inferno. Two shadowy beings in the night stood quietly, staring down at them as the beasts rampaged. One of them loomed over the other, a gargantuan thing whose limbs were all wrong...

"We know the portals may not close, but we have to do something," Randall said. "Cover me!"

He chanted and invoked, rings on his gauntlets spinning, and the nearest portal flickered, wavering for only an instant before the incantation was over. It remained as it was. More creatures flitted through it, and Eric's chain-axe cleaved right through the parade of them.

"I'm not doing so hot," Addy said. "Vision's starting to close in."

"She's in shock," Skye said. "We have to get her to safety!"

"At this rate we'll never make it. We have to get out of here!" Eric said.

"Think about Addy," Skye said.

Randall broke.

"Fine," he said. "Target shifted. Sassy, we're going to try and go backwards—we have to try and esc—"

But he'd tripped and sprawled over something on the ground, some writhing mass of primate soil that stared at him owlishly. Its claws wrapped around his leg, and he struggled with it for some time.

"What in the fuck," he heard someone say.

He aimed a gauntlet at the creature grabbing him and blasted it with an energy bolt. It incinerated, and he hopped back up to his unsteady feet, looking around at everyone. He followed everyone's eyes. There was a blur of some sort—jumping into one portal and sealing it up. A beam of light from another portal that was hanging sixteen feet in the air, and Bailey launched from it, fist held forward, Grimm bobbing uselessly behind her like some etheric flag. She plopped right inside another portal, sealing it behind her, and then jumped out of yet another one.

"Look at her go!" Skye exclaimed.

"Now's our chance!" Eric said.

"Go Bailey!" Addy said weakly, and collapsed.

Upon the ledge, next to the campfire, Lazarus grunted. Who was this, then? This little girl before him—zipping in and out of each portal like some cryptid herself? He looked over at the towering might of the Whisper. Her six arms were spread wide, moving as if a silent symphony, and more portals opened above her head. As if she were doing an intricate dance, her arms seemed to dictate the creature's movements. Even though her Mask had no eyes, she could see in other ways.

Lazarus took aim at the whisp of Bailey as she flew. The others were guarding her, buying her time, knocking anything that the Whisper sent streaming towards her away from her trajectory. Lazarus aimed, carefully, and fired a bullet at her. It zipped past her, birthing a soil explosion from the side of a mountain. An explosion of angry, purple monkeys spilled forth, hooting wildly...

"Ah, shit," he said. "This next one'll get you, girlie."

He took aim again, his eye blaring, and then when he finally tracked her descent and angle of next appearance, he fired.

The bullet spun, crimson trail burning through the sky, carving air and everything in its path, molecules disintegrating before it as it drew closer to the spinning force of its target. And then—BLAM! He saw an explosion of red…

Everything seemed to stop. He flipped up his eyepatch and squinted, and then howled…

Bailey felt it call to her, her power, and she knew what she would have to do. She dove and flitted between the portals, sealing them and falling out of another, wielding the weird gravity of a place beyond space and time to fling her out and towards her next destination. And when she was drawing closer, exiting out of one, Randall shoved her.

She turned, watched in slow motion as a crimson bullet pierced his chest, screamed as she rolled in the dirt and tried to regain her balance. She ran to him, grabbing his gauntlet, but it was too late—the Wendigo had arisen from the portal and was dragging him inside, and it was stronger than her. Its eyes burned at her, its stench ravaging her face.

Bailey dug her heels into the ground and pulled, but Randall's limbs were slack, blood oozing from his chest. She grabbed up the gauntlet, trying to hug him, trying for better purchase, and heard him say something in her ear, but then it was done and the Gauntlet slipped off in her hands and he was gone… nothing but a bloodstain on the ground and his empty sleeve in her hands.

The last thing she saw of him was the nub of his wrist sliding in, that weird bit of smooth flesh, an elbow where none should have been…

"There's no use!" Grimm was saying. "We're outgunned and outnumbered! We have to get out of here!"

Someone was bodily dragging her, and monsters swarmed them on all sides, but Sassy crashed in amongst the crowd and began knocking heads together. Bailey twisted in the grips of Eric, watching over his shoulder at the far ridge.

The one-eyed man's eye flashed and his laugh echoed as he fired wildly into the night sky. And there—there before her eyes, a white glimmer and shine against the night sky she saw it—the six-armed conductress, something so primevally part of the universe itself it was as if she had come face to face with Divinity itself, and she found her eyes burning at the sight in her skull and she screamed, nausea in her chest and a feeling of a microphone squealing in her ears, some haptic feedback loop that seemed destined to drive her mad.

The last thing she thought of was Randall's whisper in her ear…

"Be Brilliant!" he said, face slack, skin pale from blood loss, the nub of his arm disappearing.

In her mind's eye he slipped away as her consciousness did.

PART 4: LEGACIES

CHAPTER 28:

AFTERMATH

It was a quiet ride back to base. Randall was gone—and nobody seemed to know how to respond. The van itself was towed carefully, and the remaining members of S.C.A.R.E.D. rode together, crammed uncomfortably in the back of the hearse. Skye drove. Sassy had her head and half her torso hanging out the window, to make room for everyone else, and nobody seemed to care.

Bailey felt a hot sense of guilt in her chest. She had not yet released Randall's gauntlet from her hands. She had awoken being strapped in a seatbelt—and all they seemed to be able to do was look in the distance as the crowning glory of a night full of portals loomed over them all, an open menace that had crushed them in totality.

"Everything's a mess," Skye said to herself.

"I'll handle cleanup when we get back," Eric said.

"I wonder how Barbary will take this," Grimm said.

They did not say—we have to have a funeral. Bailey was waiting on someone to acknowledge something, anything. Addy was asleep, mercifully drugged and her wound staunched. They had not been able to recover her hand, though Grimm had whispered in Bailey's ear something about a prototype he'd been working on.

And that seemed to be that. The bad guys had won. Who knew how far their influence would spread? Bailey saw it in her mind's eye, then—a black and crimson cloud of evil, flowing from the Badlands, from the mouth of the deceased serpent that created the desert. How far would this evil spread? How long before the compound was overtaken?

Nobody seemed to have the energy to think or talk about these things. And after a while—watching Skye take slow turns, watching the portals fade into the morning mists that flowed from the Black Hills, she found that her fear was slowly leaving her.

Whatever that thing was back there… she thought she had glimpsed a part of its intentions. It was horrifying in magnitude, and she hated it, utterly… yet she couldn't help but feel some sort of understanding with it. Just like the land itself, the *Thing*, the six-armed evil that manipulated the monsters from the other world, it wanted only to exist, to subsume and protect for its denizens.

It was a power she had not felt before, and it felt like something in her was changed just by witnessing it. Still… what could she do but sit on these feelings? A hot knot of self-hate, familiar, bobbed up to her throat, and she swallowed back bile. How could she feel compassion for it? When it had taken Randall? And then she turned her hate—not at herself, but outwards, towards that hideous *Thing* that done this.

It was easier to be driven by vengeance than be lost, to be sad...

Days passed by in a blur. Eric and Grimm supervised cleanup duties. Skye had disappeared into the library for days at a time. Sassy played Addy's nursemaid. The defensive perimeters were checked on an ongoing basis, Grimm heckling her and micromanaging her from behind as she logged in to the Mainframe.

Eric had conferred with Barbary about the events that occurred. The kitchen shook, with the force of an earthquake, and after some time had passed, Bailey saw her for the first time without the monstrous visage she had erected. Now she was tall, gorgeous, and lovely—long black hair down her back, and a perfectly pale complexion that put Bailey in mind of Elvira or some other gothy vamp from the sixties. Their meals improved after that—and Barbary had taken to stalking the edges of the Manor, shaking a pile of dangling skulls from a thread, waving her broomstick, and muttering enchantments. Bailey did not know exactly what Barbary was doing… only knew that she could feel an extra wild sense of protection grow up and over the compound.

The local news did not report on much at first. Drivers were cautioned to avoid the Black Hills area, for fear of avalanches and migration season. A slew of missing people started popping up, one by one… and all Bailey could do was sit back and watch as the chaos slowly leaked into the surroundings.

She kept Randall's gauntlet on her night stand. Nobody had felt inclined to come and take it from her. She did not know how she felt about that. She considered trying it on, but Grimm had been constantly complaining about Randall's bizarre desire to have a prosthetic powered by magic that didn't have fingers. It was an outdated prototype, he'd said, and they had the tools and technology to do so much more...

Still, it was her reliquary. Something she held while she thought about the past. She did not feel like she should have been here for this—she was too new, too green for an event of this magnitude. She did not have the closeness with Randall that the others had. There was something… almost disrespectful about remembering their conversations, how belittled she felt. The last major thing they'd talked about, and she had called him on the carpet and been so stubborn.

She drummed, and meditated. She did not pierce into the Other World; she was too terrified of her power, of opening a backdoor into the place they were in. For all the good her powers had done, Randall had died because of her—because she couldn't control her instinct to rush in and save the day. She was too conscious of the effect she'd had—didn't even feel like she was due any emotional support.

Still, she did her best to be friendly and helpful when she could be. She brought food and drink in to Skye, who was practically squatting in the library, knee-deep in books and often falling asleep over a pile of notations. Eric and she took turns running the perimeter of the compound. She brought food in to Addy when she could, and checked her wound, listening to her rant and sob about her personal failures.

Addy cried into her chest one day, and Bailey tried not to feel bitterness. Her tears, too, were stuck in her heart. She could only feel the blackness of guilt and torment writhing alive in her, like some cancerous beast growing, which she always replaced with hate towards the orchestrator of all this.

At nights, she went with Sassy to the outside of the house. Together they sat and said nothing—which was fine, since Sassy's presence was more than enough to comfort her. That she and Sassy both could not voice what their thoughts were comforted Bailey in a way that she could not quite put her finger on. The both of them were creatures of silence, given over to heavy emotions.

One night, Bailey's watch told her it was around 3 AM. Sassy motioned to her from a bare patch of dirt she'd squatted over. Bailey walked over, watching, and Sassy's gigantic finger carved some crude stick figures in the ground.

Two giant apes—one with a bow in her hair—one mad and angry, a vast circle in between. A stick figure arm had reached out from the one without the bow. There were lines, something like wind in the circle. It was funny how such an elementary drawing could portray so much. Bailey felt privileged to have been there, and when she gave the she-squatch a hug, she could feel thick, hot tears soak her back.

"You'll find him again," she said, and Sassy squeezed her even tighter.

Bailey's self-imposed tasks she found herself doing meant she worked her way to the kitchen most days. Normally Barbary was very insistent she steer clear and stay only in the doorway, but after about a week, Barbary relaxed the wards on the door. Bailey came in and found herself watching as pots scrubbed themselves, knives chopped food, and Barbary leafed through an ancient leatherbound book, reclined at the far back table.

"What are you doing?" Bailey asked.

"Steak tartare, with potatoes julienne," the Rusalka replied, taking a long drag off of a cigarette, her elegant voice only slightly hoarse at the end. "A variation of a family recipe. Some of the ingredients are a tad hard to source nowadays, but times were different back then. You could pluck a human child from its home and you'd be doing the family a favor. One less mouth to feed, and you ate relatively well for a month."

Bailey blinked.

"How long ago did you stop eating people?" Bailey asked.

The Rusalka stared at her, seemingly lost in thought.

"Mmm, I think Randall tended to frown on it, so when we wound up together, I kind of went cold human. Of course, you miss it, but I'm told humans are mostly sentient and self-aware these days, though if you watch that Youtube it makes you think."

"I quit eating octopus," Bailey said helpfully. "They can open jars. There's not much difference between them and us."

"Ooh, that's a good idea for a dish," Barbary said. "What brings you today?"

"I need to talk about Randall," she said.

Crimson tears welled up at the corners of Barbary's porcelain face, and she dotted at these with a bloodstained handkerchief she had tucked away in her bosom.

"I do so miss him," she said. "We've been together for, oh, eighty, ninety years, you know. We met in the roaring 30's. Knocked me out with a paddle and tied me up in his basement. Took my coat right away from me. It's still here, somewhere, and I could find it if I tried. But I've never really tried too hard. He was a young buck with a can-do attitude and knew how to fillet a fish with a grace that was quite shocking for a young man with no hands."

"Wait, he kidnapped you?" Bailey asked. "And did you say ninety years? How old is he?"

"Ah, by my recollection he's nearing one hundred and twenty. It's mostly been good years. There's nothing quite like that delicate dance of power between a married couple. He does so remind me of my father—chains and all. He really knew how to treat a woman—find her minding her own business out on a spray of coral in the ocean, and threaten them with either permanent disability or perpetual enslavement to their every carnal desire." She let out a rapturous sigh at this. "Oh, how I miss him. And Randall, too, of course. That's part of the deal, though. And don't look so shocked at the kidnapping part. Of course he knocked me out with a paddle. I would have eaten him and gnawed on his bones for weeks had he done it any other way."

Bailey blinked a few times, trying desperately to remember why she'd arrived.

"I wanted to apologize," Bailey said. "It was my fault. During the battle. I tried to rush in, and he pushed me out of the way to save me."

Barbary rolled her eyes and laughed. Her bosom, cleavage practically obscene, wriggled with every motion.

"Dear, you can't go blaming yourself for everything bad that happens. Randall made his decision. He was always a very stubborn man. Very headstrong. Always had quite a bit of fire in him, though. A very driven man, despite his inadequacies. I found his lack of hands somehow erotic. Tell me, have you ever had the pleasure of a man's wrist nubs circling your areola? There's something so obscenely rewarding about it—feeling that scar tissue sandpaper its nubbly way around your erogenous zones."

Bailey was not quite sure how to process this, so she tried not to choke as she responded.

"Can't say I've ever had the pleasure," she said.

"Good, because you'd be tomorrow night's supper if you had," Barbary said. "Now get out of here with your self-pity. You're a young, beautiful woman in your prime. Go seduce a man and eat his heart, or whatever you young human females get up to. And on your way, could you drop this by the library? It's a bit of an old concoction—you'd blush if I told you what went in it, but Skye's not yet slept in the past 72 hours and I hear you humans get ill-tempered and cranky without sleep."

"No problem," Bailey said, who was mostly eager to leave.

Bailey knocked on the door to the library. Skye's voice called out to her in a patchy way. Bailey entered and found the place stank of old sweat and grime, the eldritch vanilla smell of knowledge bound on dead trees an intangible stink that mixed with a distinct lack of feminine hygiene.

Skye looked like death. Her bronze skin had an unhealthy pallor to it, and her hair was half-hanging from a scrunchied ponytail that had only been erected with half a brain. Her hands shook around a cup of lukewarm coffee that only half-made it to her mouth.

"How long has it been since you've had sleep?" Bailey asked.

Skye's voice was a hoarse whisper.

"Can't sleep. Have to stop them. Bailey, I think I'm close. I think I—hic—found it. I'm right there. There's. It's the scars, Bailey."

Bailey nodded, and grabbed the coffee cup from Skye. She held the brimming vial out to Skye.

"Barbary said this improves concentration," Bailey lied. "Drink it down."

"Fingers aren't working," Skye said.

Bailey unscrewed the top and held the vial to Skye's mouth. She tilted it back, slowly, watching to make sure it was all drained, and then had no more time to stow the vial away in a pocket than Skye began to slump over. Bailey dragged her to the mattress someone had dragged in the room some days before, and carefully covered her up.

"It'll be here in the morning for you," Bailey said.

"It's... Bailey, listen to me. Read the paper on the desk. We have to find the Scars, Baileeeeeee!"

And then she began snoring.

CHAPTER 29:

SCARS

The next morning, Bailey woke up with a feeling like someone had punched her in the stomach. As soon as she opened her eyes, she looked up at the top of her four poster bedframe and realized something was off in some deeply fundamental way. Well, more so than the last week or so had been.

She rose to her feet, sliding on slippers, and made her way to the dining room. It was passing through the lounge that she found Addy and Eric staring at the TV.

"Authorities are saying this is the 51st missing person in South Dakota in the last week alone. The high frequency of these cases has necessitated the formation of a missing persons task force, and Senator Lankstein has requested a special investigation through a joint cooperative task force with the FBI. In the meantime, citizens of South Dakota, specifically in the Black Hills and Badlands area, are warned to be very careful when travelling alone. Never leave your children unattended, and make sure that you have firm emergency backup plans in case such an event happens."

Eric turned off the TV.

"It's getting worse and worse," he said.

"Can people not see them?" Bailey asked.

"They can hide themselves if they want," Addy said. "One of their many talents. Odds are likely Lazarus and whatever that monstrosity was with him are slowly expanding their forces."

Bailey stared at the muted TV screen, but a siren started to scream and an intercom buzzed. Bailey's hands went over her ears.

"ATTENTION, ALL TEAM MEMBERS OF SCARED—PLEASE REPORT TO THE DINING ROOM FOR A BREAKFAST BRIEFING. THIS IS URGENT. ATTENDANCE IS MANDATORY."

"Sounded like Skye," Addy said.

"Hope she's made some progress," Eric said.

The three of them marched together to the dining room. The floor shook as Sassy loped her ambling way into the hall with them.

Skye was seated at the head of the table, looking much more put together than Bailey had seen her last night. The sleep had done her some good after all. Even Barbary slunk in around the corner, smoking an obnoxious-smelling cigar with streamers of blue smoke cascading up into the corner. Grimm was perched in the background, legs crossed and floating about three feet off the ground.

"Is this everybody?" Skye asked. "Headcount's—" She blinked.

"You're counting Randall," Grimm said gently, from behind her.

"I know." She paused for a moment that extended onwards, closed her eyes, and took a deep breath before she continued. "Okay. Looks like everyone's here. I know we've been in panic mode, and you haven't heard much from me, but I've been considering what we can do. The truth is, we're in a bind. Our main power source is gone, and so is the head of operations. I know we all wanted to bust Randall's balls about how much of a hard ass he was, but the truth is he had a great sense of direction and an uncanny knack for what we needed to do next. We're overpowered and underqualified, and what's worse, we've lost our best brain."

"That's arguable, darling," Barbary said, from the corner. "For what it's worth. Randall always told me how proud he was to have someone like you around in case a situation like this very one arose."

Skye smiled at her briefly before continuing.

"The truth of the matter is. We're out of options. Randall was the heavy firepower. He was the magic. And without him, we just lack the resources to continue. At least... as we are now. I've already spoken with Grimm about duplicating the energy of the Lantern. I'll let him talk about it."

"Short and sweet: It's impossible," Grimm said. "The Lantern's energy was specifically attenuated with Randall's talents. Without him around, it's impossible to replicate. So we won't be using any new or advanced technology that I could potentially create. Not without another power source."

"Randall said the Lantern held something valuable," Bailey said. "And you—you were talking about them last night before you fell asleep."

"Which brings me to my next topic. I've been researching Scars. I had heard they were rare. And the truth of the matter is, they are. Extremely rare. But I heard word of a couple different things. Did some research. Just about drove me insane, but I think I have a basic understanding of the concept. Scars are crystallized essence of suffering. It's a tangible energy source that functions much like a beacon of sorts to cryptids and other monsters. Scars are developed when one has an interaction with some immense amount of suffering. Hauntings—those are caused by Scars left on the grounds by the horrors that happened within. But they're not just a passive energy source. I mean, they can be. Okay, this is a hard concept to relate. Bailey, you remember my story about Weak River, right?"

"Right," Bailey said.

"Weak River was a shaman. His powers functioned differently than yours, but if you'll notice, in the story, his eyes glowed crimson when he used his power. He fought and struggled with the illness that kept him down. My hypothesis is this. That the inner work Weak River was doing allowed him to access the direct power of his Scar, and he was able to use it to control his powers."

"There's a lot of questions that come up from that, though," Addy said. "Is everyone's Scar internal? How'd Randall get his out of his body? And why would he go through all that trouble?"

"I'm not finished," Skye said. "Scars are rarely internal. Scars are usually externalized, semi-condensed memories of suffering. So I was looking at a lot of different cases. This might get a bit esoteric, but consider that, for a lot of human existence. We've fought against Suffering. That's kind of the story of humankind, right? There's a. Okay. So a Scar is not just your inner trauma. It's also the interaction of the Crimson Pulse infused with human memory and pain. It's the intersection of these two things that results in a Scar being imprinted into the aether. Or whatever you want to call the baseline of energy that exists all around us. This synthesis is a beacon, calling Cryptids and other creepy things from wherever they come from. But, since this is such a unique human energy, it's also capable of being utilized by human beings. To enhance their natural abilities. It unlocks things. Powers. Strength. Each one has a different sort of intrinsic ability depending on the person."

"So it's like a power up," Bailey said.

"I wouldn't call it that necessarily," Skye said. "There's internal work that needs to be done to overcome that trauma. It's really an issue of reaching into the Scar to pull out the remnants of your humanity, the pieces of you that were locked away."

"I agree with Bailey, that sounds like a power up," Eric said.

Skye looked completely dissatisfied with this.

"Look, it's not that *simple*," she said. "There's a case I was tracking. The Leeds family. Mother Leeds, had twelve children, lived in New Jersey during post-Civil War times. It was a sweet spot, somewhere between 1870 and 1890. You have to understand what pregnancy was back then, in Victorian times. It was enforced enslavement, to an extent. A woman was bound to take care of her children, to suffer through the pregnancy, and the odds were good it would come close to killing her in childbirth. That a woman lived through six, let alone twelve, should tell you how serious the situation was.

"After the first twelve, when she was nearly fifty, she found out she was pregnant again. Fifty was a remarkable age considering the lack of access to basic health necessities. And it was far past what most people considered prime fertility. She was an old woman, with an already wrecked uterus and a life that was spent basically locked in domestic servitude to a husband that clearly did not have the decency to pull out, or use a lambskin condom besides. So you have to imagine her state of mind. The twelfth child almost killed her. The thirteenth? That one was destined to hurt, and she knew that at her age she'd be hard-pressed to even be mobile afterwards.

"The mental anguish from this, from all the suffering she had gone through and would go through. Well, my hypothesis is that this embedded itself into the child. The myths and rumors all say she cursed her thirteenth-born. But the truth of the matter is, that suffering she had was left unchecked. It embedded itself into the Crimson Pulse, both her anguish and the spectral energy from another world. And when the child was born... well."

"The Jersey Devil," Bailey said.

"Exactly," Skye said. "Her Scar was her mutated child, who took flight shortly after birth and returned to terrorize the entire family and the surrounding countryside. This stuff isn't so much a powerup as it is a unionizing substance. It will literally let us meld with the substance of the Other World. For better or worse."

"With great power comes great responsibility," Grimm intoned, floating upside down and miming hanging on an invisible web.

"There's a middle ground," Skye said. "That's all I'm saying. Randall was conscious of this corrupting influence. Of the possibility of reclaiming even the darkest aspects of one's personality, but coming out worse. That's why he used the Lantern. It was a stabilizer. If he didn't directly interact with the Scar, there was less of a chance he would be warped beyond repair by utilizing its energy."

"So what are you suggesting with all this?" Eric asked.

"I don't know about all of you, but when I look around this room. I count six shining faces. Faces who have fought this terrible Other World—faces who have been catalyzed by its damage. Faces who have their own Scars. Our only chance—if we want to stand a chance in all this—is going to be by reclaiming our darkness. Searching deep within and going back to where we all started, to find the Scars that brought us here. Reclaiming our power. Fighting fire with fire."

"Where would we even begin?" Eric asked, voice hot. "You expect us to find some physical remnant of our suffering—our very first impact with the Other World, you're saying—and then bring it back here? Do you have any idea how wild of a goose chase this is going to be?"

"She didn't say it'd be easy, darling," Barbary said. "She said it was your only chance."

"Retrace your footsteps. Reclaim your power. Regain your Scar. And if we gather enough power—we can go and return that bastard Lazarus and everything he's summoned to sender."

"Oh man, I got chills," Addy whispered to Bailey. "She'd be a great boss, if we all live through this."

"To summarize," Grimm said. "Your orders are to introspect and travel back to where you came from. Gather your personal Scar. Merge with it. And in so doing—try to power up."

"Goddamnit Grimm!" Skye said. "If you had a physical body I'd kill it."

Grimm shrugged.

And just like that... the meeting was done. They all ate a solemn breakfast, thinking heavily, the weight of an unknown future hanging over their head. Even Sassy seemed particularly pensive.

"Just gotta find my Scar," Bailey said, into her oatmeal. "Retrace everything that happened to me since I got here."

It wasn't much, but it was something—a small glittering sparkle of hope for her future.

CHAPTER 30:

SASSY'S DANCE OF PASSIONATE TRAGEDY

They did not have these leaves where she came from; where the air smelled like thick jungle, rotted undergrowth, and the primal smell of her tribe's musk. These were not words she knew—these were memories she had, of days long gone by, and at night, when the small ones would putter to their bedrooms and lay inside like children frightened of the dark, she would sit beneath the stars and watch the moon and remember.

The small ones—the small naked ones—(and that had thrown her for a loop—in this land, the dominant two-legs had undergone some horrible malady that made their fur fall off. Apparently it had been a worldwide disaster. She had seen their littler people in the box they kept on the wall inside their ornate cave. They were all naked, too. Everyone covered themselves, as if to hide their shame, but Sassy had been too polite to bring it up.)

Their forests here were different. The animals were different. *Everything* was different. She saw similar things—knew that, as far as herbs and plants went, the rules were basically the same. Spiky bad, red poison. Of course, the plants here didn't put up near the fight that she was used to. Somehow, an acorn didn't taste quite as sweet if you didn't have to punch the tree in its angry face to subdue it before you took and ate what you wanted.

They gardened—though of course she did not know that word, but understood the concept. There was a spiky bit of metal surrounding a bare patch, and any time she had ventured in to grab something the shape-shifting she-beast with the sharp metal knives ran out screaming at her. (And metal, that was something... somehow they'd been able to melt rocks into something extra durable and shiny, but the exact specifics of it was lost in translation, though the floaty pale guy had once tried to draw a diagram.) She soon realized that one could grow your own vegetables, and the thought intrigued her to no end. If she ever got back—

It was one of several inner emotional chains she went through. The amusing antics of the naked ones were enough to distract her during most days, but when she was by herself, all she seemed able to do was to focus on the past. Now, however, there was more crowded into her mind.

They had drawn a diagram for her. She'd got the gist. Naked speech was mostly tone, but some things she needed them to draw out plainly. She was to go out in the woods and find... well, something. Find herself. A little part of her that she'd lost. And she would grow strong again. Stronger. Maybe enough to stand up to all those creatures.

Of course, she still had all her fingers and toe-fingers. She used one of their shiny metal things to check herself out, much like she had used the lake back home. Her tail and all her fur was there. Even the ridiculous pink affectation they had bestowed upon her head was there. So what was she missing? What was part of her that she couldn't find?

Again, she thought about home. Home was a dank swamp, a comfortable tree root, a cave where one could sleep against Him. She tried not to think about Him, but as often happened, she found his scent-image and her mind-pictures bringing him back up. Where was He? When had they gotten separated?

She'd wandered for many sun-and-moon times in these woods since the naked ones had sent her away to find her missing piece. She had wandered, and wandered, and wandered, and finally found where she had arrived. An indentation, shaped like herself. Old leaves and sticks and branches had fallen into the hole. Here was where She had come from, wasn't it? Surely, if She had lost some part of herself, then it would be here.

The tracking had been easy. She remembered that day. The small one, with the long dark hair. *Addy*. She knew that name, just like She knew that they called her Sassy. Addy had found her, face planted on the ground, barely able to move and aching from a fall that felt like she'd jumped off the highest tree in the forest and lost hold of the vine. When she'd gotten to her feet, an outline of where she had landed had creased the ground.

Of course, She thought, though she did not think in these words, but rather felt these things. This world was not hard—how much her first impression had told her about this world? Back at home, if you slipped from the tallest vine, the ground did not give. It devoured. One would fall and crack open like a ripe melon, and all of the skittering things with claws and mandibles would crawl from beneath the leaves to eat your remains.

This world was easy. Everything was weak. She could tear most of it open. And its dominant two-legs had become weak as well. What else could She do? She knew she needed to protect them. They were small, they were weak. Though, the ones that took her into their tribe were strong in their own ways.

The one with no hands. He could summon lightning, force the world itself to do his bidding. That was not something she had often seen. Addy. She was fast—stealthy as a stick insect on tree bark. She envied the naked one's speed. So many were so strong in so many ways. And She knew that if there was something to be done for them, She would have to grow even stronger.

But what was She missing?

Again, She thought of Him. Felt the memory of Him as powerful as if he were there with her. She closed her eyes, leaned into the recollection, tried her hardest to smell him…

It came back to her. That perfect day they'd had together. Swinging through trees, chasing each other. Him nearly drowning. Rolling around together in His cave. She had lost so much when She lost Him… and if only She could get Him back, She felt that she would be the strongest of them all, of anyone in this weak world.

The wind blew around her, cycloning up in a wide circle. She opened her eyes to her fur rustling, and smiled into it. Leaves from the indentation she'd left danced in the breeze, surrounding her with a riot of oranges and yellows and greens and pine needles, and she held her hands up to experience the moment. Hadn't this happened that same day they had met?

Tears spilled from Her eyes, and she blinked as a big red leaf the size of her head slapped into her face. She pulled it off, and stared at it. It was shaped like a heart, and seemed to glow like the cave mushrooms back from where She had lived with Him. And, of course, it was gigantic. She had not seen something like this here before…

Still, She was not an overly sentimental creature. She wadded it up, and pressed it to her face, as if to clean it and wipe up her tears. But She could feel something dangling between the leaf and her face as she pulled it away.

It was something stringy, something... glowing? She put a hand out, thinking she had hocked up a loogey, but her fingers went through it, and the phantom afterglow trailed up her hands and wrapped itself around her arm. She could see it travelling up her, this spark, and watched, eyes round 'O's of shock as she began to glow like a beacon of light.

The image of Him and their perfect day came to her again, striking to the core of Her like a hot piece of metal, and this time, She could not stop it in its tracks. It rolled over her, a fallen oak of emotion and raw ache, and she bellowed, loud and low and ascending to a shriek. Birds took flight around her, and the stars themselves fell from the sky, twirling around her yearning need...

He arrived, in a dusty plain, with nothing but hunger in his belly, and the same ravenous anger that had swallowed him ever since She was gone. The portals had opened everywhere—all sorts of the beasts where He had come from had taken flight in them, and He knew that in this land, where everything was weak, He would be strong.

He would destroy everything, He knew, if only because He could not have Her.

But something glinted in the heavens; some wayward constellation, perhaps a shooting star. And with it came a strangled scream.

He bared His teeth, shoulders aimed. Whomever had screamed, whatever had screamed... it was now going to be His lunch. He took off at a lunge, diving past sand and plateaus and horrible creatures with too many legs. He hit black tarmac, was nearly broadsided by something square and fast and vibrating that he tossed off the road with a backhand. He could hear shrieking coming from it as it exploded.

He passed the black snake road, and plunged into the dense forest. But then the cry came again... the timber changed, and something in his glowing red eyes began to soften. There was something... familiar to the scream, something so intimately appealing to Him that He found Himself stopping in His tracks.

He smelled the air. He could see something shining brightly off in the distance. He could feel its warmth radiating out to Him. And as He drew nearer and nearer, anyone passing by would notice that His eyes had begun to glow blue.

Trees, vines, bushes, and scrub parted before Him. He made it to a clearing, hesitant, moving slowly... fingers parting the branches where the light lay beyond.

He saw Her.

And She saw Him.

There was a rush of movement, the sound of thunder. And their light illuminated the forest around them, a pyre of celestial brilliance that shot into the cosmos itself.

And if one were near enough to see the light, one would also be near enough to hear the hurried, rushed, intimate sound of "Ook... Ook! OOOK-OOOK-OOOOOOOOOKKKKK!" as it echoed through the forest around them.

CHAPTER 31:

ERIC'S DANCE OF DESTINY

"Caesar."

"Eric?" The voice on the telephone sounded shocked. "Creator above, where have you been?"

"Away." Eric's voice was short and clipped.

"Have you heard the news? There's people going missing. The Elders are saying we can't go out past dark. Where are you?"

"Fifty miles or so away. Could you use some company? I need to come back."

"You disappear for years and call no one and now you just decide to call one day? And you expect me to put you up?"

"Yes," Eric replied.

A pause. "You pig-bastard," Caesar said, eventually. He sighed. "I'll have a cot rolled out for you. When are you coming?"

"Tonight."

"We'll have to have a hog fry to celebrate. She-she talks about you all the time and the kids will want to see their Uncle."

"I'm glad," Eric said, and then hung up.

"Hello?" Caesar asked into the phone line. "Eric?"

He rolled onto the Rez at night-time, headlights shining in the gloom. No people were out. There was nobody waiting for him; no stray dogs wandering as they were wont to do. There had been some construction done here and there—new houses, new plots of land split and separated from the others. The passage of time meant that his people had slowly, bit by bit, accepted the trickling slide of the white man—that urge to modernize, to separate, to divorce themselves from others. Whereas before one was lucky to have barbed wire fences to keep chickens, now there were fences everywhere.

Fences, walls, gates. Who could blame them? When the world was as dark as it was, sometimes, one needed to lock themselves away. How many of his people had stayed here, on tribal land? Stayed behind these fences and did not venture into the world at large? How often had they decided that safeguarding their ways was more important than mingling?

His time away had changed him. He was no longer a young warrior filled with grit and a desire to escape his past. Now he needed to come back home. To find who he had been. What had shaped him. What had caused him to leave in the first place.

He'd left because of terror. Here in the wilderness, on tribal lands, he knew there was darkness. Had seen it—had seen the signs, the omens. Watched the horrible Unktehi slither its way into the compound, watched his Grandfather transform into something terrible and awe-inspiring. The Thunderbird of legend—his Grandfather had smote the evil serpent in its path, sacrificed himself, and flew away into the clouds.

It was madness. He'd tried to escape it. He could not live in a land of monsters and people together. Something about it quickened his blood, scared him. He'd wandered, trying to disappear into the modern world, getting lost in its own mindless, evil pattern. Working contract jobs. Laying foundation. Construction. Making a paycheck. Taxes were a comfort and their own intrinsic frightening thing. He'd stared at a 1099 form with the same trepidation he imagined he'd have when facing a bear.

Still, that fear that he, too, would become a monster drove him. He got involved in inner-city work. Signed up to be a park ranger. Gave climbing lessons to white people escaping from their skyscrapers for the weekend. He was always handy with a rope and chain…

A life of dull modernity. He'd started playing video games to escape even from it. Wasn't that his pattern, he wondered? You were unhappy, terrified of what you may turn into, terrified of who you were, of who you'd let yourself become… and you tried to escape.

He'd seen more than enough burnt out junkies to know what drugs did. That was an early lesson—alcoholism, meth, shoot outs. That was what his people had done to escape their horrid little lives. Drink themselves away, tweak themselves out, make mountains out of molehills. Better for him to stay alone. To stay hidden.

He didn't know when it had begun. The isolation. He'd locked himself in his apartment one summer. The heat outside was unbearable, an utterly grotesque Kansas City heat that was damp and unforgiving. He'd done contract work—well paid contract work—and decided that, for him, he'd had enough of the real world. He dove in to the internet, to electronica, to the febrile fake connections that other isolated people took joy in.

He streamed. He played games. They paid him for it. He was losing himself, losing the little pieces of himself bit by bit. He was no longer Eric, grandson of the Thunderbird, but now he was some ghost behind a screen staring out at a world that didn't exist and hoping it would provide him some sense of normalcy.

Yet still, he could not escape from those memories. And the Darkness that clung to him seemed to follow him wherever he'd gone…

Brief thunderous booms. A glint of something sparkling, weaving its way through trees. The feeling that the Sun itself was staring down at him. The untold weight of a past that he had pushed out of his mind as too unrealistic.

Another early morning like all the rest. It was Kansas City summer, again—the early sunlight blared through the kitchen window and stung his eyes, and he woke up to make his coffee, skipped the shower, and ate an old bagel that was sitting on the counter for a few days. He was scheduled to stream at 9 AM, and for a lack of anything better to do that was how he was going to spend his morning.

He did not expect to find his living room trashed. Cereal boxes had been dragged from the cupboard and upended all over the coffee table. His DVDs and game jackets were thrown about the room. A large butcher knife—and it surely wasn't his—was embedded in the couch cushion, directly in the ass-groove he'd sculpted from a year of comfort and relaxation.

The front door was locked. The windows were locked. There was no way someone else could have been inside his safe space. He blinked. Checked the baseboards for mouse holes. (Though honestly, a little part of him thought, what kind of mice could drag around a butcher knife?)

"Hello?" he called out. Maybe it was the super, checking in, and he'd locked the door behind him, and there was some sort of explanation for all this that was implausible.

But nobody responded. The apartment was silent. Abandoned, except for him. A cereal box, sitting half-empty on a corner table, poured the rest of its contents onto the ground and slipped, hitting hardwood floor.

Eric got a broom and a dustpan and swept up the mess, and by the time the afternoon had rolled around he was so caught up in his gaming there was no bit of warning or recollection left in his brain. Except the subtle snag when he shifted on the seat of his sofa.

It was another Sunday. He didn't remember how close these incidents were together, except for some unknown feeling that they were in the vicinity of the same month. The air was hot, again, and he was supposed to meet up with a woman in town. He'd gone into the bathroom, annoyed at the idea of going out, and found, again, another mess.

A shaving cream can had exploded. Parts of the mirror were cracked. White foam was everywhere. Shrapnel from the can was embedded into the bathroom door. A finger— someone's finger, or something like a finger, had etched words in cream on the remnants of the mirror.

"Son of Thunder." That was all it said.

He snapped a picture of it, of the mess in his bathroom, and used a washrag to wipe out the words. He thought about them, over and over again, as he squeezed and cleaned and washed the rag under hot water.

When he was done, he called the super. Asked for the locks to be changed. Called up his date, and told her today wasn't a good day.

And he sat and played games again, alone.

He'd posted the photo on a forum. He liked forums. They gave him the ability to talk and withdraw. There was no back and forth, no additional need to give something he knew he'd never get back.

He needed answers. He did not want to return home, did not want to think about the old times. He was a city-slicker now. He was in the modern world. Things like ghosts were superstitions. Beliefs little children had. Beliefs young men had.

Someone suggested he get a camera, and record himself in his sleep.

"Better if you get a camera for every room," someone else said.

Someone sent him a YouTube video. It was of some girl named Bailey—a young girl, extremely young, who documented case files of weird, unexplained phenomena. This particular video was about a poltergeist. Despite her age, Eric found something important in what she was saying.

"Some armchair theories suggest that Poltergeists are man-made; psychic powers left untreated and untouched, neuroses exploding outwards uncontrollably to wreak havoc on unfulfilled, unhappy lives."

He got cameras the next week. Went over his budget, but there was always new work to be had in the future. When he came back in to his apartment, the coffee table had been split in half. Glass was everywhere.

After he swept up, he set up the cameras.

He reviewed them, slowly, carefully. Nothing happened for weeks. Until he was woken up by his bed shaking. The side table lamp slid as he watched to six feet out in the middle of the air, then heaved itself bodily at the wall. His candle display floated, revolving. He sat up and told everything to stop.

At once, everything fell to the ground. He cautiously reviewed the tapes. Watched with fervent eyes on his laptop as something shining, something glittering, sat up out of his body and waved its hands, orchestrating the event. When he opened his eyes on tape, the thing slithered back inside him, some shadow made of phosphorescence that glowed in black and white.

He posted this to the forum as well.

Someone private messaged him. It was a man named Grimm.

Grimm and Randall came out to meet up with him. They waved sensors up and down his body. Randall asked him a series of questions about the events. Eric tried not to gape at the fact that Randall had no hands.

"Tell me, have you ever had any trysts with something, or someone… out of the ordinary?" Randall asked.

Eric's face was a mask.

"You mean, other than all this? I don't know what you mean. I just stay at home and play video games. Sometimes I go out and work when the money dries up. I'm normal."

"Normal is such a subjective word," Randall breathed, but he seemed aware that he had hit upon a touchy subject, and dropped it.

"Did a scan of your apartment," Grimm said. "It's clean." He took a sip of coffee that Eric had made him. "I know Randall doesn't want to say anything, but the problem is you."

"Me?" Eric blinked. It was hard not to get up and throw the men out immediately.

"You've got something embedded in you," Randall said.

"Major surge of psychokinetic energy," Grimm said.

"I just play video games," he said, again.

"You showed us that picture earlier," Randall said. "What does the phrase 'Son of Thunder' mean to you?"

"Nothing," Eric said. He was tired of this, and tired of crazy white people reminding him about his past. He sighed. "Please leave my apartment."

"We haven't even got to the good part yet," Grimm said.

"There is no good part about this," Eric said. "I want to play my video games and live my life in peace, and if you don't get out right now, I'll throw you out myself!"

As if to punctuate his point, the same butcher knife from before menacingly floated into the room and took turns weaving between the two interlopers.

"You can clearly see this is a problem, can't you?" Grimm asked, and ducked as the knife flew at him.

"I'm not doing this!" Eric said. "It's not me."

Randall had his cloak wrapped around the knife, which was trying to lunge at him.

"Please tell your attack cutlery to back off," the handless man pleaded.

"Look, I don't know what to tell you. I don't even know how to start."

"Start by asking your knife to go back to the kitchen, maybe?" Randall said.

Eric rolled his eyes.

"*Get back!*" he snarled, in Lakota.

The knife paused, mid-stabbing motion, then turned around to him and floated somewhat glumly back to the kitchen. Randall chased after it to get his cape.

"It started when I was a teenager," he said, and here he thought of only the basics. "My friend Caesar and I watched my grandfather perform a Sundance. To fend off a monster that came to attack our village. He turned into the Thunderbird, and flew away."

Randall and Grimm looked at each other for a moment before saying anything.

"Makes perfect sense," Grimm said.

"Absolutely," Randall said. "Son of Thunder. Here I thought you were a basketball fan. Poor taste of college teams, I thought, but who am I to judge. No, we'll get you fixed up right away."

"What are you going to do?" Eric asked.

"Put a dampener on your latent abilities," Grimm said.

"An old spell which should quiet any unnecessary funny business with your subconscious. My theory is that you witnessed some deeply disturbing phenomena accompanied by an evil force. This caused a traumatic psychic scar, which you carry with you. Perhaps the dance you helped your Grandfather do exposed you to some of that which he had. Either way. It's a simple enough spell. We'll simply pull the scar from your psyche, bottle it up, and you'll have to give it to someone you fervently trust."

"I just play video games," Eric said, again.

"Sure you do," Randall said, soothingly. He turned his head to Grimm. "Bring me my knife from my bag, would you?"

It was like a sterile surgical procedure. Randall had chanted; the lights dimmed, and a glowing orb broadcast a halo over Eric's body, which was spread out lengthwise on the couch. He tried to keep his eyes closed, but the two men had him disrobe, and he was a little suspicious of two men he hardly knew, white men at that, standing over his bare chest with something sharp. It sounded like something his drunk uncle Jaime would rant about over family dinners-silly stories about the Illuminati.

His ancestors would be spinning in the sky if they could see him now.

"Okay, can we talk about the elephant trunk in the room?" Grimm asked, sneaking a peek.

"Shut up, you puerile child," Randall snapped. "Athame." *A-thame*, he pronounced it.

"Athame." *A-tha-may*. This was Grimm, handing over the utensil.

Eric watched the knife float on its own, bobbing with precision from Grimm's grip. Randall moved his handless wrists, and the knife slowly, carefully, etched a small square of flesh from Eric's chest. It was almost painless. Eric watched, fascinated, as the patch of skin lifted itself up. Something dark over his rightmost breast glowed, a dull crimson color.

"Clompy things," Randall said.

"Forceps."

What looked like tongs reached out, down, and plunged into the exposed flesh. Eric hissed—the muscles in his right breast seized up—he could taste bronze in his veins, copper electricity as it sparked through his entire nervous system, and then before everyone's eyes a sizzling jagged piece of ruby was unearthed. It buzzed, gleaming in the haloed lights.

"Containment unit."

"Glass jar from Costco we scribbled on with permanent marker."

Randall moved the forceps and the squat lightning ruby down into the jar. He drew a star with blood from Eric's chest on the underside of the lid, then screwed it closed and sealed it up tight. The whole thing lit up like a beacon, crackling with energy.

"And there we have it," Randall said. "Don't drop it."

They patched him back up. Once he was dressed, Randall had packed his tools back into his kit bag, and Grimm had disappeared into Eric's back bedroom.

"I'd like to talk to you about something else now," Randall said. "How do you feel about travelling?"

"I just want to play video games," Eric said.

Randall looked back down the hallway, then turned round again to Eric.

"What's your construction job pay you?"

Eric told him.

"I'll double it. Though don't mention it to Grimm, he'd kill himself for a pay raise."

Eric blinked at him.

"And what would I be doing?" he asked.

"Fighting monsters, on occasion. Mostly analyzing them. Going on trips to neutralize different situations. Travel stipend. Decent insurance. We also provide free room and board."

"I'm good," Eric said.

"You're sure?" Randall asked. "I have a nose for talents, and you seem to be very gifted."

"I just want to live in peace," he said.

"Alright then, a compromise," Randall said. "You come live at the Facility for a few weeks. We'll monitor your progress as far as healing goes, and make sure nothing relapses. Then, when you're done healing, you're free to go."

"What do you get out of that ?" Eric asked.

"The satisfaction of knowing someone with power like yours is no longer a threat. Of course, you'll be living in the historic Black Hills region of South Dakota. Lots of open land, lots of gorgeous vistas."

"That is awful close to home," Eric said. "Alright. I'll stay. But you can forget about me working for you. Those days of monsters are over for me."

"Fair enough," Randall said. "But you know. We can probably find your Grandfather for you. If he wants to be found."

"Alright," Eric said, after a moment. "And what was that about a paycheck?"

Kansas City had seemed like a lifetime ago. Asides from a brief trip to drop off his lightning ruby back at the Rez, he'd never really left the Compound. And how could he have? There were pretty girls, expensive tech, and they even had a Sasquatch on duty. The Wi-fi itself was amazing—streaming was a thousand times easier. And spending money came cheap… usually as a result of little back and forths to stomp out tiny monsters here and there, or capture some for research. There was something to the way his resolve had eroded, over time, when he thought about it…

Somehow or another he'd followed in his Grandfather's footsteps, even if he'd had to take his own path in fighting the good fight. And now he was back here… to take back what had been bestowed upon him as his birthright, to fall in line with the old ways, like he had been running to avoid his whole life. He was just like his Grandfather, then… fleeing forever once he'd performed his sacred duty.

He found Caesar's little squat at the far end of the living quarters, near the center grounds and the banquet hall. Even Caesar had given in, over time, to modernization. His chickens were up for the night, but the rooster had escaped. It strutted around, dead-eyeing everything around it, whipping around at the slightest breeze. All of its feathers and even its comb were at high alert in the dark. The coop itself was a wraparound chicken wire knock-up, winding around the back side of the trailer. Eric tromped up the wooden ramp in lieu of the stairs, and knocked on the front door.

There was a commotion inside, laughing and carrying on. The smell of someone grilling in the distance carried over on the breeze. Eric looked at the coop again, at the agitation of the rooster. He had a strong feeling it wasn't smelling foxes…

The door swung wide open, and She-she's beaming face greeted him.

"Eric!" she gasped.

"She-she!" he said. He felt a warm glow light up in his heart that he had not allowed himself to feel for some time.

"Come in, come in," she said. "Dinner's at the main hall tonight, but we're letting the kids eat so we can put them to bed early."

"Not too early, I hope?" he asked.

She grinned.

There was a Disney movie playing on the VCR. The kids had briefly greeted him, but were put off by the fact that he hadn't brought them any souvenirs after so long.

"Ten years without a single birthday present," the oldest, Haley, all of fourteen years old, had said. "You have catching up to do, Mister."

He felt bad. This was his family; this was his tribe, the tangible chain of people he had run away from so long ago. It'd been so long he hadn't even thought about presents. He thought of his reputation as an Uncle. Oh well. Life would find some other way to disappoint them in the future…

She-she and Caesar sat with Opa at the table, playing Uno and dealing him in as they chatted. Haley had said ten years, but hadn't it been closer to twelve? How amazing to see the ravages of age on his loved ones. Opa was looking more and more like a mummy every day. He'd once seen her cut the head off of a snake with a dull trowel, in one stroke. She was on her hands and knees picking vegetables, even at sixty-five, when he was a boy. And now… what, she was nearing eighty? It didn't seem fair. Her arthritic knuckles popped as she shuffled the deck and passed out cards. Her glasses seemed thick enough to fry bacon with.

Well, time still passed, even if you weren't here to see it, he told himself.

"And how is life in the big city?" She-she asked.

"It's life," he said. "Moves too quickly. You lose track of time in the city. Makes you think things are always going to be the same."

"Look at you, waxing about the passage of time," Opa said, gums flapping. "You're a young man. You have plenty of time left."

Eric cut a glance at the distracted girls, their legs kicked out behind them in front of the TV.

"I missed out on so many years," he said, voice soft.

"Is that why you haven't been back?" Caesar asked. "City life?"

Eric shook his head.

"I couldn't continue here," he said. "You know what happened. I had to try to find Grandfather again. And the journey took everything out of me."

"It wasn't anything else?" Caesar asked. His patient tone, and the kindness to his words, seemed to cut the worst of all. "We're your friends, you know. You can confide in us."

Eric stared into his mug of coffee, refusing to lock eyes.

"I don't know what to say," he said. "I'm a guest here. If I spoke my true feelings, then maybe I would not be so welcome."

Opa made a 'haaaaa' noise, as if to clear her throat or shush them.

"You invite him over, and you guilt him, and pepper him with questions about the past!" she cried. "Was the only purpose of his visiting here to be scorned and abused?"

"It's fine, Opa," Eric said.

"It's not fine. Let us enjoy your company; and if it is a pleasant enough visit, then you can come back and visit again. This time fearing no guilt. You've lived with guilt enough on your own. Let it not roost here. Now let's play a round before supper's done."

Eric smiled at her, and they began to play, just like old times, She-she grinning her warm, loving smile, and Caesar and he joking like they were young men again.

When he was a boy—hardly yet a young man—it had been him, and Caesar, and She-she. A trio of friends. And somehow or another. They had come to certain conclusions about one another.

Caesar liked She-she. Eric liked She-she. But She-she only had eyes for Eric… at least, at first. It was a delicate power dance; an unwieldy détente in a polite war of words. All three of them loved each other as best friends. And each of them knew that their delicate triangle would forever be lopsided and destroyed if just one aspect of it came out of place.

Still, it happened. Eric and She-she had been lovers, meeting at the old Pine at the edge of the Reserve, standing under the moonlit night and embracing one another, watching the people move around like ants, seeing the houses as anthills. They hid it from Caesar; a dagger's edge dangerous game that they both knew would break the three of them if there was one little slip-up.

Things came to a head that night, with the imminent arrival of the Unktehi, and the boys heading off to help with the Sundance.

Eric and She-she had met by the old pine out at the far edge of the property as dusk fell.

"Why did you call me out here?" Eric asked.

"I'm scared for you," She-she said. "I don't know what I'd do without you, if something happened."

"It'll be fine," Eric said, lying.

"You don't know that," She-she said. She bit her lip, and then spoke. "This is dangerous, and you know it. And you and Caesar are both going? What will I do if you're both dead?"

And there was something in her eyes, then. Some hidden thing that she hadn't said. And Eric felt a hot flame of jealousy boil up in his heart, sparking with anger and things he'd seen that he now knew differently about.

Eric did not stay long after his Grandfather flew away. He, too, planned to fly away.

He met She-she again by the old pine.

"I have to go find my Grandfather," he said. He was thinking about their conversation from earlier. "I'm leaving."

"But what am I to do?" she asked.

"What you must," he said. "Caesar will still be here."

Her eyes were shimmering in the moonlight, but he turned and left.

"Eric," she called.

He did not turn back to her.

And so he beat a retreat, searching endlessly for his forebear, trying to forget about betrayal. But a year or two in the world didn't do much to make Eric think his Grandfather would ever be found, or even wanted to be found. Brief glimpses here and again—strikes of lightning that struck a certain resonance in his chest. The sound of a flap of wings here and again. Sometimes, he would see the sun blotted out around him, feel the air cool... and he'd look up, high at the sun, wondering.

Eric came back and visited, in the first year. He'd discovered something that hurt even more... but did not surprise him.

She-she and Caesar had forged their own alliance, with him out of the way. They were married. And there was more. They'd made something in his absence... a child.

"You never told me," he said, when he'd seen the swelling in her belly.

"We didn't know what to say," she'd said. The 'We' of it bothered him, but he'd left... and wasn't that part of his penitence?

Whose was it? He didn't know. Caesar didn't know, did he? She-she surely didn't know. Nobody knew. He never asked again—never pushed any further. Never asked them how they felt about things. How they had finally decided on the betrayal. What lies they told themselves to soothe up the fact that Eric had gone and abandoned them both, or that they had abandoned him. Had they taken comfort in each other in his absence?

This must have been that third wheel feeling Caesar talked about.

So instead he was an absent uncle, and lost himself in the imaginary world, because in the real world, the lines were too blurry and out of focus for him to know what he should do.

Eric told them, the two of them, the might-be-his-daughter and his niece, all about ghost stories that night. He told them about things that crept and things that slunk, about things creeping over from another world. He told them to stay safe, and to listen to Opa, and to call them if they needed anything, but that he would do his best to protect them all.

And he and She-she and Caesar went to the main hall, to treat with the Elders, everyone who remembered that once upon a time the Son of Thunder had lived in this place with everyone else.

It was like a family reunion. Opa stayed at home with the kids, but all of the tribe that lived within walking distance had arrived, and someone had fried a hog. Someone else had made fry bread; someone had made grape dumplings. Fruits and vegetables were on trays, little cheeses, hors d'ouerves both new and traditional.

After they ate, and Eric caught up with everyone he cared to, Elder Tallchief spoke to the whole room.

"We have had a crisis rear its head," he said. "And in our time of need, the Son of Thunder appears again. Tell us the reason for your visit."

"I'm lost, and need to find myself," he said. "I know where my power lies, but I am frightened of embracing it. I'm terrified that if I embrace it, then all the darkness inside me will spill out. That I will no longer be who I am. That jealousy and anger will devour me alive, and take those I love away from me."

He could feel She-She and Caesar's eyes on him, burning holes in him.

"Then you need guidance," Elder Tallchief said. "Go to the Lodge. Stay there until you have a vision. Let the spirits of our ancestors guide your footsteps, so you know how to tread forward into the future, without stepping on those you love."

And so Eric did.

Four days. Four nights. On the fifth, the walls began to bleed. His grandfather appeared at his side, in a cloud of smoke.

"Grandfather," he said. "Where have you been?"

"I flew to the heavens, to rejoin with the sun," his Grandfather said.

"I don't know what to do," Eric said.

"What do you think you should do?"

"Reclaim my power. Put the scar back in my chest. Feel it inside me again. That old ache."

"You have the power to walk between," his Grandfather said. "You are not just you. You are not just my grandson. You are more. You must Dance, child."

"Dance?" Eric was almost delirious.

"As your Grandfather did before you. As my Grandfather did before me. You must perform the Sundance in the Moonlight."

"There won't be another blood moon for weeks," he said. "There may not be enough time."

"That's what scars are for," his Grandfather said, and then blew away like smoke.

Eric got to wobbly feet, staggering towards the door to the lodge, and collapsed on the ground. The dirt was cool against his cheek. Steam rolled over him, and someone was pulling him to his feet, slinging his arm over their shoulder.

He barely recognized Caesar's kind face before he passed completely out.

It was a little jar, now that time and the annals of memory had passed—a lumpen ruby, misshapen and jagged, but there was a dull glow to it that got brighter as the two brought it near him.

"When the Medicine Man passed, he gave this to us," She-she said.

"We held onto it for you," Caesar said.

And now that he held it close, allowing the old feelings to pass into him again, feeling the parts of himself that he was running away from re-sort and reconnect themselves, he recognized it not as a bolt of lightning, but one half of a broken heart. Lightning sparked from it, zapping painlessly out to touch his finger pads on the inside of the glass like one of those novelty lightning balls at head shops.

"I have to do the Sundance in the Moonlight," he said to them.

Caesar's face was stricken.

"You saw what happened to your Grandfather," he said.

Eric nodded.

She-she's face was hidden in her sleeve.

"It's the only thing that will protect the people I love," Eric said. "I have to."

She-she let out a strangled half-sob.

"Then you have to let us help you," she said.

Caesar nodded along with her, resolute.

"I'm scared I'll turn my power on you," Eric said. His eyes were haunted. "I'm raw still. Hurt about everything."

Caesar and She-she both grabbed his wrists.

"We know the love you have for us as friends is stronger than any amount of hate," Caesar said. "Let me help you. Let me make up for what I took from you."

"I won't stand by and leave the two of you alone," She-she said. "Not this time."

"I never meant to hurt you," Caesar said.

"We were both just so lost when you left," She-she said.

"We didn't know what to do," Caesar said.

"But I loved you enough to let you go. Because I knew you needed it," She-she said.

Eric felt something in his chest stir, then. The Scar lit up, strobing, and the hair on his head started to raise on its own.

"Let's go," Eric said, and tears he had not shed for years were unblocked. "Let's go. Now. Before I change my mind."

Opa had the kids. The three of them set off—She-she with the horns and the braided rope, Caesar with the drums. Eric held the jar with his scar in it as a lamp to light their way. It was dark out—and as they walked up to the old pine tree on the hill, they could feel the way the wind whipped and howled, and the sky clouds darkened overhead.

She-she affixed the rope around the oak. She and Caesar each used a horn and pierced Eric, carefully, one through each thick bunch of muscle in his chest. He groaned and strained and cried and sobbed at them to stop, fire in his eyes, but on they continued, until it was done and he was stuck like a pig.

Caesar and She-she each held one hand on the scar jar between them. It sparked and spit, buzzing and glowing with a crimson fire. Eric leaned back against the piercings, hanging himself from the oak, knees bowing him and keeping him in pain. Each of his friends took turns beating the drum. The beat intensified as time flew on.

Eric could feel the weight of his body suspending him against the oak, could feel the stretch of where these dual-prongs had pierced him. He thought of his family... his blood ancestors, one continuous line, each Grandfather and Grandson performing this dance. The clouds loomed, large and squat and heavy overhead. He could feel hot saline rain pour out and sting his wounds.

He thought about the actions here at this pine, thought of what he had run from, and what he had left behind, thought hard about the love they shared. As aching and painful as it had been, as terrible and crucifying as it was.

A great crimson light shone from his friends, who had begun to move around him with the drums. He closed his eyes, felt the burning static of the air around him coalescing, feeling his hair raise, hearing the drums—pounding and ever-circling, as if summoning something from the heavens itself.

And then, with a crashing noise, and the ground itself shaking, lightning spidered down from the sky. It struck the pine, sizzling its way through the rope and through the horns, completing some sort of eldritch circuit and injecting pure adrenaline into his chest. The horns burned to a crisp.

He gasped and fell backwards. Flesh fell away with the piercings. He could feel the burnt smell on his chest, feel a ragged ache deep in his flesh, and gingerly touched the wounds with his fingertips.

The drumming stopped. Caesar and She-she came close to him, holding the Scar, and it throbbed in the glass, shattering the jar and floating, suspended, in mid-air. Eric reached out and grabbed it before it fell, cracking it in half, and placed each half in the new wounds on his chest.

They fit, and he could feel the power of the earth beneath his feet sucking at him, and the power of the sky above him ready to inhale.

"Your eyes," She-she said.

"They're blue," Caesar said. "Like a glowing blue flame."

Eric found himself soaring upwards. He simply had to breathe in the air. He floated above the two of them, his friends, his family, his tribe. He breathed in, all over, feeling the power of the Scars burning inside him, and at once, he could feel a dangerous electricity envelope him. Electricity buzzed, and he flapped, and he knew he had finally found it—that power that he had locked away so long ago.

"The Thunderbird," Caesar breathed. He was crying.

And there was a split second where Eric considered it. Considered reaching down and charcoaling both of them. Caesar for his betrayal. She-she for leaving him behind. But the love he had for his friends—his family—was too strong.

He turned his attention back to the distance. He could feel She-she's love in his veins now—and Caesar's tears—new Scars bleeding such a sweet ache into his chest, and he turned and soared into the night, powerful wings of lightning carrying him, crackling ozone as he soared.

He flew away again, but this time he knew he'd be back.

CHAPTER 32:

SKYE'S DANCE OF PERPETUAL UNDERSTANDING

The newness of this situation at present was confounding for Skye. She had not been at all prepared for Randall's disappearance; now that she was here, again, in another situation where she would be forced to step up, she found herself fuming at the man. Anger had driven her like a wraith—she'd locked herself away when they got back to the Compound, screaming and spitting, cursing Randall's name and his grave and his stupid lack of hands. Still—there was nobody around better suited to take care of everything in his absence.

Barbary had tried to console her about this; it was wasted words, however, because Skye had already done the math. (And wasn't that what an effective leader did? she asked herself, because now there was nobody else to bounce ideas off.) Whoever was left in charge did the math, they calculated the considerations, they tallied the numbers. They balanced the books, checked the rosters, formulated plans.

She was now Boss, all things considered—and the biggest reason she hated Randall was that he'd left without even giving her time to grieve. She was considering what their next steps were even as she watched the bullet tear through his stupid, self-sacrificing chest. Before he even hit the ground, before he'd disappeared, she was thinking—how do we escape? How do we leave? What kind of tactical disadvantage does this give us now?

And the biggest worry of all: how am I supposed to comfort everyone in his absence?

But there was no comfort in death, she knew. Only the cold reality that in the void of power, in the chaos, someone else got pushed to the top of the garbage dump, as Lord of This Mess. And damnit all… was there ever a time she would be able to escape?

Her mother had been a hateful cow. There was something to that, something about their relationship, some horrid fault Skye had committed without knowing as an innocent child that had, for whatever reason, soured up every ounce of maternal instinct the woman had. Or at least, that was the impression she got. Her mother would never come out and say this to her; that would require acknowledging her existence in the first place.

She saw the writing on the wall though. So as she cared for her five younger siblings, she prepared herself for her own life as soon as it was legally possible. She took summer school courses on tribal scholarship, doubled up her credits so she could graduate high school early. And right as she was prepared to launch into a glorious future, the old heifer had one last surprise in store for her.

Skye had found her mother dead in her bed on Skye's eighteenth birthday.

"You fucking bitch," Skye said, to the corpse, to the heroin needle, to the grin on her waxy, broken, euphoric face.

Skye was now left, the oldest of six. None of her family would take the rest of the kids in.

"We'll have to put them in a foster home," the social worker said. "Unless, of course, you decide to take custody."

"Can I do that?" she asked.

"I don't recommend it," the social worker had said. "You're a young girl with a bright future ahead of you. Guardianship is an intense job. Are you sure you can handle it?"

"What do you think I've been doing my whole life already?" Skye snapped. "If you think someone that died of an overdose did most of the mothering, I have some news for you. You're not gonna fucking like it."

That was one thing she got from her mother, at least: her foul mouth.

Still, Skye was approved, once she got a job and started bringing some income in. The tribe helped; commods kept them eating, the Clinic was there for days the kids were sick, and one of the neighbors had helped her get her driver's license and transfer the title of the car over into her name.

Skye considered community college as her only option. She already had two jobs—Big Sis, and re-possessing cars at a loan company. These ate up most of her week. She took night classes, doing her best, and tried to major in English Literature. Folktales fascinated her the most. She would read old historical tomes, errata from chroniclers long gone, about individual people and what they practiced.

There was a surprising overlap in the humanities. When she transferred to a four year, another local state college, she found her hands tied. The best she could do when taking care of five kids was commute at nights. Half of her degree plan, however, was in another town entirely, on another campus. Frustrated and shiftless, she forged her way through with a University Studies degree, and eventually reconciled herself to the fact that at the end of six long years she would never, ever, not ever leave with anything but a pile of student loan debt and a piece of paper congratulating her on her hard work.

She'd talked to the History Head, a woman with short-cut hair and a general disdain for her. She looked like a twelve year old boy. Of course, the Head said, there's nothing we can do. Hands are tied. We faculty have too much to deal with without trying to untangle our students' issues.

"Can you give me advice about Grad school? I'm the first one in my family to go to college, and I feel stuck."

"What's your degree plan currently?"

"University Studies," she said. "I wanted History, but-"

The Dean shrugged.

"I don't think any respectable Graduate program will take you in, to be honest, not with a University Studies degree. It's fine, anyway, you get tribal benefits, right?"

Skye barely refrained from cursing her out. But once she graduated. (And that was a shiftless, cocksucking artificial experience for her, where donors, wealthy and well-off, got an hour and a half of praise—the Mayor, some feckless Nepotism-elected suburbanite, stood on stage and told a story about how he'd tricked and stalked his wife into their first date, to standing ovation.) When she was clear, she sent a very strongly worded letter to the haughty woman that told her to go fuck herself. In code, of course. She'd used the first letter of every sentence and spelled it out, signed, Anonymous. Odds were the toad at the top of the totem pole would be totally oblivious.

A year and a half of working later, and most of the kids were grown. One of her sisters, who'd married a well-off realtor, offered to take care of the rest of things.

"I may as well. I feel just as responsible for them as you do," Nina had said. "And besides. You've already done more than your fair share for our family."

It was a blessing, but suddenly she had more time than she knew what to do with. The woes of the working world began to get to her, and a small voice at the back of her head told her she was wasting her future.

She started applying to Graduate programs. Just to spite her old Professor. Anthropology had always fascinated her. She picked ten programs that looked good, paid ten different application fees, and paid for ten separate transcripts, and then waited and waited and waited. The first three rejections stung, but at least they were impersonal. The fourth was something of a shock to the system. The Head of the Department she'd applied to responded to her. She met up with him at his office, on the ground floor of a very confusing campus in-state.

He was late from lunch and seemed flustered when he saw her.

"Well, come in," he said.

She sat opposite him and waited for him to speak about the program.

"Well?" he asked waspishly. "Do you have any questions for me?"

"I'm not sure where to start. I had a friend recommend the program."

He sneered at her.

"I wondered," he said, as if that was somehow shameful, and the disdain in his voice was clear. "Let me see here. What's your transcript look like?"

"Well, I have a University Studies degree, but I've taken a lot of sociology classes, and I've always been very interested in indigenous cultures. Myths and religions, specifically, since it's so close to home."

"You realize this is a *science* degree, right?" he asked.

There was a very sharp looking ball point pen in her pocket. She considered stabbing him in the trachea and leaving, but managed to stop herself.

After a couple more pointed, demeaning questions, he started to ramble on and on about the program.

"We've done some very interesting things with the program," he said. "You should see the pictures we have set up outside. We've sent teams out to study early Delaware tribes. Done some very interesting work during archaeological digs."

"So, would you say a large part of your program is digging up the dead?" she asked.

He blinked.

"Well, yes," he said, and then continued bleating.

Whatever else he was saying, she didn't hear it.

It was a sense of defeat and humiliation that haunted her as she walked back out of the labyrinthine campus and to her truck, and she slid into the driver's seat, feeling like an utter failure, and drove back home.

The next six rejection letters were quick and easy. She tossed the last few in the garbage, not even bothering to open them to check.

She got a sense of shock, however, when she received correspondence from a college she was ninety percent sure she'd never heard of, let alone applied to.

"Hallowtide University," she read out loud, from the midnight blue envelope they'd sent it in. She opened it, and peeled out the letter.

"Dear Applicant, (-and here she'd almost chucked it in the garbage disposal; were it not for some sick sense of self-punishment she would have-)

"We have heard word that you are interested in pursuing a Graduate Level degree in Anthropology and/or the Humanities. We here at Hallowtide University have a prestigious history of successful graduate level students and are working diligently to increase the diversity of our programs."

And here she really did take a lighter and try to burn it, envelope and all, but some wax seal or another on the paper prevented it. Nor could she tear it apart with her hands; scissors she'd grabbed seemed to dull themselves on the wax. Skye, college graduate that she was, figured that a rational world meant there were rational reasons for things, and so she took this as a sign.

"We invite you to our Luncheon on our Campus. There we give an orientation for our Graduate level students, and give a tour of our historic campus. Please join us.

Yours,
Dean Cranster"

There was a VIP invite inside the envelope, with a date and time. She'd even found her phone had given her the benefit of updating itself. What a marvel technology had become, she thought, tucking her early model Nokia into her pocket.

Google Calendar would not be invented for another five years.

Hallowtide University was in Pennsylvania. Draped in greenery from the Michaux State Forest, its gabled roofs and cornices stared down at her from a distance, arising almost suddenly in her view like Disneyworld.

She passed a river—more of a brook where she drove past the bridge—and onwards into the clearing ahead. To her consternation, there were not a lot of other people there. Owing to the weird way it was addressed, she considered that it was part of a mass advertisement to drum up interested parties. But here she was, almost the only car on the lot.

Well, she considered, it was summer. Almost as soon as she thought this, she saw a white horse run through a clearing somewhere to her right, disappearing almost as quickly as it appeared. She squinted at it. Was that… a party hat on its head?

The front doors were overwhelmingly large. The whole place had the appearance of a vast transplanted castle. She felt a bit like Jack and the Beanstalk grabbing onto the knocker and swinging; but soon enough a smaller door opened nearby, and a man with wide goggles on peeked his head out. He wore a turn of the century pageboy outfit; tweed jacket, with leather pantaloons and hip waders. He smelled strongly of fertilizer, and his facial hair was entirely like an angry cartoon cowboy of one sort or another.

"Campus is closed for the summer," he snapped.

"I got a strongly worded letter… something about a VIP invite." She waved it.

The man looked at her, eyes blinking rapidly as he attempted to process this.

"Ah. I'll be back, then."

And he slammed the small door shut again. Skye stood there, unsure what to do with herself, when the doors opened again wide, and a tall, older man with a pointed hat and robes walked out. He wore half-moon spectacles and stared through them at her.

"Skye, was it?" he asked, white fluffy eyebrows squinting.

"Yes," she said.

"Ah. Banquet and Luncheon is at the Wrigley Center. Apologies for the bizarre dress and accoutrement. Our theater department runs a very lucrative fundraising event in the form of a

Renaissance Festival open to the public every summer. I'm afraid this is the Renfield Center. Are you at all adverse to walking the grounds, or would you prefer to drive? I'm afraid Campus is a bit hard to navigate at first; there are at least thirty entrances, or so I have been told."

"Is there a closer parking lot?" she asked.

"So, are you like, the Headmaster, or something?" she asked.

The wizardly-looking man peered over his spectacles at her.

"Whatever gives you that idea?" he asked.

She and Gandalf the Cosplayer, whom had not yet told her his name, rode in her Suburban over a few awkward bumps and sharp turns over backwoods roads. He pointed and demurred in a few different directions, and finally, they arrived. There were far more cars back here in this lot, and the Wrigley Center was a dark squat building with about as much flare as could be expected for a lunch room.

"Welcome to Hallowtide University," the wizard said, and hopped out.

A recent late-spring rain had puddled on the ground in places; the Wizard introduced himself as Benjamin Vickers, PHD, Department Chair for the Anthropology Department, and lifted the hem of his robes as he delicately extended a naked, furry leg over a puddle. There was a tattoo of a dragon fly on one ankle.

It was a typical lunch room. Nobody else had dressed for the occasion, asides from the Cafeteria Staff, who had dressed mostly with headbands with bobbly eyes on the top. Skye got herself a plate and sat near another woman at the far edge of the room.

"Welcome, Prospective Students, to Hallowtide University," a portly man in a suit with red cheeks said. "We hope you enjoy a delicious luncheon on us. As you eat, we'll go over the history of our, ehe, Hallowed institution, and give you some insights as to the nature of the programs we offer."

The actual President of the Institution was a nearly silent, gaunt-skulled man, who looked as if he were vacuum-sealed to prevent moisture every night before he went to sleep. He said nothing, but stood and bowed when introduced. Of course, he didn't need to say anything. The portly man, Dean Cranster, did all the talking. What started at first as an illustrious overview of Hallowtide's long history extending back to Colonial America soon devolved into a hard-to-follow well-practiced diatribe on their various programs and activities, their extracurriculars, and local events the University was involved with. Skye stopped trying to follow fifteen minutes in; she knew most of this information would be either on the website, or in a brochure, the ones she could see sitting by the potato salad on the side board.

Eventually, she could take no more of his monotonous self-indulgence, for she raised her hand. He stopped, sputtering, seeming cut-off, and turned to her.

"You have a question?" he asked.

"Yeah. I saw a horse earlier near the Renfield Center. I might have misheard you earlier, but did you say you had an Equestrian sports program?"

He blinked a few times.

"No," he said.

There was a bizarre look on his face. Across the hall, thumbs twiddling, Dr. Vickers stared at her over his fake wizard beard.

"Perhaps it's something to do with our very popular Renaissance Festival," the Dean continued, and then launched into its history.

Skye tuned out. She was already planning out her return trip in her head. When it was over (after an hour that had felt like an eternity) most of the prospective students filed out, in huddled groups with their prospective advisors. Dr. Vickers remained seated by the door. Skye put her tray away, and made for the exit, near Vickers, but his hand reached out and tapped her wrist, delicately.

"Hold on a second," he said. "Tell me about this horse."

"It was white," she said. "Looked like someone put a party hat right over its forehead."

"Is that so?" he asked. "Well, I'm involved with the Ren Fair Committee. We scheduled no horses. We don't even have the setup for it. One of the main planners hates horses. Well, his mother was bit by a horse when he was a kid, so he's kind of got a thing about it. Can't blame him, really."

"So you're suggesting I saw a wild horse in Pennsylvania?" she asked.

"Not exactly," he said. "You look like you're a little impatient, am I interrupting you?"

"I think I changed my mind about this place," she said. "I appreciate the invitation, but I'm looking for somewhere that's a little more. Respectable, I suppose."

"Look, we play hard, sure, but we also work hard here," he said. "I have a feeling you really know what you want to do with yourself. If you could do anything—absolutely anything with yourself—let's just play pretend for a minute. Let's say money wasn't an object."

"It is," she replied. "I'm a little too old to play games, Dr. Vickers."

He pressed his hands up to his face, pressing against his eyes with stress, and then looked up at her.

"Look, I understand what you're saying and where you're coming from. But we have a very specialized degree plan I think you might be perfect for. I looked over your transcript, and I specifically invited you myself. Your overall degree plan was, well. Kind of haphazard, but the individual courses you took and your GPA are outstanding. I'd really take it as a personal favor if you just spent a few hours with me this afternoon so I can explain our program and showcase the Department we have."

"You guys don't dig people up, do you?"

"Only to put a stake in their heart," he said, grinning, eyebrow cocked.

This got a chuckle out of her, and despite her plans to leave she relented.

The Anthropology Department was located in the Fortner Building. It was offset a bit from the main campus grounds. It looked, more than anything, like a gigantic fortress at the back half of the property.

"Impressive," she said.

"You haven't even seen the inside yet," he said.

He was still dressed like a Wizard. When they entered through a side door, the building was dark. Linoleum tile, freshly waxed, clinked underfoot. He walked her to his office, and opened the door.

Skye blinked. She could have sworn she saw a broom standing up entirely on its own, suspended by nothing, mid-room. As soon as the lights came on it tipped over. Dr. Vickers frowned at it and scooped it up, sitting it in the corner.

At Skye's face he grew sheepish.

"Lots of pranks here," he said. "We have fun in this Department. It's important what we do, but you know, when I was going through and getting my PHD, everyone was so. I don't

252

know. Stuffy. Red-faced and belligerent. Intent on prestige and fame and respect. I think that's important, but I also think that ensuring your work here gives you the impetus to create a better tomorrow is important. And I kinda have a rule: no assholes allowed."

Skye grinned at him. The broom seemed to rustle against the corner; even Dr. Vickers cut a side eye at it, then peered up at the vents in the ceiling.

"Little chilly to you?" he asked. "These vents are like turbo fans. Blows papers all over the place. Alright. Well, normally I would have a student mentor for you, to sort of guide you around, but I guess you'll get the whole deal from me."

He showed her the various parts of the Fortner Compound, as it was called. Graduate students had their own Offices here; enrollment in the Graduate studies program gave them an option to bunk on campus, on the basement floor of the Fortner Building.

"I did not come from wealth, moderate or other. Grad school for me was a nightmare-negotiating rent and work and everything. I want to make sure my students are taken care of, so they can focus on this research as their bread and butter. You'll be a TA at first, if you choose to participate in Work-Study. It's entirely optional, but you seem to have the bearing to care for a group of idiots and walk them through a difficult concept."

"You have no idea," she said, thinking about her whole life.

It did not take Skye long to agree. Soon she'd packed up and moved to Pennsylvania, and Dr. Vickers took her under his wing, his newest protégé.

It did not take long after moving in for Skye to realize that something was fundamentally *off* about the Fortner Compound. The study room was a massive fireplace, well-furnished and well-stocked with refreshments. There did not seem anyone to come in and refill them; every evening there was a fire going at 5 PM sharp. Despite the heat of the summer, the room was always the perfect temperature. And she never saw anyone lighting the fire...

An old Art Room that had been bricked off and was no longer in use was used by some of the undergrads between classes. Some old movie posters decked the place; the walls were an off-blue, almost too cheery. But after hours, when the Building was empty save her and some of her other unfortunate colleagues, she would always get the weirdest feeling pulsing from the room. She'd decided to give in and confront her wild imagination after a few weeks of staying up late and working on her thesis. She'd lifted the key from Vickers' office, unlocked the lounge, and stepped inside.

There was a painting at the far end of the wall, behind glass. She stared at it with a feeling akin to terror in her veins. It was white—so bright it was almost phosphorescent. Yet now that she looked at it, with the overheads off, all she seemed to be able to see was a pair of brightly shining eyes—an off-lilac color, glowing gently. And as she stepped back, she could see some sort of an outline. It was a figure, some kind of ethereal looking glammed up person... maybe...

The vending machine light kicked on next to her, the lights inside humming, and she jumped.

"Boo," someone said behind her, and she screamed.

She turned around, intent on killing, but it was just Dr. Vickers.

"I see you've perceived some of the glory here," he said.

"What is that painting?" she asked.

"Kind of an enigma. Fortner Compound used to be the Art Building, way back in the day. This painting just kind of appeared in the gallery here, or so they say. Never really sure who the artist was—nobody came out and claimed it. Pretty spooky, right?"

Skye sighed and breathed out.

"So it's not just me," she said. "This thing sticks in your mind. I dream about it sometimes. It just looks so familiar to me... Like there's some reason it's so important..."

Vickers gave her another one of his x-ray looks, then, and sucked in his teeth before he spoke again.

"Well. Here's the thing. I see the hard work you're doing. Your teaching is brilliant. Your research has been stellar. But have you ever wondered about. Well, how do I put this... Field Research?"

"Do we do that kind of thing here?"

"We have funding for it," he said. "Skye, we certainly do have an academic fast track program here. I want to see you succeed in this. But I've been thinking. Are you sure you're not ready for more?"

"Is this a come on?" she asked.

He shook his head, laughing.

"No. This is going to sound weird, but I need you to follow me. I have to show you something. It's a special project some of us in charge of the Department have been working on. Have you ever wondered why we have you cover so many classes?"

"Can I speak freely?"

"Absolutely," he said.

"I thought maybe you guys were just taking advantage of the help."

Dr. Vickers shook his head.

"No. We're working on something pretty fantastic. It's just this way."

A bit of skepticism on her face, Skye nevertheless followed the man through the winding stairways of the building, down to the bottom floor. He unlocked a door she'd never seen before, and ushered her in, locking it solidly behind him.

Three more locked doors-one a keypad, one a signet ring, and another a separate key altogether.

"Alright," he finally said, at the last door. "Behold."

He opened the doorway and gestured her inside.

To her great surprise, it was like a fortified bunker, military specs and all. She looked around, eyes agog. A holo-dome at the center of the work table seemed to show a three-dimensional globe, with little red x's here and there. Guns hung on the walls; various bits of technology was here and there, littered in various stacked boxes with bizarre names. 'Thermoregulator coils' she read on one. 'Essence of Asafetida," she read on one shelf. There were several small baby food jars that had been packed with herbs.

"What is all this?" she asked.

"Hallowtide's big secret," he said. "Tell me, Skye, have you ever wondered if perhaps some of those myths you read about weren't entirely made up?"

She turned to him, face in shock.

That had been the start of it, she knew. Unsure of what to do—trying her best in a bad situation. She'd gone out with various other faculty members and learned as much as she could first hand. And with that information and knowledge, she'd bumped into Randall somewhere along the way—the both of them on the hunt for some Cryptid or another. She couldn't remember. And working with him had somehow seemed a good idea, especially after old Dr. Vickers (God Rest his Soul) got blown up.

And now… now… the other old bastard she worked for had gone and gotten himself killed. The nerve of him! How was she supposed to just pick up the pieces he'd left behind?

The weight of her education, a pillory of student loan debt that she'd willingly bargained her future with, hung heavy around her neck… but it also gave her some grounding. She knew she would have to really research this.

Endless days seemed to disappear. It felt like studying for her dissertation again; tomes upon tomes were devoured by her hungry eyes. She made lists and notes with her fingers on her laptop, wrote on coffee napkins, and at one point dragged a chalkboard into the room. Anything she could get her hands on she tried to read.

Topic after topic failed her. There was nothing in any of the books to lead her in any direction. She sat and cried, more than a few times, drying her eyes on her sleeve. Again, she was reminded of grad school. But her contacts with them were dried up. When Dr. Vickers had gotten himself blown up (and wasn't that a trend, she wondered?) Skye's hated rival had ascended to head of the Department. There was no way Dr. PrettyBitch would loan her anything—she was on her own.

It was the final stretch of a good six days' worth of research. Her attention had gone sometime in the past three days. She hadn't slept. All she could think about was the numbers. The truth of the matter was, no matter how she spun it, she wasn't sure they would be able to survive if they met the one-eyed bastard again in his domain. Not unless she shifted the dynamic somehow. But how was she to do that?

But it came to her, one night, in a dream. Perhaps osmosis, she considered; she had used a book on New England mythology as a pillow and drooled all over it, but when she woke up and rechecked it there was the story of the Jersey Devil on the page, stuck with her spit. And slowly, she thought about what Randall had said—Randall with his bizarre take on everything, his unscientific theories, his magic, his twisting of the laws of here and there. He had no rulebook. He went on his gut. But Skye knew there was something more… if only she could tease out the strands of it all…

Red jewels, she found, or red something… always something left over, something left behind. She thought of the Unktehi; she thought of the Crimson Pulse; she thought about what Randall had said about his Lantern, the conversation he'd had with Bailey in the hearse, about scars... She thought about the connection between Humans and the Others; she thought about Suffering. She consulted with Grimm, and asked him a million questions about the process he and Randall had used to develop their technology.

She was delirious by the time Bailey came to her and drugged her. In her dream that night, she was seated at a table filled with people. It was just like her dissertation defense. She gave her insights on what she thought they could do. For some reason Randall was there; Dr. Vickers was there; her hateful Mother was there, heroin needle still sticking from her arm. Even Steph was there, Baby Bird helmet mangled and turned backwards, and how long ago had it been since Skye had even thought about her?

"I believe our only recourse in fighting back the scourge is taming the power of the Scars," Skye said, finally, after some explication.

"You are aware of the dangers inherent in this?" Randall asked. The bullet hole in his chest oozed and spurted over the table like a fountain.

"Absolutely," Skye said. "But I'm convinced that with respect for its power, we can tame our lesser impulses."

Randall nodded. The blood stopped, the wound holes reclosing.

"Seems like fallacious logic," her mother said. "Why use some substance to fight your fight for you? Why don't you just train yourselves more? Why not just get stronger?"

"Because sometimes, as a leader, you have to do what it takes for your team to survive to another day," Skye said.

Her mother seemed satisfied with this, and smiled at her. The heroin needle dissolved.

Dr. Vickers looked at her. He was dressed like a Wizard, eye hanging from his skull and jaw missing. His tongue flapped as he spoke.

"Are you absolutely certain you can lead the team in this endeavor?" he asked. "You won't let someone else's opinions sway your argument, or your motivation?"

Skye nodded.

"I'm driven, and I'm determined," she said.

Dr. Vickers popped his eye back in, reattaching his jaw, and grinned at her, giving her a bloody thumbs-up.

Finally, Stephanie spoke. Her voice sounded like it was coming from the back of her skull. Her neck looked throttled and twisted.

"Are you sure you can turn this situation around?" she asked.

"Utilizing our Scars will ensure we do a complete 180," Skye said.

With a great cracking of bone and tissue, Stephanie's whole head rotated back. The green lamps for the eyes lit with a sparkle.

"Then I have no objections," Randall said. "Are we in agreement?"

The four attendees all nodded.

"Congratulations," Dr. Vickers said behind her. Skye was wearing a cap and a gown; she was standing on a platform somewhere, and hands doffed a red scarf around her neck. "The highest honor we can bestow upon you. We pronounce you Team Lead."

All around her, books and notes lifted from the ground. The blackness of the scene retreated from her mind's eye, and she looked down at the hood, holding it in her hands as it glowed, pulsing.

Numbers span through her eyes—calculations ripped and tore themselves open in the air before her, and a new avenue seemed to open in her mind. She could see it all—every individual effect each action she could possibly take would have, its probability, and its outcome. Her eyes glowed blue as she perceived the future, and wrote out her notes, and when it was over, she knew exactly what her next steps would be.

She went to the panic room afterward—base of operations, Randall had always called it. And she called the Team Meeting. She would tell everyone about reclaiming their Scars… and now it wasn't just a theory anymore. She had proof in her hands, though she knew there was a ninety-five percent probability showing hers to the rest would stain their preconceived notions of what they were looking for.

And as she spoke over breakfast, she could see the future parting before her eyes, the odds ever-so-slowly rising for their chance to succeed…

CHAPTER 33:

GRIMM'S DANCE OF ETHEREAL DISCOVERY

After their Team Meeting, Grimm found himself with a lot of free time. He figured he knew where his Scar was—That Place, That Place that he tried not to think about anymore. And it would be a long gruesome fight with himself to go back there.

He wondered if you could cry as a ghost. What would the substance be made of? Still, in an effort to put off the inevitable, he bugged Skye. Just to see if there was, you know, anything else he could do. Like. Anything. At all.

"No," she said. "There's a good eighty percent chance you're procrastinating."

"That's not a standard deviation," he said.

"Still. It's vital that you attempt to retrieve your own Scar."

"I just don't see what the point is," he said. "I'm intangible. I can barely fiddle with the radio station knob."

"Look," she said. "Get your ass out there. I know you don't want to go back there—"

He gasped in mock horror.

"Back where?" he asked. "I ain't afraid of no... Scars."

"Yes, you are," Skye said. "I crunched the numbers. You're the Tim Allen of fighting Cryptids. Anything you do you either do big and fuck up, or you go home. Your reticence informs me that it's a high probability there's an emotional factor involved."

He blinked.

"When did you become a robot?" he asked.

"I saw Stephanie in my dream last night," Skye said.

She'd plopped it down in the middle between them now, like some rancid surprise. Grimm steadily hovered and considered this.

"How was she?" he asked, and hated the way his voice shook when he asked.

"Good," Skye said, but she didn't meet his eyes. After a moment more of uncomfortable silence, Skye cleared her throat. "Look. The odds are high that everyone else will return in about two weeks. Things will get real hairy after that. I don't care what you do in the meantime. Treat yourself. Get some sun, hit the beach. Just do what you need to do. Find that Scar and get your ass back here afterward, when you've had enough rest."

"So basically I have a vacation until then," he said. "Neat."

"You really should be applying yourself to this," she said.

"Yeah, but isn't this a quest of introspection? Sometimes you have to leave to find what's really there all along."

And Skye's eyes burned blue; and she smiled at him. It creeped him out, to be honest.

Two weeks then. He studied up on Carl Constance's Treatise on Astral Theory he'd found online; after working some kinks out with Eric on getting a voice recognition program going, he was able to surf the internet again on his own, though it was a bit like yelling at a very stupid infant.

There was one theory that interested him. According to Carl Constance, once one had projected, the limits of time and space were virtually yours to command. He attempted this a few times—envisioned himself appearing in the local Circle K, next to the Cornito display, but he was stubbornly stuck in the computer room. He tried various visualization techniques—ambient noise, white static, ceremonial music. He tried touch sensation—remembering how it felt to stand on the linoleum, drunk and grabbing convenience store Tacos at 2 AM at the end of another long week of hunting monsters. Even that didn't work. He tried to use Affirmations—"I am a powerful being of light and source, and I have the ability to transfer my consciousness to anywhere in Time and Space."

Still, nothing.

In desperation, he tried to envision licking tortilla chip dust off his fingers. To his surprise, he felt himself shift and ripple. He opened his astral eyes, and his surroundings had been replaced.

There was a woman with her baby in the cart, an aisle over. She hadn't noticed him, but the baby did. Grimm stared at it. The baby stared back. Grimm tried to make a face; the baby giggled, arms reaching towards him.

Grimm used to hate kids, but if they were all this awesome…

Then the Mom turned, saw him, saw that he had no reflection in the security cams overhead, and screamed.

"There's some strange ghost after my baby!" she shrieked.

"I'm not that strange," he called after her. "Also, not a ghost. And I don't want your fucking baby!"

A big burly African-American security guard pounded down the aisle, sliding to his knees with his gun out, in position behind a queso and salsa display.

"Sir, or whatever the fuck your pronouns are," the security guard said. "I'm gonna have to ask you to leave. Now."

"Dude, Jordan. It's me, Grimm. I come in here every Saturday like clockwork. You know me, man."

Jordan looked over the revolver.

"Do not push me. Vacate the premises immediately. You have until the count of three until I open fire. Three."

"Dude, seriously, it's not what it looks like."

"There's too much strange shit going on for me to take the word of a ghost. Two."

"Dude, I'm literally transparent. Look at me. Bullets won't do shit."

"One."

"Would this be different if I wasn't white? Wait, hold on, that didn't come out like I—"

A bullet fired, whizzing through him. Cornitos exploded everywhere. They both looked equally shocked. Grimm looked down, patted down his body, and Jordan frowned, reholstering his gun.

"Well, that's about what I figured, but I don't like it," the security guard said. "Is that really you, Grimm? What the hell happened to you? You look like a shade of your former self."

"Ha-ha," Grimm said. "Honestly, been a weird month."

"Shit, you're telling me. Last week we had a centipede with a human face come in. Took all the scratchers with him when he left, and called me something racist."

"So you tried to shoot me?" Grimm asked.

"Oh, sorry. Buried the lead. He ate a man's face off, too. I mostly got reamed for the lottery tickets. Been deputized, and the County's policy is shoot first and ask questions later."

But a muted sob came from the next aisle over. The two of them looked down at their feet. A big red puddle had trickled through from the aisle behind Grimm and the Cornitos display.

Their eyes met in mutual looks of shock.

"We should probably check that out," Grimm said.

The two men inched their way over to the next aisle, meeting each other's glances and nodding before they went in.

A woman with blonde hair in a high cut sat in the aisle, hands crimson. She sobbed up at them, holding something in her arms.

"How could you?" she cried.

Jordan moved forward, bending down.

"Let me see what happened, ma'am."

She shifted and moved, holding up a broken bottle of wine, tears in her eyes.

"It was the last bottle of Red in the county," she wailed, to them. "How could you? You know nobody else is coming with deliveries! Not with everything happening…"

They both exhaled, and Jordan called someone on his walkie to come clean up.

"I fucking hate this place," Jordan said, in the next aisle.

"If you could use a job, we have a few positions that opened up," Grimm said.

"What, the undead police? Creature Patrol? No offense, but I ain't cut out for that."

"I don't know man, you held your ground. We got a little more advanced tech available than just guns. Give me a call if you change your mind."

Jordan nodded.

"Just. Try and come in the front door next time," he said.

Grimm nodded, then closed his eyes. He imagined the night he vomited up everything he'd ever eaten after a nice big plate of rabbit stew Barbary had made. There was a rippling in his consciousness, and soon he found himself in the toilet at the Mansion.

Addy did not seem pleased, and shrieked at him until he left.

"That seems really inconvenient," he said, through the door. "We gotta get you an extra hand."

"Fuck off."

He floated away, smirking.

On he travelled. He imagined eating crusty baguettes, and popped out in Paris. He floated up to the top of the Eiffel Tower and photo-bombed an oblivious couple's picture. Liver and Onions took him to Alabama, strangely, in a dairy where the cows seemed pretty unhappy. He managed to phase into an udder in dire need of a milking and gave the next person to use the milking machine a heart attack.

Crawfish Etoufee brought him to New Orleans. A homeless man with a paper sack of vodka saw him blink into existence, shook his head, and poured out the whole bottle onto the street. Grimm slipped under the ground and swam through the dirt with the maggots and burrowing moles; avoided one or two suspiciously preserved, angry-looking fops with fangs. He flitted through the soil and surfaced for sunshine, finding himself in Lafayette Cemetery. There were others like him—maybe just a bit different, more thin and stretched and listless, but they were there, lazing away the afternoon, recumbent in their tombs and coffins. He rallied them all to stretch their invisible legs and soar into the breeze. They had a fun afternoon of antics, swooping through the headstones and scaring the tourists, making bets on who would crap their pants first.

He was stuck for flavors after that, and had to find a donut shop to get himself back on track. He tasted supermarket Key-Lime Pie in his mind, and found himself in Palm Springs. There were a lot more naked fat men than he was expecting, though the music was good. He imagined Deep-dish Pizza, and found himself in Boston, where an elderly couple mistook him for someone cosplaying Al Capone's ghost. They asked for directions, but he'd only passed through before in life—he lied, and then followed them for most of the day as they got lost and disoriented.

And then, struck for anything else, he imagined Apple Streudel. He was whisked away to the outside of a cottage in the woods, with black pines all over. No doubt this was somewhere in Czechoslovakia, though why he knew this he never understood. He heard screaming from inside the cottage, and slid in through a strangely sticky side door. An old woman was screaming, being prodded with sticks, into a man-sized oven by two pre-teens.

She stopped screaming and looked at him, relief in her eyes.

"Dark spirit!" she cried, in Czech, and strangely, he could understand it. "You've come to save me!"

The kids stopped and stared at him. He stared back at the scene.

"This is exactly what it looks like," the boy said, in Czech.

There were books upon books of spells on the sideboards, and a cleverly illustrated vellum parchment showing how to disembowel and prepare a teenage boy was next to a cutting board that had seen better, less-bloody days.

"Check the fridge," the girl said.

Grimm popped his head in. A man's severed head stared back at him.

"I've seen all I need to. Carry on," Grimm said. He waited outside until he heard sufficient elderly screaming, before he popped away.

Grimm thought of the taste of Gruel.

He found himself in a dark, stone cell. There was an echoing, lonely feeling to the walls, and he could hear muttering all around him. Countless other ethereal hands seemed to reach their way from the bars in the hallway outside his room. He pointed himself up towards the sky and imagined himself like a balloon, soaring ever-upwards. When he breached the ceiling, he looked down, soared ever-higher, and saw he was in the Bay, floating over Alcatraz. He soared in to tour San Francisco. Again, a lot more naked fat men than he was expecting.

He imagined Limburger cheese, expecting Germany.

He was cold. The sky had gone black. He stared all around himself. There was an American flag flapping idly in the breeze, and a set of exaggerated footprints on the sand. There was some sort of celestial humming in his ears, and he felt himself very loose and airy.

When he looked out to the sky, he could see the spinning globe of the Earth in the distance. And still, there was this bizarre sucking feeling on the back of his neck...

He floated around the Moon for a bit, hovering and gliding, pretending to jump and leap like an astronaut. When he hit the equator, and the Sun was gone, he found himself staring up at something putrid in the night sky.

A horrible gash in the air—crimson and pulsing, some practically vaginal glitch in the system. It seemed to beckon to him, ever-closer and closer...

He closed his eyes and thought of milk. Opened them again. He was in a pasture, at night. A cow gave him a side-eye. He floated there for a second, and then hovered closer to a commotion further in the herd. Something spiny and hairy, looking a bit like a Chihuahua with mange, had affixed itself to a cow leg.

"Chupacabra?" he said, out loud.

It retracted its fangs and hissed at him.

And then he closed his eyes, and the taste of Bread Pudding came to him all at once. He tried to fight it, to open his eyes back up, but it was no use. He was back in the forest again; back where he had been avoiding going in the first place.

It was a grove of trees. The same grove of trees he had gone Pixie-hunting for. He'd known it was here the whole time. Heck, hadn't all this been the reason he'd come after the little bastards in the first place?

He dropped to his feet on the grass. Stephanie used to make the best Bread Pudding. She would make it for their picnics; they'd walk out here, in the middle of the woods, and they would sit and stare at the stars and talk about their hopes and dreams and eat whatever deliciousness she had packed. Grimm had thought he'd found his true love. And she had loved him—in her shy, sensitive, sweet way.

He'd gotten up and left her alone, during a Blood Moon, of all times.

"I gotta go drain the tank," he said to her. And what putrid last words he'd said. How much of a failure was he, really?

When he returned, she was disemboweled, head twisted practically off. A horde of the flying little bastards were picking through her pieces and singing their shitty rhymes to one another. Of course, she could fight—that's why he left her alone—but why she hadn't, that question had plagued him forevermore afterward.

Of course, he took to stalking them. The little alien-looking mother fuckers. He saw how their wings could paralyze their prey. He thought of Stephanie with every pixie he'd crucified. If he could, he'd make them all pay...

Trust that they were out tonight. He could see their bulbous, lamp-like eyes in the perpetual Blood Moon that had hung in the sky since all this started. They were sitting on branches, clinging to tree bark like geckos, whetting their tongues and staring at him.

Something else was flickering there—something half-formed and partial. He floated close to it. It was a hand—he grabbed it and pulled, leaning, and found Stephanie's shade gasping for air.

"Lookit the dead boy and dead girl," he heard something tiny whisper.

"True love, the poor bastards," something else said.

"Grimm?" she asked. "What happened to you? Where did you go for so long?"

Grimm stared at her for a long time before replying.

"Life happened," he said. "Why are you still here?"

He'd seen this before—he wasn't a ghost, not really—nor was she. She was something left behind—a staticky, confused remnant of emotion confined to the spot where her horrible death had taken place. Not quite a scar, but an echo.

"I've been waiting," she said. "Waiting and waiting for my hero. And here you are."

He closed his eyes. Winged things buzzed around them.

"Hero?" he heard something ask, and laugh mockingly. "Couldn't even get revenge, could you? Couldn't even properly survive a fight with Mr. Wendigo, could you?"

"You have to move on, Stephanie," he said to her.

She looked lost.

"But I don't want to," she said. "I want to stay here with you."

"Aw, her boyfriend's a coward, and he wants to send her away," something said, flitting by his head.

He saw red. He reached out with his hand, like he was knocking a fly ball from a tennis court, one nice long backstroke, and the pixie slammed into a tree, dust sparkling from its wings. It slid to the ground in a pool of its own viscera.

One of the pixies cursed. The rest of them scattered.

Grimm looked down at his hand. It was pulsing red, then calmed down again.

"It's time to go, Steph," he said quietly.

"Just hold my hand, and we'll look at the stars one more time. And then after," she said.

His ethereal fingers laced with her echo. A green pulse came up between them, and Grimm found himself crying—crying hard.

"What's wrong?" Stephanie asked. "Why so upset? This is the perfect evening, isn't it?"

Grimm closed his eyes, and let himself believe for a moment.

"I never said the words," he sputtered. He turned his bleary eyes—and how could a ghost even cry, he wondered? to her face. "I never got the chance."

"Just say it," her echo said softly.

"I love you, Steph," Grimm said.

She smiled at him; he could get lost in her green eyes forever, but she blinked and faded, until all there was was her hand in his, and he looked at it until he saw the green of her gaze stain his fingers. It spread, pulsing, covering him like a warm embrace, further up and up and up, and when it reached his heart… he howled, the taste of Bread Pudding in his mouth.

He breathed in, breathed out. Got angry—found himself strobing red. Got calm. Glowed blue. Thought of Stephanie—and glowed green.

He tried to pick up a stick—tried hard—his intention was to flatten the little blue bastards all around him, one by one—but no matter how he glowed he couldn't.

"Well, this will require some experimentation," he said.

He only looked back at the grove once, before he dove off again. In the distance, as he flew, red, blue and green flashes followed him, little fireworks in the night sky…

CHAPTER 34:

ADDY'S DANCE OF ENLIGHTENMENT

Meditation. Zazen. The art of knowing that something is and is not—the acceptance of something that could be, and that something never was. Addy had come out here, to the place where she had met Randall, and had been here every night since Skye had told her what she should do.

It was penance; self-flagellation, perhaps. She thought of the rhyme she had learned from her childhood. Thought of her parents, long dead. Thought of her *Oji* Tenzen.

"What is the sound of one hand clapping?" she asked the darkness, and the stump of her missing hand cried out in pain, a phantom memory...

Every night they drew closer. She could block them out some days—other days she would retreat, muttering some sutras in her wake as the smell of their rot infiltrated her space. She had studied under Randall—read books by American authors, Frenchmen, even, on the mystical rites of her people. How bizarre, she thought, that she should travel so far away and yet still her only solace was that of the rites her people had passed down.

The woman in white seemed persistent in her efforts to drive Addy insane. She was their leader; she was Addy's ever-loyal banshee, a wailing creature intent on terrifying her personally. What had she done to deserve this? Addy wondered. The Blood Moon hung high overhead—it was never-ending now, its pulse, and Addy could feel and sense *them*. There was always a frigid tang to the air as the *Yurei* drew closer and closer...

What was her Scar? She wondered. Was it her missing hand? Her parents' death under the shadow of Mt Fuji? The explosive confrontation in the forest when she'd first arrived here, so many moons ago? What was she missing? What had she said, what had she done, what crime had she committed to have a life like this? The Blood Moon looked like a cursed star overhead. Perhaps her existence had been an affront to the Gods, she thought—maybe it was some cosmic timing, some sheer dumb luck. Maybe all the world was one vast cosmic dice board, and she'd rolled really low stats before she was dumped here.

Cackles in the evening breeze. She shut her eyes. Tried to focus on the feeling of herself, her awareness, her oneness with everything. If she cleared her mind, she would clear their sighs, clear their presence. Make them blink out and disappear. There was nothing here with her but the trees, and the breeze, and the elements all together, and the evil eye staring down at her from the sky…

"Addy-chan," she heard, from the trees.

Despite herself she opened her eyes. Saw the woman in the white kimono again. She was a sentinel, with staring bloodshot eyes.

"What do you want from me?" Addy snapped, shrieking. "What are you? *WHO* are you?"

The woman smiled at her, head tilting, teeth razor sharp and gleaming. There were other things that rustled in the trees… bat-winged things, things that slurched and dragged themselves. Addy shut her eyes closed again as they began to move, to taunt her. She breathed deeply. Didn't respond—knew they would not move when she did not acknowledge them.

They would not move upon her until she acknowledged their existence. That, at least, was something useful; but the lines between knowing and unknowing what was real were weak, especially in the past few weeks, and reaching the mental state of emotionless uncaring she required to throw them off was nearly impossible.

The hair on the back of her neck rustled with a cool breeze, and a voice whispered 'Boo!' in her ear. Addy shrieked, jumping up and turning around, entering her combat stance… but it was just the floating specter of Grimm.

"Damn you!" she said. "You're going to kill me if you don't stop."

"Have you found your scar yet?" Grimm asked, spectral face gleaming.

Addy shook her head. She looked all around her, at the shadows on the eaves of the clearing.

"No," she said. "Every time I try to reach deep down, to find that inner truth, they come out of the woods to find me."

Grimm turned and looked at them. He seemed to be counting.

"I think I can help," he said. "But I need you to promise me something."

Addy narrowed her eyes at him.

"Promise you what?"

"Promise me, afterwards, you'll be my hands," he said.

"I'm a little under-qualified," Addy said.

"We'll make you a replacement," he said. "But you have to promise me. You'll help me build whatever I need to build, and I'll keep you safe from these things."

"My concentration is shot," she said. "I can't keep this up anymore. Soon they'll be on me. Once they've scared me to death first. So yes. If you can help me out, I'll help you. I'll be your hands in this world."

Grimm grinned.

"Great! That's all I really needed to hear," he said. "Watch this."

He breathed in, closed his eyes, and began glowing red. Flickers of power extended slowly over him; and then a wash of green billowed through the mess. Addy could see the surroundings lit up as if by a lamp, and shielded her eyes. Soon, there was a brilliant strobing of green, and Grimm's visage had changed.

Addy moved her hand from her eyes, and beheld. There he was—the same old pale, haunted, stretched face, with crazy hair and sunken in eyes. But where his eyes had been there was now flickering green flames. A majestic black robe billowed down around him, and in his hands a sharp scythe gleamed in the light of the moon. He was still translucent, but now he looked deadly—like some sickly woodcut of Death come to life.

"I'm the fucking Grimm Reaper, baby!" he exclaimed. "Sending all lost souls back to where they belong."

As one the crowd of Yurei moved forward—the woman in the white kimono's nails growing and slashing, things in the trees screeching and uncoiling themselves. Grimm dodged and weaved through the air, striking and cutting. Where his blade passed, blood spattered. Yurei parts fell, dissolving into green ethereum which he paused to suck up, skeletal fingers conducting it towards his open maw, and his eyes flared brighter.

Only the woman in the white kimono was left. She stood, floating, considering her next move.

"Go back," Grimm's voice intoned. "Burden the living world no longer."

She howled, hands outstretched to throttle him, but he moved past her. A green streak of energy hovered in the air where he sliced—and soon she dissolved, a white spark spiraling up and up and up to the sky, where it winked out.

A dying, plaintive sigh on the breeze… *"Addy-chan…"* and then nothing.

The robes uncoiled, the scythe dissolving, and Grimm's gaunt face grew more fleshed out. Soon, he was just like his regular old annoying self again, only slightly translucent.

"That was amazing," Addy said, breathing deeply.

It was as if the burden of a thousand years had fallen off her shoulders. How long had they stalked her? She wondered. Had their torment drawn her mother and father into their suicide? Was that woman…

She shook her head. They were gone now. Answers and truth were human ideals. In the world they lived in, there were more things than human experiences in it. More things than human logic. More things than human comprehension.

"That must have been your Scar," Addy said.

"Absolutely," Grimm said. "And now, your part of the deal. Report back to the Mansion once you find yourself. We've got a lot to do, and even more to build."

"I'm not even sure where to begin with this scar thing," Addy admitted.

"You want advice?" He blinked. "From *me?*"

"No!" Her face was flushed. "I want to ramble at you and use you as a sounding board for my thoughts. Is that okay?"

He shrugged.

"Not any worse than Randall," he said.

Addy nodded, continuing.

"I just don't think I've ever really known who I am, to be honest. Most of my life I've had to stand on the precipice of two realities—two views of life—I'm either crazy and delusional, or actively being targeted for something I had no control over. All I could do was try to make the *Yurei* disappear, to ignore them, to invalidate their existence. My whole life has been a reaction to them. What is the self when it's simply a shell built in opposition to a reality that might not even exist?"

"Okay. Hold up. You're not thinking about things the right way," Grimm said. "These things—the *Yurei*—you think they're targeting you because you can see them. You think, even now, after all we've been through—even with a missing hand, *taken by them,* you think that you could possibly be insane."

"Could I possibly be sane in this world? Could anyone?"

"The world's not sane. It's not fair. Nothing's fair. There only is what there is, and there isn't what there isn't. There's no human-based way of looking at things that can add or subtract from the mystery of the equation. This whole time you keep looking for an answer outside of yourself. Some piece of the puzzle that you don't have, when the reality is it's simple. You exist. They exist. Willing them away doesn't work. What remains is that you've focused on making them disappear from your sight, instead of asking how to remove yourself from theirs."

265

"You're a douche, but damnit, you make sense," she said.

He smiled another crooked-teethed smile.

"We aim to please. Come back to the Mansion when you're all zipped up."

"Might be a few more days," she said.

"Yeah, yeah," he said, turning and floating away.

Addy sat for some time chewing this over, and then decided she would debate the nature of it with herself. She sat in silence, in lotus position, attempting Zazen. Clearing her mind-considering the nature of a thing that existed and did not exist. Reality was implausible; how bizarre, how unlucky she was, to have been born under a cursed star, to have been birthed into a tragedy. Was anything she'd ever thought about herself true? Was she even real?

"There exists only that which is, and that which is not," she said to herself, looking at her hand, and her missing hand. "It's not that they're not real... it's that I'm not real. I'm not something—I'm nothing. If thinking means one is, then by not thinking, one is not."

And she cleared her mind. Focused on her breathing. Felt something stirring at her feet, saw red and green colors blasting before her mind's eye, and when she opened her eyes again, she found that she could not find herself.

"I am," she said. Her body came back.

Yurei stirred in the trees; ever more, she thought, and a weariness came over her.

"I am not. I am nothing." And her body faded away again.

She walked past the Yurei in the bushes, who sniffed the air, but could not see her... and she knew that in nothingness, she had found her power. This time it was her phantom knives, her *sotto voce* sutras, her one-handed muttered mudras, bellicose words that stained the air with green that she erected and chanted all around them that did the trick. When she walked away, a passing shadow, she slapped her remaining hand against her leg, idly, as if to release her work.

The howls of the collected *Yurei* as her spellcraft exploded behind her did more to soothe her than anything she'd ever felt in her life.

CHAPTER 35:

BAILEY'S DANCE OF DESPAIR

When she was younger, Violet was her closest friend and confidante.

Violet, with burnished purple hair. Violet, every inch of Bailey's height, who wasn't afraid to wear jeans and jackets and temporary tattoos and soccer cleats. Violet, she who was sassy, Violet, she who was brave. Violet, she who wasn't afraid of anything.

Except, of course, for the howling from the woods…

Bailey's Dad told her to stay inside the tent. Then he crept his careful way outside, only to scream in the darkness, once, and never return…

Violet and Bailey sat and stared at one another inside the tent until the dawn rolled around, shivering together for warmth…

When the stink had gone, Violet had hunkered down, purple eyes gleaming in the light of Bailey's flashlight, holding her index finger over her own mouth and said, without speaking, that Bailey needed to be quiet.

It was Violet who had gone out first—Bailey unzipped the inside of the tent, slowly, then scurried to the far corner. Violet stumbled out—and then Violet had shrieked, seemingly forever, when she saw what had happened.

"You can't stay here," Violet said, trying to block Bailey's view, but Bailey was curious, and pushed her out of the way, and for the first time Bailey beheld Death in all its foul ripeness. There her father was—impaled on a gig out by the river shore.

Violet was worried, more worried and more frightened than Bailey had ever seen her before. And that was probably what scared Bailey more than anything else.

"We have to find you some food," Violet said, after sending Bailey back into the tent.

"What's wrong with Dad?" Bailey asked.

Violet shook her head, eyes closed, and whispered something in Bailey's ear.

"What's dead?" Bailey asked.

"Dead is when you don't move anymore," Violet said. "Dead is when your soul's gone. When someone dies, that means they go away forever. It means they're hurt, and they're hurt bad, and it won't ever ever heal itself, and then they quit moving. And they'll never talk with you again."

"Oh," said Bailey, and for the first time in her life, she felt sad.

Violet, her therapist had said, years later, was her internalized trauma. Violet, her therapist had said, was her brain's insidious way of rewriting her memories. Violet was, her therapist said, an imaginary friend—some figment of pretend Bailey had conjured up in an attempt to block out the horrific abuse she'd been subjected to. Violet was her intense suffering given form—Violet was her anguish.

"Your father was clearly a cruel man," Dr. Satheem said, with a clear and undemanding tone. "Your subconscious created these memories to shield you. That is why Violet showed up to protect you—why she showed up to give you advice. This process of negotiation with one's self, it creates delusions, you see, especially in such a young person as yourself."

At the time, Bailey nodded. Years afterward, when she had completely sank herself inside the internet, consuming and devouring information streams, filtering through every stray possibility that existed for a world outside the one everyone was trying to convince her of, she realized that Violet, her imaginary friend, may have been a Tulpa…

Violet had been there with the Old Couple. Violet had steered her there, clearly unwary but anxious, some innate need for Bailey's survival foremost in her mind. She had flown up the mountain top after she swam away in the stream. She was gone for a day and a half, Violet was, and left Bailey with some berries and some nuts and some of the supplies Bailey's father had left behind. Bailey sat there and watched nature. She drank water slowly, with little sips, like Violet asked her to. She went and talked to her father, who stank more and more as the day dragged on. Night fell, and Violet parted the bushes, lilac eyes staring pointedly, waving Bailey over.

"There are people on the mountain road," she said. "I'm not sure if you can trust them, but they might have a phone, or some food. Bring as much as you can carry with you."

Bailey thought it was a good idea, and off she went, slipping on rocks and skinning her knees. One particularly bad scrape is how the rescuers would find her, weeks later—DNA analysis from the campsite would compare and the Search and Rescue team would track her to the cottage, knocking down the doors, pistols drawn, demanding everyone in the house to get on the ground.

Eventually, however, she would find herself at the door to the cottage, knocking on the door gently with a six-year old's fist. She would overlook the mountaining pile of stinking garbage collected in piles, horseflies buzzing angrily. She did not know what to think of the junk heaps in the back, the starved dog all skin and bones collared to a corrugated tin doghouse near the decaying tire swing. She was too young to know any better. Violet, however, buzzed with anxious energy, and told Bailey to be careful.

Violet even told her what to say.

"I came here with my Daddy, and I can't find him," Bailey said. She questioned why Violet would tell her to say this later, and never really understood it. "I need to call my Mom. Do you have a phone?"

The old man stank of tobacco, and he leered at her, chin a broad field of white stubble and mouth chewing.

"We ain't got no phone, little girl," he said. "But you'd better stay here until we can find your Pappy."

The look he gave her chilled Bailey to the bone. Violet did not like the look of him, either.

"I made a mistake," Violet whispered. "You have to leave! If you do stay—I think he's going to hurt you."

"Will I be dead?" Bailey asked, in her head.

Violet's eyes, tinted eggplant, brimmed over with tears.

"Maybe worse," she said. "Tell him you left your backpack outside."

Bailey said this, and, perhaps sensing her discomfort, the old man grinned again, spitting on the floor near her feet. She jumped, and he moved forward and padlocked the door from the inside.

"We gotta keep little girls like you safe," he said. "You don't know what kind of crazy things live out in this mountain."

"I really need to find my Daddy or Mommy," Bailey said.

"Don't worry," he said, horrible leer on his face. "We'll be your new family now."

They couldn't ever see Violet—never at the table, telling Bailey what not to eat, never at night, when the Old Man came in with a medicine bottle that stank of mothballs. Bailey did not eat their poison; she did not drink their ether. She dodged when the Old Woman made to pull her hair, to comb it, to dress her up like one of the many horrifying porcelain dolls buzzing with flies against their bedroom wall, but could not escape—the Old Woman had hit her, whipped her with a belt for insubordination.

"You're not my parents!" Bailey shrieked. She gasped in air, again, to shout: "I want my Mommy and Daddy!"

"How dare you!" the Old Woman gasped, slapping her. Bailey fell. "If we're not your parents, then you're not my child. And if you're not my child, but you're living in my house, I guess you're a dog! And you'll sleep in a crate like one!"

They'd jabbed her, fed her dog food for a week. Forgot on purpose to water her. And here some of the memories fuzzed out. She remembered Violet saying something to her—that if she didn't drink she'd die, she had to, she had to even if she couldn't stand it, even if the water tasted funny—and then the next thing she remembered was the blessed light of the front door being kicked open, streaming into the darkness of that tin hovel, dust particles falling in the beams, the screams, the shouts. Policemen yelling. Gunshots.

When it was over, and the Old Couple were both dead like her father, they took the Jaws of Life to the lock on her cage and she trotted out on all fours to them. One of the men picked her up and hugged her, weeping over her. She remembered something like helicopter blades, and flying, flying into the sky…

Somewhere between there and home, Violet had disappeared, but it was so long ago, Bailey never could understand why…

Maybe Violet had been too much a part of what happened. Maybe Violet on the forefront of all those memories soured Bailey's subconscious towards her. Whatever the case was, Bailey did not think of her—at least not until she'd turned fourteen, and started thinking about getting out of the house for once.

Puberty was hitting with the force of a sledgehammer. She had been inside most of her life at this point—at least for most of the preceding five years. At most she'd ventured onto the stoop to grab the paper, and then slipped inside again, locking the door behind her, struggling between her sense of safety and her need to talk to people, and losing.

Her whole life had been a cage. She'd been in it for so long that it was a comfort, but this was the real first part of the longing she had, the stirring of her invisible wings. The lure of the outside world—and boys her age—called to her.

She was lonely. She had no friends. She wished, more often than not, that she could conjure someone up out of the blue to talk to her. And that's when she found the deep parts of the web, the parts about Tulpas…

A Tulpa was a shard of one's personality. Thoughtforms—artificial spirits, alternate personalities. Depending on the user's paradigm, it was given different origins. The practice was first documented in a journal of an American traveller, who found Tibetan monks that used it as a way to distance themselves from material reality. A Tulpa was an imaginary friend, but a voluntary hallucination. By *forcing* them into reality, or manufacturing the image, the sight, the smell, the feel of them in one's mind, one could make them appear, fully formed, before one's eyes, by thought transference. At least. That was the theory. The practice was harder.

She thought of Violet; thought of how Violet had been there for her, in her darkest of times, thought of how Violet had explained things to her that didn't seem to come from Bailey's own mind. Hell, she needed someone on her side, didn't she?

She made a picture of her. (And here some echo of something she'd seen once, long ago, in her father's bedroom, came back to her, but it was a fragment, and so illusory she supposed it was a part of a dream she'd had once.) The woman had violet eyes. She was Bailey's age, with bad-ass purple hair in a Mohawk, and her labret pierced, and she dressed like she just waltzed straight out of a Hot Topic, like she didn't care about the outside world or all the terrifying people in it.

Then Bailey started to imagine her. This was hard. The forcing—she somehow had to superimpose the feel of her own skin on this other person's body. She had to feel what it felt like with her fingertips to touch coarse hair, to touch smooth metal. She had to imagine what she smelled like. Lavender, Bailey supposed—that was purple enough, wasn't it?

The first few weeks Bailey laid the groundwork, meditating for hours, visualizing with open eyes a girl by her side. It didn't seem to do anything. And then one night, Bailey squeezed her eyes shut, and she was guided… by something, some inner instinct, some residual echo of a voice in her skull, some alternate train of thought that whispered "Imagine the air splitting before you."

And Bailey did so, and then suddenly, as if animated by some spark, Bailey could finally see her, touch her, smell her… hear her.

Violet was back, sitting on her sofa, smiling.

"I'm a split personality?" Violet asked, looking confused.

"You're a fragment of my consciousness that I've disconnected from," Bailey said.

Strange how their roles had reversed; Violet seemed a bit new to all this, and walking her through their new living situation was something Bailey had to take the lead in. Bailey knew it would be hard, from her perspective, to be a part of a mind in a body she didn't control, at someone else's beck and call. Still, this was the Violet she remembered, because unbidden Violet would talk about things they'd done as children. Some things Bailey did not remember; some things she did, with startling clarity. It was a whirlwind.

They did not talk about Bailey's father. It was a hazard zone, and the both of them knew it.

But the basement was not enough for Violet. "It's so cramped down here," she said one day, jiggling her knee. "I don't understand how you can put up with all this. Day in and day out. Not even a bit of sunlight. It must drive you mad."

"Company helps," Bailey said, clicking away at the keys to her PC.

Violet walked over, perching on her shoulder with an elbow. Bailey could feel her touch like static on her own skin.

"What are you working on?"

"Editing some Youtube videos," Bailey said.

"And what's Youtube?" Violet asked.

Bailey looked at the screen for some time before responding.

"It's. Think of it like TV. You can watch individual shows. Sometimes they're short, sometimes they're long, sometimes it's whatever people want to make a video about. I run a channel about monsters."

"What kind of monsters?"

"Like the kind that got Dad."

Violet grew quiet at this.

"I'm so sorry," she said. "You're sad still, aren't you?"

"A lot of the time," Bailey said. "But I don't feel so sad anymore when you're around."

"I'm glad," Violet said. "But don't you think you'd feel happier if you met more people your own age?"

"I'm fine," Bailey said, and her voice was clipped.

"I really don't think you are," Violet said. "Look. I might just be your imaginary friend, but I want what's best for you. You're just wasting your life down here. Not making connections with people. Don't you want a boyfriend?"

"More than anything," Bailey sighed.

"You don't want to stay the rest of your life in this cage, do you?" Violet asked, perhaps thinking the tricky subject had been broached. "Isn't that what happened when you were a little girl?"

Bailey looked up at her, and felt fire flow from her belly.

"If I hadn't left the tent," she said, voice daggers, "None of that would have happened."

She and Violet stared at one another for some time. And wasn't it strange, Bailey thought, how a situation could feel so awkward, when you were really talking with yourself?

"I just want what's best for you, Bailey," Violet said, after a moment.

"Yeah, well, I know what's best for me. It's staying here, inside, in a place I'm familiar with, where I know I'm safe," Bailey said. Her voice was like ice. "Where I won't get attacked, or beaten up, or almost killed."

"I know how you feel. I was there with you. You're just scared," Violet said, trying to be the voice of reason. "And it's understandable, but you can't just. You can't let it hold you back like this, Bailey."

"I have a life here. I'm safe. I wouldn't even know what to do with myself if I went outside."

"I would. We'd talk with boys, if you want. I know you're nervous, but we can swap. I can go out for you. It'll be like Cyrano de Bergerac. I drive, but you're the one getting the man."

"I haven't even read that yet," Bailey said. "How do you know about it?"

"I think your Dad and Mom were talking about it once. You guys had that movie Roxanne on VHS. You were little."

For some reason, the fact that Violet could remember her parents better than her pissed her off, and she snapped.

"I don't want to leave, don't you get it?" Bailey said, and now she was angry. "If you're so unhappy here, why don't you just leave?"

"Fine," Violet said back, and she just seemed tired. "I just want you to know. I'm not mad at you, Bailey. I'm worried about you. When you're ready to listen again. When you want to talk. Just call me, okay?"

And off she went, climbing through the basement window and out of Bailey's life.

"Even my imaginary friends won't get off my ass," Bailey huffed.

And out of resentment, Bailey'd never, not ever, called her back. But her sister had heard her—heard her talking to herself, found the things she was doing. Scheduled another appointment. This time with a different therapist.

The flow of her future was changing… and after four years of therapy, Bailey found herself strong enough to walk down the sidewalk by herself again. And dismissing the whole Tulpa thing, the imaginary friend thing, as a twisted distortion of her mind caused by too much time spent by herself… a violet illusion of anguish painted in vivid imaginary Technicolor…

In times of great distress—the greatest, really—she often thought about Violet, silly as it was. "What would Violet do?" she often wondered. "What would Violet tell me I should do?"

Bailey had trekked here on foot, knife in hand. What good it would do she didn't know. Not a single Cryptid greeted her. Just the remains of the campfire she and her three friends— four, if she counted Devin—had put together so long ago. Some of their supplies were still out here. Someone's cellphone, long-since dead, lay as a monument to their struggle.

The grass had grown. Water had come, rising from the creek and swallowing some of the scenery. The place still remained like a Mausoleum, however, and not a single insect sang. The broken down church in the distance called out to her, and she decided to head back there. The earth was calm now, here, and she could feel the soothing sigh of it in her bones.

She sat in a pew and bowed her head. Overhead, bats rustled their wings. She tried not to feel her skin crawl.

"Violet," she whispered, into the darkness of the cathedral where her friends had died. "What should I do?"

"Hey," Violet said immediately, in her ear. "Long time no see. You sure know how to hold onto a grudge."

Bailey jumped, biting back a scream.

"Didn't mean to scare you," Violet said. She had both of her legs balanced on the row of pews in front of them. "You seem distressed."

"I'm supposed to be looking for something," Bailey said. "I can't find it. Not sure where to look, really."

"What is it?"

"A piece of me. A scar. Something animated by my trauma. Something that, if I reclaim it… could help me out. Thing is, I don't know where to go. Don't know which incident to pick. Everything's sucked. My whole life has been one big tragedy."

"I think I can help," Violet said. "Come here. Give me a big hug."

Bailey's arms reached out to grab her, and for a second, if anyone were to look at the two of them, they might see their limbs conjoined, as if Bailey were some humanoid pinwheel.

There was a blast of blue and red light, mixing and merging, a tunnel that opened before Bailey's eyes, and soon Bailey felt all of Violet dissipate, even as she held onto her, even as she watched her smiling friend's face disappear, until all that was left was a plastic tiara in her hands, with a purple jewel in the center.

Like a movie reel, she saw things start to unfurl in her mind's eye…

She was five years old. Bailey and her father were having a tea party. Dad had gotten her her own Princess crown. Bailey had put it on her stuffed animal, a regal looking tigress with two legs.

"That's for you, silly," her Dad said.

"No, it's for Violet. That's her name. She's named after the color of the jewel."

"Well, maybe you should be crowned," her Dad said, laughing. "Maybe you should be violet."

"I can't be somebody else," Bailey said.

"You can do anything through the power of imagination, Bailey," her Dad said. "Always remember that. You can go anywhere. You can do anything. You just have to believe you can. The first step to doing anything is imagining it."

Another loop, tape deck skipping, VHS speeding. More things resounding, pounding in her brain.

She and Grimm were falling in the tunnel, but it wasn't a tunnel, was it? It was flesh—some vast uterine lining that pulsed throughout. He'd landed, with a thud, on purple grass. His limbs were broken. Pixies were tearing and gnawing at him. Bailey reached down and grabbed him, pulling his soul back up through the schism behind her, through which she could see the grime of the cave they came from. The sky in this land was clouded with dark mists—the seas boiled red in this new land. Bizarre creatures of all shapes and sizes lurked in the trees and fought one another as foreign suns and bizarre day lengths passed.

Speeding up even more—now she was back at the Badlands.

Now she was diving in and out from the Portals—feeling the seams of the world open and close, feeling them separate, feeling them meld around her. Watching a crowd of monsters, mutinous and hungry, fighting and snarling at one another, fighting to be the first ones through. Feeling her hands and her imagination open and close the entrances with just a blink. Radiating power from every pore of her being~~~~

She sat up from where she had been slumped over. Bailey hesitantly placed the tiara on her head, closing her eyes, and then... her eyes began glowing purple. The loop was rewinding now, back and back and back until she was fourteen, where she had heard Violet's voice whisper in her ear.

"Imagine a split in the air before you," Bailey said, but it wasn't her voice, and she moved her hand down in one fell swipe. Reality tore open before her, a crimson stain in the air that roared with the suction of wind. With an upward swipe from her left hand, it closed again.

"Let's do this," Violet said, in her ear.

Bailey grinned.

CHAPTER 36:

THE FOURTH HORSEMAN

Two weeks since everything started. Still the Whisper spoke to him, commandeering her forces with a wave of her multitudinous hands. They had devoured, en masse, the surrounding towns one by one... first a street, then a strip mall, then a neighborhood here and there. Fire and destruction, wailing people, and suffering were all that was left where the dark forces rode. Lazarus rode with them sometimes, other times watching only in spirit, using his Eyes to pierce and see what may be. He watched, laughing, as he saw the beautiful suffering all around him.

A woman and her children devoured, torn limb from limb. That had delighted him to no end—cars and electricity and all the terrible things of this modern world were crumbling before him. Power lines overhead were snapped by the flying fiends—people would poke their heads outside, wondering what had happened, and then the other fanged beasts would strike, dragging them away.

Some people had shotguns, some had pistols. Some people fought back. Always joyful to watch—some humans were able to survive, but some were eaten, some tortured, some flayed. Lazarus found himself watching these little games with nothing short of amusement.

There was one little girl—she'd gotten so far. Escaped, as if her luck were somehow protecting her. Things had started happening around her—a monster would try to get her, but some sheer circumstance would save her. It was delightful, he thought. To see how innocence squirms as it tries to evade the true horror of the world. Her family had gone first—she barely escaped when a hound had overshot her and launched itself off the balcony. She sped down to the street, where a squawking flyer swooped, intent on lacerating her skull. A swinging power line got it, snapping from some unseen tension here and there.

She ran to the neighbor's house. They let her in, but soon she realized that they were all shapeshifters—changers kept safe from the terrors outside by the terror they themselves could become. She watched them shred each other to pieces fighting over her—comparing her to a veal cutlet. All that was left was death in her wake. She escaped again, getting a ride from a horrible man who had nothing but foul intentions for her. Their car spun out from a Sasquatch flipping them—the explosion and the impact threw her, landing her in the grass, and she stumbled, sobbing, down the broken road.

"What cruelty," he said to himself. He got to his feet and stretched, popping the kinks in his back. "I must take care of this one by myself, apparently. My lady, I must step away. I hope you will be fine in my absence?"

The Whisper did not speak for once—only manipulated and commanded, her brilliance shining in Lazarus' Eyes, arms moving in different symbols.

Shrugging, he aimed a bullet and shot off another portal. The air shimmered and opened, and with a belch of hellfire, Lazarus found himself face to face with his promised glorious steed. Its eyes burned crimson, like rubies, and its pearlescent skin sagged where decay had set in. Lazarus walked up to it—it neighed, champing at the air, mouth frothing.

"Perfection, as always," he said, and used its exposed rib to pull himself up into an ungainly side saddle.

He sat there astride his pale horse, his own Eyes glowing as fiercely as that of his mount, and he shrieked in indolent despair: "For I am Death, and Hades follows close behind me!"

And off he galloped, in a cloud of smoke that sparked where hooves hit the ground.

He found her. A sobbing nine year old. Two monsters had fought one another to death in front of her.

"H-h-h-help me!" she said to him.

His compassion bloomed for her. He slid off the horse, more gracefully than he had mounted, and stepped over to her, boots squashing the blood-crusted earth.

"Come to me, child, and let me ease your suffering," he said, kneeling.

She sobbed, diving into his arms. He curled his right hand up to stroke her hair, and then. If someone were to see him from behind. They would have heard a great snapping sound, and watched his shoulders jerk, like he was twisting the lid off a stubborn jar…

Crows cawed and took to wing as he placed her body down on the earth, whispering something over her. Then he stood.

"Death, in the end, is a comfort to us all," he said, and mounted his horse again.

He shot more wild, glowing shots into the sky. Monsters streamed forth in great crowds, and he himself led the charge, pistol drawn and aimed forward, laughing and laughing…

The Black Hills rose up in his view, and the Mansion on the plateau above gleamed as his forces made their way further into the woods…

BATTLE FOR THE BLACK HILLS

Illustration by Anton Tolstobrov

CHAPTER 37:

BATTLE FOR THE BLACK HILLS

"Lazarus," he heard, whispering in his ear.

He turned, and found himself face to face with the white mask of it—the Whisper. So great was her power that she could move without movement—appearing here and there, wherever she went. She shone, even here, on the edge of the forest, like some statue of divinity itself come to life.

As much time as they spent together, however, it did not stop him from wanting to scream.

"My lady," he said, pulling on the reins of his pale horse to turn it. The stallion whinnied, smog and sulfur bellowing from its nostrils, as they faced the Whisper. Her face, occluded by her Mask, was higher from the ground than even than he on his mount. He had to crane his neck upwards to see. "We have held off as long as we could. This petty destruction, this wanton killing. I admit, I have participated. I continue to do so—to listen to your words. Gladly, even, do I do this, knowing of the salvation of it for my people. Knowing how bound we are in this world, to the chains of logic and reason, when such paradise awaits us all in worlds yet to come. And yet. My hands quiver still."

"Oh?" the Whisper's voice was cold.

"That child came to me for comfort, and in her time of need, I could offer her only our brand of salvation. The fear she had in her chest... the quiver of her tiny body in my hands. I am ashamed of my weakness, and ashamed more of my actions towards her. I fear that... in some ways... perhaps this may be too cruel of a solution."

"Your faith in my Purpose is weak, then," the Whisper said, and its voice was not disappointed, but merely sad.

"My lady, I believe in you. I believe in what you have shown me. My faith is not in question. You who have given me this awesome power—this strength beyond, this body eternal. I have seen your children, in all their glory—defying all odds, all biology. I have incanted the Holy Words you whispered to insane scribes so long ago. I have listened only to you, and remain your devoted disciple in these times of darkness yet to come, which will usher in the crimson light of a new dawn. And yet..."

A hand came out, darted—skin pale, like light personified. It gripped him by the throat, and lifted him into the air, disengaging him from the horse. His feet dangled, and his undead steed skittered backwards, kicking and neighing.

"And yet, you say. Well? What does your human logic and your human compassion tell you, oh devoted warrior? That you, you who see only this world as linear, you who see only this world as a series of action and reaction—tell me, oh lowly worm, what your advanced *human* insight tells you that one of my caliber has not already considered endlessly from my throne in the space beyond the confines of your dreadful golden star?"

He gulped, hands grasping at her fingers and drawing in gasps.

"I… I meant no disrespect, my lady," he babbled. "It is yet hard. Being born among these sheep, to hear their bleating… though a sheep alone knows how guilty and truly decrepit the thoughts and feelings and emotions of other sheep are, those who veil themselves in false accoutrements of virginal snow… and yet the lambs, truly pure in their wool, they cry out as they are slaughtered for your children's supper. Might we not. Might we not deliver unto them a sermon of some sort? Ask them to willingly join our ranks… to ensure that those who have not yet had a chance to suffer the cruel slings and arrows of this world yet… perhaps we could send them directly over, my lady, to avoid… avoid...."

He was going to say 'excess suffering,' but then gulped and swallowed the words back. Still, she seemed to understand his intent, for her countenance grew stormy.

The hand, feeling as large as the Statue of Liberty's, squeezed ever-tighter about his neck, and he could feel his consciousness draining… until she released him, and he fell, hip banging against the ground, wheezing and gasping for air. If he had not already been blessed with eternity, he knew, the fall would have killed him…

He sat up and breathed, old lungs rattling.

"I understand your plaintive sobs," She said, after what seemed like an eternity. Her Mask did not seem to soften, but her voice appeared more reasonable. "Despite your many failures, you have yet been loyal to my cause. Despite your grotesquerie in every imaginable situation, you are yet the only one of your kind close enough to a wolf at this juncture of history, capable of being my General and mowing down these blithering, pathetic, polluting, parasitic worms. Still, try as you might, you cannot unpin yourself from human concepts of morality and reason. To your detriment."

He got to his knees and bowed as he spoke.

"Perhaps my Lady has feared I have grown too soft," he said.

"Get on your feet and face me, you miserable coward," the Whisper demanded, voice booming. Lazarus' hair was blown backwards by the force of her words.

Lazarus swallowed and dragged himself to his feet.

"Do you know, Lazarus, why I am here?"

"To turn our world into a paradise."

She reached out with one hand, dangling something wet and awful over his head. It was his eye. Bizarre to be staring back at it.

"This," she said. "This is a marker of your suffering. This is the unique interaction between my Divine Pulse, and mortal suffering. This is your *Praxis*, putrid worm, and without it, you would be naught but a fragile, wizened, dead cowboy, buried six feet in the ground. You would be bones. Paradise? You think my aims are to baptize this world in fire, and cleanse it?"

She threw her head back and laughed.

"This world is unique amongst the cosmos. The alignment of the planets in this solar system creates an energetic frequency which allows my Divine Pulse to surge into the confines of this dimension in conjunction with your lunar observations. Yet again, another interaction—a synthesis of two things, which is greater than the individual parts."

"My lady? What are you saying?"

"I aim only to trigger the confrontation between humankind and that of the other. To push them to their limits—to have them embrace their divine suffering, their darkness, their eternal remorse. The transformation that would take place!" Her voice sounded exultant. "Only the strong, the beautiful, the unique—those who have pushed themselves to become more-than will survive in the hellscape I turn this land into."

"But to what end?"

"There is no end," the Whisper said. "There is only suffering-a cycle that continues, endlessly, generating more and more conflict, causing more and more destruction, causing more and more of your kind to reach deep into their darkness and grab hold. Survival—at any cost. That is evolution. That is synthesis. That is the conjunction—a beautiful dance of endless torment."

Lazarus stared at the beast before him, trying to mask the emotions thundering through his head.

"A system like that cannot be sustainable, My Lady," he said, voice wooden.

"Systems? You think I care for systems, for reason, for anything other than witnessing the beauty of suffering before us?"

"My Lady surely has a purpose for cultivating such power."

"Indeed," she said. "You are shrewd, in your own rat-like way. I admit, my quest—my aspiration—is not just the destruction of this place. I am not merely a connoisseur of pain, some collector of rare emotive relics. My own aims. I have had no one to confide in these many long eons, so I suppose, given your limited intelligence, some discussion on the point would be necessary. These *Praxes* that your people develop. Their *Scars*, to put it plainly. They are the keys to my own ascension."

"Ascension?" Lazarus asked.

"You think me an all-powerful Goddess, and yet, I am but an echo of what I may yet be. What use is a single planet to lord over? A single dimension? No, I seek ever-onward. I aim to elevate myself—to become one with a new plain of existence, to Become All That Is. Only by using this *Praxis*, this *suffering*, may I absorb more power."

"And? What will you do?"

"Become one with all," she breathed. "To join with all. To see the sights, to smell the sounds, to feel the excruciating pain of all existence—to shoulder that burden, to become, as one, something new and divine… and in so doing, I shall make the entirety of the multiverses *suffer*. So that the entirety of existence itself will grow ever-more powerful!"

She's mad. Madder than I am. And I was mad enough to trust her seductive whisper in my ear… Lazarus thought.

"There are Six who have already awakened," the Whisper said. "The same damnable mercenary crew that insignificantly battered themselves against our Great Flood before. Retrieving their *Praxes*—their inner sparks, their synchronization and manipulation of the Divine Pulse. The stability of my manifestation in this plane will thereafter be heightened by my synthesis with their power."

"So My Lady's presence on this world will no longer be threatened?"

"The chief worm's intellect is astounding," the Whisper said. "This will be our Proving Ground. Our world of strife, through which we can harvest ever-more fruits of suffering."

"Was this part of your plan all along, My Lady?"

"Dare not to doubt me again," she said. "My patience and benevolence towards you grows ever more miniscule."

Lazarus' mind spun. He thought quickly—how could he convince her?

"My Lady. I beg you. Consider my words from before. I will help you on your quest. But how shall we handle our innocents? Surely… surely we must ensure more humans will. Will reproduce. If this be your divine garden of suffering, we must keep seeds—ensuring they remain pure, so that they will root."

The Whisper was silent for some time before she spoke.

"In my infinite wisdom and compassion, I have heard and considered your words from before. And though it disgusts me, I am not yet without mercy for your weak affectations. It is true, perhaps, that I have not thought of a *system*. A bargain, then, between us. Bring me the Six *Praxes* from the group of fools you are destined to meet. If you are successful, then we shall do as you ask. Ushering your lambs through the vast cracks between worlds, where they may be divested cleanly of their human ideals."

"My lady!" Lazarus cried, and bowed again.

"Celebrate not for your human compassion and your lingering moral virtues! The purer the soul, the purer its transformation, and the more useful its power once it has received Our Divine Revelation. This is purely a perfunctory action born of logic and calculation."

"I understand, My Lady," Lazarus said.

And then the Whisper was gone again, the forest dark and teeming with her unclean soldiers. Still shaking, Lazarus beckoned to his mount. Its hideous visage drew nearer, nuzzling him and nipping, until he mounted it again. A terrifying neigh came from it as it kicked the air, champing, hoofs tearing streaks of flame in the night sky.

Dark clouds had begun to move in. The slight trickling of rain overhead burned acidly. Dark things flapped in the sky, their crimson eyes glowing. A vast fog had begun to roll around and behind him, carrying the Whisper's creatures in its bosom, and Lazarus found himself with a new resolution.

He would end the pitiful people on the Hill, and save everyone he could…

Lightning flashed, and thunder cracked on the mountainside. Bailey stared up at the sky. Raindrops poured, stinging as they hit. She ran, legs pushing her onwards, further and further towards the Mansion in the distance. The Earth was groaning beneath her feet; the forest itself was crying out for compassion. Shadows were stirring on the horizon…

She hit the Mansion doors with a thud, heart nearly beating out of her chest, and Eric's voice called to her. He had a can of spray paint in his hands, and was on his hands and knees near the van, under a parking canopy.

"You look like a drowned rat," he said to her.

Her plastic tiara was enwrapped with tangled snarls of her hair, and she knew she looked ridiculous in it… but there was nothing for it now.

"I did it," she said. "I found my Scar."

"You're the last one home," he said. "Hey, come help me up. I'm old and my knees don't work like they did when I was younger. Too much time in my ass groove playing games."

She walked over to him, grabbing his hand. There was a spark between them—like she could feel the chi of him thrumming… But he got to his hands and knees, and then nodded his chin towards the van.

"What do you think? I could have used a stencil or something, but…"

Bailey found herself laughing. Whereas before, it had said 'S.C.A.R.E.D.,' now it said 'S.C.A.R.R.E.D.'

"Seems pretty appropriate," she said. She looked up at the sky. More lightning cracked. The sky itself seemed heavier. "I don't like this weather. The land here seems worried."

He nodded.

"The clouds aren't natural," he said.

"How do you know that?"

"How do you know how the earth feels?"

"Point taken," she said. "Come on, it's too wet out here, we'll melt."

The two walked inside, and Eric gave her a quick side-hug before he darted off to wash his hands and change. Bailey felt something snag from under his shirt against her own, and stared at his retreating form. Were those… nipple piercings?

She heard stirring in the corridors, could feel something in the bones of the house itself that stirred nervously…

She walked through the various rooms. Skye greeted her from the open doors in the library, poring over computer readouts, blue eyes glowing. Sassy was in the dining room, drawing a large heart on the table with a salt shaker, looking very much happier than Bailey had ever seen her before. Even her fur seemed slicker, and the bizarre musk she'd always given off was now tanged with something else… something pheromonal, something almost like a citrus smell…

Grimm and Addy were in a spare bedroom they had turned into a workshop. Grimm floated behind Addy, telling her what to do with what tool and what to turn where. Addy seemed annoyed but resigned; Bailey noticed that her hand was a functioning prosthetic. They were at some kind of lathe, working on something that looked familiar, but Bailey had less than no time to process this before an announcement went up over the intercoms.

"All available team members please report to the Library," Skye's voice said on the intercom.

Grimm and Addy met her eyes, and the three of them looked terrified.

"Thought we'd have more time to prototype this," Grimm said. "Addy, don't let Bailey look at anything yet. Scoot! Go to the library! Shove her if you have to, Addy."

"I don't want to spoil the surprise either, Grimm. Honestly, you can just tell me what to do instead of micro-managing me."

"Yeah, but that's not fun."

"ALL AVAILABLE TEAM MEMBERS PLEASE REPORT TO THE LIBRARY NOW!" the intercom buzzed again, and everyone held hands up to their ears as the PA screeched from decibels that went on and on.

The three of them bobbed and walked, and found themselves being edged out of the way by Sassy thundering in. Eric was standing near an old TV he'd hooked up in the library. He and Skye were staring at the news. The screen rolled, twice, before Eric banged it with his fist and the image stabilized.

"Reports are in that a number of small towns in the Black Hills area have fallen prey to violence and looting, with total electrical outages in some areas and numerous natural gas explosions. Survivors are frantic, and the whole county appears to be in a state of emergency. National security experts from the Government have assured us here at News-5 that it is likely that the Black Hills area has been subjected to a rash of homegrown domestic terrorists with weaponized neurological agents, with the intent of sowing discord, mayhem, and panic in their wake. Citizens are advised to protect themselves at all costs. Citizens are also advised… ah." The news anchor found another document, adjusted his glasses, and then read: "Despite reports of monsters, the National Guard wants to ensure all citizens that any reports of bizarre sightings are a result of weaponized biological hallucinatory agents, and have no basis in reality. Nevertheless, in the chaos and confusion, citizens are advised to stay indoors at all times."

"Bastards!" Grimm snarled. "Don't want to admit it, even when things are this bad."

"What else do you expect?" Skye said. "The government's not ready to let an Apocalypse scenario happen under their nose. They have to save face and rationalize this."

The news anchor continued: "Still, the FBI and the Military are treating this with the utmost concern and respect. As we speak, the National Guard has been mobilized to the area and, in conjunction with state and federal investigators, have created a cordoned-off quarantine zone. If you have travel plans to visit the Black Hills area, you are advised that a quarantine is in effect due to possible potential biohazardous fallout. Travellers are urged to take alternate highways and avoid at all costs all resort and outdoor areas of the Black Hills. If you live within the Black Hills zone of impact, the National Guard will not allow you back to your home. If you are displaced, you are urged to visit one of the Red Cross stations set up within miles of the Quarantine Zone. If you are currently in danger in an area in the Black Hills, you are urged to make your way to local law enforcement stops for further help. Law Enforcement stops can be found—"

Eric turned off the TV.

"The situation is bad," he said simply. "It's only going to get worse. Have we all done our work?"

"Fuck yeah!" Grimm said, eyes glowing green.

"Maybe, but then again maybe I did nothing," Addy said, tilting her head, blinking in and out of existence as she thought.

"I operated my mission parameters within the exacting limitations of our situation with one hundred percent accuracy," Skye said.

"Ook," Sassy grunted, and she smiled.

"Yes," Bailey said. "We did."

"I think I got my spark back," Eric said. "That makes all of us, then. All of us with a Scar."

They remained quiet for some time, until someone said something.

"Hate to be the first one to stir the pot but... If you look at the towns they've hit, it looks like they're on a path headed straight for us," Grimm said.

"How quickly do you think they'll be here?" Bailey asked.

Skye's eyes gleamed, and then after a moment or two of careful consideration, she put her pen down on some paper and jotted some quick calculations.

"T-Minus 30 minutes, give or take," she said.

"Give or take what?" Eric asked.

"Depends on if our enemy has any idea of what we've been up to. If I'm right, the non-linear nature of time in the Other World ensures that observation of outside events is not scoped. What that means is, it's possible that the Primary Target, the Mass Event we witnessed before, has observational skills not linked with our current understanding of time and space. In other words, our enemy may be able to perceive non-locational events. In which case the probability is high that it's learned we have all gained more power, and is en route as we speak to wipe us out before we become too big of a threat."

"You couldn't have given us a little more time to prepare?" Addy asked.

"Seriously, I'm still wearing wet clothes from my night in a graveyard," Bailey said.

"Fun, isn't it?" Grimm asked.

Bailey blinked at him.

"The scope of my power isn't limitless. If I lack information on a subject, then my calculations will err. Consider me like a computer. Variables go in, and numbers are crunched."

"I do not like this new robot shtick," Grimm said.

"There are two outcomes to this situation, given our knowledge," Skye continued. "Outcome A: My calculations are off, and the observational skills of our Enemy are limited in scope. That means we will be safe until we approach them on their territory. The likeliness of this is minimal. Outcome B: My presumption was correct, and the ensuing battle results in mass casualties. This scenario is highly likely."

"Then what was the purpose of our Scars?" Eric asked, voice heated.

"Understanding both of these situations and outcomes as either likely and fatal, or unlikely and therefore low priority, I studied up on some of what Randall had spoken of, regarding rituals that Lazarus may have used. I believe I have discerned a third option—that of eliminating the effects of the *The Invocation of Arsha'kamal*. In order to summon entities of great power to this plane, there must be a protective symbol that keeps them tethered and in a constant state of manifestation."

"What do these symbols look like?" Bailey asked.

Skye shrugged.

"That I have no idea on. There is a suggestion that keeps popping out, something in the notes that states that an entity is bound by our laws once here. It's likely they will be physical objects. They could even be particular Marshalls in her army, though I have doubts the Mass Event would entrust its sanctity here to what it likely considers cannon fodder. Likely it will be an object the Mass Event keeps close at hand."

"Well, that's something like a plan," Grimm said. "I guess it's time. Come to the Workshop, Bailey. Everyone else, too—we've got lots of goodies and presents for all."

It was a tight squeeze, but they all fit in, even if Grimm had to float half in the wall.

Skye was given numerous arrows, with different properties—some with C4 attached, some with oil packets in the end, and a striker-chip that would cause ignition upon velocity. Some had explosive nitrogen capsules, which would freeze most flesh in its tracks.

"Excellent," Skye said. "I've already calculated how to use these the most efficiently."

Grimm stared at her for a moment or two, and then moved on.

"Eric, this is for you, homeboy."

Addy handed a gleaming chrome guitar to him, with barbed wire strings. He stared down at it, eyebrows arched.

"What is this?" he asked.

"It's a Battle-Axe," Grimm said. "I figured we needed some extra badass quotient this time around. Different finger positions on the frets cause different interactions. There are three components to it. The fret-bar at the top is your command stick, and the handle. Notice the titanium, diamond-encrusted bottom edge. That's sharp as shit. You can use this to overhand strike, and sweep underneath. And if you toggle the finger grips here and here…"

Eric did as instructed. The neck extended out, like a spear, and a sharp point at the end shoved out.

"A halberd," Grimm said. "And if you do a C Flat—"

Eric did so. The extension on the neck folded in on itself, and gleaming chains suddenly turned it into, more than anything, an axe mixed with a morning star.

"I've never liked a weapon so much as this," Eric said, and his eyes seemed to sparkle.

"And we mustn't forget our girl," Addy said. She grinned. "Come here. Where'd your boyfriend run off to? We made him something, too, but it's not quite ready yet. Let me see those hands."

A pair of what looked like brass knuckles made of scrap metal were fitted over each knuckle. Sassy squeezed her elongated grip, and smiled an orangutan smile.

"Addy," Grimm said. "I made you something, too. When you weren't looking, with Eric's help. An upgrade. Look in the second or third drawer."

Addy looked confused, but went ahead and dug around obediently. She pulled a pair of twin blades out. There were switches on the bottom of them. When she triggered the hydraulic trigger, the blade exploded outwards into three different serrated edges.

"Pretty," she said, looking obsessed.

"That should interface with your neural prosthetic," Grimm said. "Alright. Now it's time for Bailey's surprise."

The others stared at her as Addy presented her, reverently, with Randall's gauntlet.

"You're the closest thing we have to a wizard nowadays," Grimm said. "There's a neural net inside it, which is useful for stunning and capturing creatures. It also has an SSD on-board—that's Scar Synchronization Device. In essence, it synchronizes with whoever wears it, draws power from their Scar, and emits a weaponized pulsar blast. You can basically use magic missiles. The same sort of blasts and spooky-action-at-a-distance that Randall used."

"Guys," Bailey said. Her voice choked up.

"Here," Eric said.

He presented her with an old Plague Mask. A tribal rose was engraved across the side of it, with another flower engraved. Bailey tucked the Gauntlet under one arm and used both hands to stare at the mask.

"You're one of us now," Skye said. "I hope you understand what that means."

Bailey placed the Gauntlet over her arm, and it tightened, neatly sealing her limb inside it. She could feel a number of different energy forms in it... and if she could just reach out... She aimed at the far wall, and focused.

An explosion of purple energy flew out, screaming and torched a couple of books.

The fire alarm started shrieking. Everyone held their ears, and Eric, being the closest, knocked them to the ground and stomped them out. Sassy picked Addy up; she pressed the button to stop the alarm.

"Maybe not so much an indoors weapon," Grimm said, when the noise had ended.

"Put on the mask!" Addy said.

And there was a feeling of immense rightness as the tightness of the mask fit over Bailey's face. A number of different readouts popped up before her eyes as the Mask activated. She found she could focus and switch the energy type of the Gauntlet.

"Looks like a fit," Grimm said.

There was a frantic thump against the far window. Bailey looked over—there was a waterlogged bat slapping its wings against the window. Bailey wasn't a big one for sky rodents, but it looked weirdly familiar...

Sassy pried open the window and grabbed the bat, wiping it off on her fur as it shrieked. There was an explosion—some kind of sulfuric burst of fog, and then a ragged-looking older woman screamed and banged at the Sasquatch's chest, dangling from a foot.

"Put me down, you oaf!" the woman snapped.

"Barbary?" Bailey asked.

Sassy dropped her. There was a thump as she landed on the floor and awkwardly arranged her tartan skirt. She got to her knees, hands shaking, and then sat herself in an armchair. Her gray hair was in a messy bun, and she seemed to shake, staring off into the distance.

"You okay?" Grimm asked.

"No. Anyone have a cigarette?" she asked, voice cracking.

Eric wordlessly tossed her a pack, and she lit one, smoking nearly half of it in one puff that didn't seem to end. Her eyes were red-rimmed, and she looked like she hadn't slept in weeks.

"So what's up?" Addy asked.

"There's a man outside," she said. "A man on a horse."

There was another silence then.

"Buried the lead, I guess," she continued, lighting another cigarette off the old one, and swallowing the lit end. "Grounds are swamped with stinking cryptids. There's an army that goes off into the distance, farther than the eye can see of the ugly bastards, and we're completely surrounded."

There was a silence between them all for some time.

"I suppose it's time," Skye said. Her eyes flashed blue. "You remember what we talked about?"

"Already done!" Barbary snapped. "That's the last time I do *that*. A damn Mothman nearly caught me on the way back."

"Battle stations, people," Skye said. "This is it!"

The six of them rushed to the front doors. Skye sketched out battle coordinates for them, and then they opened the door.

The smell of putrefaction rolled in to greet them. A teeming mist out in the trees; the hissing and mumbling, the presence of monsters in the hundreds. And there before them stood their enemy... or at least one part of the equation.

Lazarus, on an undead horse, his eyes glowing. His steed: sulfur drifting from its snout, and devil light leaking from its eyes...

"Friend or foe?" Skye called.

"I would prefer if we could be friends, but I expect you to call me foe."

"Why have you come here?" Skye asked.

"Threefold reasons," Lazarus said. "The first—you are an impediment to My Lady's plans."

"Who is your Lady?" Skye asked.

"She is the Guiding Whisper, the one who sits beyond the Crimson Moon," Lazarus said, voice reverential. "The voice who speaks to one at the end of their sanity, who compels them to transform ever onward, into a glorious new state of evolution."

"We all transformed without her assistance," Skye said. "Evolution doesn't require something from the outside. Evolution requires you take what's happened to you, and learn from it."

"Ah, but My Lady has such marvelous plans for the future of us all," Lazarus said. "Your human logic will not sway me so easily, young lady. I have trod the path of darkness so far on this journey... to not see it through at this point, that would be naught but cowardice. For what greater purpose can there be than the rebirth of this wicked world? No... I have done too much evil to give up now. The annals of history would paint me a traitor... a weakling, with no spine..."

He seemed lost, momentarily, thinking heavily on things.

"What's your second reason for coming here?" Skye asked.

"Revenge," he said. "You attempted to fight me; to disrupt my plans. I cannot take that personal affront and not pay it back in kind."

"A fair assessment," Skye said. "Yet is revenge necessary? Surely you understand the virtues of forgiveness? You understand we were acting in the interest of humanity. To end as much destruction as possible, as quickly as possible."

"Ah, human virtues. I suppose we fight on opposite sides, pitted against each other on our disparate paths."

"And how is that?"

"I shan't give away too much, shall I?" Lazarus asked. "Once this world has been cursed with fire, we will usher humanity into its next stage of being. Living in that Other World—one of many. Our forms will no longer be bound to logic or reason. We will be pure creation itself! What needs are survival when imagination, pure creation itself, can fulfill all of our desires?"

"Is there not something to the confines of being human?" Skye asked. "Cruel as life is, it's shaped us, and without it... what would we even be?"

Lazarus thought on this. He seemed hesitant....

"My third reason," he called out, after moments passed. "The future of all remaining people."

"And how's that?" Skye's voice was a demand.

"The Whisper has promised to save the innocent, in exchange for removing your power and returning it to her. We will usher our innocent into the Other World, peacefully, and allow their transformation to occur naturally."

"And yet she's only promised this to you in exchange for something? Sounds like a devil's bargain. You say she comes to make peace, but she doesn't understand humanity. She doesn't truly understand Suffering, does she?"

"The Whisper understands Suffering more than most," Lazarus said, but his voice faltered. "Why do you speak to me like this? Knowing, as I'm sure you do, of my forces awaiting in the eves beyond."

"You're still a human being, and I assume you can be reasoned with," Skye said.

"Aye, true enough. And yet I hope the same of you. Tell me, young lady. Think on this. The six of you consider this, and speak with one another. Disarm yourselves. Deliver unto me your relics—those symbols of your transformations. Once delivered, I promise your safety and security. And I can guarantee that this wanton killing will stop."

"You're asking us to cut ourselves open," Skye said. "I won't allow it. There's a high probability that this Whisper you speak of will do anything she wants when she has the power she needs."

"Two sides that want the same thing, but each with different approaches," Lazarus said. "Have you not in this conversation embraced the struggle of suffering? Have you not yourself espoused the beauty of transformation?"

"If we didn't struggle, we would have learned nothing," Skye said. "Our struggles, our Suffering. It's part of what makes us human. But once we're removed from that, then there's no telling what we'll turn into."

"A fear of the future, then?" Lazarus asked.

"A fear of the zealotry of a madman, and the beast from beyond the stars he worships," Skye said. "I fear only that what we know of as humanity will be destroyed."

"And yet, you still speak," Lazarus said. "Seems as if you are as hesitant to draw first blood as I."

"No," Skye said. "I was just distracting you."

There was a flash—glowing green *kanji* scribbled themselves in a circle around Lazarus and his horse, and with a noise like a laser phantom daggers exploded inwards and through his gut. His horse whinnied, staggering, and Lazarus was bent over, holding his gut. One lame arm went up to his throat, where a dagger was lodged in his Adam's Apple, and he pulled this out, staring at it, watching as it dissolved in his hands and blood dripped onto his fingers.

Another arm reached out to his side holster. With great effort he aimed his Colt up to the sky, and its crimson glow sparkled as he shot into the sky.

"Now!" he cried, spitting blood, one hand over his rapidly healing trachea, and the denizens of the forest rushed out en masse.

Grimm glowed, sparking into his Reaper form.

"Bailey, you attempt to seal the portals," Skye said. "I'm going after Him."

Bailey slipped her mask over her head and nodded.

"It's time to be FUCKING BRILLIANT!" she howled, eyes gleaming purple.

Skye withdrew an arrow, rushing out with Sassy as her cover. A crowd of swarming worms with snake heads tried to attack, but Sassy grabbed some, ripping them in half, using her feet to kick away others. Skye had already taken wind speed, direction, and attempted a calculation for velocity as she spoke. She stared across the field at Lazarus.

He was slowly de-knifing himself. Bound as he was by the *mudra* Addy had put in place, he could not move. He did not seem close to death, however—something which worried Skye. She took aim with a nitrous arrow, which cleaved him perfectly in the heart. An explosion of near-zero Kelvin air surrounded him, and he breathed in, clutching his chest slowly, trying desperately to yank the arrow out. She sent a C4 arrow next, engaging it as it drew even with him. The explosion knocked him clear of the saddle—something she had not considered was the physical limitations of the *mudra*, which occurred to her as dirt went flying. The horse lay on its side, bones and flesh scattered, and Lazarus had rolled clean of the trap.

Grimm spun and flashed off in the forest—green vitae splattering from ephemeral *Yurei* in the trees. Addy's ginuntings sparked as she slipped in and out of shadows, carving beasts in threes and fours. Grimm tried to go for a stampeding, flesh and blood thing coming straight for Eric, but missed—his scythe-blade slashed through, seemingly doing nothing, and he sparked different colors as another *Yurei* came and tackled him.

Eric played a chord on his Axe, and the neck extended out. He used the polearm, both hacking and slicing, twirling around in a circle and clearing the heads off an angry swarm of horned rabbits. A knight fashioned from shadows, with a glowing rapier, darted toward him, coming in quickly, and Eric played another chord. The polearm retracted, into an axe, and he swung it around hard. The helmet of the knight flew into the distance. Its body, headless, kept moving, however, and Eric parried another blow with the body of his Battle-Ax. There was a *twang* as the barbed wire strings caught and diverted the sharp tip of its otherworldly fencing gear. Eric twisted the guitar around again, snapping the rapier from the torso's arms, and grabbed it by the hilt, turning, leaning into it and shoving the tip into the heart of the knight, stabbing it and two other creatures in a shish-kebab that embedded itself in a tree.

Eric picked his axe back up, slicing and dicing as body parts flew…

Bailey had found a portal nearby—her eyes flashed purple as she held her breath and dove in. The passage was quicker than she remembered—she found herself hitting the ground in the Other World with a shockwave that sent creatures flying. She switched her Gauntlet to neural net, erecting a barrier that seemed to sizzle when monsters hit, and then turned her attention to the portal at hand. She closed her eyes, feeling the energy accruing in her, and then breathed out and squeezed, aiming with the Gauntlet. A ripple, and then the seams of the universe began to close themselves again…

Bailey turned, carving open another Portal, and dove. It sealed behind her as she popped back into the Black Hills. A riot of colors met here—blue, green, purple, crimson, all strobing under the canopy of trees. The portal she'd escaped from closed behind her, and off she ran again, for another one.

Sassy punctured a turtle-armored deer in the throat with her brass knuckles, then ripped its head off, her eyes glowing red and howling. A serpentine wyvern descended, snatching her by the shoulders and flapping away. Sassy struggled with it for some time before grabbed ahold of its talon, snapping its ankle. They fell together, a heavy weight smashing a group of chittering skulls into bone powder.

Skye let loose another few volleys of arrows—each of them piercing Lazarus to seemingly no effect. He grabbed at the bare ground and heaved himself up. The explosion had taken half of the skin off his face and blistered it raw. Meat and gore and exposed tissue faced the world. He aimed high, in the sky, and squeezed off more shots.

Something tackled Eric, snarling and snapping against his throat. They rolled, Eric kicking it off and smashing it with the axe's barbed-wire side. It howled—a savage looking wolf, with purple fur—and he lopped its head off, too. He got to his feet, and found himself surrounded with a pack of similar beasts. Eric strummed another cord, releasing the chain, and began whirling it around himself. They snapped, growling, stamping the ground, seeming to patiently wait for his energy to go…

"There's too many of them!" he cried.

Bailey was jolts of purple streaks as portal after portal closed in the distance, and here Eric was all by himself, surrounded… More portals gleamed overhead. Gigantic winged things pulled themselves out, and flew toward him.

Eric threw his weapon down. He closed his eyes, breathing heavily. Took off his mask and shucked the front plate of his armor. Static filled the air around him. The piercings on his chest began to spurt blood. He spread his arms, and lightning arced down from the sky to greet him. The clearing lit up like noon-day sun, flying creatures dropping on all sides, and Eric's eyes glowed from red to blue.

The wolves lunged, but lightning flew from his body as he flapped his new wings, taking to the sky, and they were flash-fried...

"Bailey," he called down, and dove, scooping her up under her armpits with his hands.

"Aim for the Portals!" he cried.

"Right!" she said.

He tossed her towards one, and she dove inside. Two gigantic crows tried to smash him on either side, but he spun, sparking, and feathers flew. He soared under another portal, and Bailey dove from it as it sealed, landing on him. Again they repeated this, over and over.

"Look!" Bailey cried, pointing to the distance before she dove again. "There's—are those tanks?"

Eric spun again, flashing and striking crowds on the ground, and got into an aerial dog fight with a gigantic, flapping moth, its lamplike, multifaceted eyes pulsating and gleaming. Each of its barbed hairs was laced with a terrible poison, as foul as the worst nuclear radiation. Eric flew high into the sky—there were people on the horizon, with guns, coming up the mountain trail—and felt a sharp sting enter his leg. He turned as he fell, frying the giant bug as he spiraled down and smashed into the earth.

Down below, Sassy smashed through crowds, howling into the aether. *Where was He?* She wondered. She wound up a punch that exploded a two-legged spindly bull into ground beef, and found strong hands on her shoulders. She spun around.

She and He faced each other. They smiled, each reaching forward to punch a creature approaching them from the other side.

Around them, a whirl of violence—Bailey's streaks of purple and neural nets flashing—Skye's arrows discharging, Eric's thunder snapping. Addy slipping in and out of shadows, Grimm blazing green.

But for just that span of time, an eternity seemed to pass as their fingers touched. Their love flowed between them, a message as old as time itself. He opened his wide arms, to embrace her—and she fell into his arms, heavily, and they spun together, until a loud gunshot boomed in Their ears...

A white horse ambled past, its rider holstering its gun. Sassy pulled back, a strange look on her face. There was a dot of crimson blooming on her pristine fur. He reached down to His own chest fur, staring at his fingertips, now covered in fluid, then looked back at her. The dot was bigger—a steady trickle, a spurt, which he tried to hold his hand over. He grabbed her with one arm around her back.

Her face was illuminated in a lightning strike—pale and drawn, mouth open in surprise—and then darkness fell and she collapsed. He howled, falling to his knees as he slid her body to the ground. His hands probed her face, pushing and prodding—Her eyes fluttered open and met his.

She moved a hand up to his, and held it, until her grip grew cold and fragile. He cried primal tears, great ripping sobs from his chest, and felt Her warmth leave Her, and when Her grip finally released, He could feel something ancient, something violent, unlock itself in His heart.

He did not seem to notice the Men arrive in the clearing. He looked around—eyes intent on the man on the white horse, and every savage instinct he'd ever had rose up within Him. He pounded over the ground, craters under his galloping leap, and did a flying clothesline at the man on the horse. As they both dropped, rolling, an arrow zipped into the horse's flank, exploding in an incinerating fire, and it screamed a dying scream as they tussled.

"I guess I shot the wrong one," Lazarus said as they rolled, trying to knock him with the hilt of the gun. "How does it feel to know you lived when She could have?"

The He-squatch screamed, roaring like King Kong, canines and spit flecking, winding up his fist and punching Lazarus in the face. The man's nose broke, but he laughed, and leaned forward, knocking into His skull with a hard crack. He's eyes rolled, and soon they began to punch one another, breaking and splintering bones, until they were both exhausted piles of near-jelly.

A purple flash somewhere in the distance behind them—Bailey was standing at the edge of the clearing they were in, and a neural net she'd sent at them missed them as they rolled.

Lazarus struggled to turn the Colt around, trying to aim up-close, but a backhand from Him knocked the Colt away, spinning over the forest floor. Lazarus stretched for it, but again He grabbed the human underneath him, shaking his shoulders and pounding his head into the dirt. A normal man's skull would have turned into applesauce. Lazarus' feet coiled up and tried to push—The He-squatch only slid a little back, but grew winded, struggling forward. Lazarus' eyes glowed, and an explosion of crimson light knocked Him away, back cracking into a nearby tree.

"Finally!" Lazarus wheezed. The Colt was only two feet away, and he struggled, reaching for it and crawling on his elbows. His fingertips were even with the handle, but an orange cord of glowing energy wrapped around it, snagging and tossing it farther into the trees. Lazarus' eyes traced the cord back to... to...

She stood there, plastic tiara on her head, tribal rose on her Plague Mask.

"Got an Upgrade, bitch," she said, snapping the whip again. It wrapped around Lazarus' ankle. He looked down at it, and then back up at her. A Portal had ripped in the air behind her, and she smiled, falling backwards into it. He felt himself dragged, ever-onward, through a split in his sanity through the Portal—down and down and down they dived, air rushing past, growing hotter and hotter, until they at last emerged.

Bailey rolled to her feet, boot stamped against the whip. The smell of sulfur was all around them—the wailing intense.

"No," Lazarus said. "No. Not here."

His grandmother had always told him, when he was a boy, that there was a place beyond Purgatory where all sinners went when they died. It was a place of hellfire and brimstone, a place of darkness, where foul beasts dwelt. Each man was punished according to his sins; each man was tormented, accordingly, per what he was owed.

Lazarus sat up and looked around.

"No. No. Not here," he stammered.

Magma boiled in the distance. Men and women in chains were attached to the walls. Some of them were growing into the wall-fleshy statues, human forms that once were separate from this place. Strange fungal pods everywhere pulsed noxious fumes. A towering throne of skulls at the opposite end of the room had two braziers sitting before it. A beast—Lazarus thought of whispers his grandmother had spoken to him, of the Goat-Devil, the Baphomet, that tortured men eternally...

"What did you think would happen?" Bailey asked.

"A punishment like this?" he begged. He crawled forward to Bailey, hands on the hem of her outfit. His voice was pleading. "I did... I did only what was asked... Please..."

Bailey kneed him in the eyepatch, and he fell back, clutching it.

"This is your reward. You yourself caused this. You yourself have become a source of Suffering. And that can never be forgiven."

"Please," Lazarus begged. "Show mercy upon me... All I did was what was asked!"

The furred demon at the end of the chamber spread its vast black wings and snuffed, goat-head roaming. It strode over, majestic erection swelling, and Lazarus stared at the beast in horror.

"Please—" he said, one more time. "Please, you fucking bitch! You can't leave me here with him!"

"I think you two will get along just peachy," she replied, giving him a thumbs up.

Bailey opened a portal behind her, waving as she walked backwards into it, and the air sealed itself up again.

"Please," Lazarus muttered out loud, but he was saved the pleasure of speaking as the Baphomet's hands gripped his head and his mouth was forced open.

His eye blazed, and he turned, looking up from the page, staring at YOU, the bobbing goat cock pulsing and ready.

"I bet you've been wanting to see me fucked for a while," he said. "I'll save you the punishment of seeing what I'm about to deal with, and maybe you'll feel a little more forgiveness towards me when you see what really happened."

One last mental image blooms up, unbidden, before Lazarus' mind.

The thought of the little girl he had laid down, the incantations he had muttered over her, the way he had whispered to her: "Go with the crows. Play dead until you are safe and away from here."

Tears in his eyes, and guilt and punishment sticking in his throat, his eternal body trapped now in this place, tortured for all eternity…

And somewhere, somewhere outside of the cordoned-off Quarantine zone, the lucky little girl was placed onto the ground by the crows. She got to her feet and brushed herself off. The sunlight was streaming down from the sky, and the dark clouds that surrounded her seemed to clear. And she laughed into the dawn until she wept.

CHAPTER 38:

AFTERMATH

Bailey zipped back through a Portal, feeling the wind tug at her. Crows were picking through the refuse. Bodies—human and otherwise—were everywhere. It was like she'd stumbled into the aftermath of a slaughterhouse. She glanced at every pile with trepidation. Bullet casings were all over the ground. In the distance, the sun was rising, and Bailey looked past it into the trees, squinting her eyes to try to make out more.

The sound of men laughing in the distance. Someone nearby was coughing. Bailey stepped through pools of gore and misshapen parts and crouched down near a bush. The grass around the area had been fried—Eric lay there, shirt gone, fresh scars on his chest. He hissed. There was another man kneeling over him, packing and dressing his wounds.

"Bailey," Eric gasped. "Glad you made it back. Wasn't sure how long it would take you."

"What happened?" she asked.

"Some of the Warriors from the Rez came by and saved your asses," his nursemaid said.

"I don't think we've met," Bailey said.

They shook hands.

"Caesar," the new guy said. He bent down and slapped Eric in the chest, scooping his hand behind his shoulders and lifting him to a sitting position.

"There were National Guard soldiers here, too," Eric breathed.

"Where is everybody?"

"Where's Lazarus?" Eric asked. "We saw you drag him into a Portal, and then everything went crazy. Soldiers stormed the woods. Bullets flew everywhere. We mostly just had our hands over our heads and prayed we wouldn't get hit."

"Lazarus is taken care of," Bailey said. "He's not coming back from where I left him."

Eric nodded.

"Good girl," he said. "I thought I saw Skye talking with some troopers over towards the Mansion. Grimm's a spotter, doing some mop-up detail. Addy… she said she had something to do, and that she'd be back."

There was a bizarre look in his eye that she'd never seen before.

"What about Sassy?"

Eric set his jaw, stared at the distant trees.

"That's what Addy's taking care of."

"Eric," she said, but then trailed off.

Bailey tracked Addy down to a clearing some way off in the distance. A group of Lakota men in jeans and blazers had hunting rifles on their shoulders as she passed. She heard them talking about cleanup duty…

Addy was crying, standing with a shovel over a freshly disturbed pile of dirt. A frilly pink bow atop two crossed twigs was planted at the head of the hole.

Sassy lay in the hole. Someone had crossed her long arms, and laid a leaf atop them.

"Hey," Bailey said, reaching out and grabbing Addy's shoulder.

Addy looked up, wiping her face with her sleeve.

"Hey," she said back.

The two stood in silence there for a minute or two, leaning on one another. The breeze blew behind them. It wasn't fair, Bailey thought, that this happened like this. Not with the sun cheerily warming their backs. Not with the day being saved. She lay there, beautiful in Her own way even in death, face relaxed and peaceful.

They took turns pitching the dirt in, one scoop at a time. Bailey used her hands. With every clump of dirt that hid more and more of her shaggy body, Bailey felt an unwelcome feeling of horror in her chest. Surely, a little part of her mind screamed, surely this isn't happening. She'll wake up. She'll open her orangutan eyes and say 'Ook' and dig her way out.

But soon the hole was covered, and they tamped it down, and that was that.

They walked, hand in bionic hand, back to the Mansion, to the sounds of soldiers laughing…

Skye was directing people back and forth from a chair on the front porch. Her hair was a mess. She and another few people—an older Lakota man, and a military officer of one sort or another, judging by his suit, were drinking coffee from a mobile canteen. Eric and Caesar were here, too.

"I take it Lazarus has been dealt with?" Skye asked.

Boy, all steel nerves, wasn't she? Bailey wondered, and a bit of spite rose in her craw.

"Yeah."

"And Sassy… where is she, ah…?"

"We marked the spot with a gravemarker and her bow," Addy said.

Skye nodded, bending her head down to the table before her, hand swiping at her nose as she sniffed. She rubbed the back of one eye with the same hand, and then straightened up. Her cheeks were wet.

"I'm sure you've seen the bodies," Skye said. "This is Elder Longmire, and Corporal Lancashire. They're head of the Black Hills Lakota Warrior division, and local National Reserve officer, respectively. They assisted in the rest of the cleanup operations. They've assured me that most of the monster problem we're facing should be gone within the week."

"Thank you for the help," Bailey said.

Elder Longmire nodded.

"My people have been fighting these things for many years. It's part of our sacred duty."

Lancashire said nothing—a soldier had come by and whispered in his ear. He sat up at attention, and then stared at the man.

"Is that right?" he asked. He whipped around to Skye and Longmire. "Advanced scouts say a bogey is moving in. Something big and hot on the radar."

Something in Bailey's gut bobbed and snagged, and the Earth seemed to scream beneath her feet...

"I wondered when this would occur," Skye said. "I know this has been a tough fight, but hopefully this next bit will be the end of it. You see, there was one more part of my plan that I kept hidden, even from you. I contacted the Reserves and treated with Elder Longmire using Barbary as a proxy. They were our backup contingencies in case we failed. And now that everyone's here. GRIMM!"

Skye screamed this last word, and he popped up from the ground.

"Reporting for duty," he said.

"Battle positions," Skye said.

"You're not serious," Addy said, and she looked lost.

"Mass event approaching," Skye said, eyes blazing blue.

The sky turned dark—the cheery dawn bleeding into cosmic purple. A vast tear in the sky pulsed, edges bleeding, and then, a blast of eldritch light as the radiant form of a six-armed masked woman stood behind them. She towered over them all.

"Now!" Corporal Lancashire called.

Hidden men descended from their sniper positions, rifles aimed.

"Fire at will!" Corporal Lancashire hollered.

The sound of gunshot was deafening. With plinks and dings, like metal, the six-armed figure stood gracefully, white dress billowing around her gargantuan legs. She stepped, and stepped again, then twirled. Light dazzled as she spun, and soon there were at least fifteen of her. They blinked out, one by one, and reappeared, bent to ear level with the men around her.

Silence in the clearing, except for the sound of fast whispers, voices low. One man's forehead started sweating, and his pistol clanged as his shaking hand turned around and pressed the sizzling gun to his temple.

"Please," he gasped, and pulled the trigger.

His was the start. One by one blood and brains exploded outwards from the men, until they all were neutralized. Arrows fired from a distance—one by one, as they pierced her illusions, they disappeared, until one final arrow from Skye caught her in the Mask with a full-bore explosion. There was a chipping noise, and the *thing* fell to one knee, hand over her right eye. Parts of her mask were laying on the ground...

"Phase Two!" Lancashire screamed.

Bazooka missiles tore screaming from the ground. The figure held up one hand, whispering something else, and then suddenly the air felt like sludge.

The missiles exploded in a concentric ring, explosive force radiating outwards. But in its wake there was a sudden heaviness to the air, and the smoke cleared. The Whisperer stood, unscathed, missile parts and shrapnel falling in mid-air in slow motion. Bailey struggled through the sludge, moving forward, and felt her energy pulsating all around her. A beam of purple light flashed from her forehead, and she found herself rolling forward, Gauntlet aimed directly at the creature.

"Stop where you are," Bailey snarled.

The figure laughed, raucously.

"So it was you that did it," the whisperer said. "In a way, I suppose I have to thank you. I would have done it myself, given enough time."

"Did what?"

"Disposed of that horrible man," the whisperer said. "He was a means to an end. Messy, and tricky, as all mortals appear to be." She looked up, one hand held over the chipped part of her Mask, and then picked the piece up with another, lower hand, fitting it in under her palm. There was a snap, and a dazzling light, and Bailey shielded her eyes...

Grimm blazed green, his clothing burning into a black, steaming robe, as he released himself. He held his scythe out and moved forward, screeching a battle cry, slashing… but one hand grabbed him, another snapped away his scythe, and yet another one wedged its way down his throat.

His green flame eyes seemed to be pleading with Bailey, as the whisperer's humongous arm reached down his etheric throat. When she got to the end, Grimm gagged, and Bailey watched with horror as the whisperer withdrew what looked like an emerald hour glass and clutched it tight in her hands.

"Perfect," the whisperer said, releasing Grimm. He phased back to himself, and grabbed at his throat, floating backwards, a terrified look on his face.

"What are you?" he screamed.

The whisperer's mouth curled into a wicked smile beneath her Mask. She dangled the hourglass by a chain from two fingers.

"The power to destroy the ethereal," she crowed. "I thank you for your sacrifice."

An explosion of glowing runes decked the area around her, and Phantom Daggers flew in a cloud of networked cords, all seeming to bind her hands to her body. The whisperer leaned against the visible sutras, and hissed as they burned her.

"Now!" Addy screamed from the darkness. "Bailey, go!"

Bailey focused, aiming with her Gauntlet, and then let loose. A purple plasm reached out, spinning and screaming, and the whisperer folded in on herself more. One of her legs reached up, arcing overhead like a ballerina, and fielded the energy, diverting and shifting it down into the darkness. At first Bailey thought she'd just knocked it away, but the sutras began flickering, and the whisperer reached a porcelain hand out to grasp at empty air. She held something nobody could see in her grip, and another of her hands extended down, disappearing.

"Addy!" Grimm shrieked.

A burst of lightning from one side. Eric limped over, jumping off the porch and into a wobbly high-rise. He phased, flickering, back into the Thunderbird, and as the Whisper extracted its prize with one arm it burst its bindings with the others. The Phantom Daggers and their cords were used as a lasso by the Whisperer's free hands—these struck and knocked the lightning blasts back, and soon the whisperer laughed, tossing a traumatized, now-visible Addy into a roll back to the porch. A scroll of vellum, black and glowing, was clutched in another hand.

"Another gift," the whisperer said, voice arch. "How wonderful. That of nothingness. The power of the void."

Lightning struck again, but each time she blinked and disappeared, reappearing somewhere new. Bailey loosed a few shots, which spun in a bola, but missed. Finally, another arrow came tearing from nowhere. The whisperer caught it in one of her remaining hands, and then it exploded.

The mask went spinning off into the darkness. She howled, and then disappeared.

"Eric!" Skye called. "Summon a rainstorm! Bailey, grab her Mask! Odds are that's her anchor!"

Eric cawed, and then flapped up to the clouds above. Bailey sprinted into the woods, and found the Mask sitting on the ground by itself. She picked it up, and for a split second, she felt a bizarre urge to slide it over her own face...

But a cold, clammy grip on her wrist froze her. Bailey tried hard to turn her head, to see what the Whisper looked like, under the Mask, but the two of them seemed frozen for some moment longer… it was as if a great force was repelling the two from each other. Bailey could even feel the Whisper's body fighting, too—and where they touched a radiant ache began to spread, like her muscles were made of jelly…

A spare hand slowly, achingly, agonizingly reached to Bailey's grip and grabbed the Mask from her, and then Bailey's wrist was free, and light danced its weird way from behind her. Bailey aimed the gauntlet at her—it was starting to rain, thick drops from the clouds overhead, and where she was hidden a great torrent of water showed where the whisperer was hiding herself.

Bailey moved forward, out from the hidden alcove.

"I told you to grab the Mask!" Skye screamed.

She nocked another arrow and let loose, and Bailey felt her grip on the Gauntlet slip. The neural net sparked outwards, and Skye's arrow flew wide.

"Sorry!" Bailey called, through the rain. "It was an accident!"

Skye's blue eyes blazed at her, but the neural net had done its work. The Whisperer was stuck, blinking in and out.

"Now! Eric!" Skye called.

A massive thunderbolt cleaved the clouds in two, and struck the earth so hard Bailey went flying backwards and her ears rang. She pulled herself to her feet, staggering over to where Eric and Skye had the whisperer pinned.

Skye had an arrow nocked and at the ready, nearly head-on, and Eric was providing a steady series of crackling bolts that kept the whisperer pinned.

"Grab her!" Skye screamed. "Rip the Mask off! Take her back where she belongs."

Bailey reached down, but again that weird resonance from the whisperer. Her hand seared as she drew it closer, and the whisperer screamed, and Bailey pushed, trying hard to grab onto a bit of skin or cloth, or something…

A stray hand came up and grabbed her by the hair. Bailey screamed, and soon there was a terrible pull and a yank, and her plastic tiara was gone, now clutched in the whisperer's hands.

Another curled-lip Mona Lisa smile, and the Whisperer disappeared, the ground beneath her ripping open. A hand appeared from a rip behind Skye, clutching at her and yanking the scarf from her neck. Skye dropped her bow and grabbed, choking as the hand lifted her, and then Skye twisted like an acrobat and spun, falling to her knees as the scarf unraveled, and she vomited as she gasped for air.

"And now for you," the Whisperer said. Her eyes glowed blue, and lightning struck again, and she travelled with it, up the arc, and soon there was a noise like a fly in a zapper…

Eric fell to the ground again, one last spark of power flapping and softening his landing before he fell and rolled. The whisperer's last two hands tore into his chest, where his piercings were, and retrieved a gleaming jewel.

"I thank you," the whisperer breathed.

All of her hands were filled now, save two.

"Bailey," the whisperer said. "Oh, Bailey. Thank you for this."

"Mine doesn't work until you wear it," Bailey gasped out.

"What are you doing?" Skye asked.

Bailey looked at her and panted.

"Trust me," she said.

Bailey got to her feet and dragged herself closer to the Whisperer, whom was placing the tiara upon her own head.

"Violet," Bailey whispered.

There was a cold breeze on the back of her head.

"Hey hey," she heard.

"I think it's time you drove," Bailey said.

"Been waiting on this for a while," Violet said, laughing, and then Bailey felt something click.

Purple energy flared up from her footsteps. No longer was there the weird echo between Bailey and the Whisperer... now Violet stepped forward, unafraid, Violet with her messed up hair and devil-may-care-attitude and no fucks to give.

"What are you doing?" the Whisperer gasped.

"Putting you back where you belong," Violet said, with Bailey's voice. Two free hands came up to throttle her, but Violet leaned in, shouldering the tall figure in the stomach, and they fell through a rip in the fabric of everything that opened...

Down they fell, struggling and punching. Violet snagged the hourglass from her grip after they fell and hit a craggy outcropping in some world filled with endless sand. The hourglass shattered against the ground where Violet threw it. They rolled off the ledge and into another split. Here they were swimming in a deep, freezing ocean. The vellum moistened, losing its structural integrity and disintegrating—and the scarf was soaked, so when they bobbed up to a surface where there was air, it was somewhere frozen. Violet took two sucker punches to the jaw, but snapped the scarf in half, and watched it sink into the ocean as she was pummeled. Another split in the sea, and with a whoosh of water spilling through, they found themselves in outer space. Violet could feel Bailey's corpuscles swelling up, expanding, so the two of them struggled, spinning, into a world where a volcano was just beginning to erupt. Violet knocked the jewel from her hands, and spit and bit, and the Whisper froze as an explosion of magma started to come down, and they rolled into somewhere else—

A world made of flesh and ruin, sulfur springs fuming, ground pulsating. They fought and tore and snapped and smacked and punched and tore through to another plane. A world of gleaming metal, all chrome edges and passive orbs that watched, humming questions to themselves. Another rip: a hot, tepid jungle, with a pyramid lorded over by a great giant squid-faced behemoth who bellowed into the sky.

"You have to go back, Bailey," Violet said.

Bailey's body was shaking.

"What will you do?" Bailey asked. "Can you fight without my body?"

"Even if I'm only ever a whisper, I'll survive," Violet said.

Bailey felt a surge of power, and then found herself in the driver's seat again, Violet's energy a purple cloud hissing from her skin. The Whisper tangled with Violet's cloud—both struggling for Bailey's tiara. The Whisper was screaming, shrieking, as Violet tore a split in the universe open again. Bailey watched, shielding her eyes. This portal was so bright her eyes were burning...

One last uppercut, and another stomp... and the Whisper's Mask dislodged and fell. Soaring heat so bright from the Portal that Bailey felt like all of her skin would burn... still, she ran forward, scooping the Mask up... feeling another weird urge to put it on...

"No!" the Whisper shrieked. "No!"

Bailey threw it in the hole, feeling her eyes dry up, and then there was an explosion that happened so fast she could barely seal the Portal up in time.

The Whisper fell to its knees, hands over its face. Violet's energy buzzed and snapped around it like a swarm of angry bees.

"One day you will remember this," the Whisper said, and it sounded so... morose, so defeated, so sad. "And you will regret every action you've taken on this day."

Two of her hands made a *mudra*, and another Split happened, and the Whisper faded into glittering pieces of light, sparkles that floated through the final crack in the worlds. Violet began to coalesce as the Portal shimmered behind her… but there was a look of shock on her face.

"Bailey!" she shrieked.

Bailey reached for her, but the Whisper's light had gripped her, and with a snap the two of them, white and purple energy clouds both, were sucked back into the next dimension. The hole in the fabric of the world sealed itself again.

And Bailey stood, catching her breath, feeling intensely lonely on an alien world. The ground shook underfoot—the beautiful behemoth in the distance was calling to the heavens, great stone pillars lowering themselves from the atmosphere, the water itself dancing in time to the moving of its mandibles that hung, gigantic worms dangling from its face.

She, too, split the air—trying to find where Violet was, to follow her again… but the land around her did not speak, and it was as if she was blindly grabbing onto a wall. But there was something else. A call to home. She felt her way back again, peeling through each layer she had come from and pulling herself bodily back into a familiar clearing.

The sky was normal now, and she lay on her back and breathed in deep, savoring Earth's air, savoring the oxygen in her normal world again…

CHAPTER 39:

SEPARATE WAYS

Two days' worth of bed rest, minimum, Barbary had exclaimed, when the bodies were cleared up and everyone had finished giving witness statements. Bailey dove into her four poster, feeling ever-so-comforted in the cage of bars and hanging curtains around her, and sobbed into her pillow when she woke up from another terrifying nightmare of alien worlds and people being sucked into portals.

She heard voices come and go, but simply watched her dead friends' Youtube channels, staring at the comments on the pages, thinking about where they had gone. Down into the incinerator, she knew… ashes to ashes, dust to dust.

Barbary brought her food on occasion, and she ate greedily, reserving her strength. She was exhausted. Violet had torn her body up something fierce—she and that weird Whisper creature. Bailey tried not to think about it, but soon forty-eight hours had passed and she felt the tiniest spark of annoyance with herself.

"You're wasting your time in here by yourself," she said, and slipped on her slippers, padding into the hallway. There were muttered voices coming from the next room, and Bailey stopped outside the library to listen in.

"I don't know how this is going to work without hands," Grimm said. "Honestly. I don't mind taking the helm here. But aren't you getting a real weird Scooby vibe from all this? You know, single ghost lives in a Haunted Mansion on a hill with a great property value…"

"Only difference is you're actually a monster," Skye said.

"Ha. Ha." He did not sound amused.

Bailey stepped into the doorway. Skye and Grimm stared at her like they were seeing a ghost. There was a suspicious amount of cleanliness in the room…

"I heard you guys talking in the hall," Bailey said. "What's going on?"

Eric bustled in past her, lugging some heavy equipment and sitting it on a desk. He nodded at Bailey.

"Surprised to see you up," he said.

"It looks like everyone's packing."

"Well, I guess we can skip the pleasantries, then," Skye said. "We're leaving."

"What, everyone?" Bailey's voice had more of a whine in it than she liked. "This—this isn't *fair*. We just overcame our first major foe. I just got my official equipment. You can't tell me we're breaking up the team now."

"We're not," Skye said. "Think of it like long term reassignments. We'll still talk with each other and share information. Should our locations cross, it would be an ideal time to collaborate. But the data center here, and the remote location, makes it highly inconvenient to set up operations from here going forward."

"I'm staying," Grimm said. "So there's that. And I was just telling Skye I might need an extra set of hands. You could stay with me, if you want."

Grimm grinned in a way Bailey knew was supposed to be comforting, but made him look like the primary haunt in a horror movie. She grimaced.

"So where is everyone going?" Bailey asked.

"Hallowtide University," Skye said. "It's about time I buried the hatchet with Vanessa. They have one of the more advanced international Anomaly measurement systems I've seen, as well as an exhaustive database that I don't have access to from here. I need to find more information on... Well, right now it's just a hunch... Let's just say I'm trying to make sure what happened here doesn't happen again."

"We're not the only team that does what we do," Eric said. "I've been hiding myself away here, getting comfy and complacent. I need to learn what I can. To try and protect more people. I'm heading Arizona-bound. Got a friend in Phoenix that'll let me stay for a few weeks. There are some *naguals,* shape-shifting sorcerors, in the Southwest that I heard word on, and some Navajo healers. The air elementals told me to look there, when I asked after grandfather. Two birds with one stone, guess you could say."

"And where's Addy?"

"She left yesterday," Skye said.

Bailey felt like someone had punched her.

"It was hard on her, what with Randall and then Sassy," Skye said. "She couldn't stand to say goodbye, so she left a note. She's on a return flight to Japan as we speak. She intends on doing some more monastic work at a few of the more specialized Exorcism temples. Hoping to learn more about her family history, as well."

"Still not sure how she's gonna get that prosthetic through customs," Grimm said.

"Maybe it's better we don't have our Scars, for that matter," Skye said. "Can you imagine travelling with those? I was just thinking what would happen if I lost my scarf..."

"Good riddance," Eric said. "My chest feels. Well, like someone did breast reduction surgery on me, I guess, on the one side. Still not back at one-hundred, but something must have been leftover—still got my scars, and then some. I am gonna miss flying, though. Maybe that's why Grandfather never came back. Didn't want to give up the sky..."

"I do miss being able to calculate wind velocity for the perfect overhand trashcan shot," Skye said.

"I'm gonna miss being the fucking Grimm Reaper," Grimm said, voice soft.

Bailey nodded. "I'll miss Violet."

Skye's eyes narrowed slightly.

"What did you just say?"

"Violet," Bailey said. "She was. Ah. My imaginary friend. The Tulpa. We talked about her—how she helped and everything."

Skye blinked, and it seemed like an eternity before she spoke.

"Are you familiar with the phrase 'Violet Anguish?' " Skye asked.

Bailey blinked, thinking. Now that she thought about it, wasn't... wasn't that something her therapist had said to her? Still, it was too coincidental—just the same words in the same general vicinity, rather than a phrase. Bailey shook her head.

Skye seemed to think on this, before her face grew calm again.

"So what am I supposed to do?" Bailey asked.

Skye shrugged.

"Whatever your heart tells you to. There's always a place here for you."

"I really could use the extra help," Grimm said.

Bailey closed her eyes. She really didn't want to be here still, not when everyone else was leaving. If only she could think of something important she could do… something radical.

And then it came to her, a thunderbolt of brilliance.

It was a week later. Skye and Eric had left. Just an old witch, a ghost screaming at the architecture and trying desperately to program an Alexa, and Bailey in a mansion. She made up her mind after doing a little bit of research on where she'd been before.

"I'm taking a vacation," Bailey said, to Grimm, who was knuckle deep in a work project, trying to egg on a pair of forceps powered by steam.

He turned, bobbing, his face curious.

"When will you be back?" he asked.

"I have no idea," she said.

Grimm disengaged from the workbench, floating there for a moment and looking lost. He looked around the room, as if trying to find someone responsible enough to say something, and then realized it was *just him.* He seemed to hate himself even as the words came out of his mouth: "Just be careful. You should really try and leave some notes or something about where you're going, your plans, just in case I don't hear back from you. I don't know how I'd do it, but just in case you wind up needing rescued."

"I'll think about it," Bailey said, and then left.

Now she was outside on the ledge before the mountain path, the slope of the Black Hills forest below her spreading as far as the eye could see. She was staring, again, at a moon that seemed too full, a moon that seemed too foreign. She had the Gauntlet on one hand, sealed over her arm. She had a knapsack on her back filled with food and other survival supplies. Attached to a carbiner on her belt her Plague Mask hung, tribal rose seeming to gleam in the light of the moon.

"All set, I think," she said out loud, as if talking to a friend. "Okay, old man. If I were a magician with no hands, then where in the hell would I go?"

She waved a hand, and a seam in the air rippled before her. She nodded, as if to steel herself, and then ran and jumped off the ledge into the tear, the wind rushing past her ears and her hair streaming behind her, grinning…

THE S.C.A.R.E.D. TEAM WILL RETURN IN:

BLACK HILLS MOON VOLUME II: THE HALLOWTIDE CHRONICLES

ABOUT THE AUTHORS

T.S. HUNTZICKER

"T.S." Huntzicker is a Social Worker, Author, Professional Photographer, and Indie Short Film Producer/Director. Thomas was fascinated with the wonders of the "para" world from a young age and was urban exploring in the 1980's before it was internationally recognized as "cool". He has an undergraduate degree in Human Consciousness and Cognition (Psychology/Philosophy) and focused his graduate work on Transpersonal Studies at the Institute of Transpersonal Psychology (now known as Sophia University). It was there that he learned to integrate the spiritual and transcendent aspects of the human experience with the framework of modern psychology. T.S. has several poems published and is an active screen writer. It was his his love for story telling that gave rise to the Black Hills Moon Universe and many of the characters and stories are a direct manifestation of his personal life experiences.

BELWOETH HARBRIGHT:

Bel Harbright is a freelance fantastic fiction writer and editor who has worked in the industry since 2015. His writing has been published in Beyond Imagination, SubverCity Transmit, and most recently, Dragon Poet Review. He has served as a content editor for Winterwolf Press, editor-in-chief of Oklahoma Pagan Quarterly, and recently was a contributing editor for Red Earth Review. He has received two Honorable Mentions from Writers of the Future for his slipstream sci-fantasy horror work, and his first YA novel, Full-tilt Exorcist, is forthcoming in 2020 from Shadow Wolf Press. He is currently finishing up his MFA in Creative Writing, with a focus on Genre Fiction and Horror at Oklahoma City University.

His homebase is in Tulsa, Oklahoma, where he divides his time between staring at a computer screen during the day and fighting the forces of evil at night.

www.ingramcontent.com/pod-product-compliance
Lightning Source LLC
Chambersburg PA
CBHW081355090726
47908CB00011B/2686